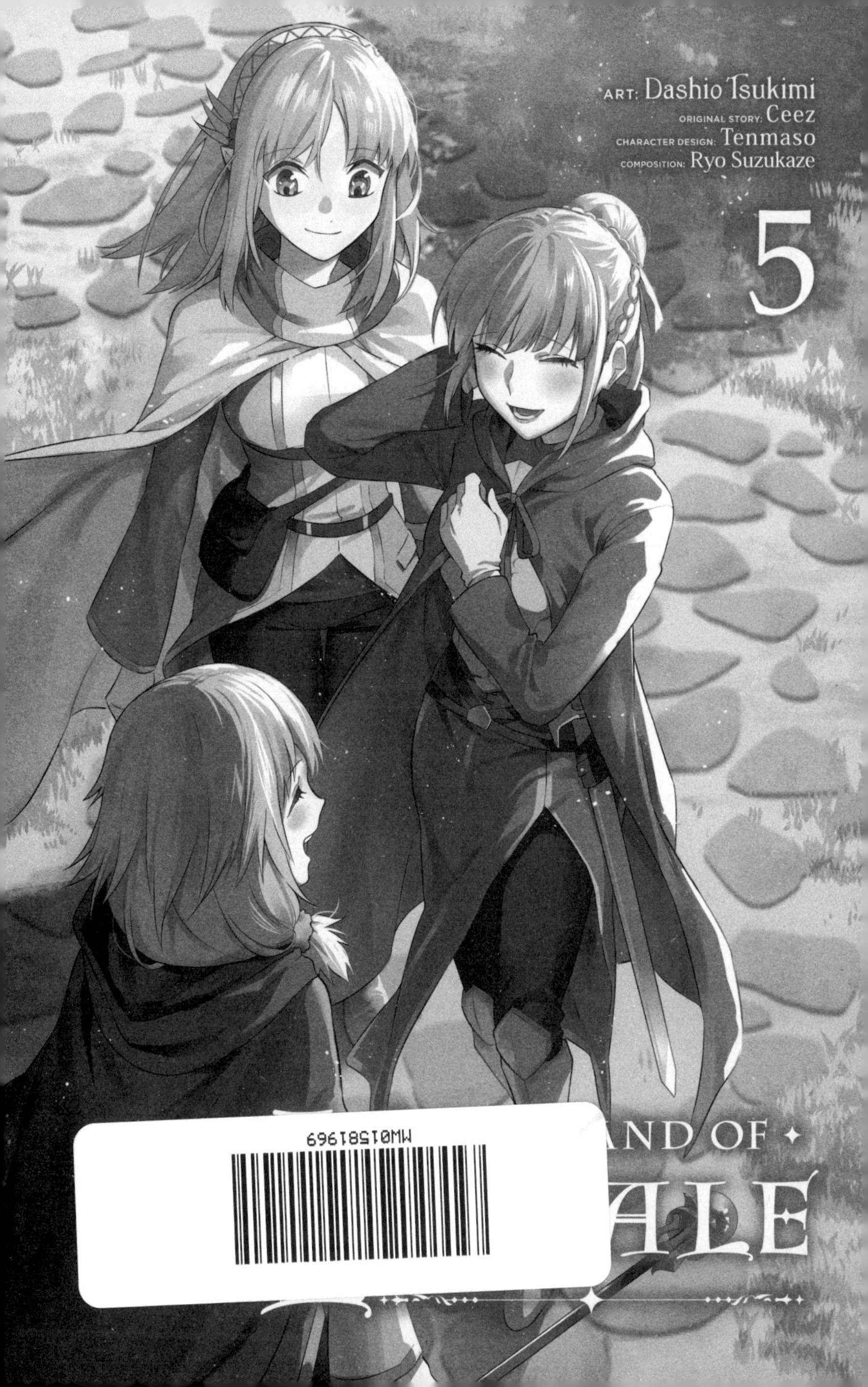
ART: Dashio Tsukimi
ORIGINAL STORY: Ceez
CHARACTER DESIGN: Tenmaso
COMPOSITION: Ryo Suzukaze
5

Contents

Chapter 19 ▷ Let's Make a Racket ········· **003**

Chapter 20 ▷ Let's Talk About Love ········· **029**

Chapter 21 ▷ Let's Protect the Capital, Part I ········· **057**

Chapter 22 ▷ Let's Protect the Capital, Part II ········· **079**

Chapter 23 ▷ Let's Protect the Capital, Part III ········· **105**

Chapter 24 ▷ Let's Take Care of the Aftermath ········· **129**

Bonus Story ▷ Time Waits for No One ········· **155**

Chapter 19
Let's Make a Racket

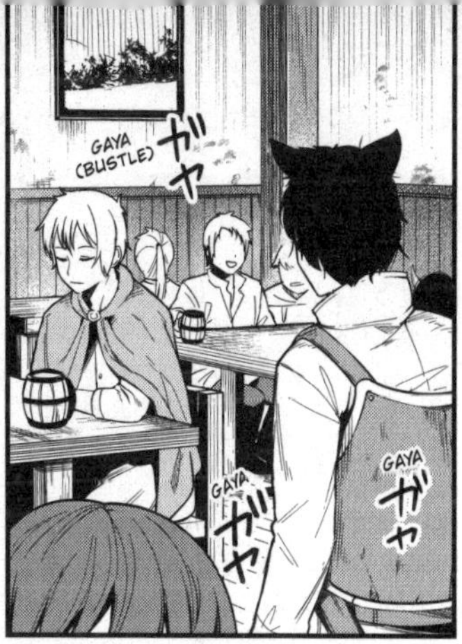
GAYA (BUSTLE)
ガヤ
GAYA
ガヤ
GAYA
ガヤ

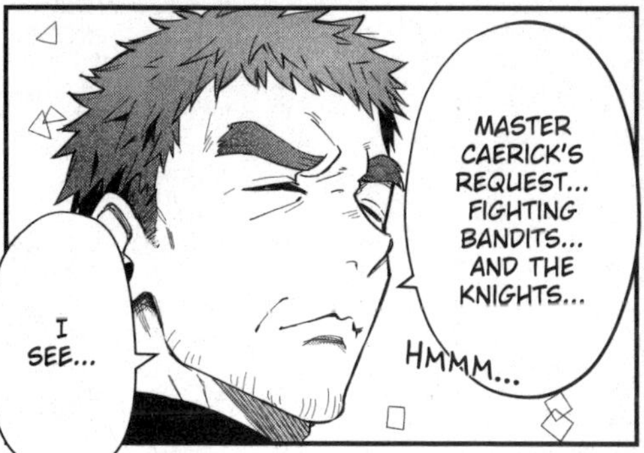
MASTER CAERICK'S REQUEST... FIGHTING BANDITS... AND THE KNIGHTS...
HMMM...
I SEE...

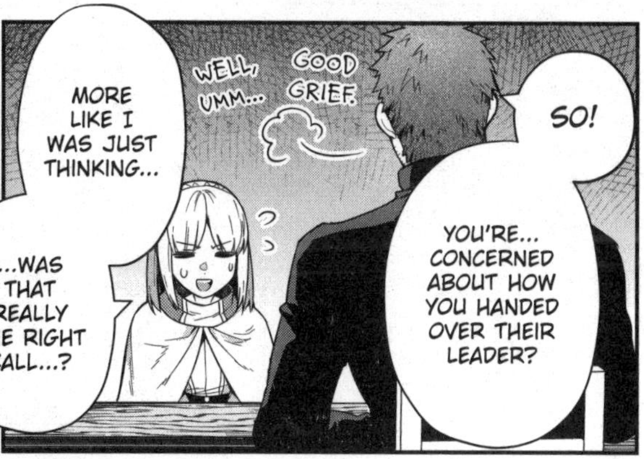
SO!
YOU'RE... CONCERNED ABOUT HOW YOU HANDED OVER THEIR LEADER?
GOOD GRIEF.
WELL, UMM...
MORE LIKE I WAS JUST THINKING...
...WAS THAT REALLY THE RIGHT CALL...?

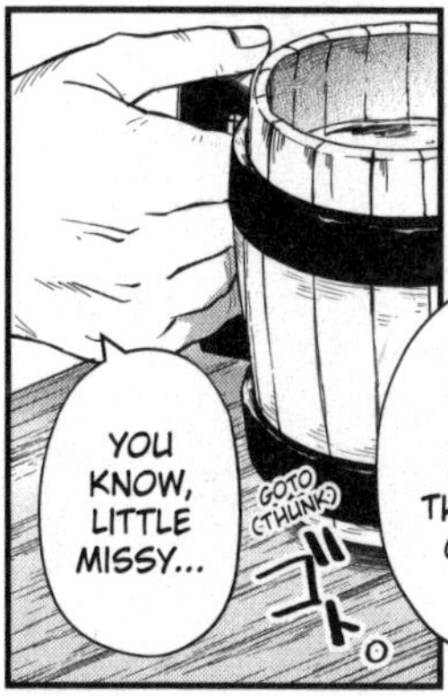
YOU KNOW, LITTLE MISSY...
GOTO (THUNK)
ゴト。

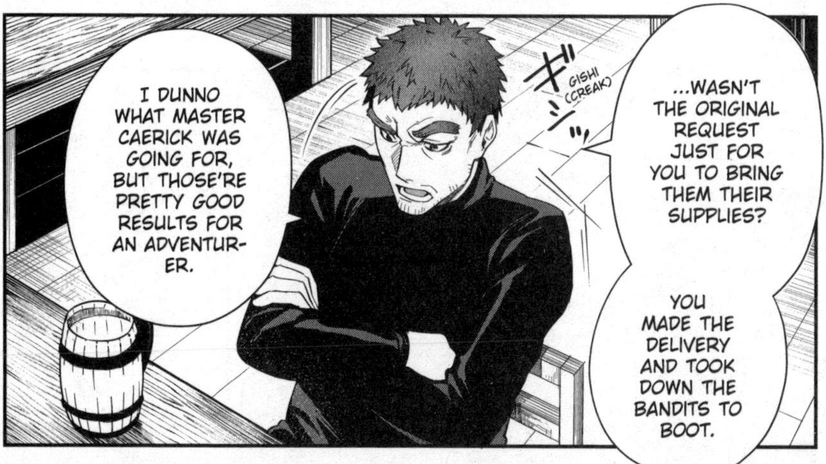
GISHI (CREAK)
ギシッ
...WASN'T THE ORIGINAL REQUEST JUST FOR YOU TO BRING THEM THEIR SUPPLIES?
YOU MADE THE DELIVERY AND TOOK DOWN THE BANDITS TO BOOT.
I DUNNO WHAT MASTER CAERICK WAS GOING FOR, BUT THOSE'RE PRETTY GOOD RESULTS FOR AN ADVENTUR-ER.

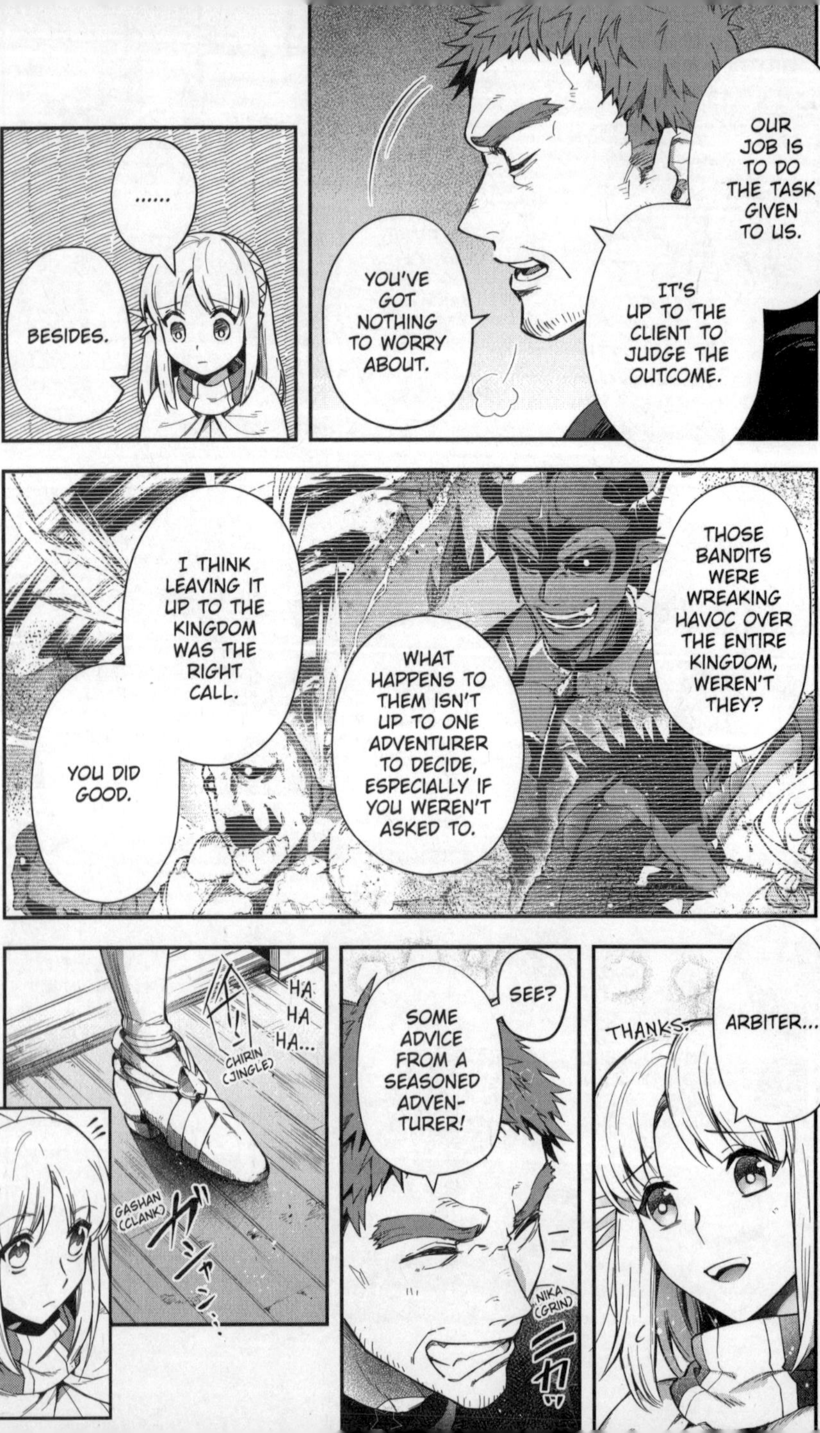
OUR JOB IS TO DO THE TASK GIVEN TO US.
IT'S UP TO THE CLIENT TO JUDGE THE OUTCOME.
YOU'VE GOT NOTHING TO WORRY ABOUT.
......
BESIDES.
THOSE BANDITS WERE WREAKING HAVOC OVER THE ENTIRE KINGDOM, WEREN'T THEY?
WHAT HAPPENS TO THEM ISN'T UP TO ONE ADVENTURER TO DECIDE, ESPECIALLY IF YOU WEREN'T ASKED TO.
I THINK LEAVING IT UP TO THE KINGDOM WAS THE RIGHT CALL.
YOU DID GOOD.
ARBITER...
THANKS.
SEE?
SOME ADVICE FROM A SEASONED ADVEN-TURER!
NIKA (GRIN)
HA HA HA...
CHIRIN (JINGLE)
GASHAN (CLANK)

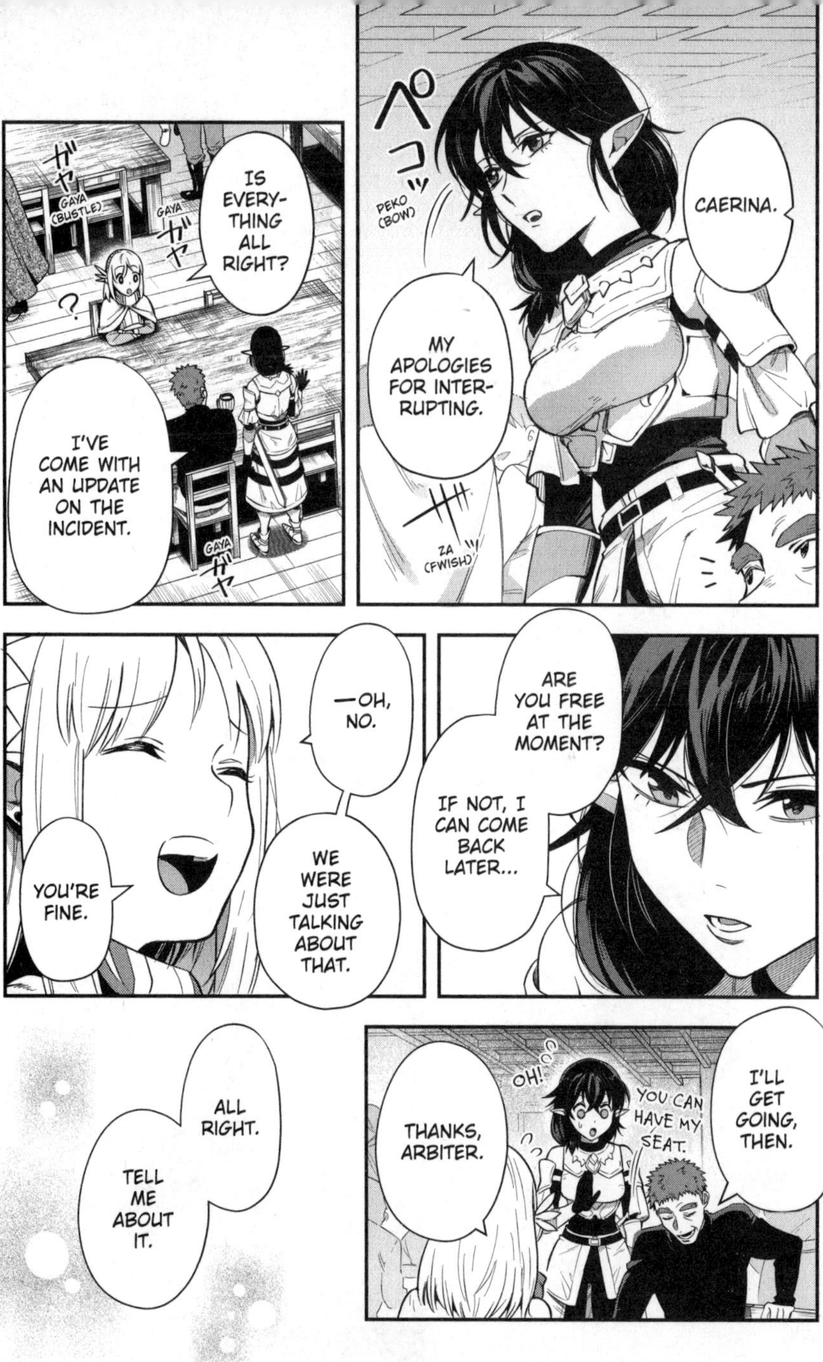
CAERINA.
ペコッ
PEKO (BOW)
MY APOLOGIES FOR INTER-RUPTING.
ZA (FWISH)
IS EVERY-THING ALL RIGHT?
ガヤ
GAYA (BUSTLE)
ガヤ
GAYA
?
I'VE COME WITH AN UPDATE ON THE INCIDENT.
ガヤ
GAYA
ARE YOU FREE AT THE MOMENT?
IF NOT, I CAN COME BACK LATER...
—OH, NO.
WE WERE JUST TALKING ABOUT THAT.
YOU'RE FINE.
I'LL GET GOING, THEN.
YOU CAN HAVE MY SEAT.
OH!
THANKS, ARBITER.
ALL RIGHT.
TELL ME ABOUT IT.

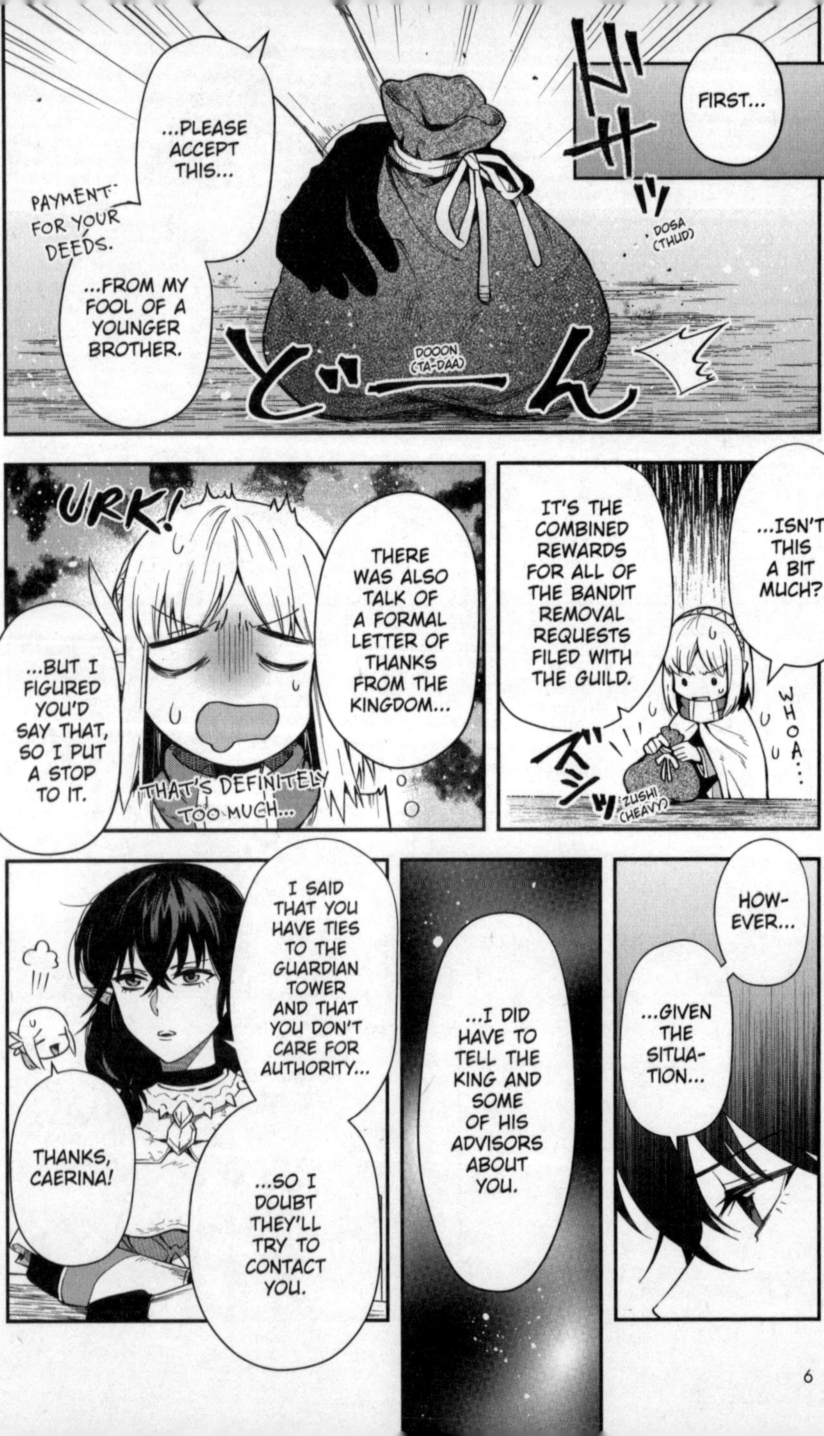
FIRST...
DOSA (THUD)
...PLEASE ACCEPT THIS...
PAYMENT FOR YOUR DEEDS.
...FROM MY FOOL OF A YOUNGER BROTHER.
DOOON (TA-DAA)
...ISN'T THIS A BIT MUCH?
WHOA...
IT'S THE COMBINED REWARDS FOR ALL OF THE BANDIT REMOVAL REQUESTS FILED WITH THE GUILD.
ZUSHI (HEAVY)
URK!
THERE WAS ALSO TALK OF A FORMAL LETTER OF THANKS FROM THE KINGDOM...
...BUT I FIGURED YOU'D SAY THAT, SO I PUT A STOP TO IT.
THAT'S DEFINITELY TOO MUCH...
HOW-EVER...
...GIVEN THE SITUA-TION...
...I DID HAVE TO TELL THE KING AND SOME OF HIS ADVISORS ABOUT YOU.
I SAID THAT YOU HAVE TIES TO THE GUARDIAN TOWER AND THAT YOU DON'T CARE FOR AUTHORITY...
...SO I DOUBT THEY'LL TRY TO CONTACT YOU.
THANKS, CAERINA!

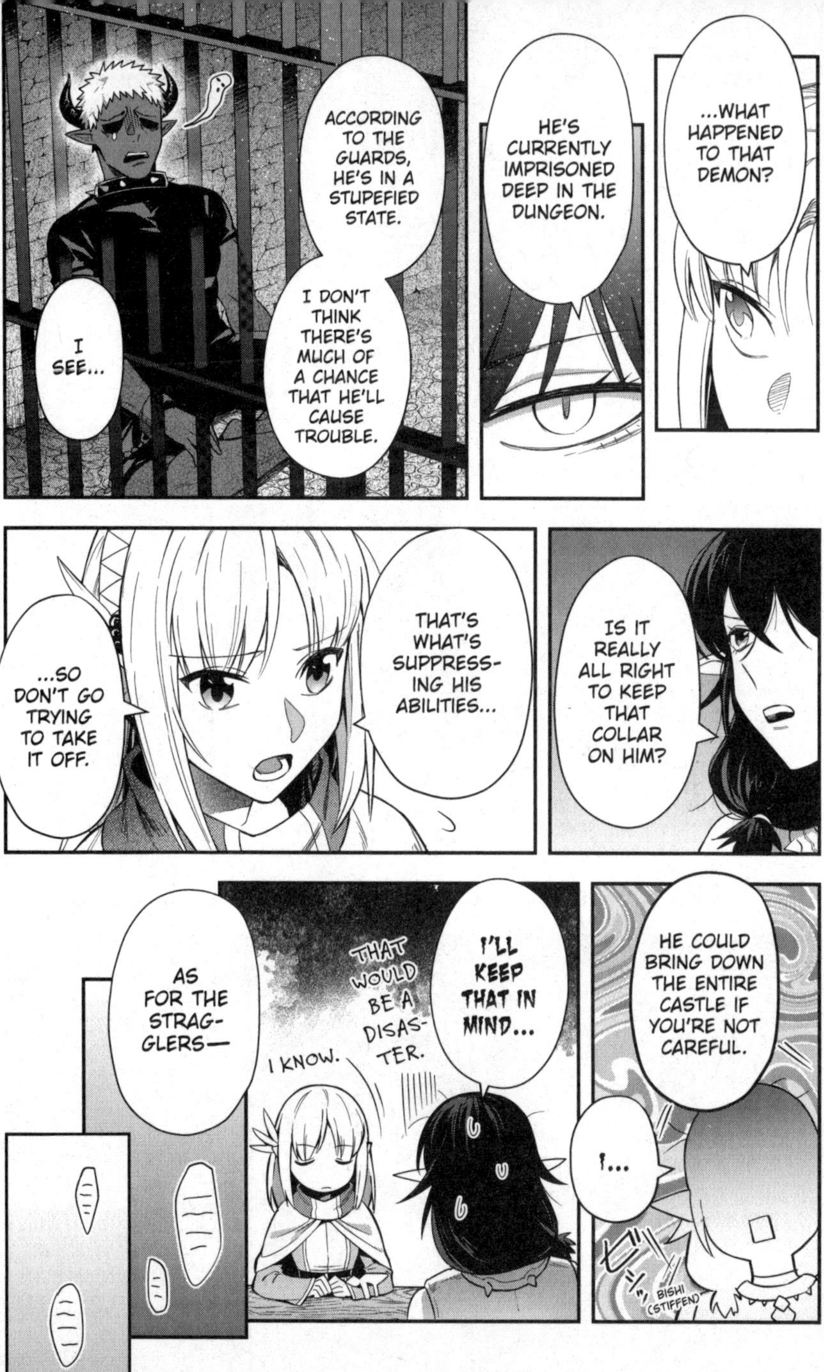
...WHAT HAPPENED TO THAT DEMON?
HE'S CURRENTLY IMPRISONED DEEP IN THE DUNGEON.
ACCORDING TO THE GUARDS, HE'S IN A STUPEFIED STATE.
I DON'T THINK THERE'S MUCH OF A CHANCE THAT HE'LL CAUSE TROUBLE.
I SEE...
IS IT REALLY ALL RIGHT TO KEEP THAT COLLAR ON HIM?
THAT'S WHAT'S SUPPRESSING HIS ABILITIES...
...SO DON'T GO TRYING TO TAKE IT OFF.
HE COULD BRING DOWN THE ENTIRE CASTLE IF YOU'RE NOT CAREFUL.
I...
BISHI (STIFFEN)
I'LL KEEP THAT IN MIND...
THAT WOULD BE A DISASTER.
I KNOW.
AS FOR THE STRAGGLERS—

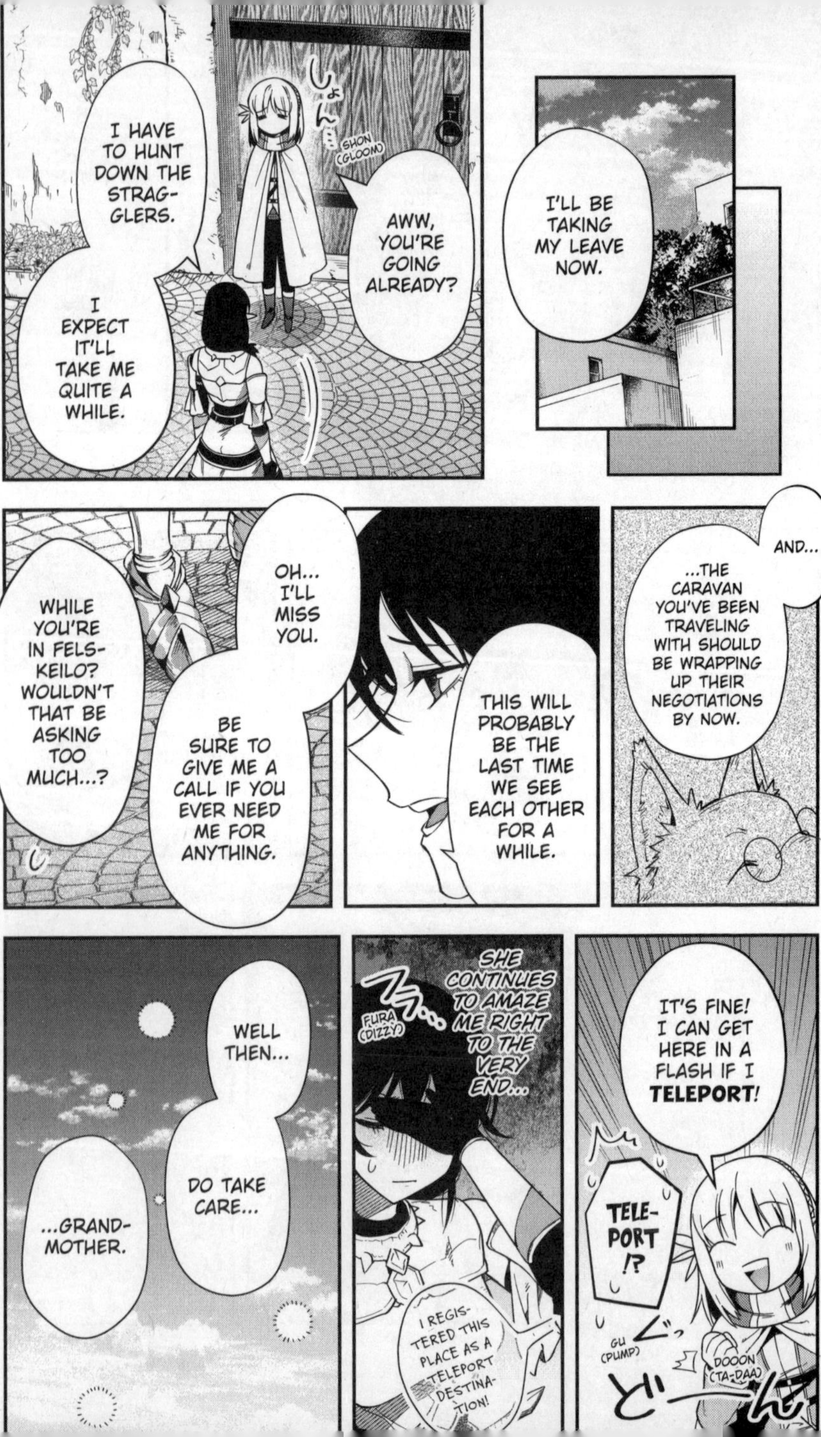

I'LL BE TAKING MY LEAVE NOW.
しょん～…
SHON (GLOOM)
AWW, YOU'RE GOING ALREADY?
I HAVE TO HUNT DOWN THE STRAG-GLERS.
I EXPECT IT'LL TAKE ME QUITE A WHILE.
AND...
...THE CARAVAN YOU'VE BEEN TRAVELING WITH SHOULD BE WRAPPING UP THEIR NEGOTIATIONS BY NOW.
THIS WILL PROBABLY BE THE LAST TIME WE SEE EACH OTHER FOR A WHILE.
OH... I'LL MISS YOU.
BE SURE TO GIVE ME A CALL IF YOU EVER NEED ME FOR ANYTHING.
WHILE YOU'RE IN FELS-KEILO? WOULDN'T THAT BE ASKING TOO MUCH...?
IT'S FINE! I CAN GET HERE IN A FLASH IF I **TELEPORT**!
TELE-PORT !?
GU (PUMP)
DOOON (TA-DAA)
I REGIS-TERED THIS PLACE AS A TELEPORT DESTINA-TION!
SHE CONTINUES TO AMAZE ME RIGHT TO THE VERY END...
FURA (DIZZY)
WELL THEN...
DO TAKE CARE...
...GRAND-MOTHER.

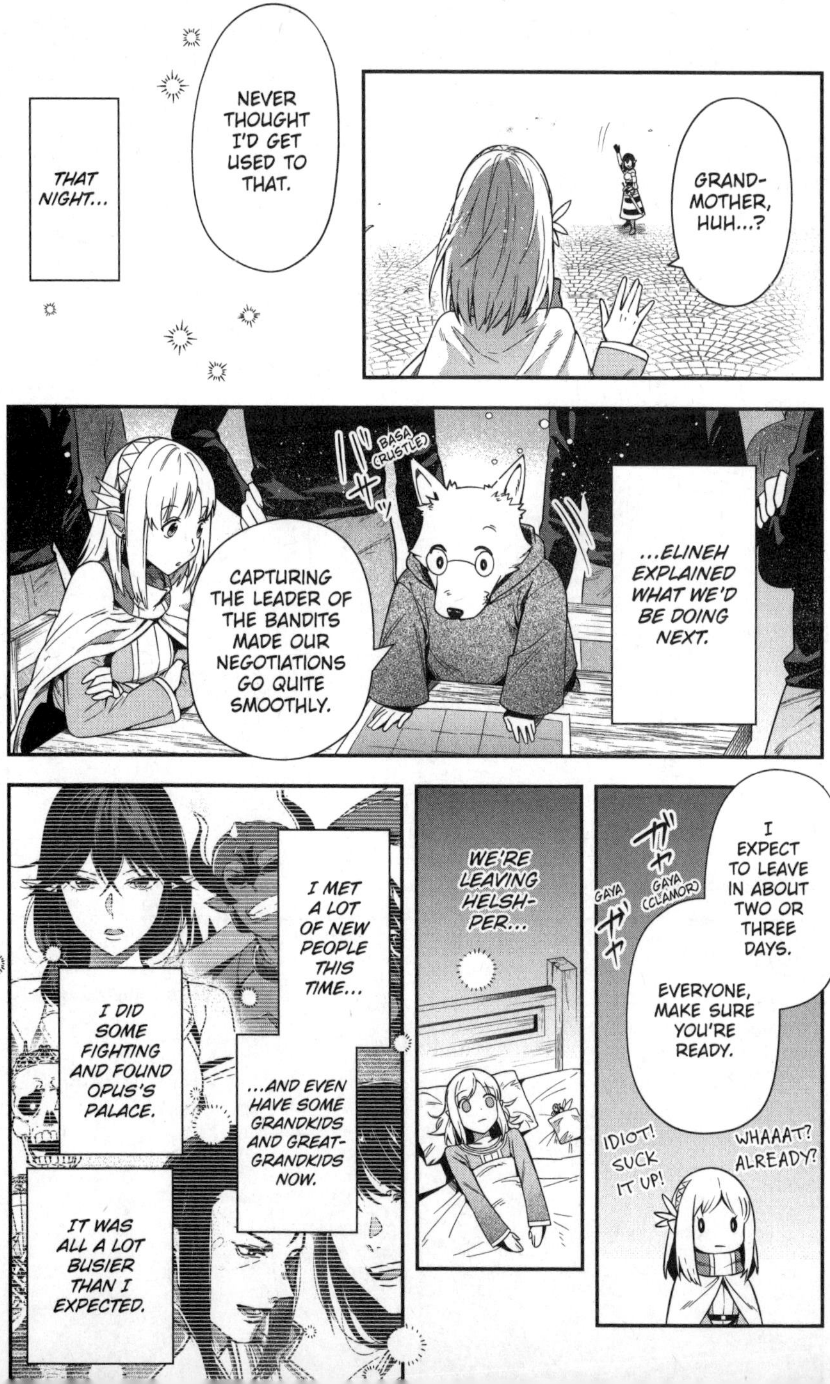
GRAND-MOTHER, HUH...?
NEVER THOUGHT I'D GET USED TO THAT.
THAT NIGHT...
...ELINEH EXPLAINED WHAT WE'D BE DOING NEXT.
BASA (RUSTLE)
CAPTURING THE LEADER OF THE BANDITS MADE OUR NEGOTIATIONS GO QUITE SMOOTHLY.
I EXPECT TO LEAVE IN ABOUT TWO OR THREE DAYS.
GAYA GAYA (CLAMOR)
EVERYONE, MAKE SURE YOU'RE READY.
WHAAAT? ALREADY?
IDIOT! SUCK IT UP!
WE'RE LEAVING HELSH-PER...
I MET A LOT OF NEW PEOPLE THIS TIME...
...AND EVEN HAVE SOME GRANDKIDS AND GREAT-GRANDKIDS NOW.
I DID SOME FIGHTING AND FOUND OPUS'S PALACE.
IT WAS ALL A LOT BUSIER THAN I EXPECTED.

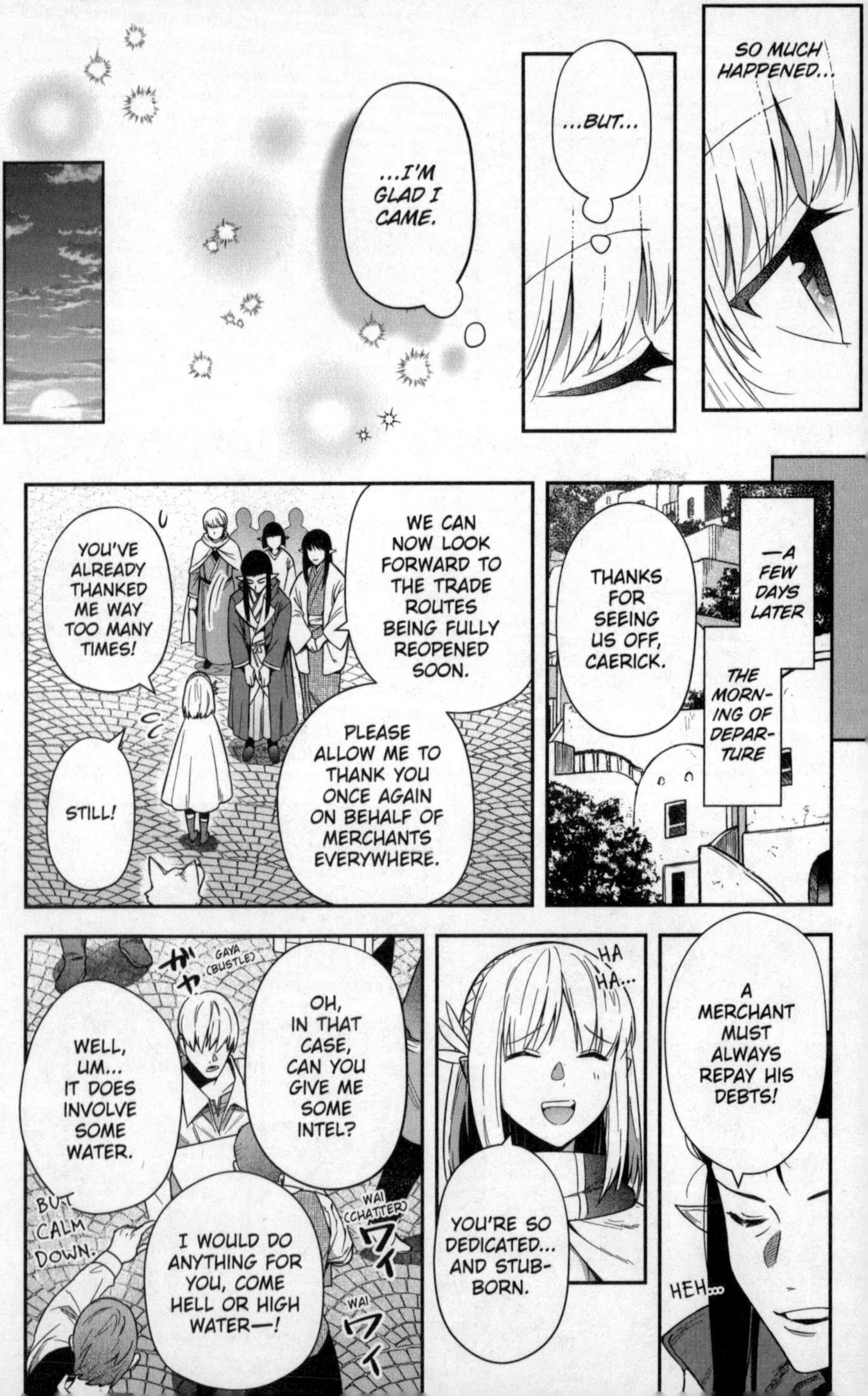
SO MUCH HAPPENED...
...BUT...
...I'M GLAD I CAME.
—A FEW DAYS LATER
THE MORNING OF DEPARTURE
THANKS FOR SEEING US OFF, CAERICK.
WE CAN NOW LOOK FORWARD TO THE TRADE ROUTES BEING FULLY REOPENED SOON.
PLEASE ALLOW ME TO THANK YOU ONCE AGAIN ON BEHALF OF MERCHANTS EVERYWHERE.
YOU'VE ALREADY THANKED ME WAY TOO MANY TIMES!
STILL!
A MERCHANT MUST ALWAYS REPAY HIS DEBTS!
HEH...
HA HA...
YOU'RE SO DEDICATED... AND STUBBORN.
GAYA (BUSTLE)
OH, IN THAT CASE, CAN YOU GIVE ME SOME INTEL?
WELL, UM... IT DOES INVOLVE SOME WATER.
WAI (CHATTER)
I WOULD DO ANYTHING FOR YOU, COME HELL OR HIGH WATER—!
WAI
BUT CALM DOWN.

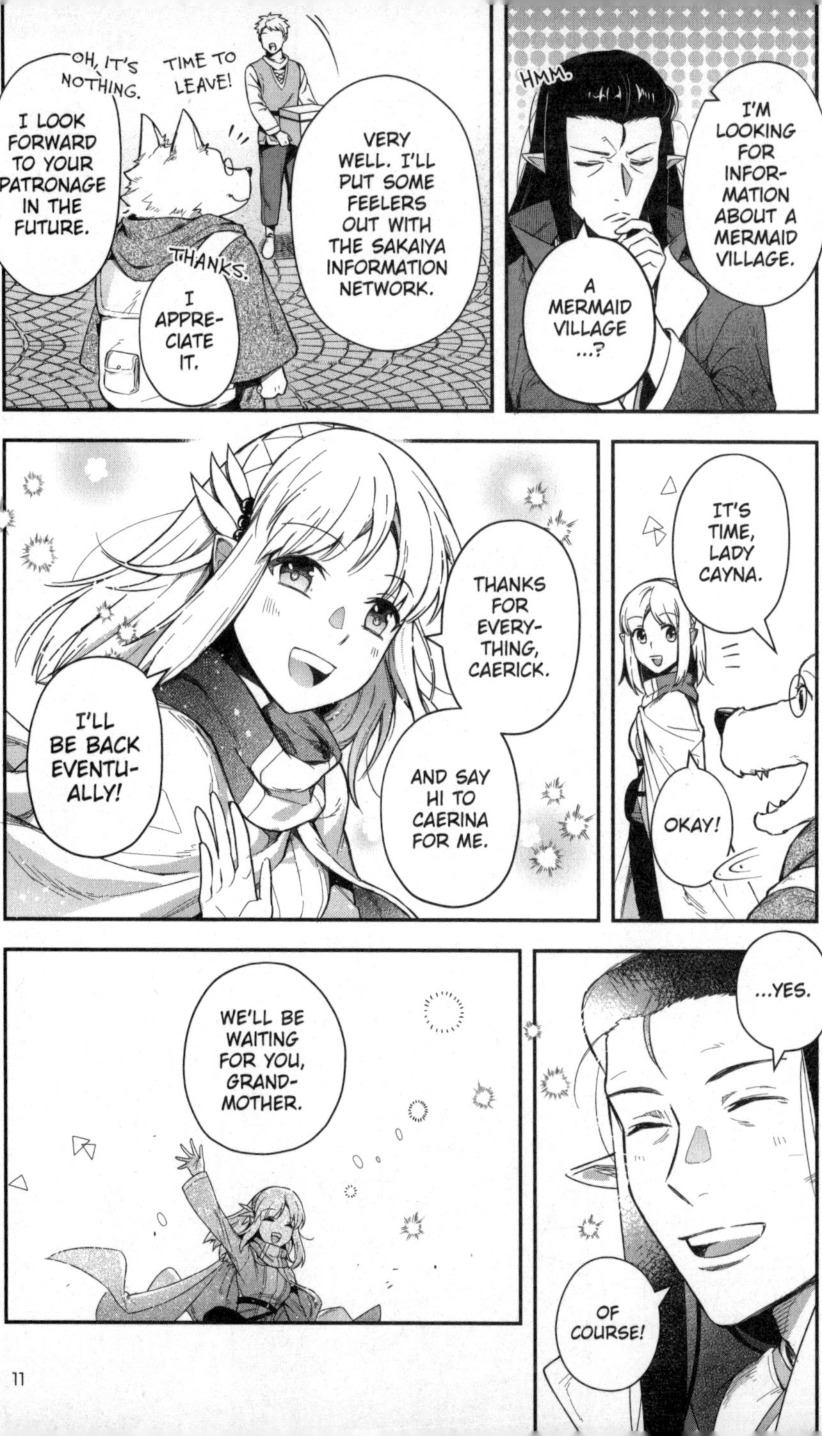
HMM.
I'M LOOKING FOR INFORMATION ABOUT A MERMAID VILLAGE.
A MERMAID VILLAGE ...?
VERY WELL. I'LL PUT SOME FEELERS OUT WITH THE SAKAIYA INFORMATION NETWORK.
THANKS.
I APPRECIATE IT.
OH, IT'S NOTHING.
I LOOK FORWARD TO YOUR PATRONAGE IN THE FUTURE.
TIME TO LEAVE!
IT'S TIME, LADY CAYNA.
OKAY!
THANKS FOR EVERYTHING, CAERICK.
AND SAY HI TO CAERINA FOR ME.
I'LL BE BACK EVENTUALLY!
...YES.
OF COURSE!
WE'LL BE WAITING FOR YOU, GRANDMOTHER.

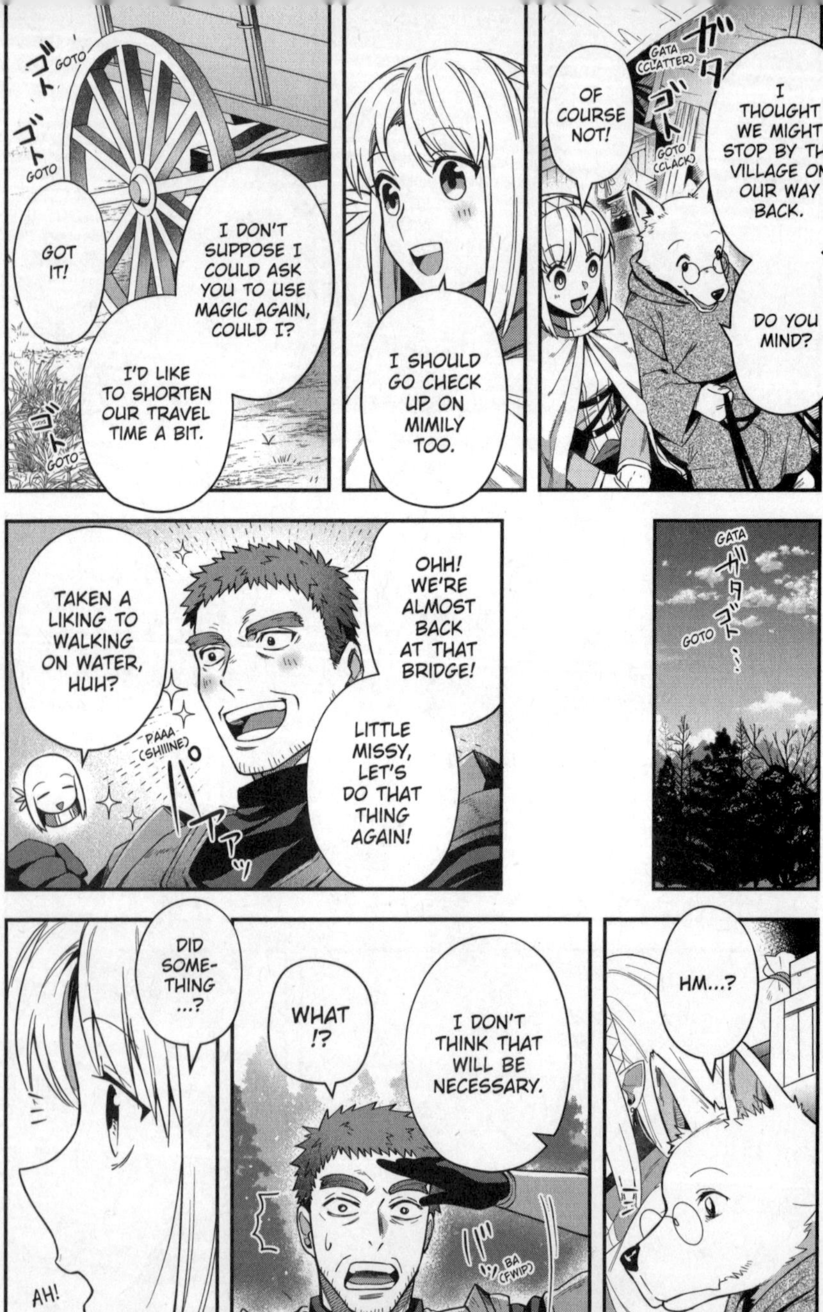
GATA (CLATTER)
GOTO (CLACK)
I THOUGHT WE MIGHT STOP BY THE VILLAGE ON OUR WAY BACK.
DO YOU MIND?
OF COURSE NOT!
I SHOULD GO CHECK UP ON MIMILY TOO.
GOTO
GOTO
I DON'T SUPPOSE I COULD ASK YOU TO USE MAGIC AGAIN, COULD I?
I'D LIKE TO SHORTEN OUR TRAVEL TIME A BIT.
GOT IT!
GOTO
GATA
GOTO
OHH! WE'RE ALMOST BACK AT THAT BRIDGE!
LITTLE MISSY, LET'S DO THAT THING AGAIN!
PAAA (SHIIINE)
TAKEN A LIKING TO WALKING ON WATER, HUH?
HM...?
I DON'T THINK THAT WILL BE NECESSARY.
WHAT!?
BA (FWIP)
DID SOME-THING ...?
AH!

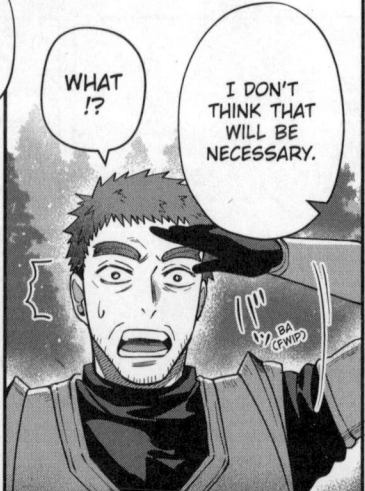

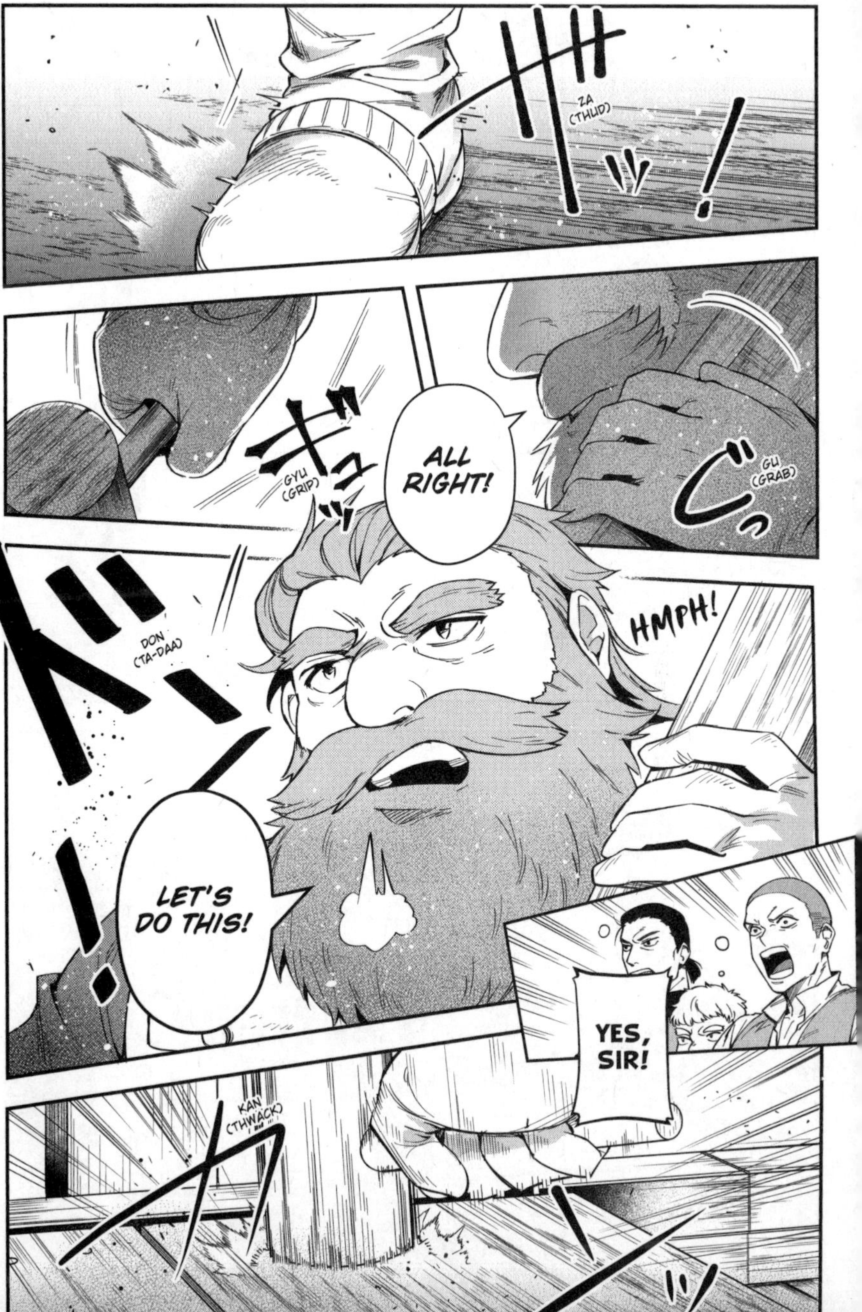
ZA (THUD)
GU (GRAB)
GYU (GRIP)
ALL RIGHT!
HMPH!
DON (TA-DAA)
LET'S DO THIS!
YES, SIR!
KAN (THWACK)

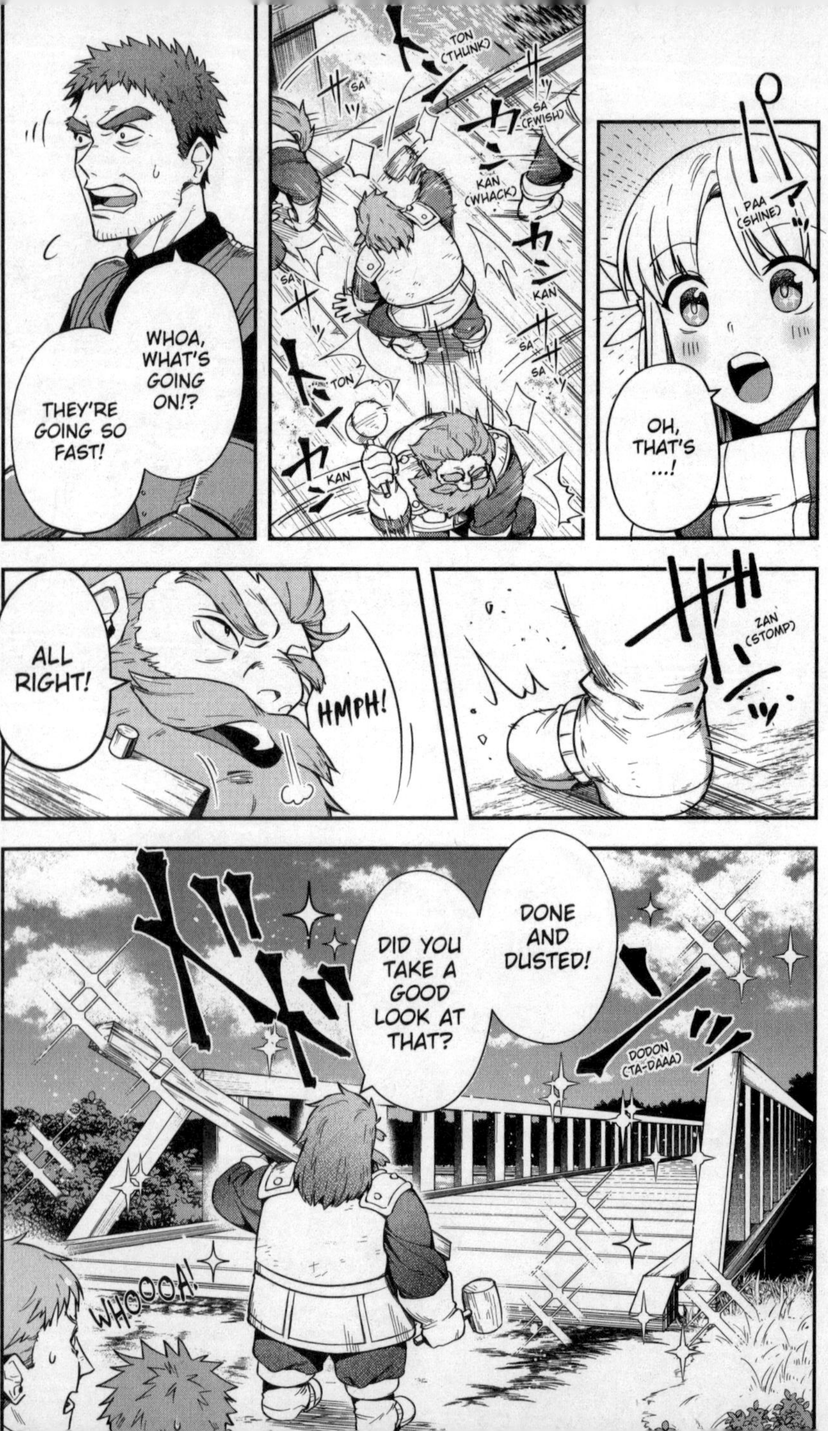
PAA (SHINE)
OH, THAT'S ...!
TON (THUNK)
SA
SA (F'WISH)
KAN (WHACK)
KAN
SA
SA
SA
TON
KAN
WHOA, WHAT'S GOING ON!?
THEY'RE GOING SO FAST!
ZAN (STOMP)
HMPH!
ALL RIGHT!
DODON (TA-DAAA)
DONE AND DUSTED!
DID YOU TAKE A GOOD LOOK AT THAT?
WHOOOA!

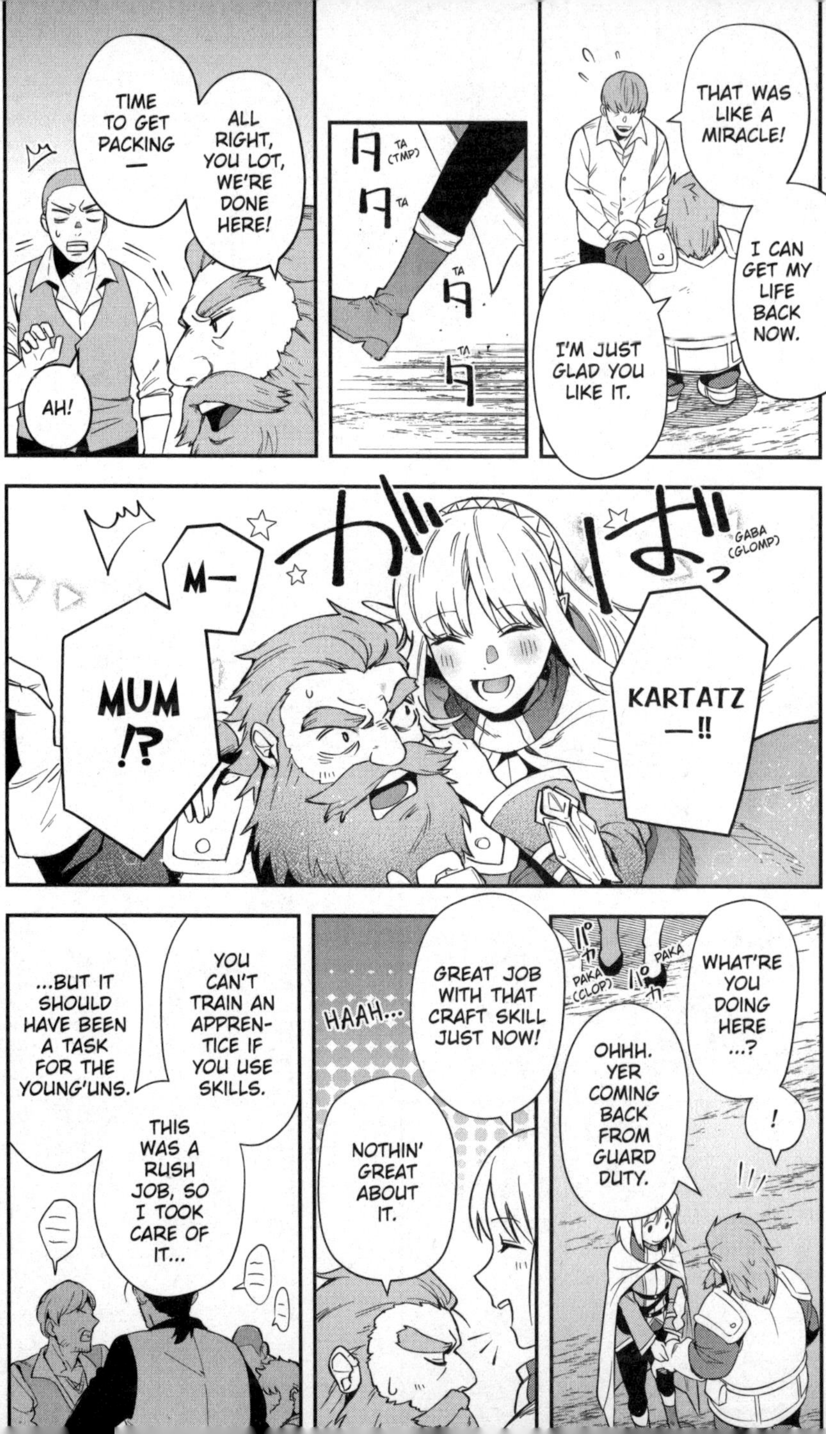

THAT WAS LIKE A MIRACLE!
I CAN GET MY LIFE BACK NOW.
I'M JUST GLAD YOU LIKE IT.
TA (TMP)
TA
TA
TA
ALL RIGHT, YOU LOT, WE'RE DONE HERE!
TIME TO GET PACKING—
AH!
GABA (GLOMP)
KARTATZ—!!
M—
MUM!?
PAKA (CLOP)
PAKA
WHAT'RE YOU DOING HERE...?
!
OHHH. YER COMING BACK FROM GUARD DUTY.
GREAT JOB WITH THAT CRAFT SKILL JUST NOW!
HAAH...
NOTHIN' GREAT ABOUT IT.
YOU CAN'T TRAIN AN APPRENTICE IF YOU USE SKILLS.
...BUT IT SHOULD HAVE BEEN A TASK FOR THE YOUNG'UNS.
THIS WAS A RUSH JOB, SO I TOOK CARE OF IT...

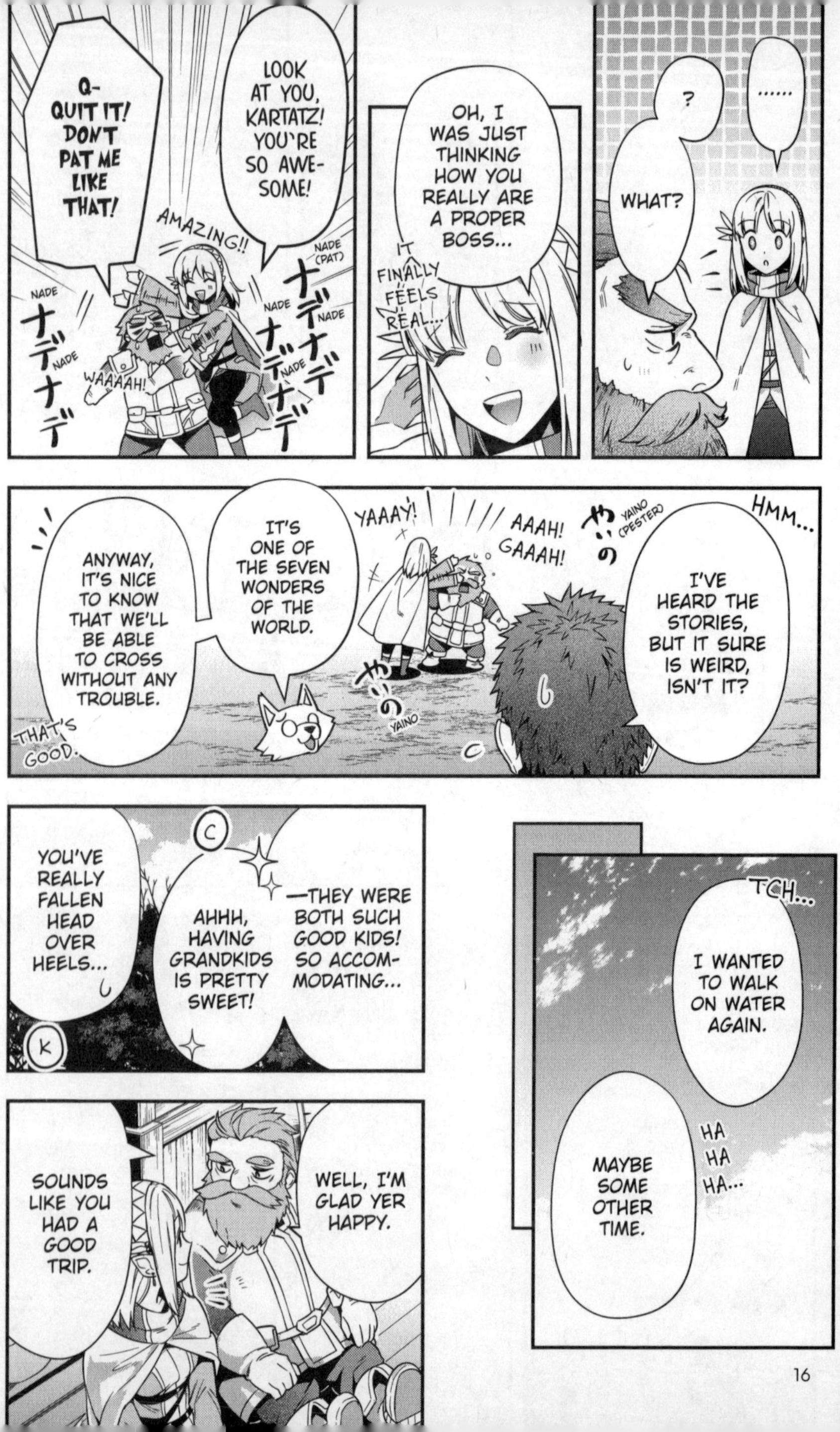
......
?
WHAT?
OH, I WAS JUST THINKING HOW YOU REALLY ARE A PROPER BOSS...
IT FINALLY FEELS REAL...
LOOK AT YOU, KARTATZ! YOU'RE SO AWESOME!
AMAZING!!
NADE (PAT)
ナデナデ NADE NADE
ナデナデ NADE NADE
ナデナデ NADE NADE
Q-QUIT IT! DON'T PAT ME LIKE THAT!
WAAAAH!
HMM...
I'VE HEARD THE STORIES, BUT IT SURE IS WEIRD, ISN'T IT?
やいの YAINO (PESTER)
AAAH! GAAAH!
YAAAY!
やいの YAINO
IT'S ONE OF THE SEVEN WONDERS OF THE WORLD.
ANYWAY, IT'S NICE TO KNOW THAT WE'LL BE ABLE TO CROSS WITHOUT ANY TROUBLE.
THAT'S GOOD.
TCH...
I WANTED TO WALK ON WATER AGAIN.
HA HA HA...
MAYBE SOME OTHER TIME.
—THEY WERE BOTH SUCH GOOD KIDS! SO ACCOMMODATING...
AHHH, HAVING GRANDKIDS IS PRETTY SWEET!
YOU'VE REALLY FALLEN HEAD OVER HEELS...
WELL, I'M GLAD YER HAPPY.
SOUNDS LIKE YOU HAD A GOOD TRIP.

—YEAH!
HEH!
I'LL HAVE TO TELL MAI-MAI ABOUT IT TOO.
WE'RE ALMOST AT THE VILLAGE, LADY CAYNA.
WE'LL HEAD FOR THE INN ONCE WE GET THE WAGONS IN PLACE...
...SO FEEL FREE TO GO ON AHEAD IF YOU LIKE.
GOT IT.
WHAT ABOUT YOU, KAR-TATZ?
I'VE GOT MY APPRENTICES' HORSES TO TAKE CARE OF.
WE'LL MET UP WITH YOU LATER.
OKAY.
I WONDER WHERE MIMILY IS.
TA TA TA (TMP)
たたたっ
MAYBE LYTT WOULD KNOW.
TE TE TE (TROT)
GUESS I'LL START WITH THE INN...
OH!

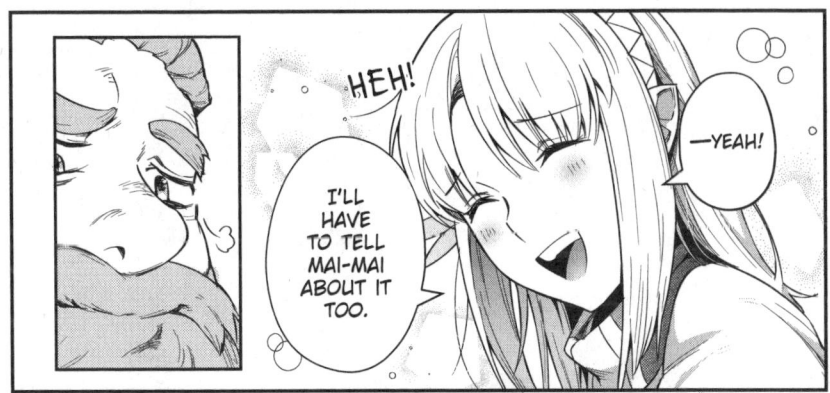

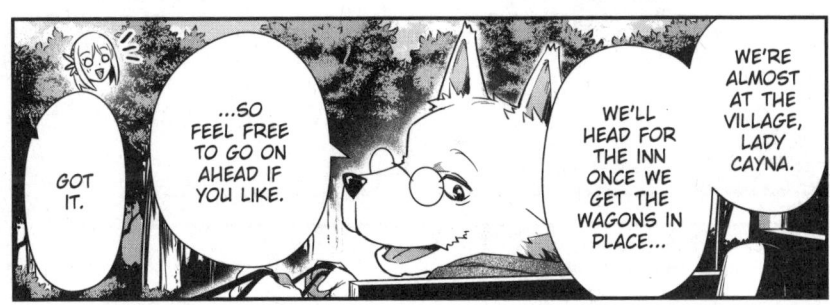

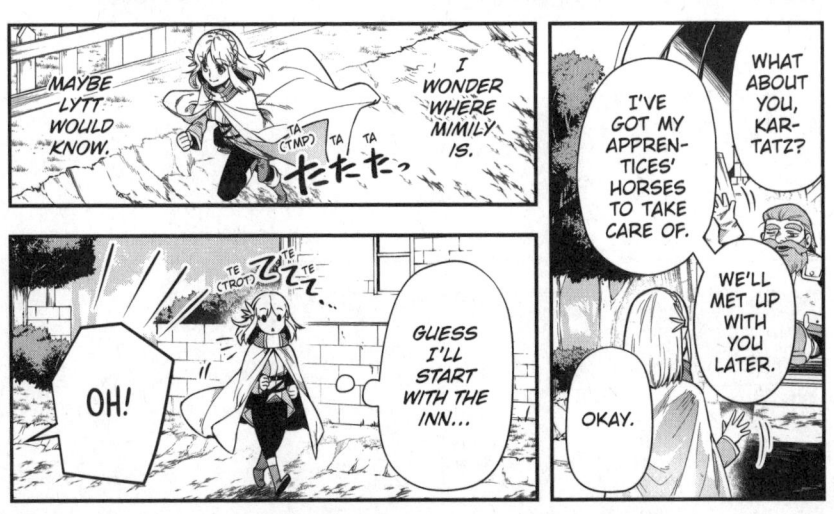

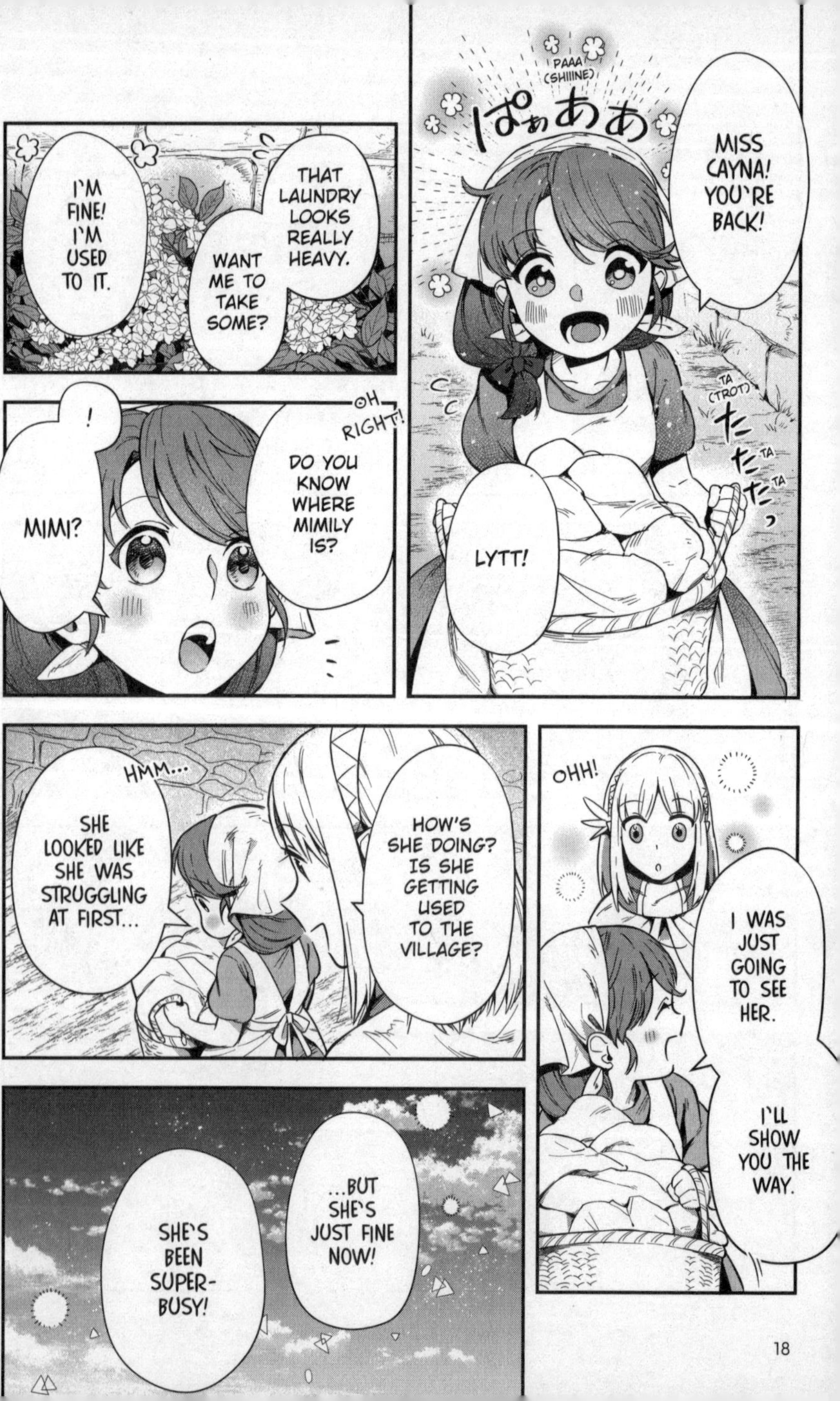
PAAA (SHIIINE)
ぱぁあぁ
MISS CAYNA! YOU'RE BACK!
TA (TROT)
たたたっ
TA TA
LYTT!
THAT LAUNDRY LOOKS REALLY HEAVY.
WANT ME TO TAKE SOME?
I'M FINE! I'M USED TO IT.
OH RIGHT!
DO YOU KNOW WHERE MIMILY IS?
!
MIMI?
OHH!
I WAS JUST GOING TO SEE HER.
I'LL SHOW YOU THE WAY.
HOW'S SHE DOING? IS SHE GETTING USED TO THE VILLAGE?
HMM...
SHE LOOKED LIKE SHE WAS STRUGGLING AT FIRST...
...BUT SHE'S JUST FINE NOW!
SHE'S BEEN SUPER-BUSY!

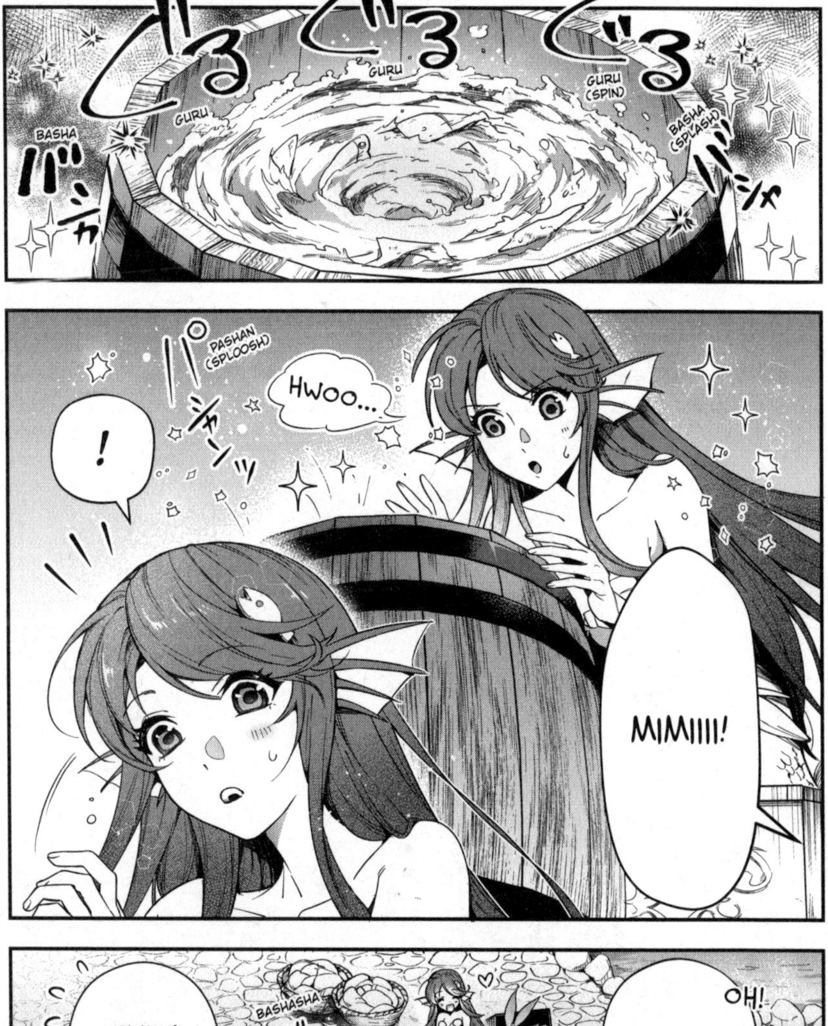
ぐる
GURU (SPIN)
BASHA (SPLASH)
ぐる
GURU
ぐる
GURU
BASHA
PASHAN (SPLOOSH)
HWOO...
MIMIIIII!
!
OH! CAYNA! YOU CAME TO SEE ME?
BASHASHA
MIMILY! WHAT ARE YOU DOING AT THE BATHS?
WITH A BARREL?

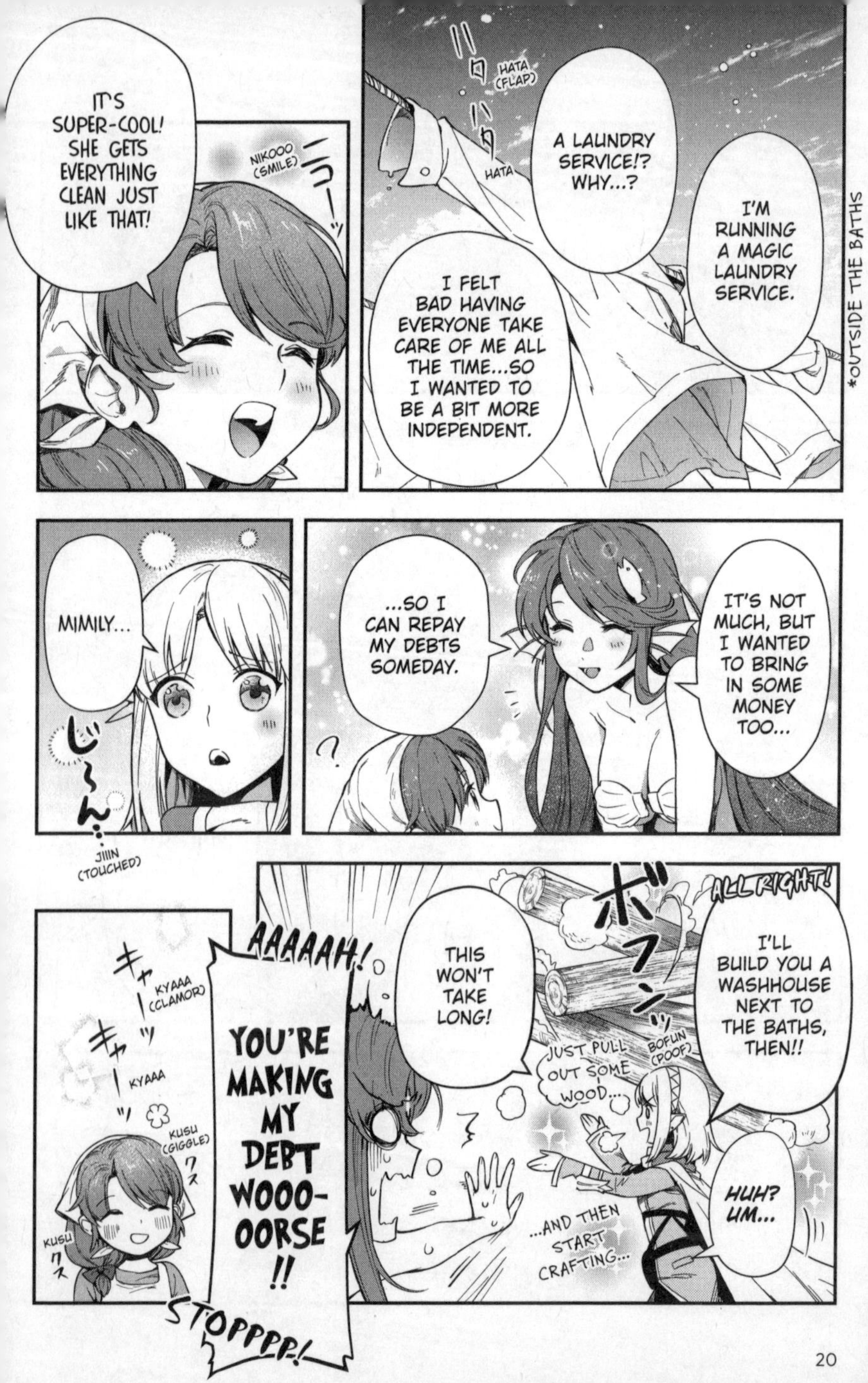
*OUTSIDE THE BATHS
I'M RUNNING A MAGIC LAUNDRY SERVICE.
A LAUNDRY SERVICE!? WHY...?
HATA (FLAP)
HATA
I FELT BAD HAVING EVERYONE TAKE CARE OF ME ALL THE TIME...SO I WANTED TO BE A BIT MORE INDEPENDENT.
IT'S SUPER-COOL! SHE GETS EVERYTHING CLEAN JUST LIKE THAT!
NIKOOO (SMILE)
IT'S NOT MUCH, BUT I WANTED TO BRING IN SOME MONEY TOO...
...SO I CAN REPAY MY DEBTS SOMEDAY.
MIMILY...
JIIN (TOUCHED)
ALL RIGHT!
I'LL BUILD YOU A WASHHOUSE NEXT TO THE BATHS, THEN!!
BOFLUN (POOF)
THIS WON'T TAKE LONG!
JUST PULL OUT SOME WOOD...
HUH? UM...
...AND THEN START CRAFTING...
AAAAAH!
YOU'RE MAKING MY DEBT WOOOO-OORSE!!
KYAAA (CLAMOR)
KYAAA
KUSU (GIGGLE)
KUSU
STOPPPP!

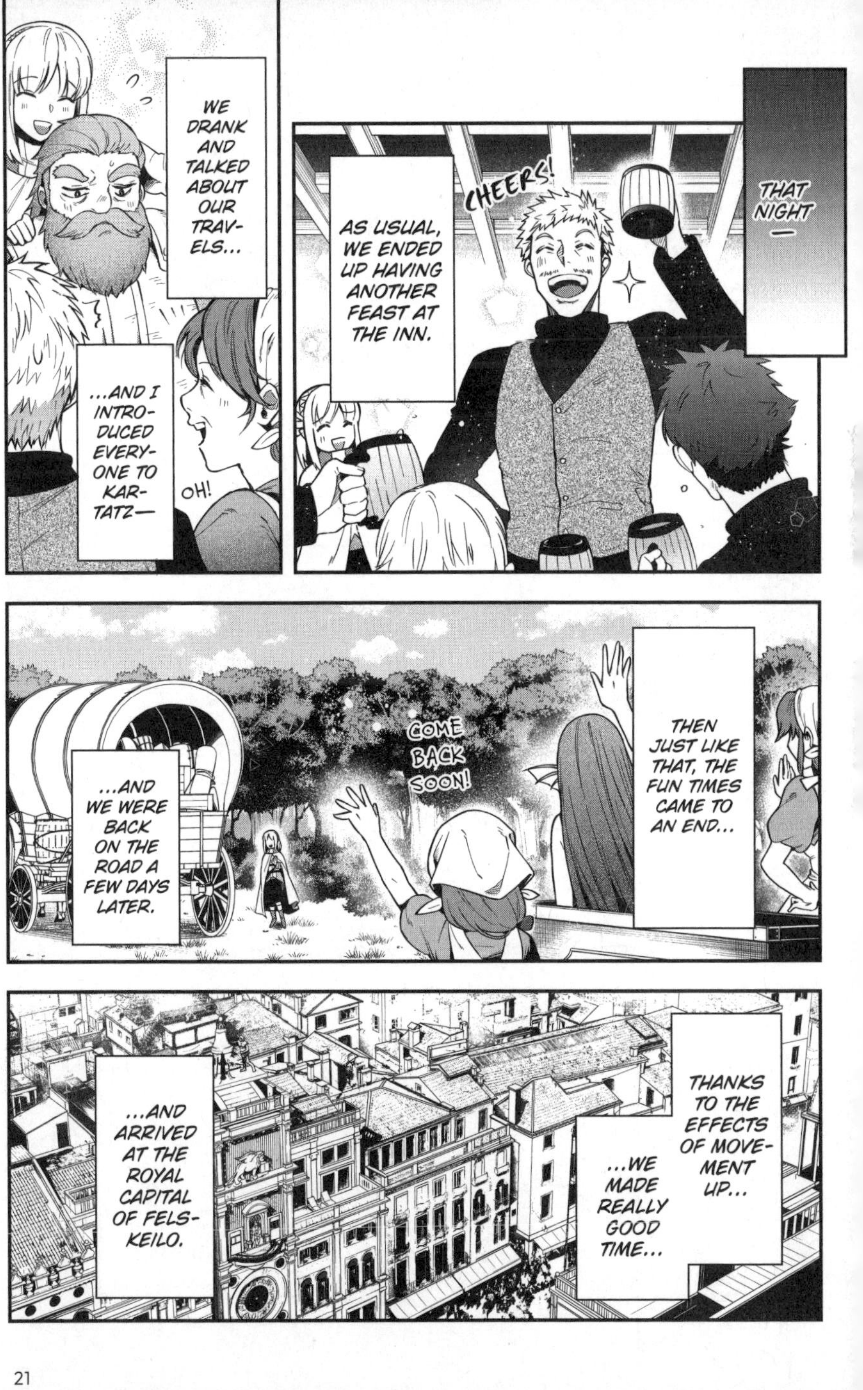
THAT NIGHT—
CHEERS!
AS USUAL, WE ENDED UP HAVING ANOTHER FEAST AT THE INN.
WE DRANK AND TALKED ABOUT OUR TRAV-ELS...
...AND I INTRO-DUCED EVERY-ONE TO KAR-TATZ—
OH!
THEN JUST LIKE THAT, THE FUN TIMES CAME TO AN END...
COME BACK SOON!
...AND WE WERE BACK ON THE ROAD A FEW DAYS LATER.
THANKS TO THE EFFECTS OF MOVE-MENT UP...
...WE MADE REALLY GOOD TIME...
...AND ARRIVED AT THE ROYAL CAPITAL OF FELS-KEILO.

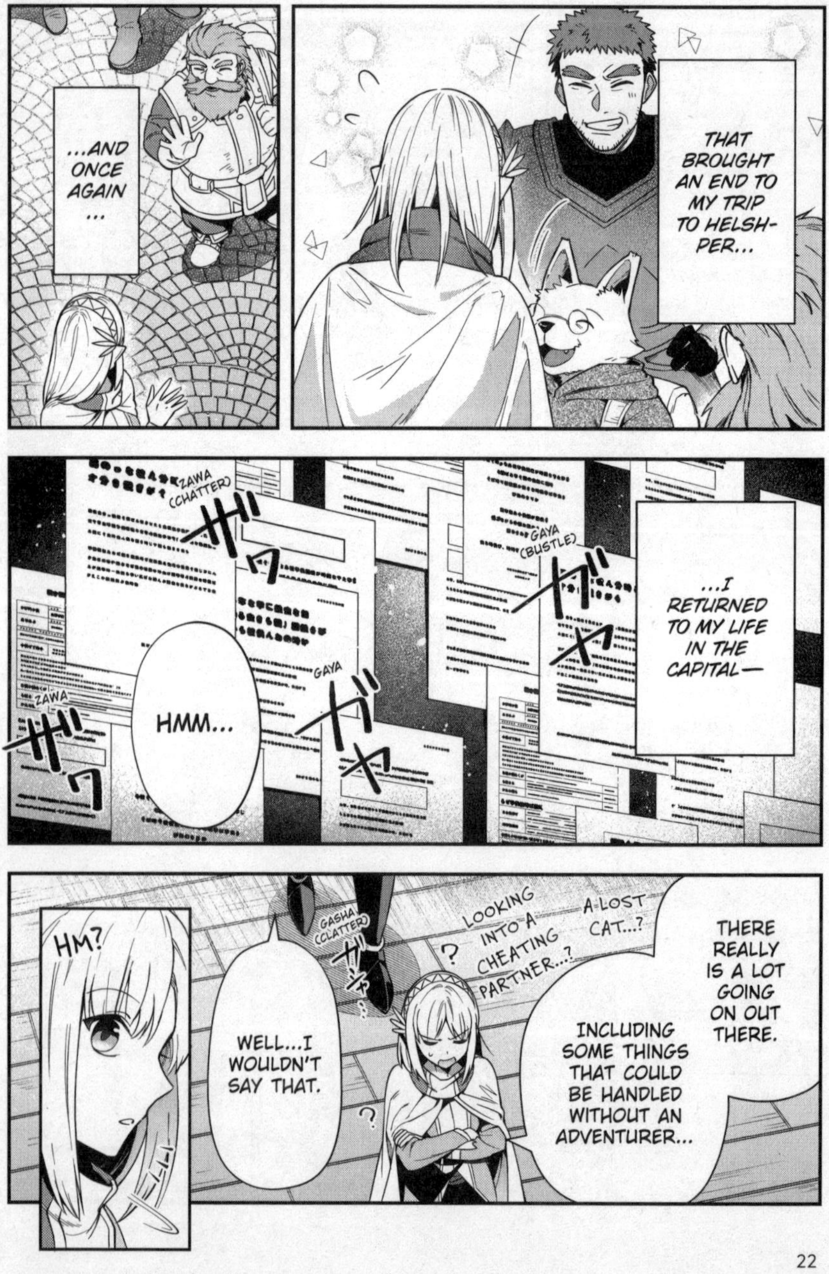
THAT BROUGHT AN END TO MY TRIP TO HELSHPER...
...AND ONCE AGAIN...
...I RETURNED TO MY LIFE IN THE CAPITAL—
GAYA (BUSTLE)
ガヤ
ZAWA (CHATTER)
ザワ
GAYA
ガヤ
HMM...
ZAWA
ザワ
THERE REALLY IS A LOT GOING ON OUT THERE.
INCLUDING SOME THINGS THAT COULD BE HANDLED WITHOUT AN ADVENTURER...
A LOST CAT...?
LOOKING INTO A CHEATING PARTNER...?
GASHA (CLATTER)
WELL...I WOULDN'T SAY THAT.
HM?

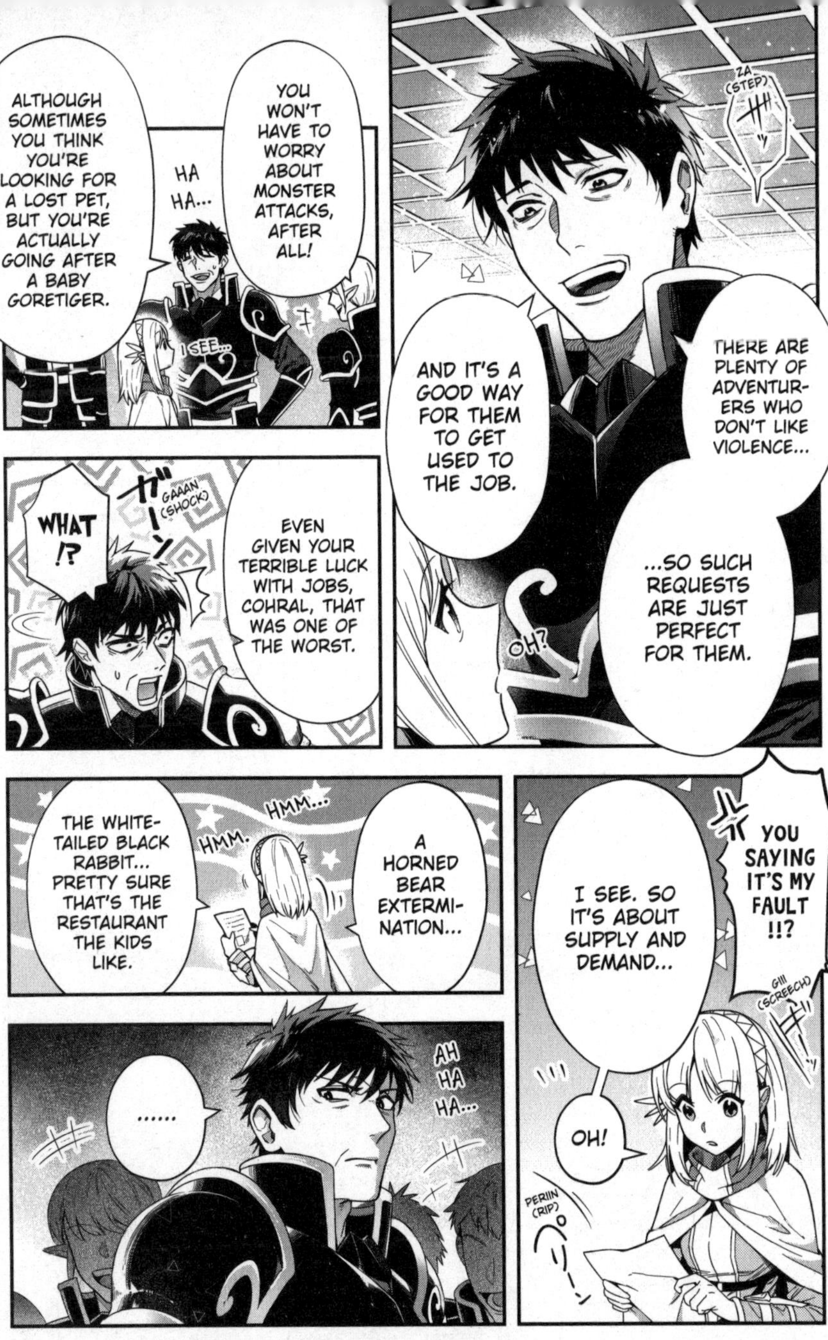
ZA (STEP)
THERE ARE PLENTY OF ADVENTURERS WHO DON'T LIKE VIOLENCE...
AND IT'S A GOOD WAY FOR THEM TO GET USED TO THE JOB.
...SO SUCH REQUESTS ARE JUST PERFECT FOR THEM.
OH?
YOU WON'T HAVE TO WORRY ABOUT MONSTER ATTACKS, AFTER ALL!
HA HA...
ALTHOUGH SOMETIMES YOU THINK YOU'RE LOOKING FOR A LOST PET, BUT YOU'RE ACTUALLY GOING AFTER A BABY GORETIGER.
I SEE...
EVEN GIVEN YOUR TERRIBLE LUCK WITH JOBS, COHRAL, THAT WAS ONE OF THE WORST.
GAAAN (SHOCK)
WHAT !?
YOU SAYING IT'S MY FAULT !!?
I SEE. SO IT'S ABOUT SUPPLY AND DEMAND...
GIII (SCREECH)
OH!
PERIIN (RIP)
A HORNED BEAR EXTERMINATION...
HMM...
HMM.
THE WHITE-TAILED BLACK RABBIT... PRETTY SURE THAT'S THE RESTAURANT THE KIDS LIKE.
AH HA HA...
......

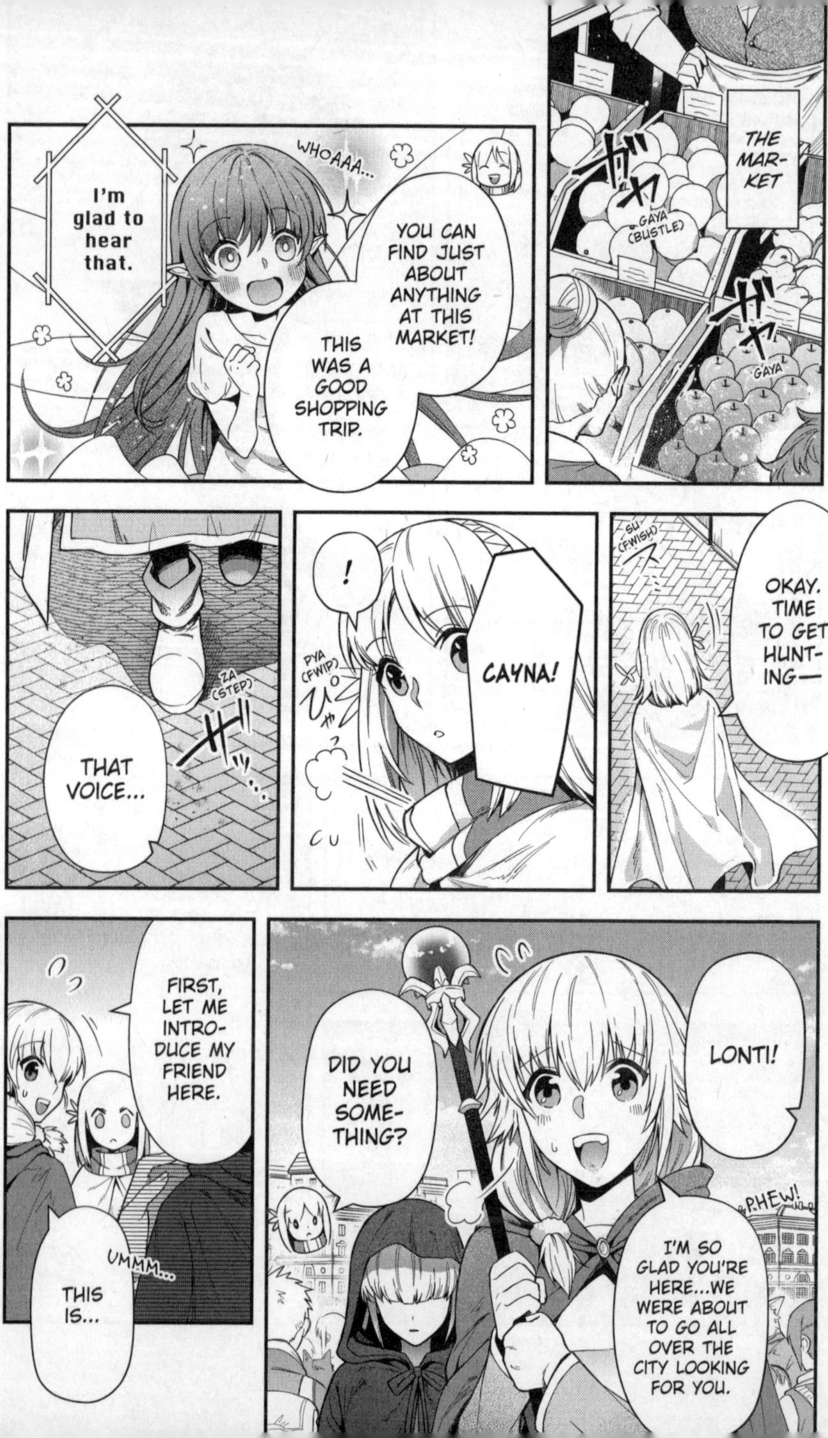

THE MARKET
GAYA (BUSTLE)
GAYA
WHOAAA...
YOU CAN FIND JUST ABOUT ANYTHING AT THIS MARKET!
THIS WAS A GOOD SHOPPING TRIP.
I'm glad to hear that.
SU (FWISH)
OKAY. TIME TO GET HUNTING—
!
CAYNA!
PYA (FWIP)
ZA (STEP)
THAT VOICE...
LONTI!
DID YOU NEED SOMETHING?
PHEW!
I'M SO GLAD YOU'RE HERE...WE WERE ABOUT TO GO ALL OVER THE CITY LOOKING FOR YOU.
FIRST, LET ME INTRODUCE MY FRIEND HERE.
UMMM...
THIS IS...

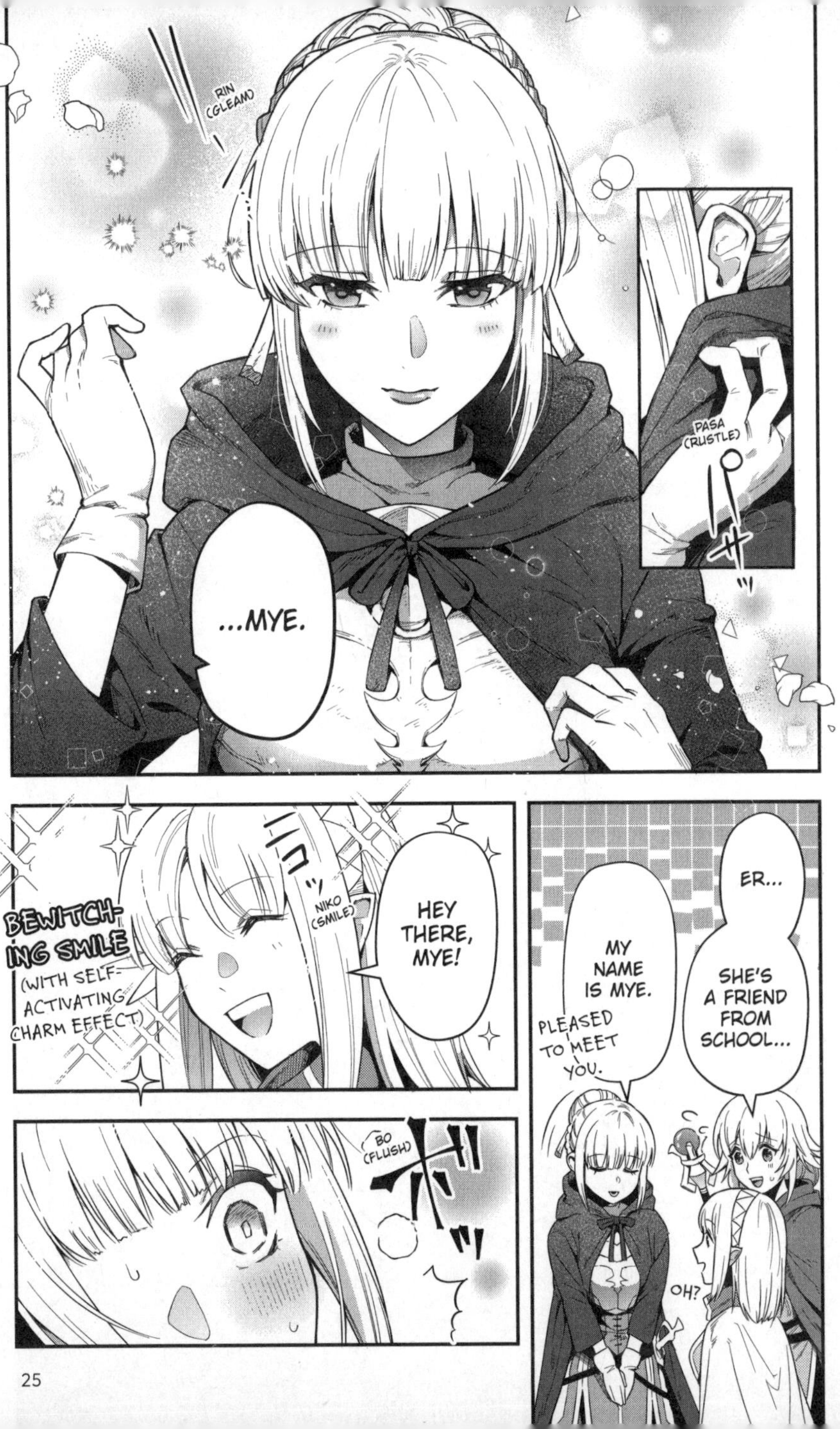
PASA (RUSTLE)
RIN (GLEAM)
...MYE.
ER...
SHE'S A FRIEND FROM SCHOOL...
MY NAME IS MYE.
PLEASED TO MEET YOU.
OH?
HEY THERE, MYE!
NIKO (SMILE)
BEWITCHING SMILE (WITH SELF-ACTIVATING CHARM EFFECT)
BO (FLUSH)

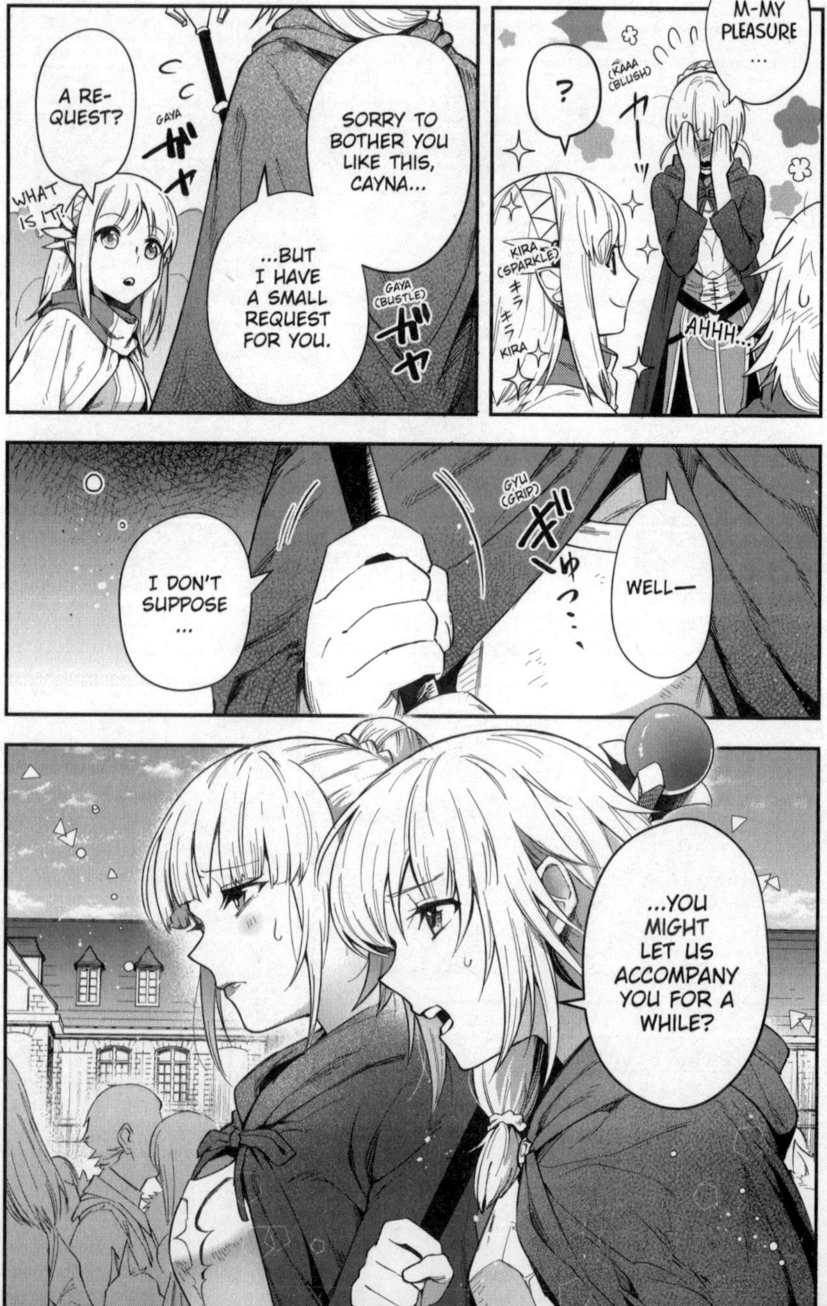

M-MY PLEASURE ...
?
KAAA (BLUSH)
KIRA (SPARKLE)
キラ キラ
KIRA
AHHH...
SORRY TO BOTHER YOU LIKE THIS, CAYNA...
...BUT I HAVE A SMALL REQUEST FOR YOU.
GAYA (BUSTLE)
A RE-QUEST?
GAYA
WHAT IS IT?
WELL—
GYU (GRIP)
I DON'T SUPPOSE ...
...YOU MIGHT LET US ACCOMPANY YOU FOR A WHILE?

In the Land of Leadale

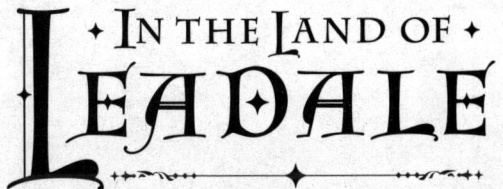

· IN THE LAND OF ·
LEADALE

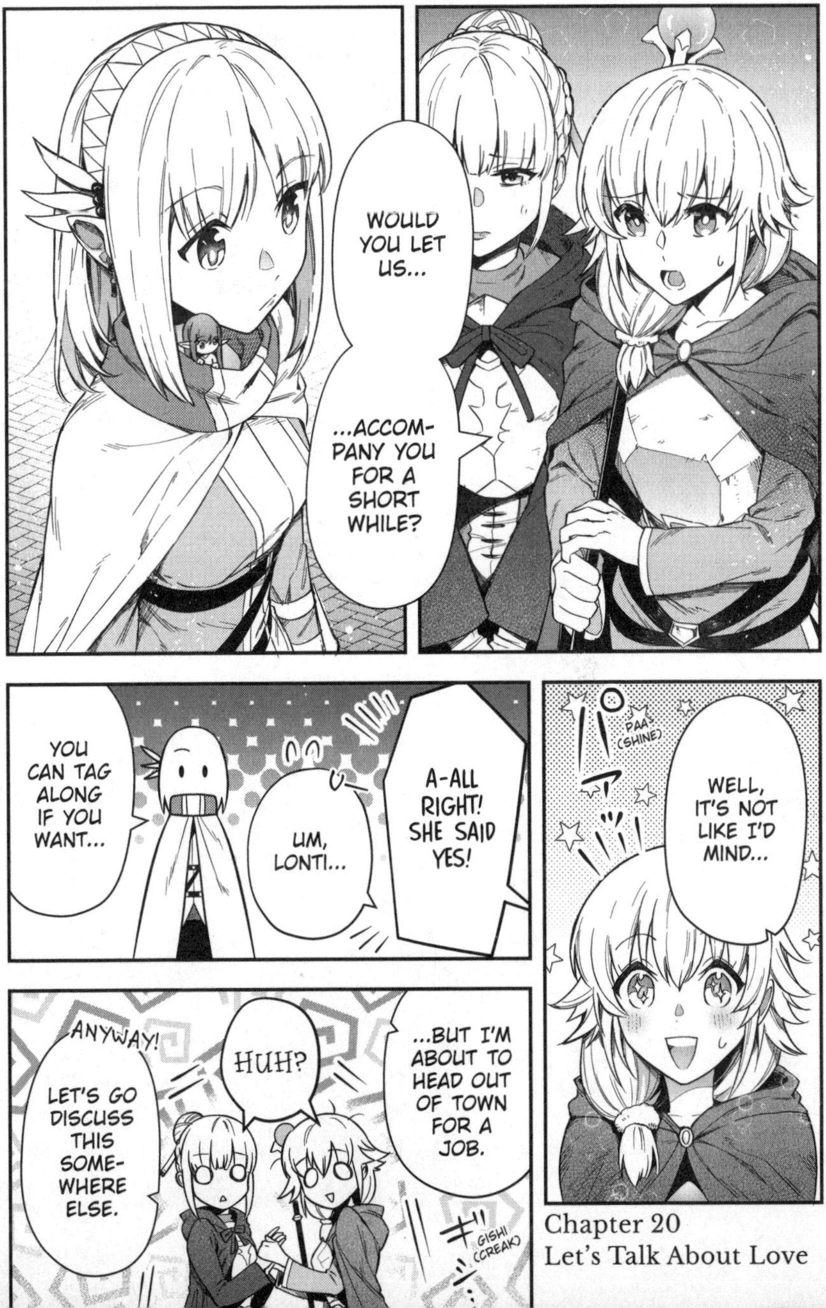
WOULD YOU LET US...
...ACCOMPANY YOU FOR A SHORT WHILE?
PAA (SHINE)
WELL, IT'S NOT LIKE I'D MIND...
A-ALL RIGHT! SHE SAID YES!
UM, LONTI...
YOU CAN TAG ALONG IF YOU WANT...
...BUT I'M ABOUT TO HEAD OUT OF TOWN FOR A JOB.
HUH?
ANYWAY!
LET'S GO DISCUSS THIS SOMEWHERE ELSE.
GISHI (CREAK)

Chapter 20
Let's Talk About Love

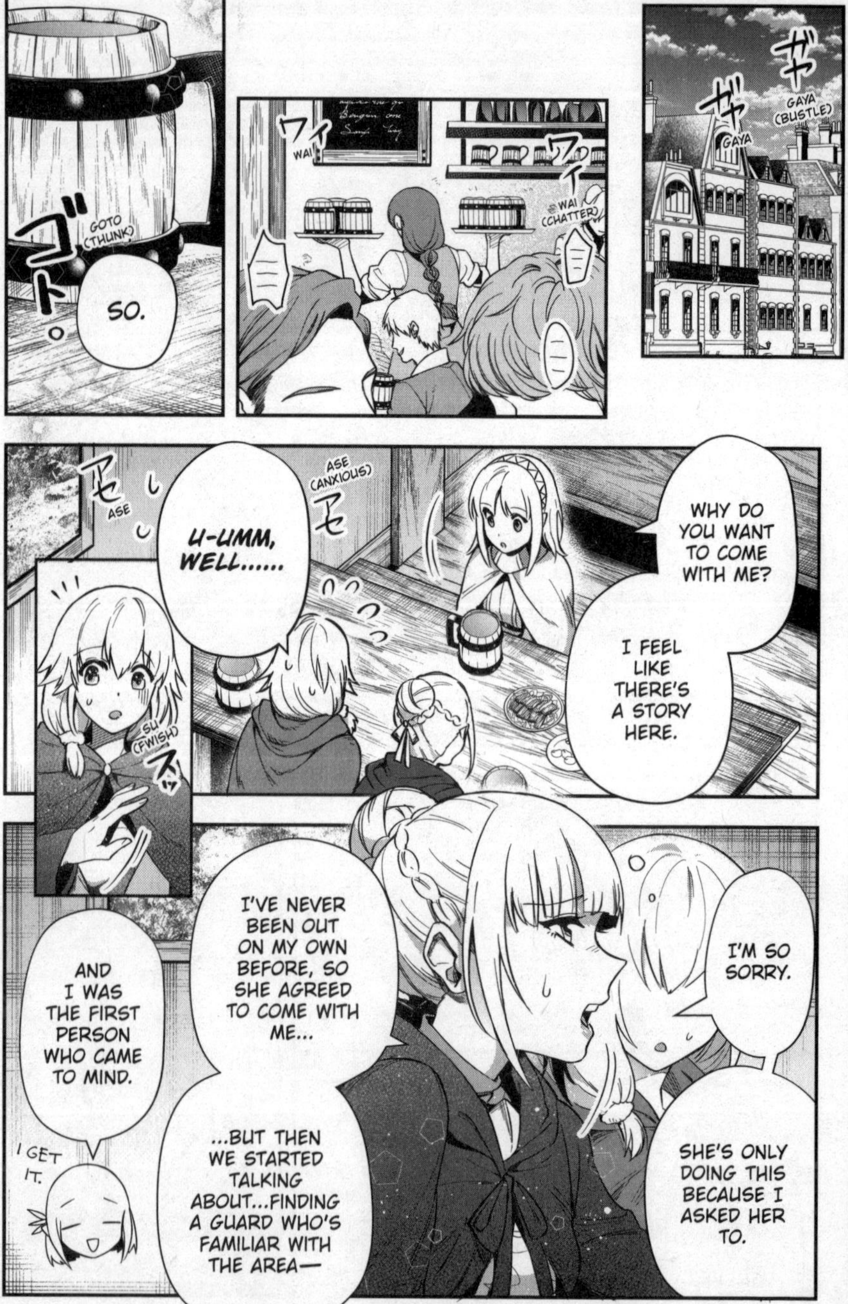
ガヤ
GAYA (BUSTLE)
ガヤ
GAYA
ワイ
WAI
ワイ
WAI (CHATTER)
ゴト
GOTO (THUNK)
SO.
WHY DO YOU WANT TO COME WITH ME?
I FEEL LIKE THERE'S A STORY HERE.
アセ
ASE (ANXIOUS)
U-UMM, WELL......
アセ
ASE
スッ
SU (FWISH)
I'M SO SORRY.
SHE'S ONLY DOING THIS BECAUSE I ASKED HER TO.
I'VE NEVER BEEN OUT ON MY OWN BEFORE, SO SHE AGREED TO COME WITH ME...
...BUT THEN WE STARTED TALKING ABOUT...FINDING A GUARD WHO'S FAMILIAR WITH THE AREA—
AND I WAS THE FIRST PERSON WHO CAME TO MIND.
I GET IT.

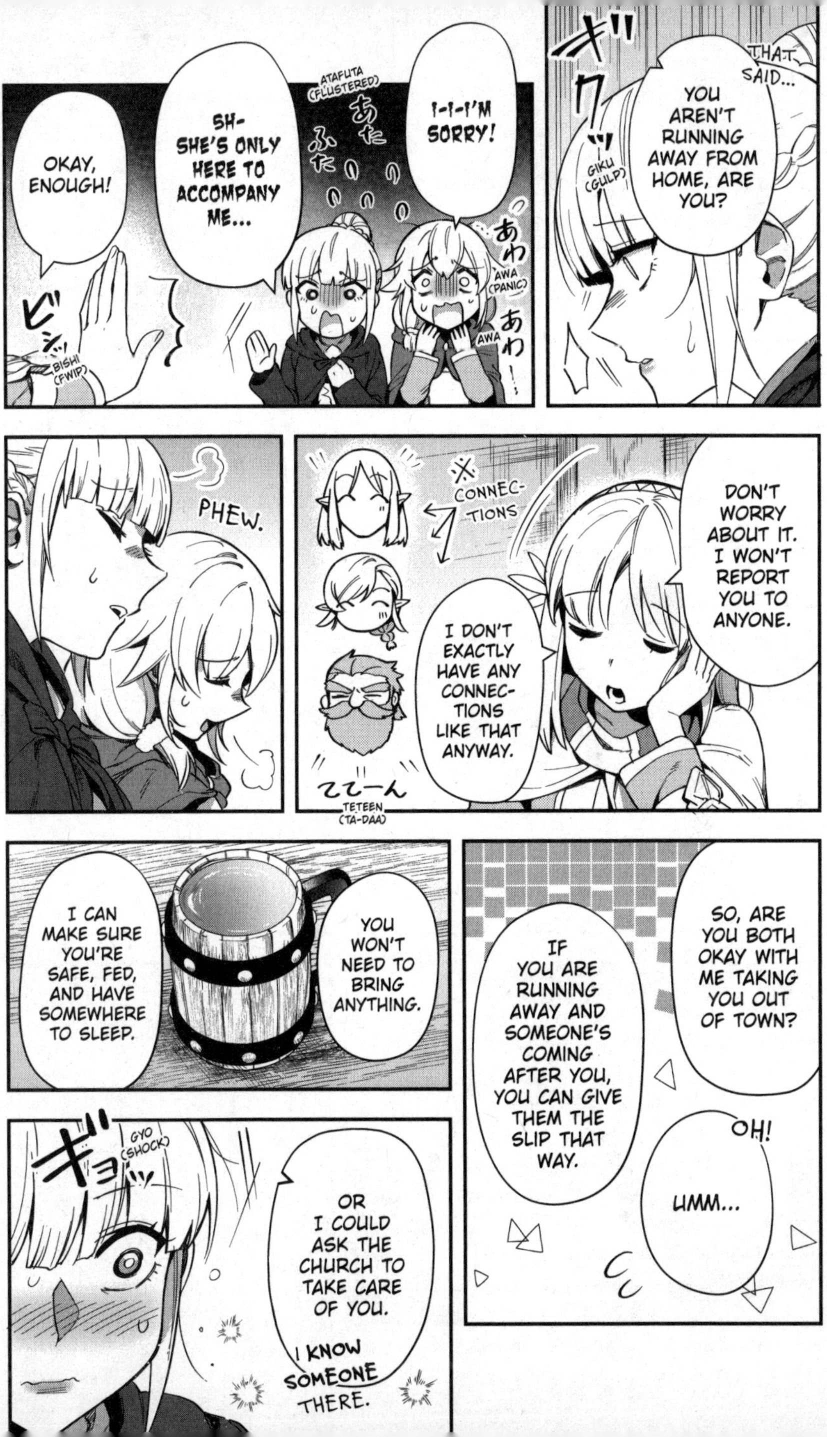
THAT SAID...
YOU AREN'T RUNNING AWAY FROM HOME, ARE YOU?
ギクッ
GIKU (GULP)
I-I-I'M SORRY!
あたふた
ATAFUTA (FLUSTERED)
あわあわ
AWA (PANIC)
AWA
SH-SHE'S ONLY HERE TO ACCOMPANY ME...
OKAY, ENOUGH!
ビシッ
BISHI (FWIP)
DON'T WORRY ABOUT IT. I WON'T REPORT YOU TO ANYONE.
I DON'T EXACTLY HAVE ANY CONNECTIONS LIKE THAT ANYWAY.
CONNECTIONS
てでーん
TETEEN (TA-DAA)
PHEW.
SO, ARE YOU BOTH OKAY WITH ME TAKING YOU OUT OF TOWN?
IF YOU ARE RUNNING AWAY AND SOMEONE'S COMING AFTER YOU, YOU CAN GIVE THEM THE SLIP THAT WAY.
OH!
UMM...
YOU WON'T NEED TO BRING ANYTHING.
I CAN MAKE SURE YOU'RE SAFE, FED, AND HAVE SOMEWHERE TO SLEEP.
OR I COULD ASK THE CHURCH TO TAKE CARE OF YOU.
I KNOW SOMEONE THERE.
ギョッ
GYO (SHOCK)

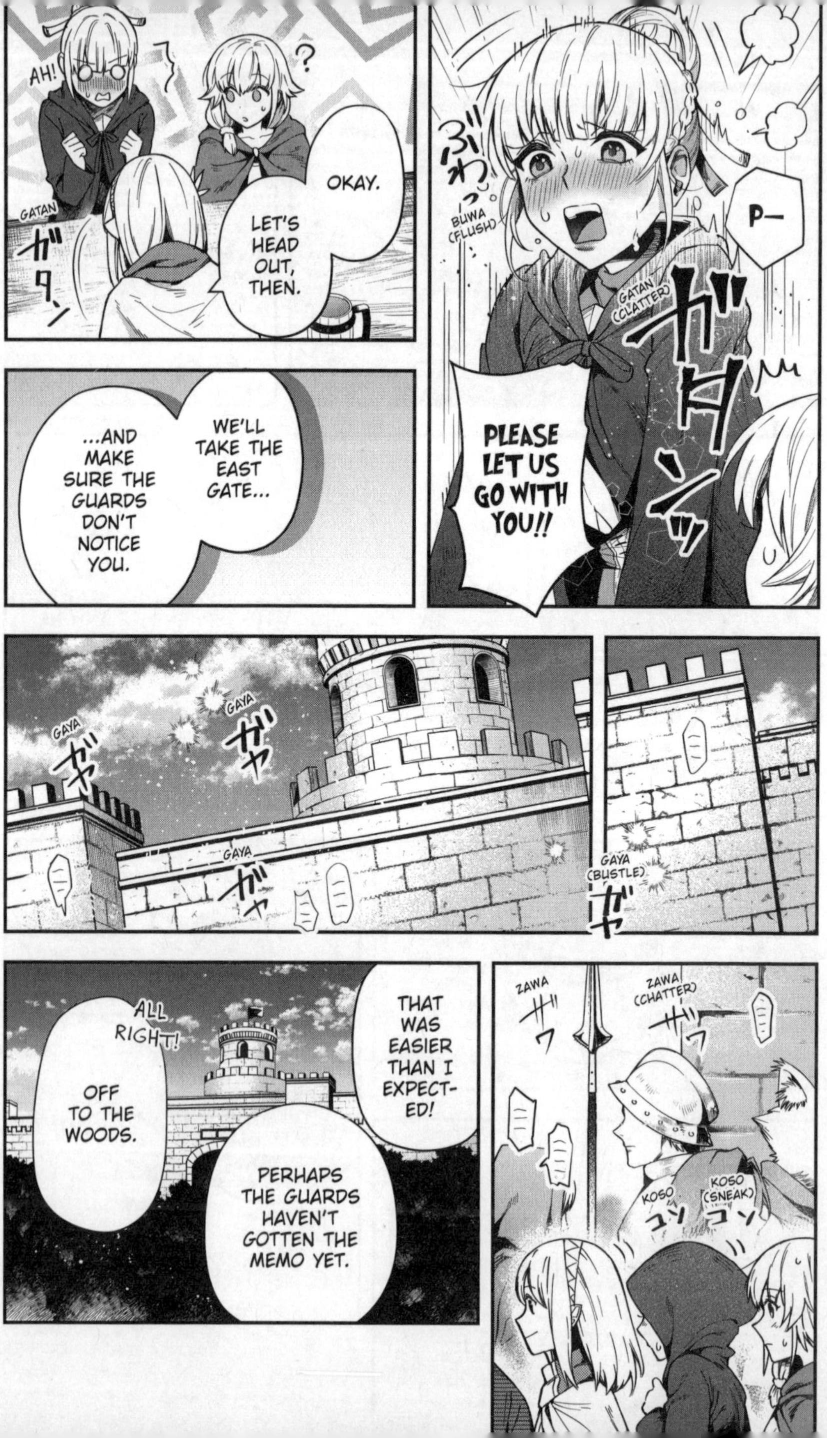
P—
BUWA (FLUSH)
GATAN (CLATTER)
PLEASE LET US GO WITH YOU!!
AH!
GATAN
OKAY.
LET'S HEAD OUT, THEN.
WE'LL TAKE THE EAST GATE...
...AND MAKE SURE THE GUARDS DON'T NOTICE YOU.
GAYA (BUSTLE)
GAYA
GAYA
GAYA
ZAWA (CHATTER)
ZAWA
KOSO (SNEAK)
KOSO
THAT WAS EASIER THAN I EXPECTED!
PERHAPS THE GUARDS HAVEN'T GOTTEN THE MEMO YET.
ALL RIGHT!
OFF TO THE WOODS.

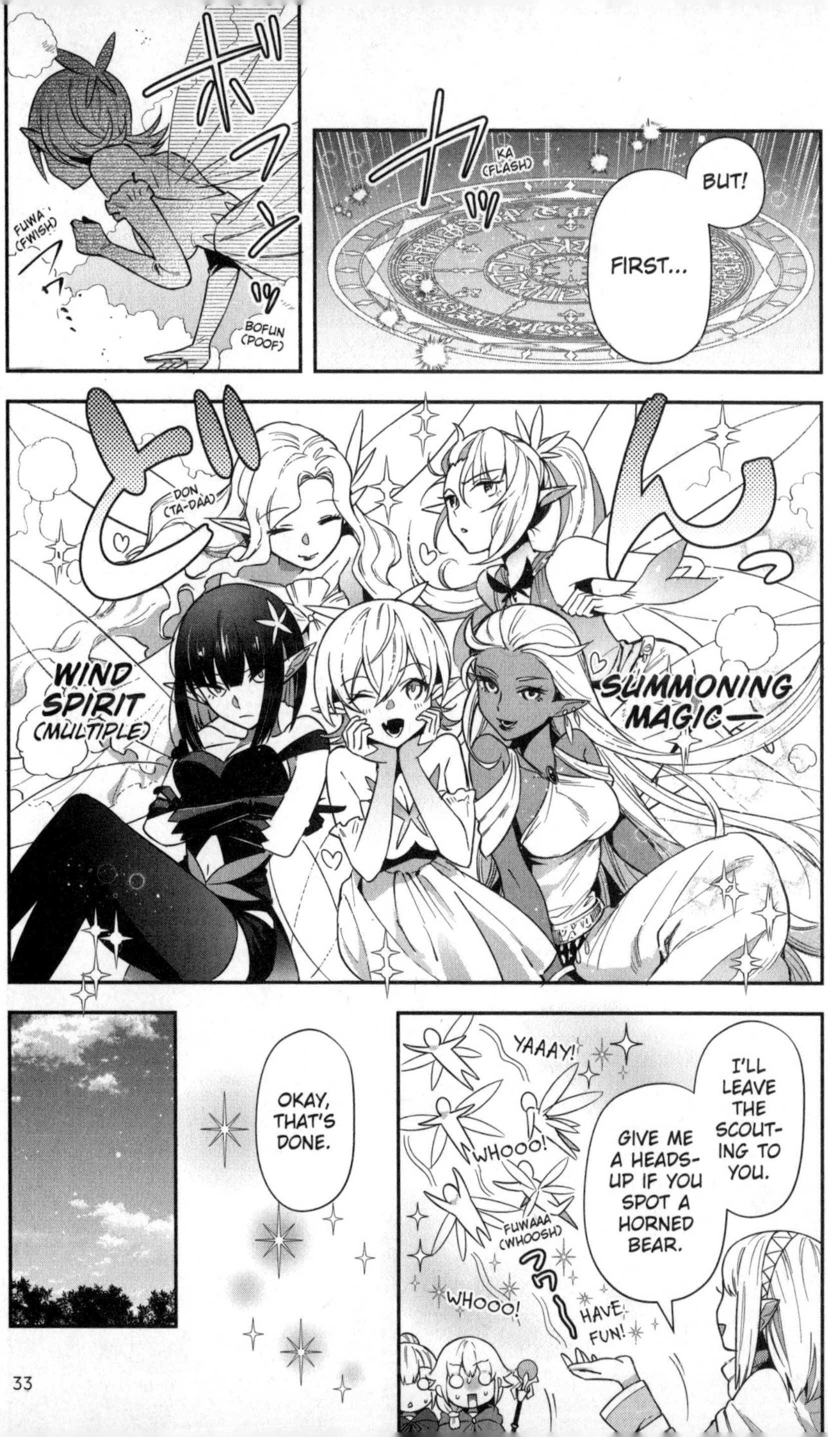
BUT!
FIRST...
KA (FLASH)
BOFUN (POOF)
FUWA (FWISH)
DON (TA-DAA)
SUMMONING MAGIC—
WIND SPIRIT (MULTIPLE)
I'LL LEAVE THE SCOUT-ING TO YOU.
GIVE ME A HEADS-UP IF YOU SPOT A HORNED BEAR.
YAAAY!
WHOOO!
FUWAAA (WHOOSH)
WHOOO!
HAVE FUN!
OKAY, THAT'S DONE.

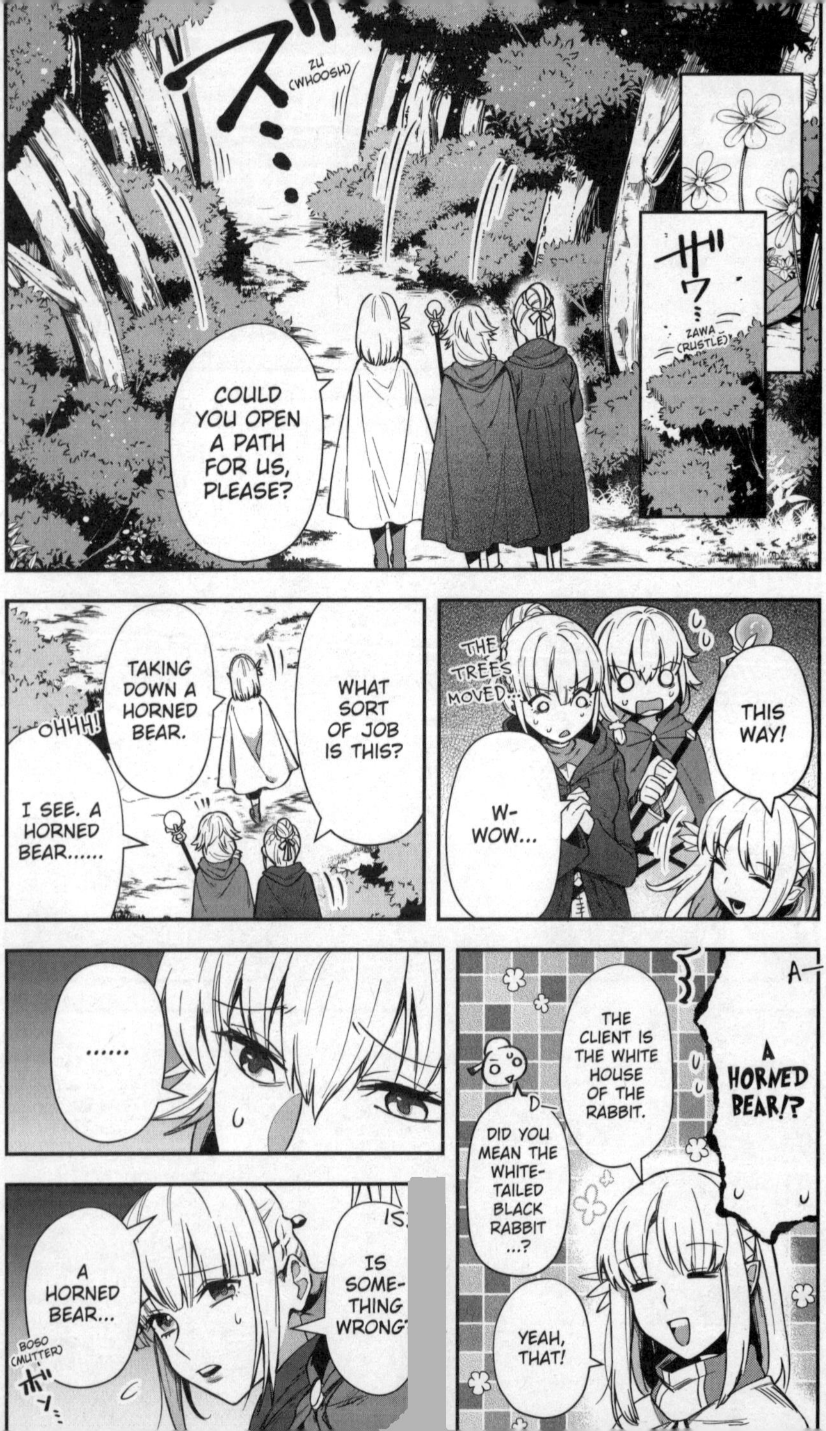
ザワ
ZAWA (RUSTLE)
ズ
ZU (WHOOSH)
COULD YOU OPEN A PATH FOR US, PLEASE?
THIS WAY!
THE TREES MOVED...
W-WOW...
WHAT SORT OF JOB IS THIS?
TAKING DOWN A HORNED BEAR.
OHHH!
I SEE. A HORNED BEAR......
A—
A HORNED BEAR!?
THE CLIENT IS THE WHITE HOUSE OF THE RABBIT.
D—
DID YOU MEAN THE WHITE-TAILED BLACK RABBIT ...?
YEAH, THAT!
......
IS
IS SOMETHING WRONG?
A HORNED BEAR...
ボソ
BOSO (MUTTER)

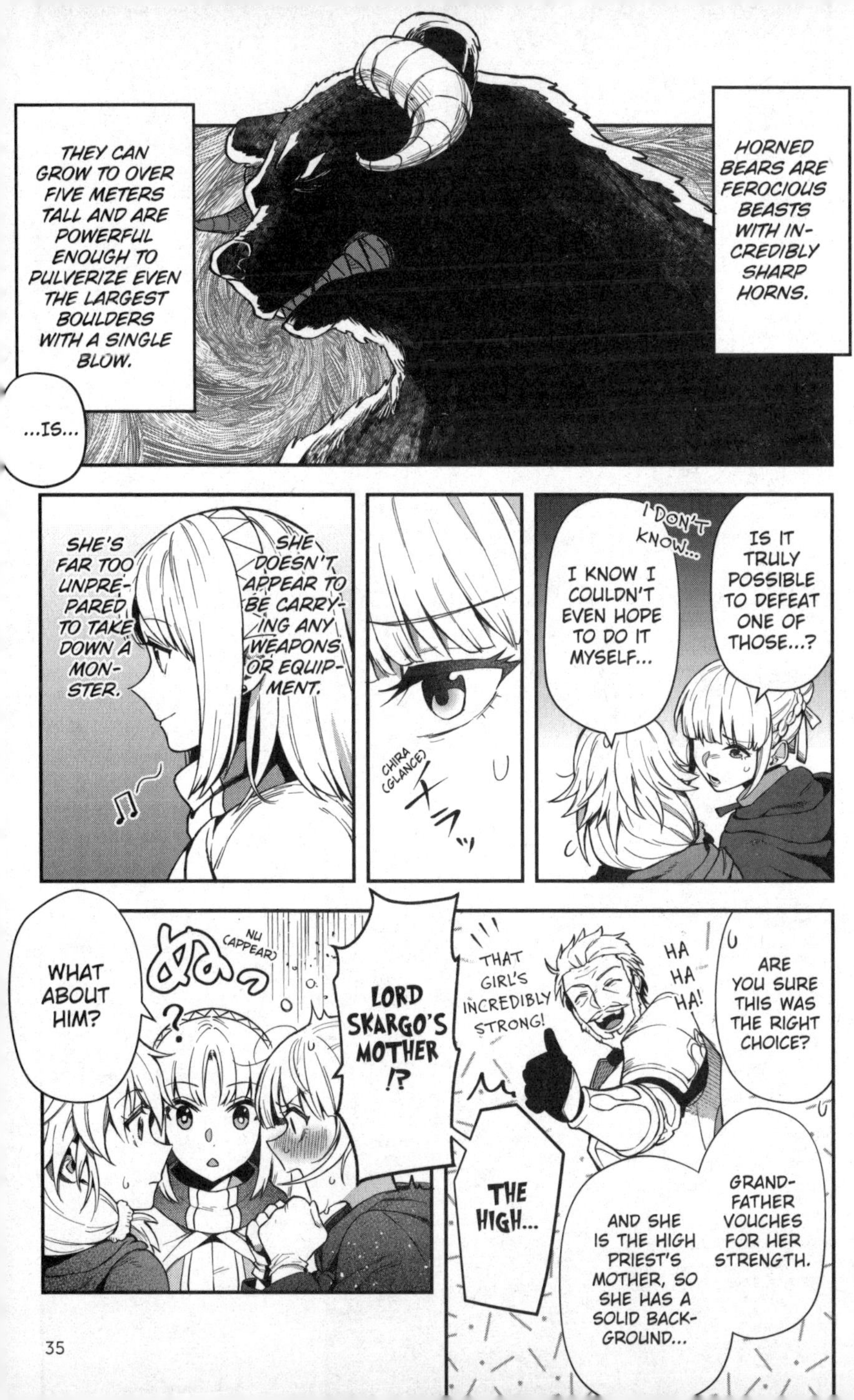
HORNED BEARS ARE FEROCIOUS BEASTS WITH IN-CREDIBLY SHARP HORNS.
THEY CAN GROW TO OVER FIVE METERS TALL AND ARE POWERFUL ENOUGH TO PULVERIZE EVEN THE LARGEST BOULDERS WITH A SINGLE BLOW.
...IS...
IS IT TRULY POSSIBLE TO DEFEAT ONE OF THOSE...?
I DON'T KNOW...
I KNOW I COULDN'T EVEN HOPE TO DO IT MYSELF...
CHIRA (GLANCE)
SHE DOESN'T APPEAR TO BE CARRY-ING ANY WEAPONS OR EQUIP-MENT.
SHE'S FAR TOO UNPRE-PARED TO TAKE DOWN A MON-STER.
ARE YOU SURE THIS WAS THE RIGHT CHOICE?
HA HA HA!
THAT GIRL'S INCREDIBLY STRONG!
GRAND-FATHER VOUCHES FOR HER STRENGTH.
AND SHE IS THE HIGH PRIEST'S MOTHER, SO SHE HAS A SOLID BACK-GROUND...
THE HIGH...
LORD SKARGO'S MOTHER !?
NU (APPEAR)
WHAT ABOUT HIM?

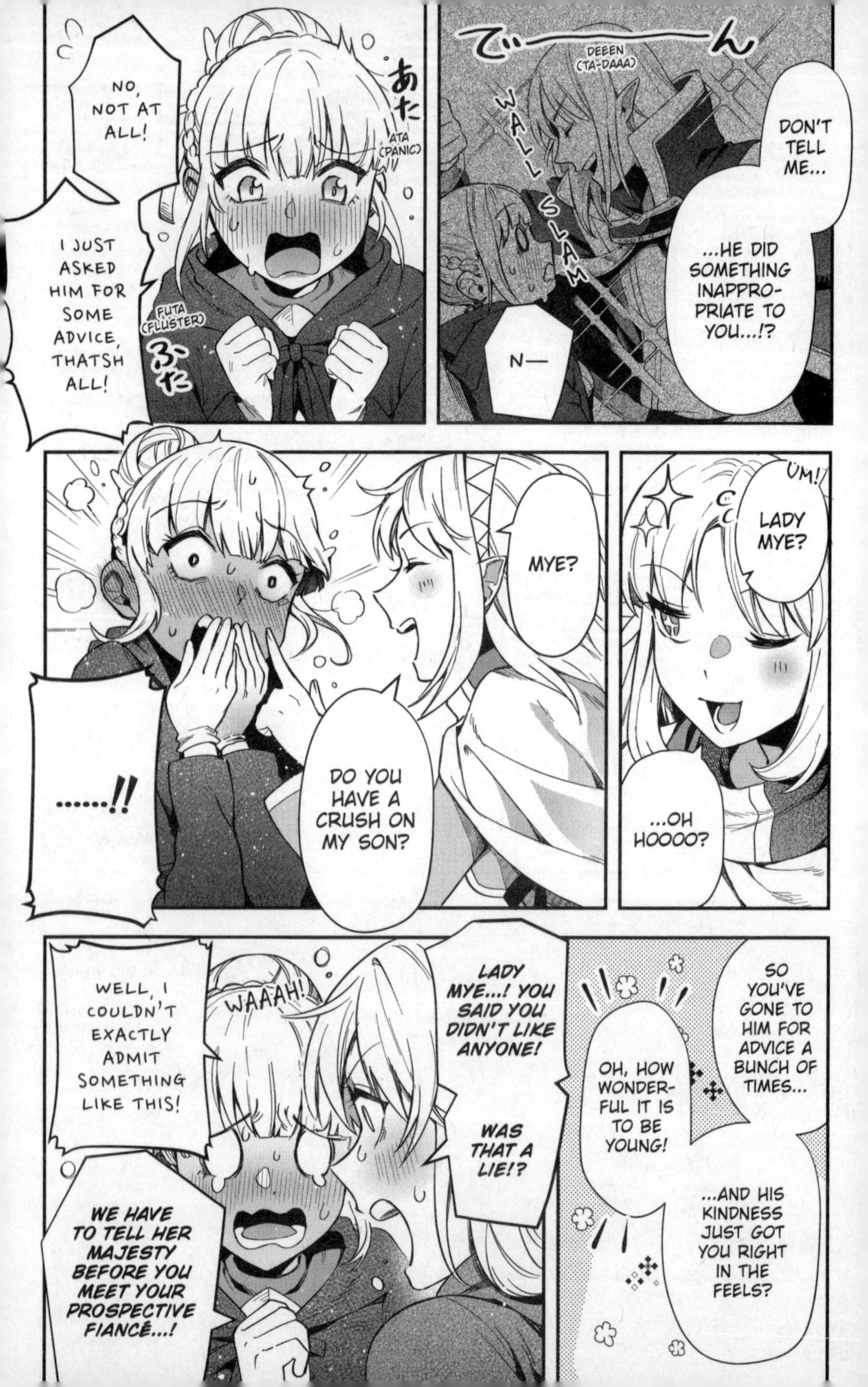
でぃーーーーん
DEEEN (TA-DAAA)
WALL SLAM
DON'T TELL ME...
...HE DID SOMETHING INAPPROPRIATE TO YOU...!?
N—
NO, NOT AT ALL!
あた
ATA (PANIC)
I JUST ASKED HIM FOR SOME ADVICE, THATSH ALL!
FUTA (FLUSTER)
ふた
UM!
LADY MYE?
...OH HOOOO?
MYE?
DO YOU HAVE A CRUSH ON MY SON?
......!!
SO YOU'VE GONE TO HIM FOR ADVICE A BUNCH OF TIMES...
...AND HIS KINDNESS JUST GOT YOU RIGHT IN THE FEELS?
OH, HOW WONDERFUL IT IS TO BE YOUNG!
LADY MYE...! YOU SAID YOU DIDN'T LIKE ANYONE!
WAS THAT A LIE!?
WAAAH!
WELL, I COULDN'T EXACTLY ADMIT SOMETHING LIKE THIS!
WE HAVE TO TELL HER MAJESTY BEFORE YOU MEET YOUR PROSPECTIVE FIANCÉ...!

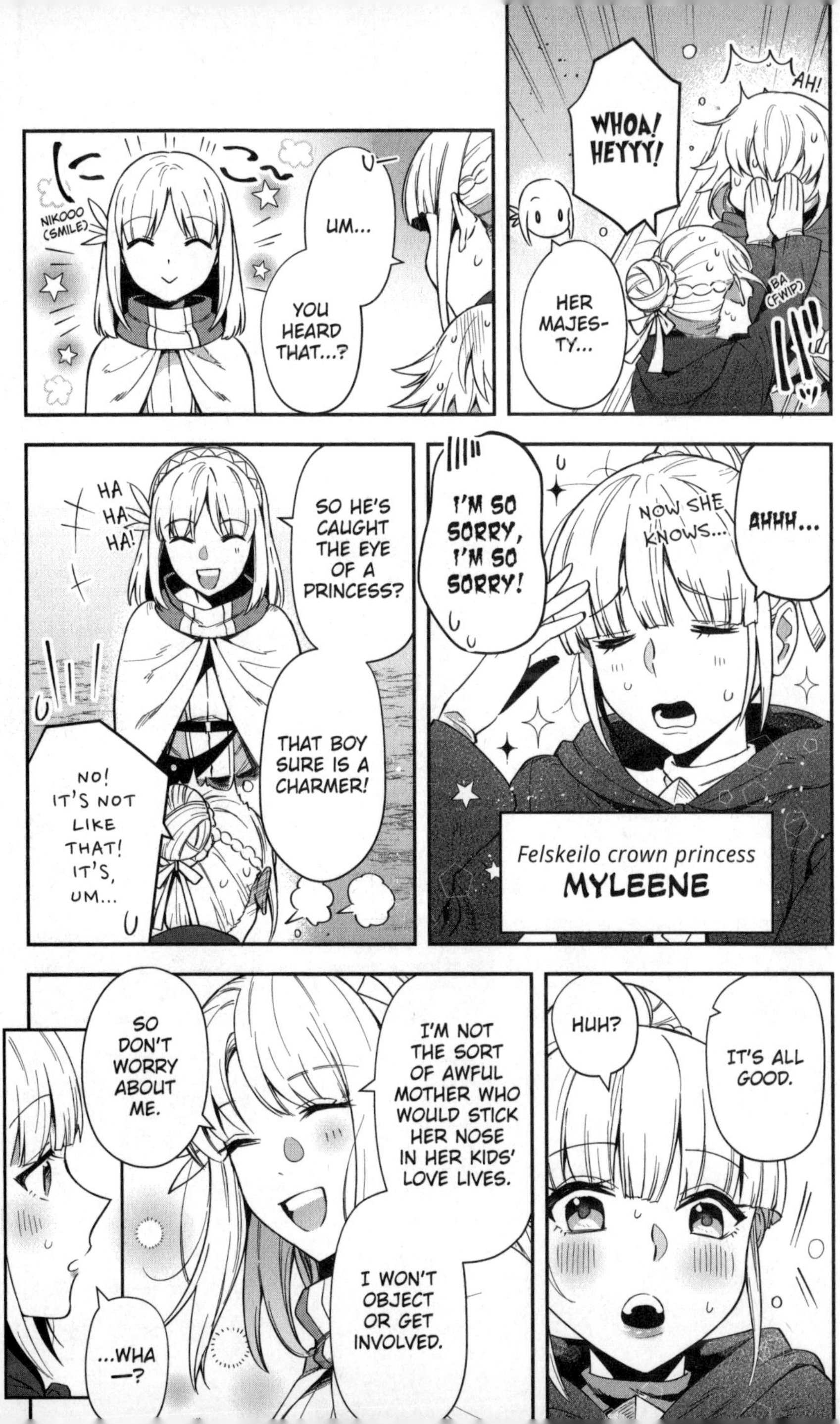
AH!
WHOA! HEYYY!
BA (FWIP)
HER MAJESTY...
UM...
YOU HEARD THAT...?
NIKOOO (SMILE)
AHHH...
NOW SHE KNOWS...
I'M SO SORRY, I'M SO SORRY!
Felskeilo crown princess
MYLEENE
SO HE'S CAUGHT THE EYE OF A PRINCESS?
HA HA HA!
THAT BOY SURE IS A CHARMER!
NO! IT'S NOT LIKE THAT! IT'S, UM...
IT'S ALL GOOD.
HUH?
I'M NOT THE SORT OF AWFUL MOTHER WHO WOULD STICK HER NOSE IN HER KIDS' LOVE LIVES.
SO DON'T WORRY ABOUT ME.
I WON'T OBJECT OR GET INVOLVED.
...WHA—?

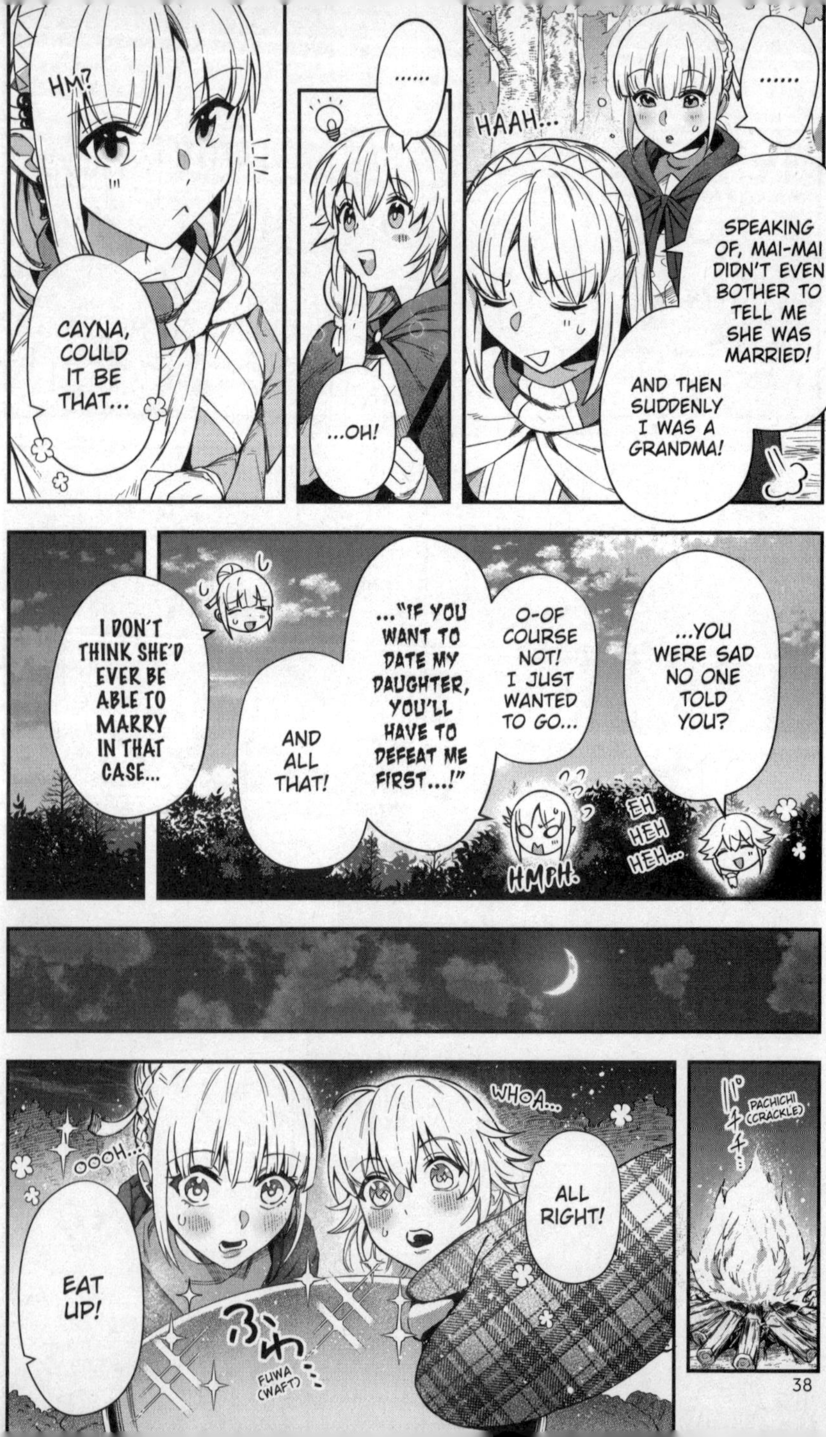
......
HAAH...
SPEAKING OF, MAI-MAI DIDN'T EVEN BOTHER TO TELL ME SHE WAS MARRIED!
AND THEN SUDDENLY I WAS A GRANDMA!
......
...OH!
HM?
CAYNA, COULD IT BE THAT...
...YOU WERE SAD NO ONE TOLD YOU?
EH HEH HEH...
O-OF COURSE NOT! I JUST WANTED TO GO...
HMPH.
..."IF YOU WANT TO DATE MY DAUGHTER, YOU'LL HAVE TO DEFEAT ME FIRST...!"
AND ALL THAT!
I DON'T THINK SHE'D EVER BE ABLE TO MARRY IN THAT CASE...
パチチ…
PACHICHI (CRACKLE)
ALL RIGHT!
WHOA...
OOOH...
EAT UP!
ふわ…
FUWA (WAFT)

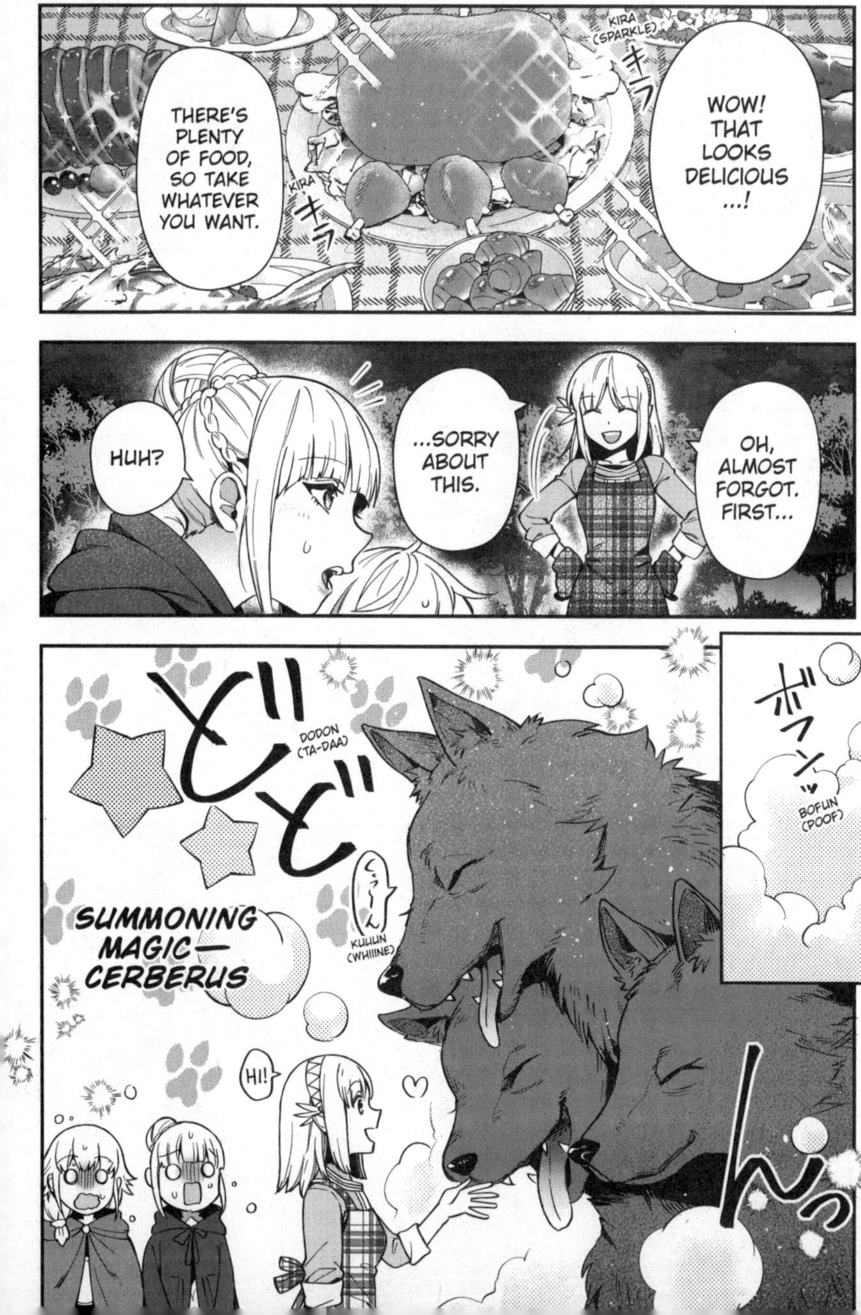
KIRA (SPARKLE)
キラ
WOW! THAT LOOKS DELICIOUS ...!
THERE'S PLENTY OF FOOD, SO TAKE WHATEVER YOU WANT.
KIRA
キラ
OH, ALMOST FORGOT. FIRST...
...SORRY ABOUT THIS.
HUH?
ボフンッ
BOFUN (POOF)
どど
DODON (TA-DAA)
くぅ～ん
KUUUN (WHIIINE)
SUMMONING MAGIC—CERBERUS
HI!
んっ

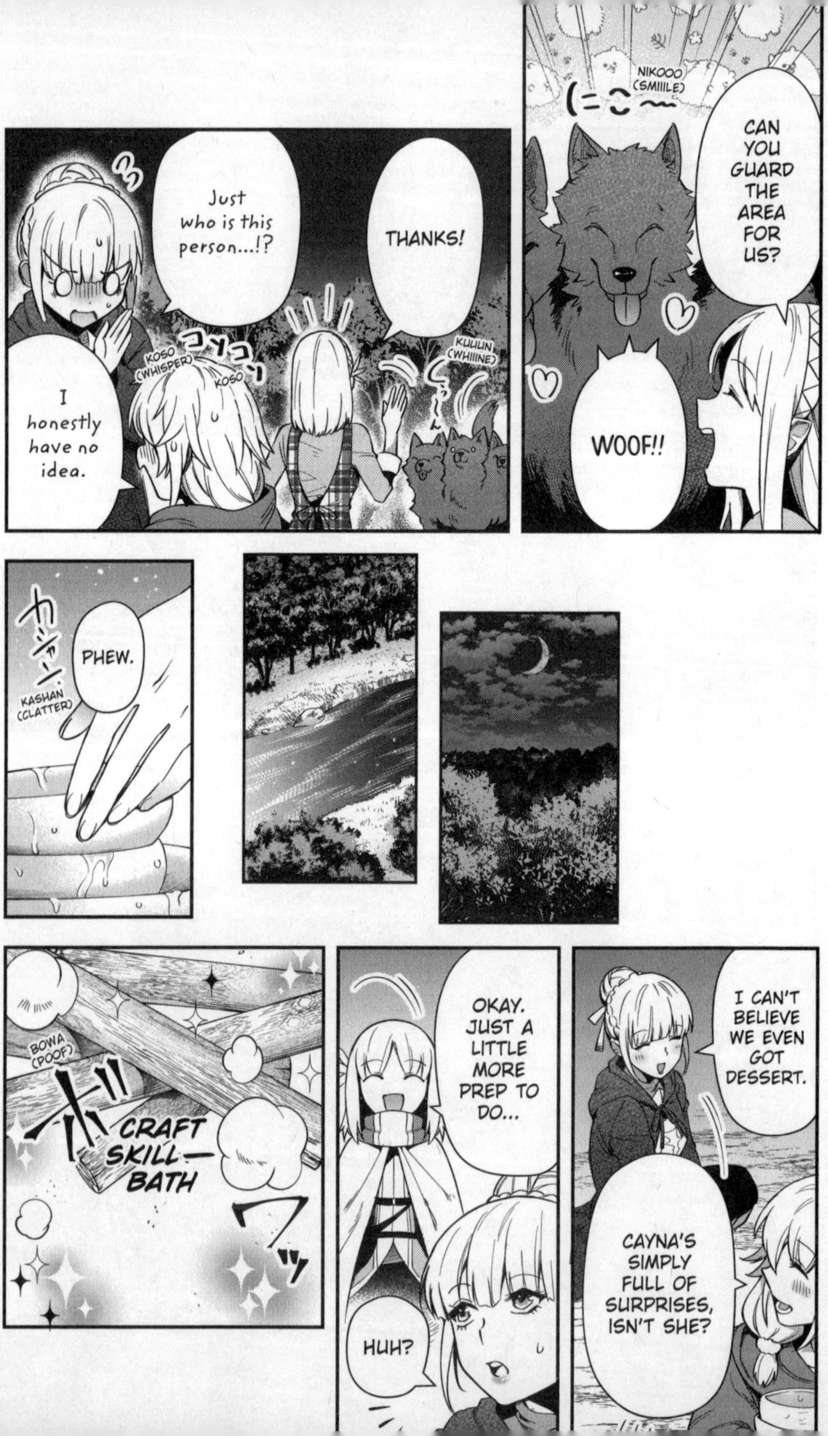
NIKOOO (SMIIILE)
CAN YOU GUARD THE AREA FOR US?
WOOF!!
THANKS!
Just who is this person...!?
KOSO (WHISPER) KOSO
KUUUN (WHIIINE)
I honestly have no idea.
KASHAN (CLATTER)
PHEW.
I CAN'T BELIEVE WE EVEN GOT DESSERT.
CAYNA'S SIMPLY FULL OF SURPRISES, ISN'T SHE?
OKAY. JUST A LITTLE MORE PREP TO DO...
HUH?
BOWA (POOF)
CRAFT SKILL—BATH

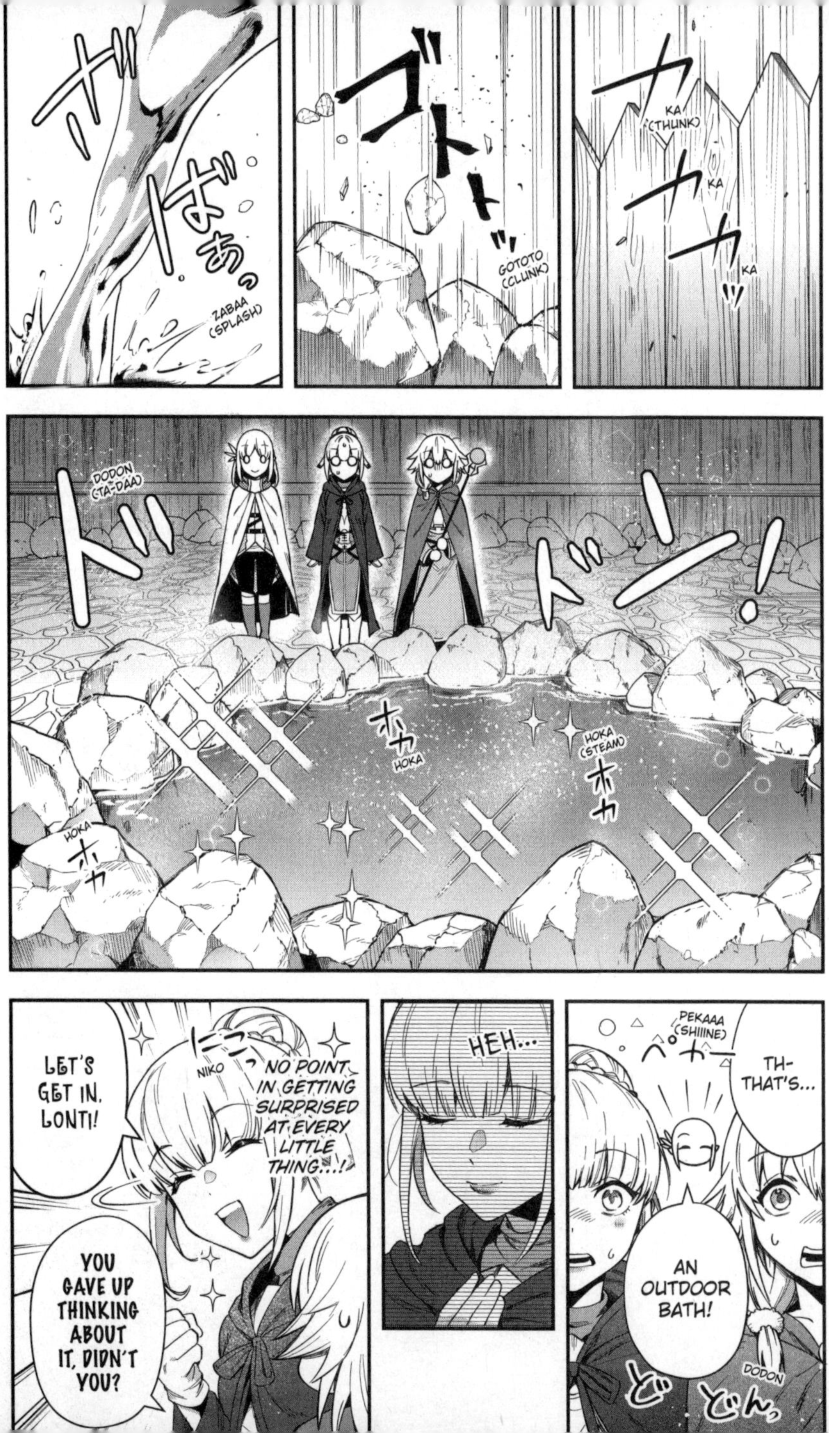
KA (THUNK)
KA
KA
GOTOTO (CLUNK)
ZABAA (SPLASH)
DODON (TA-DAA)
HOKA (STEAM)
HOKA
HOKA
PEKAAA (SHIIINE)
TH- THAT'S...
AN OUTDOOR BATH!
DODON
HEH...
NIKO
NO POINT IN GETTING SURPRISED AT EVERY LITTLE THING...!
LET'S GET IN, LONTI!
YOU GAVE UP THINKING ABOUT IT, DIDN'T YOU?

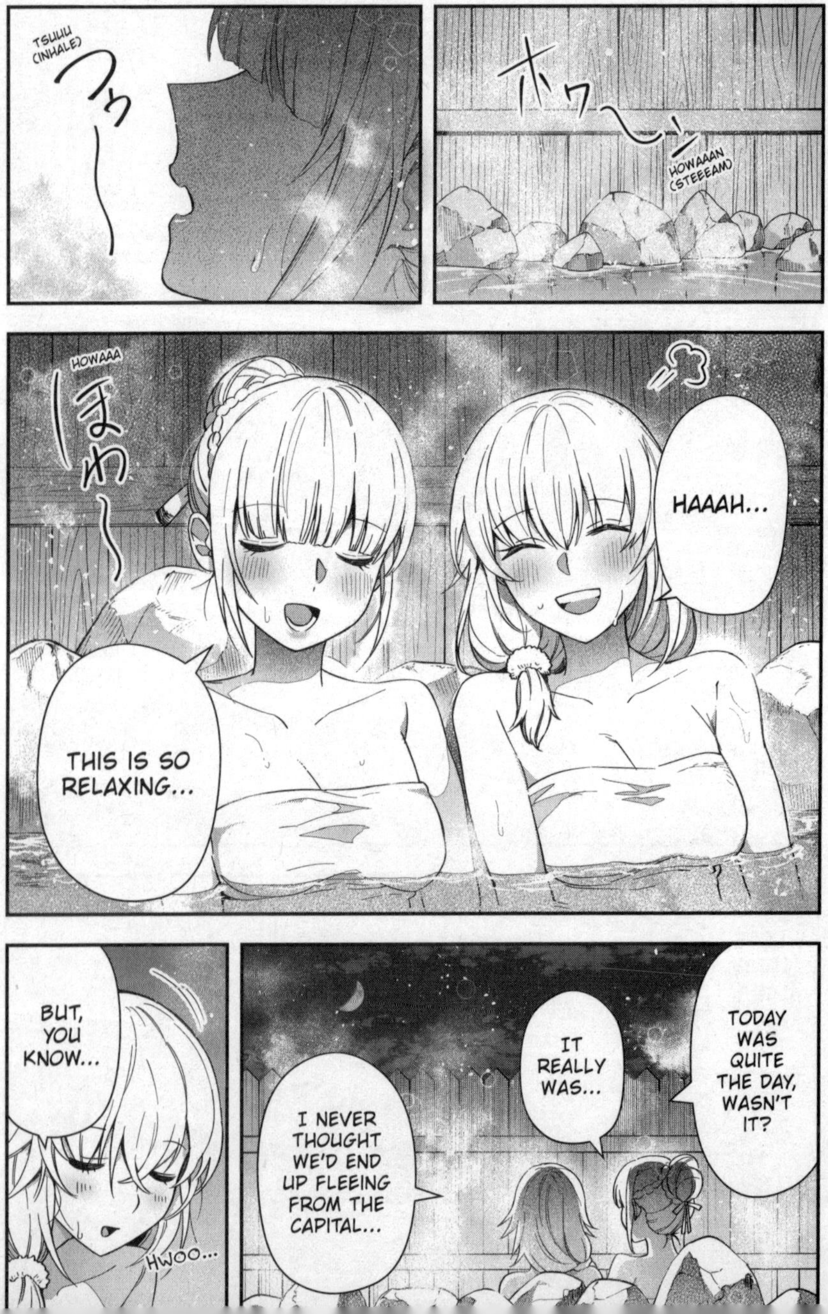
ホワ〜ン
HOWAAAN (STEEEAM)
つぅ〜
TSUUU (INHALE)
HAAAH...
ほわ〜
HOWAAA
THIS IS SO RELAXING...
TODAY WAS QUITE THE DAY, WASN'T IT?
IT REALLY WAS...
I NEVER THOUGHT WE'D END UP FLEEING FROM THE CAPITAL...
BUT, YOU KNOW...
HWOO...

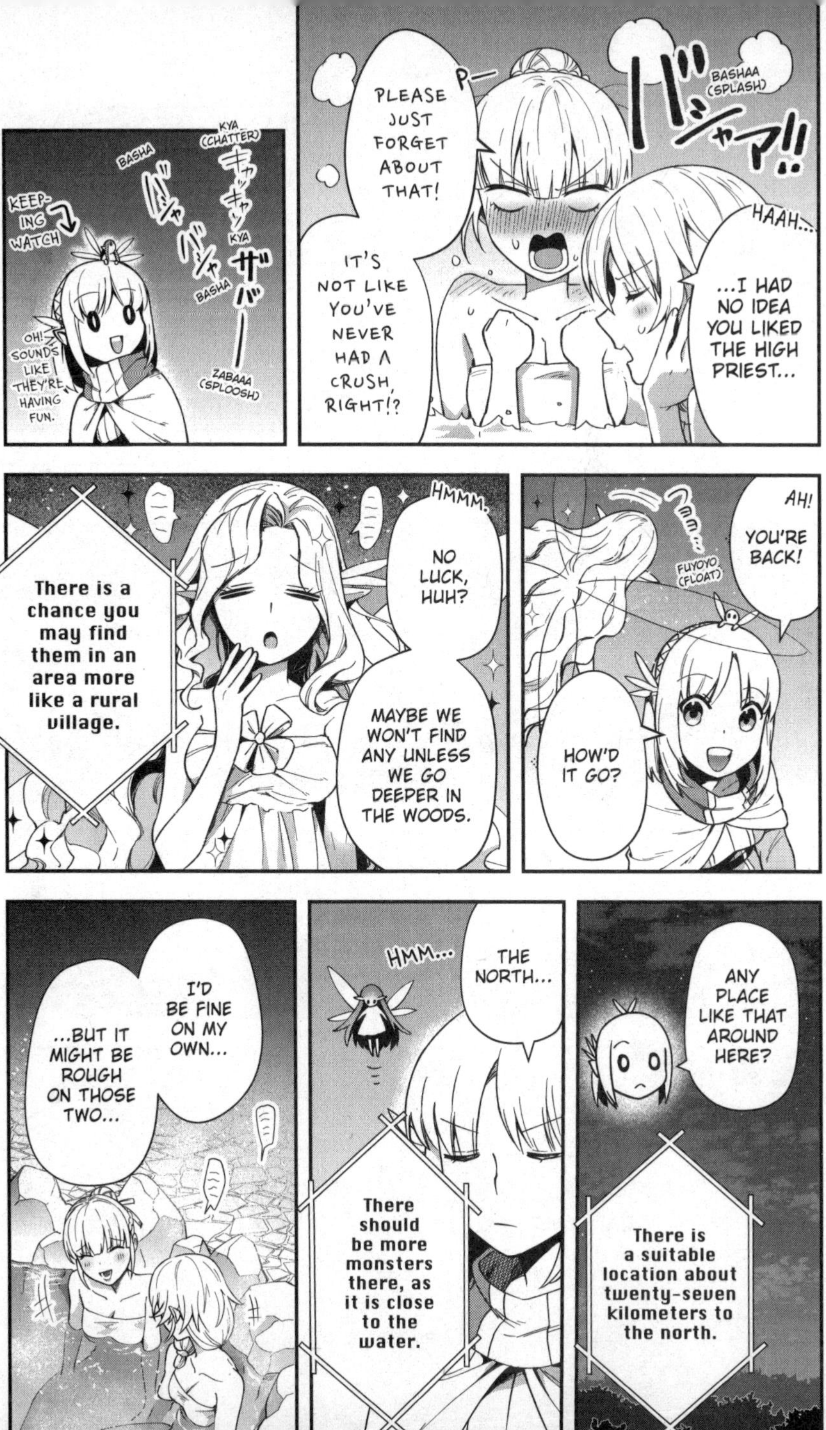
バシャア!!
BASHAA (SPLASH)
HAAH...
...I HAD NO IDEA YOU LIKED THE HIGH PRIEST...
P—
PLEASE JUST FORGET ABOUT THAT!
IT'S NOT LIKE YOU'VE NEVER HAD A CRUSH, RIGHT!?
キャッキャッ
KYA (CHATTER)
KYA
バシャバシャ
BASHA
BASHA
ザバー
ZABAAA (SPLOOSH)
KEEPING WATCH
OH! SOUNDS LIKE THEY'RE HAVING FUN.
AH!
YOU'RE BACK!
FUYOYO (FLOAT)
HOW'D IT GO?
HMMM.
NO LUCK, HUH?
MAYBE WE WON'T FIND ANY UNLESS WE GO DEEPER IN THE WOODS.
There is a chance you may find them in an area more like a rural village.
ANY PLACE LIKE THAT AROUND HERE?
There is a suitable location about twenty-seven kilometers to the north.
THE NORTH...
HMM...
There should be more monsters there, as it is close to the water.
I'D BE FINE ON MY OWN...
...BUT IT MIGHT BE ROUGH ON THOSE TWO...

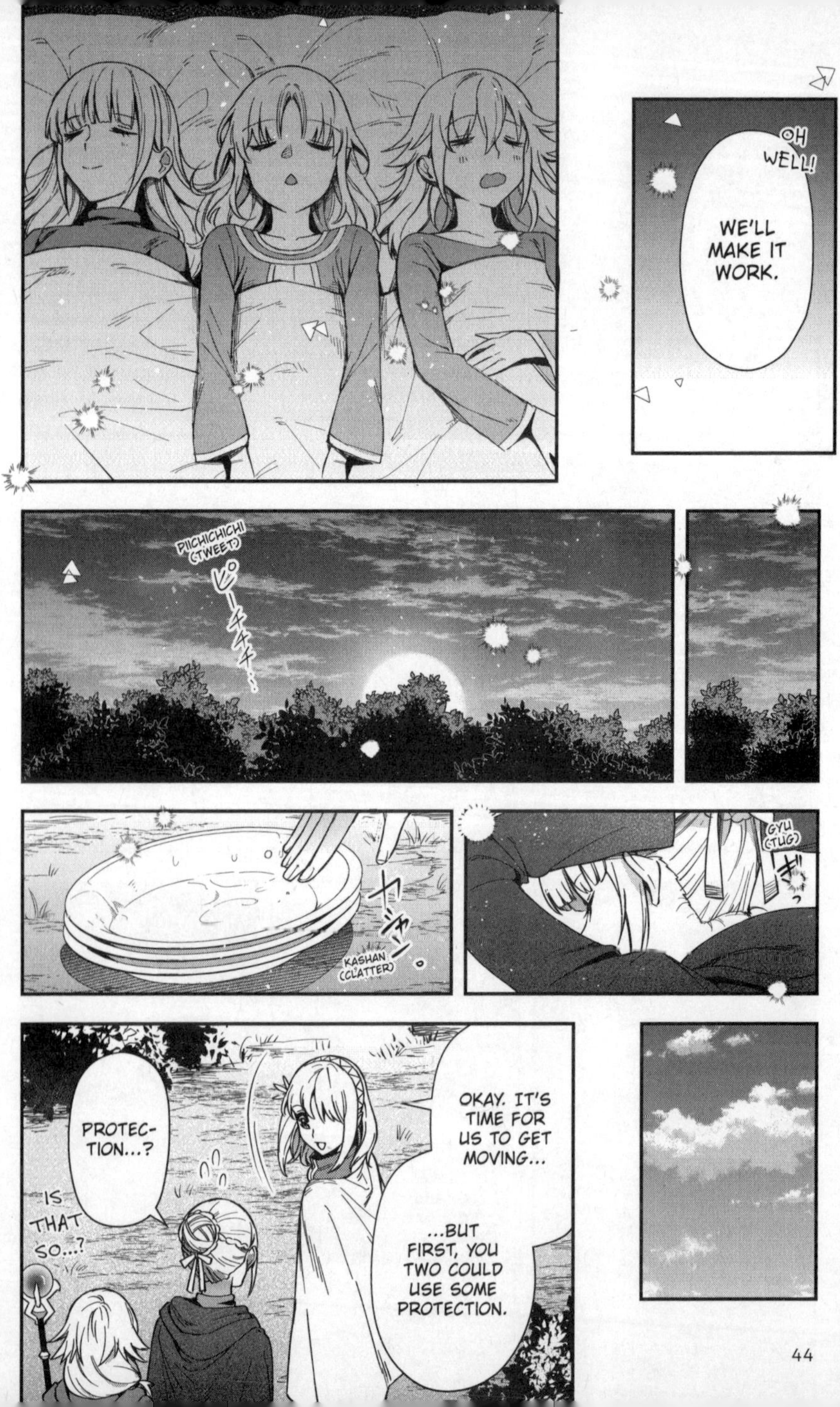
OH WELL!
WE'LL MAKE IT WORK.
PIICHICHICHI (TWEET)
GYU (TUG)
KASHAN (CLATTER)
OKAY. IT'S TIME FOR US TO GET MOVING...
...BUT FIRST, YOU TWO COULD USE SOME PROTECTION.
PROTECTION...?
IS THAT SO...?

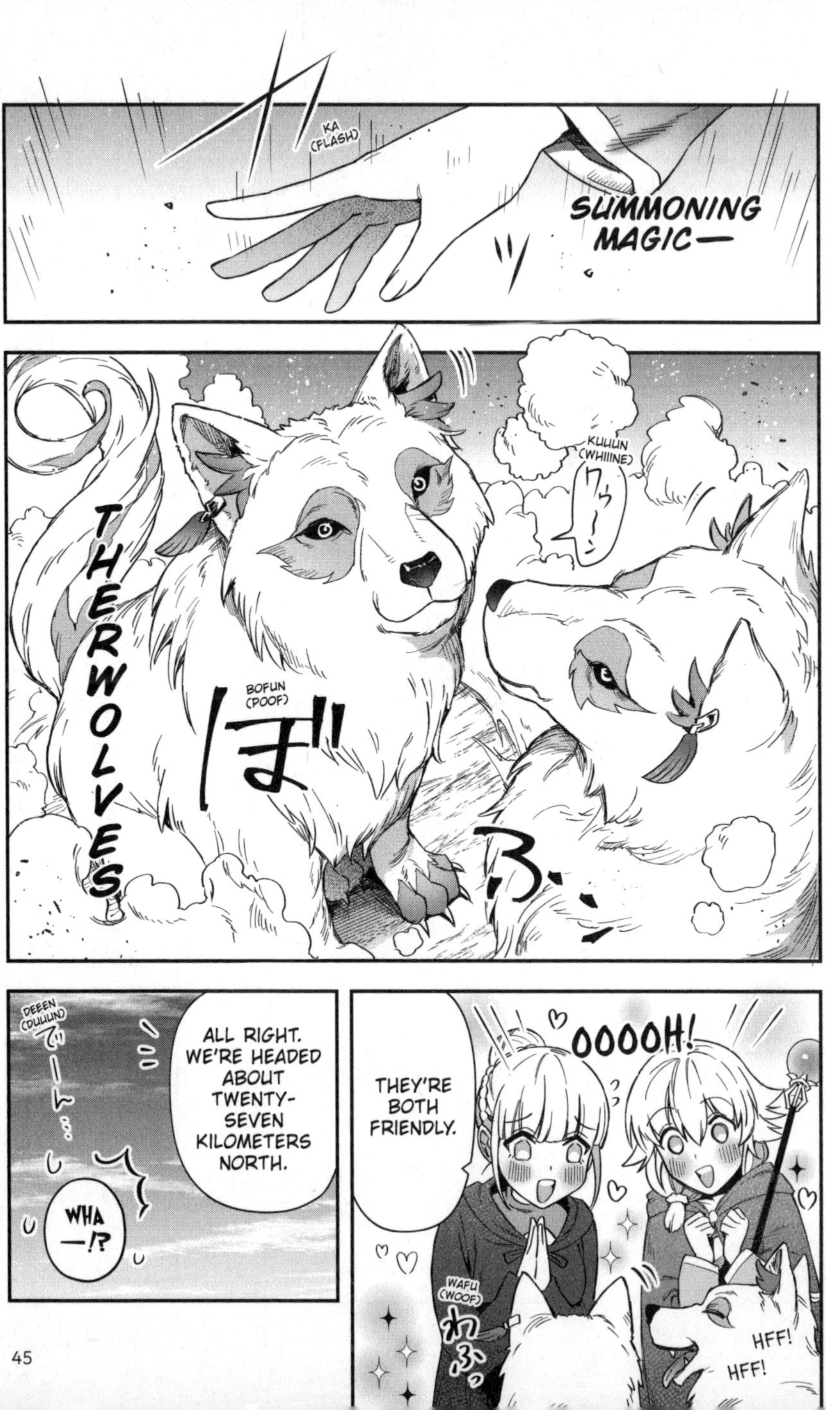
KA (FLASH)
SUMMONING MAGIC—
THERWOLVES
KUUUN (WHIIINE)
BOFUN (POOF)
ぼ
ふ
THEY'RE BOTH FRIENDLY.
OOOOH!
WAFU (WOOF)
わふっ
HFF! HFF!
DEEEN (DUHUN)
でーん…
ALL RIGHT. WE'RE HEADED ABOUT TWENTY-SEVEN KILOMETERS NORTH.
WHA—!?

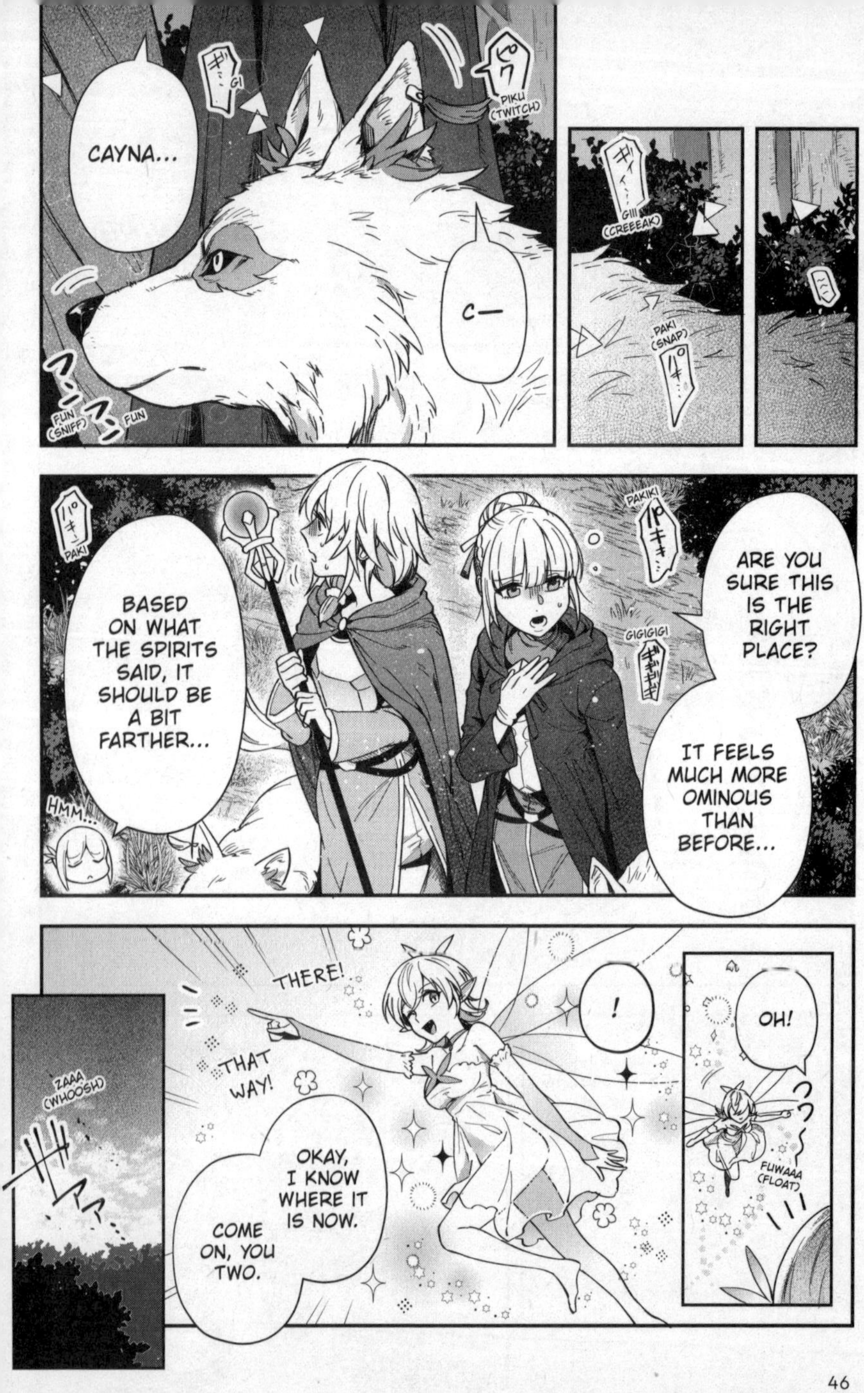
GIII (CREEEAK)
PAKI (SNAP)
PIKU (TWITCH)
GI
CAYNA...
C—
FUN (SNIFF)
FUN
PAKIKI
ARE YOU SURE THIS IS THE RIGHT PLACE?
IT FEELS MUCH MORE OMINOUS THAN BEFORE...
GIGIGIGI
BASED ON WHAT THE SPIRITS SAID, IT SHOULD BE A BIT FARTHER...
PAKI
HMM...
OH!
FUWAAA (FLOAT)
!
THERE! THAT WAY!
OKAY, I KNOW WHERE IT IS NOW.
COME ON, YOU TWO.
ZAAA (WHOOSH)

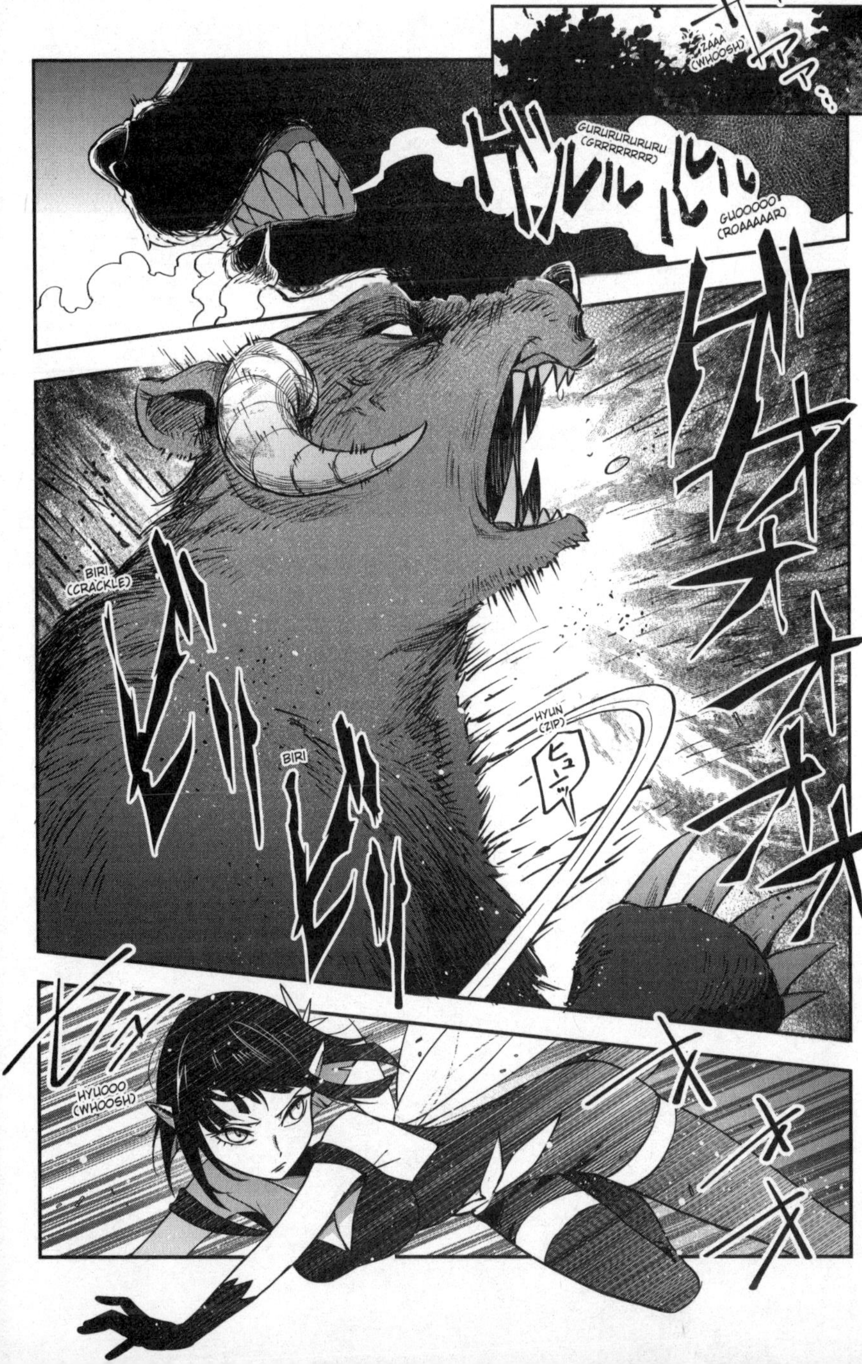
ZAAA (WHOOSH)
GURURURURURU (GRRRRRRRR)
GUOOOOO (ROAAAAAR)
HYUN (ZIP)
BIRI
BIRI (CRACKLE)
HYUOOO (WHOOSH)

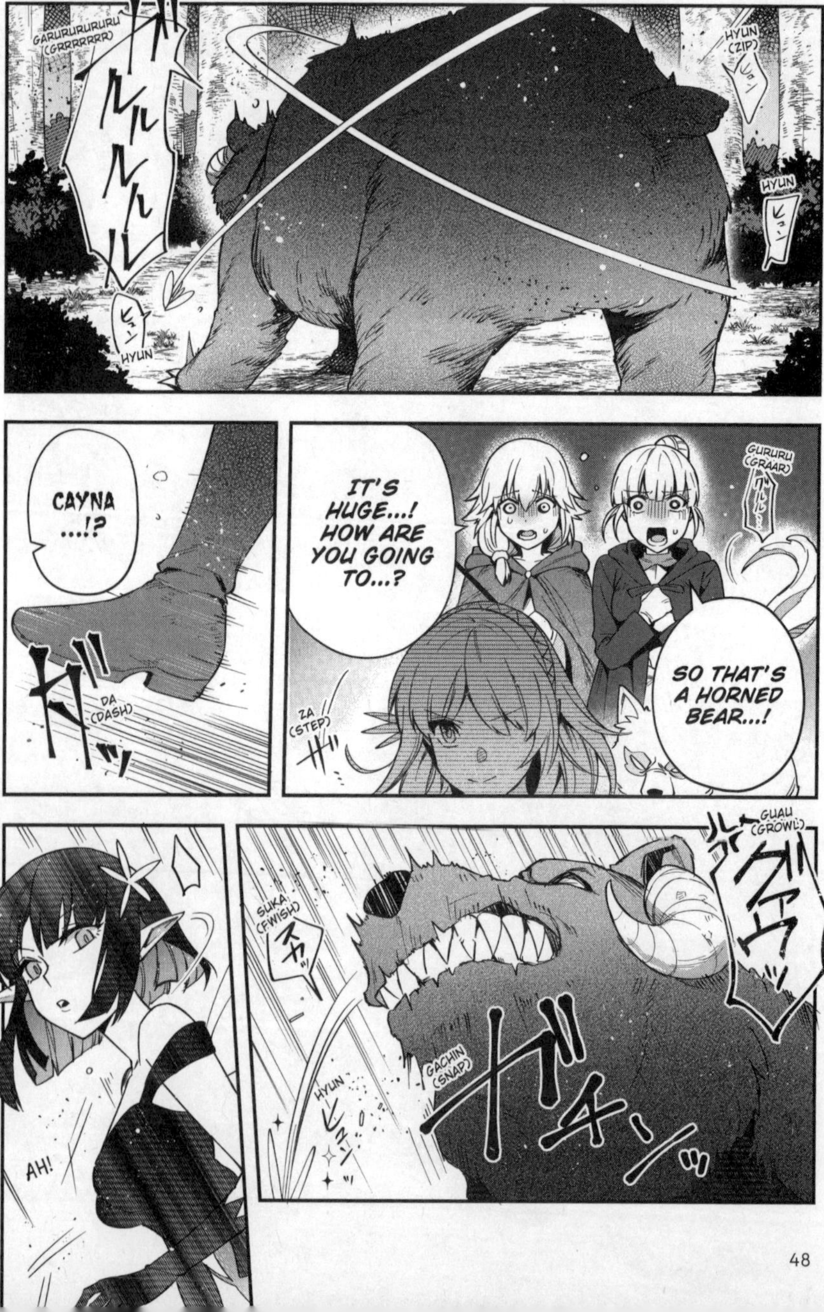
HYUN (ZIP)
HYUN
GARURURURURU (GRRRRRRR)
HYUN
IT'S HUGE...! HOW ARE YOU GOING TO...?
GURURU (GRAAR)
SO THAT'S A HORNED BEAR...!
ZA (STEP)
CAYNA ...!?
DA (DASH)
GUAU (GROWL)
SUKA (FWISH)
GACHIN (SNAP)
HYUN
AH!

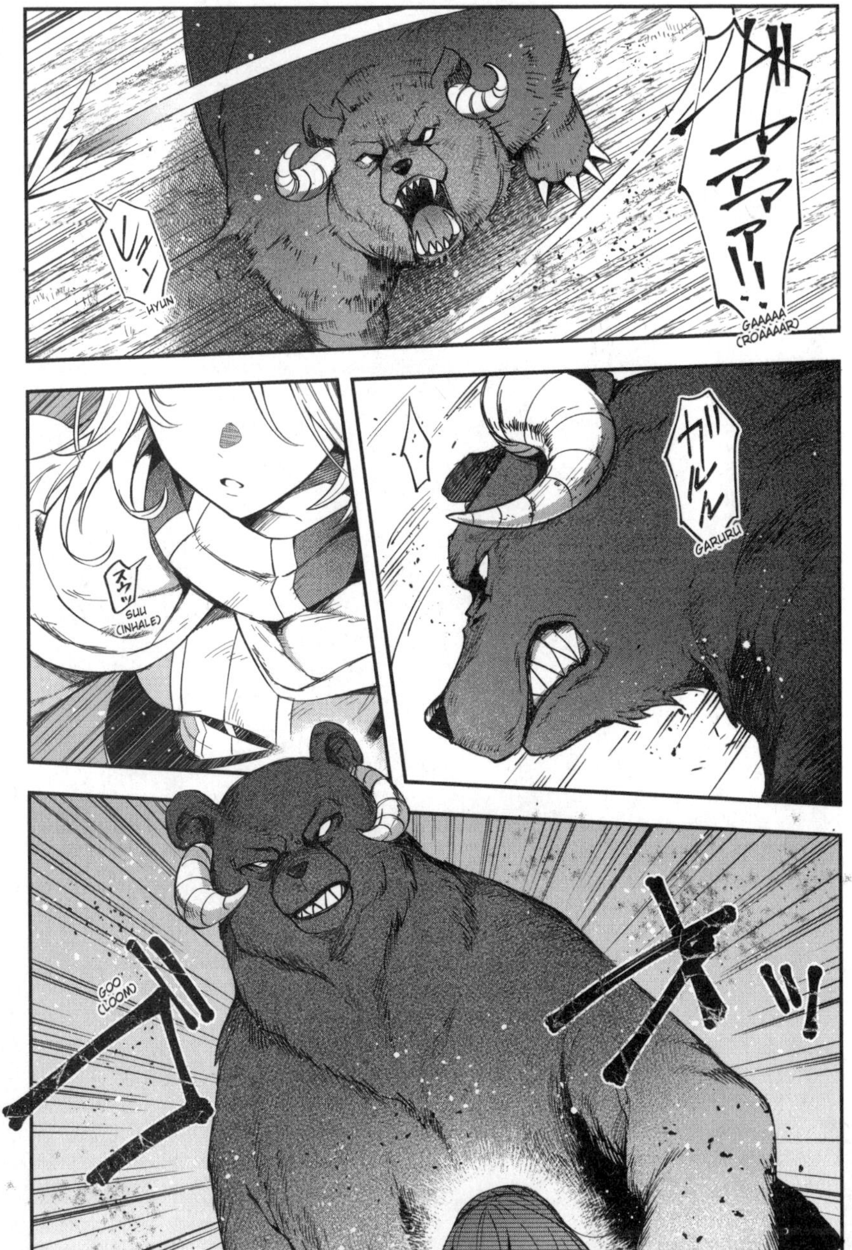
ギャアアア!!
GAAAAA (ROAAAAR)
ヒュン
HYUN
ガルル
GARURU
スウッ
SUU (INHALE)
GOO (LOOM)

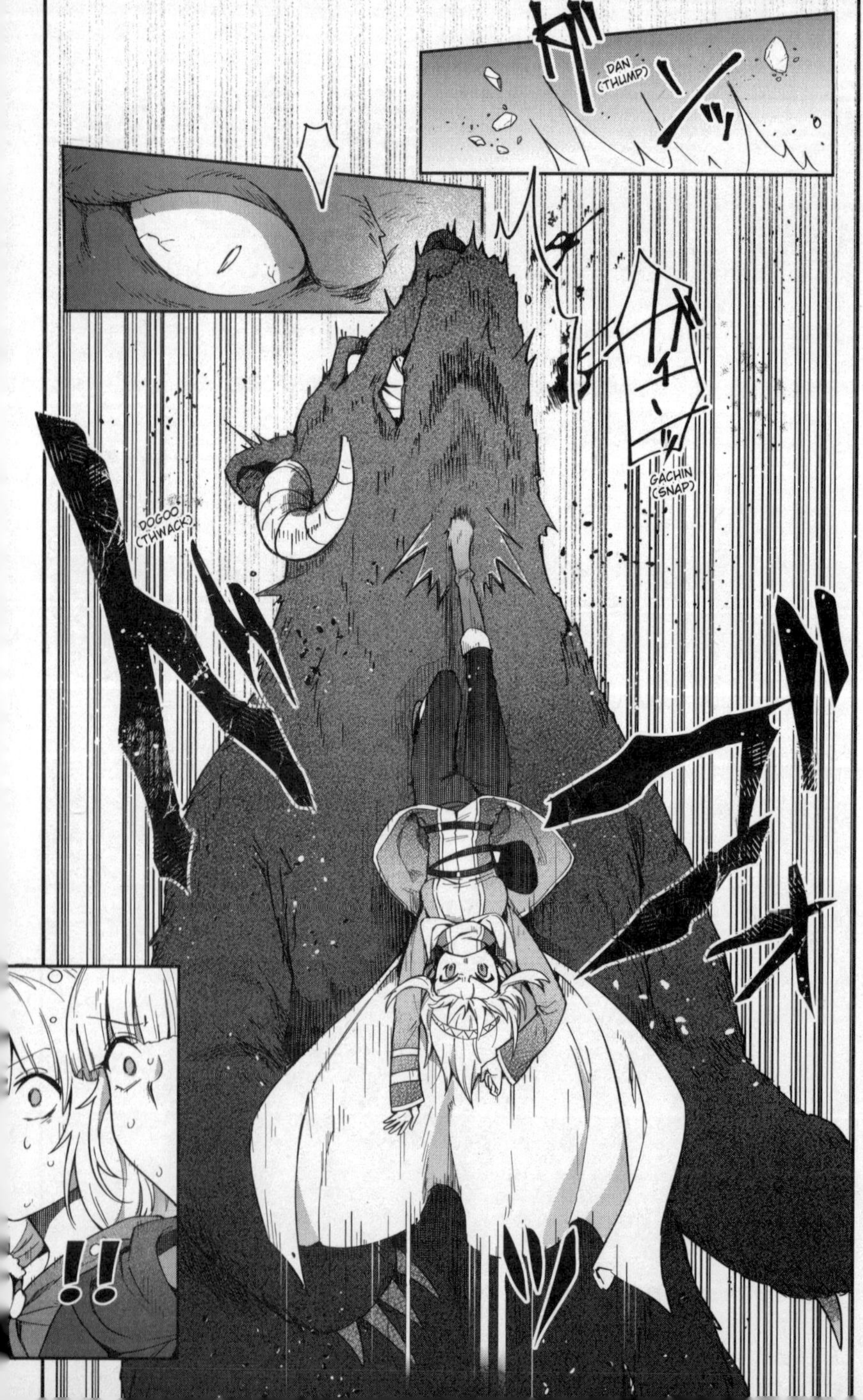
DAN (THUMP)
GACHIN (SNAP)
DOGOO (THWACK)
!!

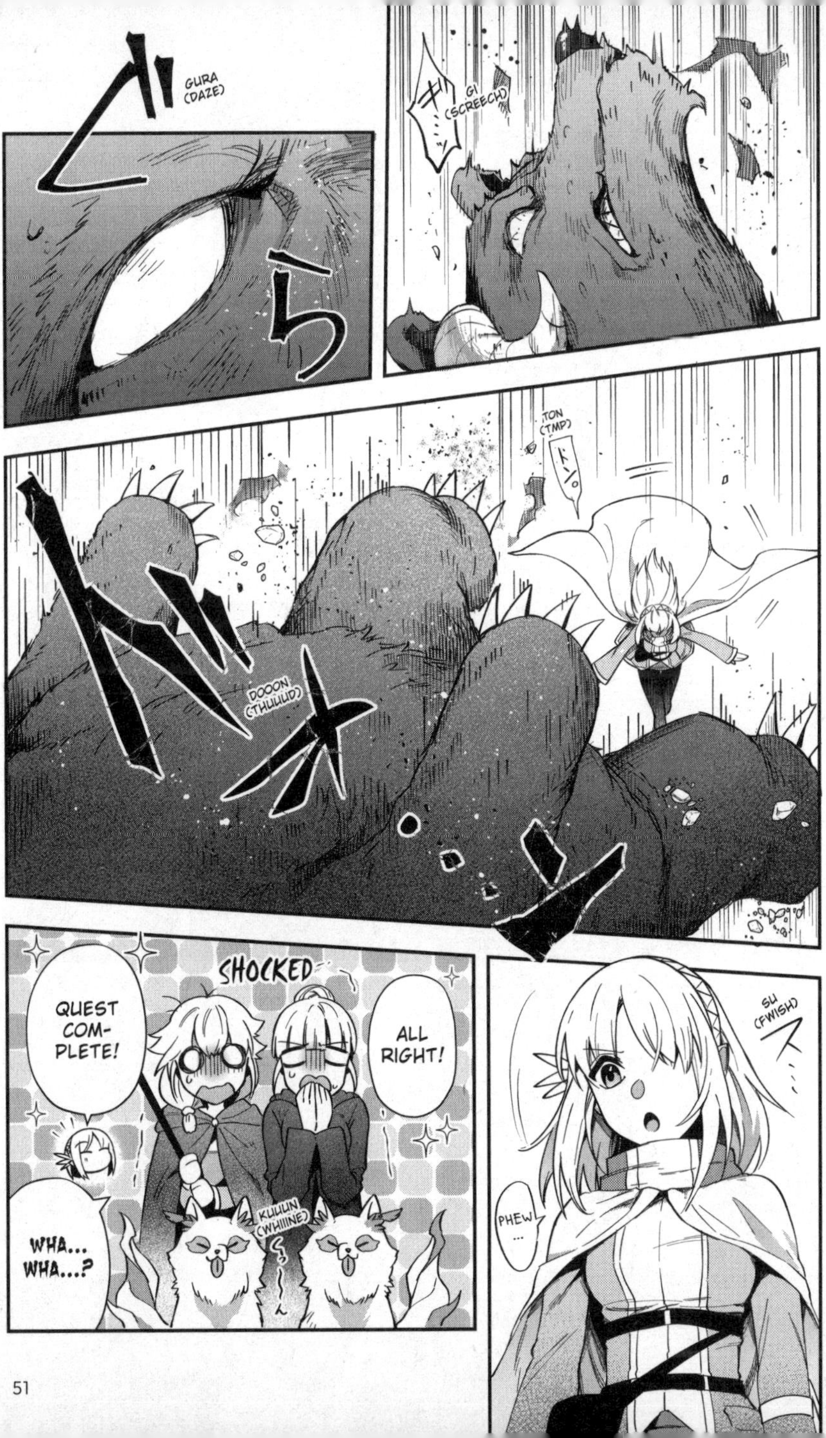
GI (SCREECH)
GURA (DAZE)
TON (TMP)
DOOON (THUUUD)
SU (FWISH)
PHEW...
SHOCKED
ALL RIGHT!
QUEST COMPLETE!
KUUUN (WHIIINE)
WHA... WHA...?

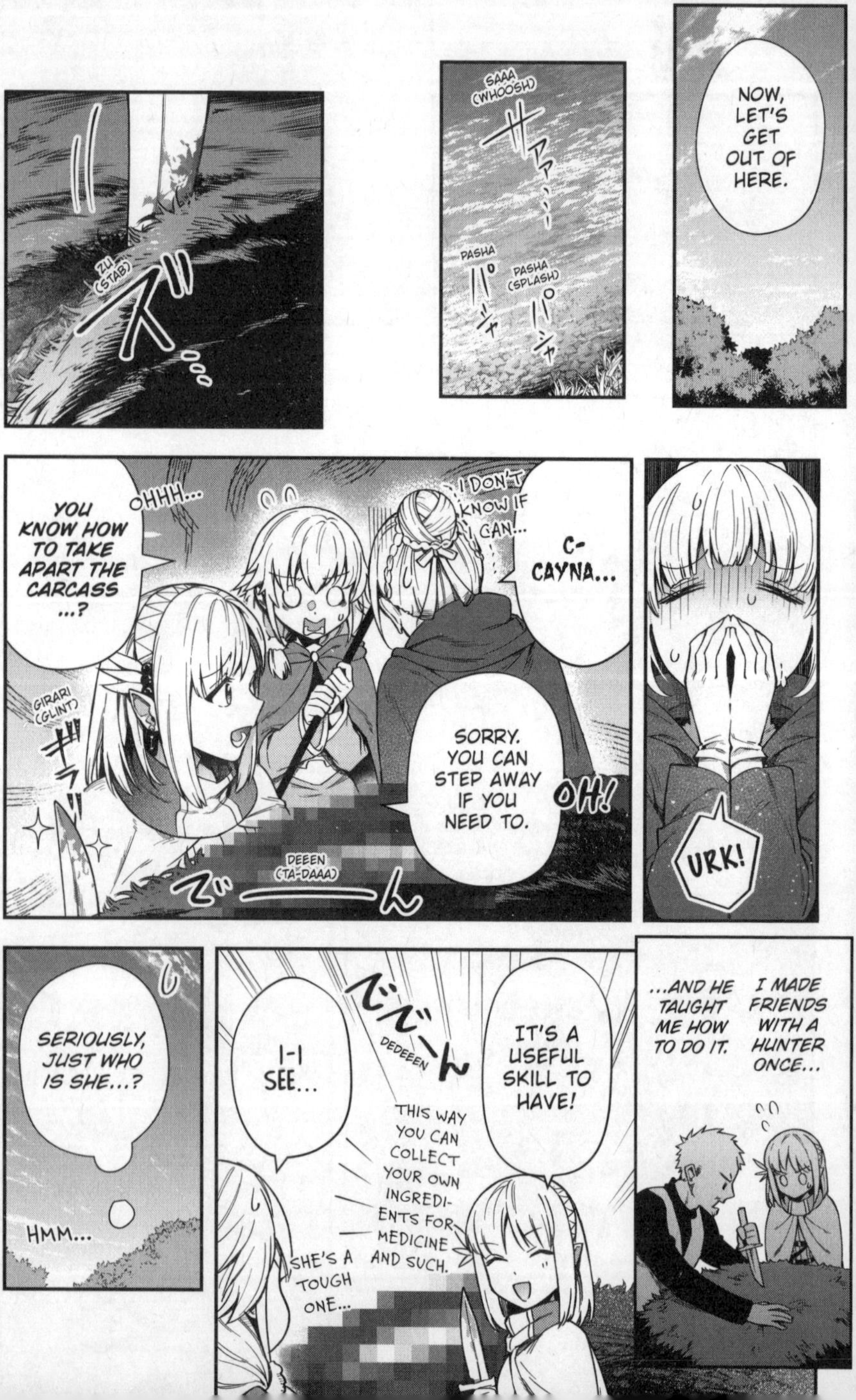
NOW, LET'S GET OUT OF HERE.
SAAA (WHOOSH)
PASHA
PASHA (SPLASH)
ZU (STAB)
URK!
C-CAYNA...
I DON'T KNOW IF CAN...
OH!
SORRY. YOU CAN STEP AWAY IF YOU NEED TO.
OHHH...
YOU KNOW HOW TO TAKE APART THE CARCASS...?
GIRARI (GLINT)
DEEEN (TA-DAAA)
I MADE FRIENDS WITH A HUNTER ONCE...
...AND HE TAUGHT ME HOW TO DO IT.
IT'S A USEFUL SKILL TO HAVE!
DEDEEEN
I-I SEE...
THIS WAY YOU CAN COLLECT YOUR OWN INGREDIENTS FOR MEDICINE AND SUCH.
SHE'S A TOUGH ONE...
SERIOUSLY, JUST WHO IS SHE...?
HMM...

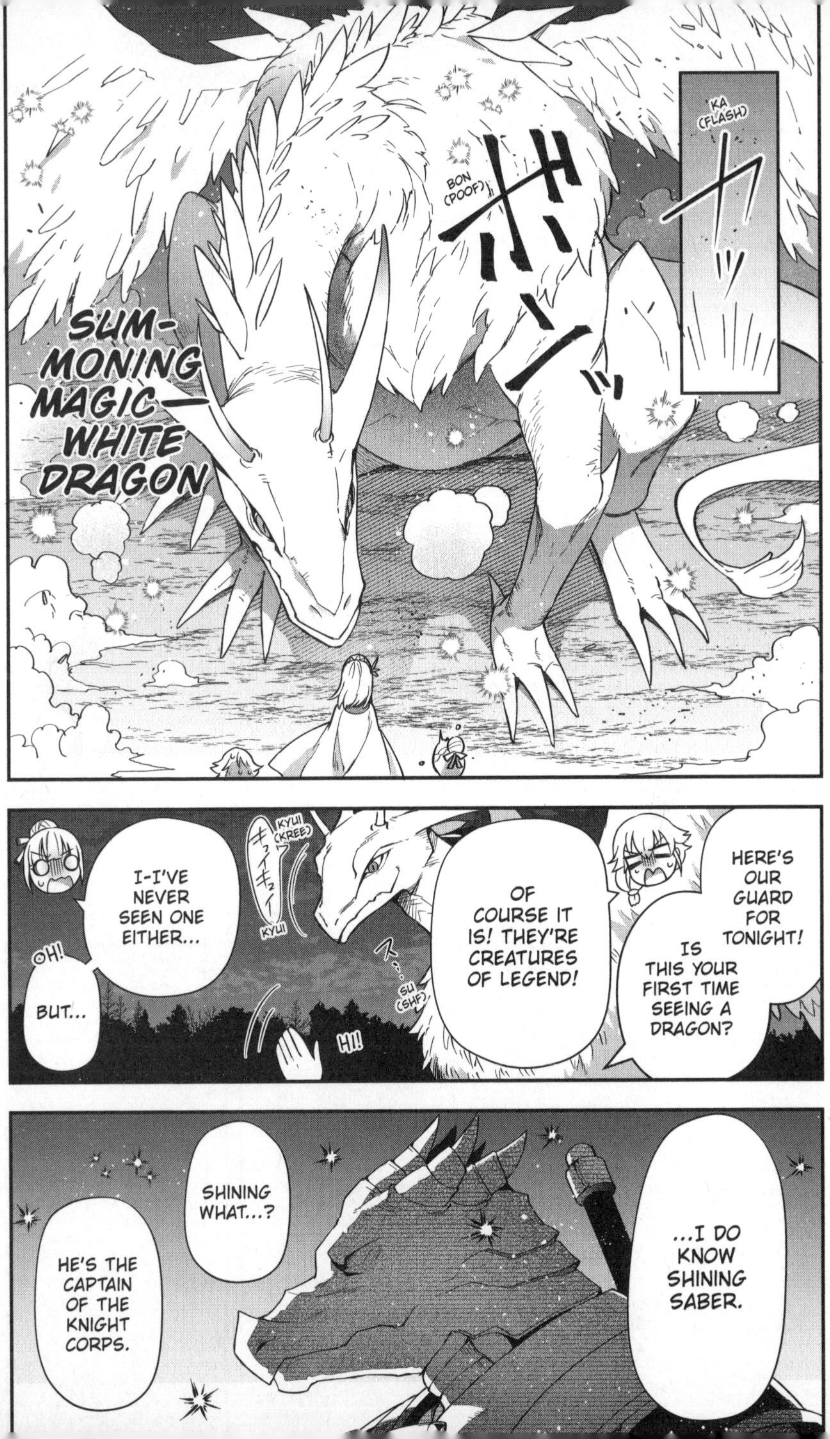
KA (FLASH)
BON (POOF)
SUM-MONING MAGIC— WHITE DRAGON
HERE'S OUR GUARD FOR TONIGHT!
IS THIS YOUR FIRST TIME SEEING A DRAGON?
OF COURSE IT IS! THEY'RE CREATURES OF LEGEND!
KYUI (KREE)
KYUI
SU (SHF)
HI!
I-I'VE NEVER SEEN ONE EITHER...
OH!
BUT...
...I DO KNOW SHINING SABER.
SHINING WHAT...?
HE'S THE CAPTAIN OF THE KNIGHT CORPS.

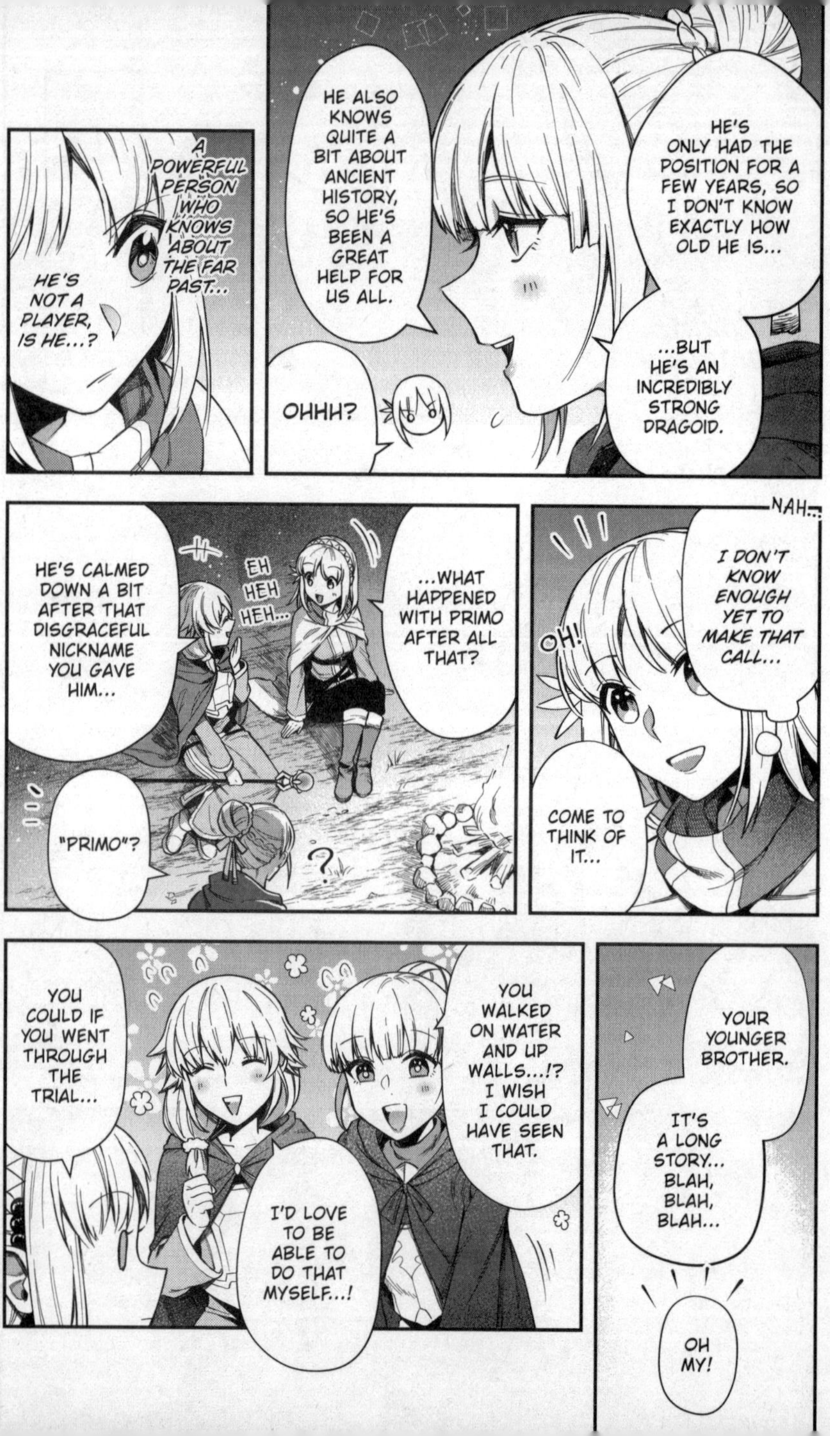
HE'S ONLY HAD THE POSITION FOR A FEW YEARS, SO I DON'T KNOW EXACTLY HOW OLD HE IS...
...BUT HE'S AN INCREDIBLY STRONG DRAGOID.
HE ALSO KNOWS QUITE A BIT ABOUT ANCIENT HISTORY, SO HE'S BEEN A GREAT HELP FOR US ALL.
OHHH?
A POWERFUL PERSON WHO KNOWS ABOUT THE FAR PAST...
HE'S NOT A PLAYER, IS HE...?
NAH...
I DON'T KNOW ENOUGH YET TO MAKE THAT CALL...
OH!
COME TO THINK OF IT...
...WHAT HAPPENED WITH PRIMO AFTER ALL THAT?
EH HEH HEH...
HE'S CALMED DOWN A BIT AFTER THAT DISGRACEFUL NICKNAME YOU GAVE HIM...
"PRIMO"?
YOUR YOUNGER BROTHER.
IT'S A LONG STORY... BLAH, BLAH, BLAH...
OH MY!
YOU WALKED ON WATER AND UP WALLS...!? I WISH I COULD HAVE SEEN THAT.
I'D LOVE TO BE ABLE TO DO THAT MYSELF...!
YOU COULD IF YOU WENT THROUGH THE TRIAL...

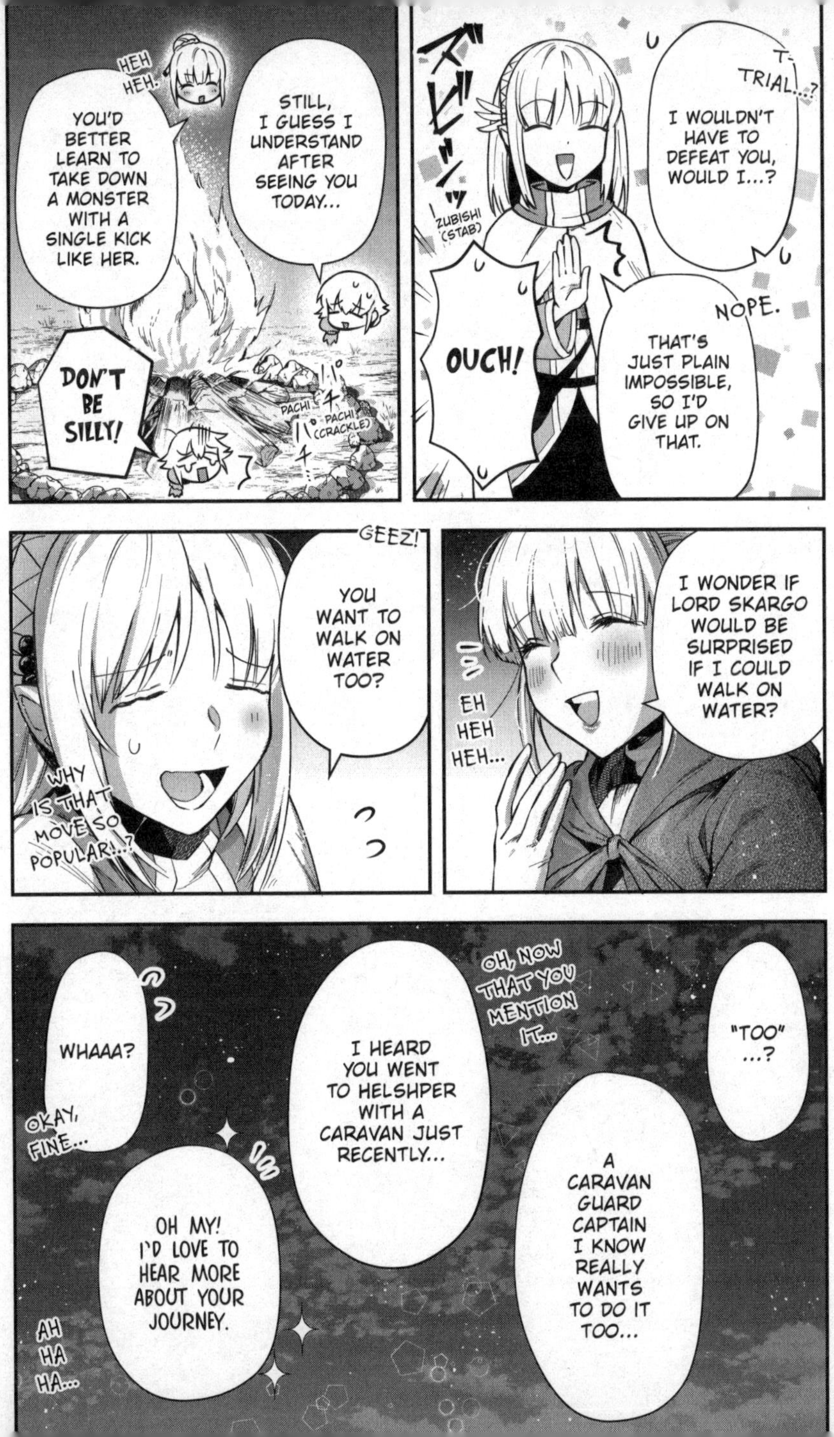
T-TRIAL...?
I WOULDN'T HAVE TO DEFEAT YOU, WOULD I...?
ZUBISHI (STAB)
OUCH!
NOPE.
THAT'S JUST PLAIN IMPOSSIBLE, SO I'D GIVE UP ON THAT.
STILL, I GUESS I UNDERSTAND AFTER SEEING YOU TODAY...
HEH HEH.
YOU'D BETTER LEARN TO TAKE DOWN A MONSTER WITH A SINGLE KICK LIKE HER.
DON'T BE SILLY!
PACHI PACHI (CRACKLE)
I WONDER IF LORD SKARGO WOULD BE SURPRISED IF I COULD WALK ON WATER?
EH HEH HEH...
GEEZ!
YOU WANT TO WALK ON WATER TOO?
WHY IS THAT MOVE SO POPULAR!..?
"TOO" ...?
OH, NOW THAT YOU MENTION IT...
A CARAVAN GUARD CAPTAIN I KNOW REALLY WANTS TO DO IT TOO...
I HEARD YOU WENT TO HELSHPER WITH A CARAVAN JUST RECENTLY...
WHAAA?
OKAY, FINE...
OH MY! I'D LOVE TO HEAR MORE ABOUT YOUR JOURNEY.
AH HA HA...

+ IN THE LAND OF +
LEADALE

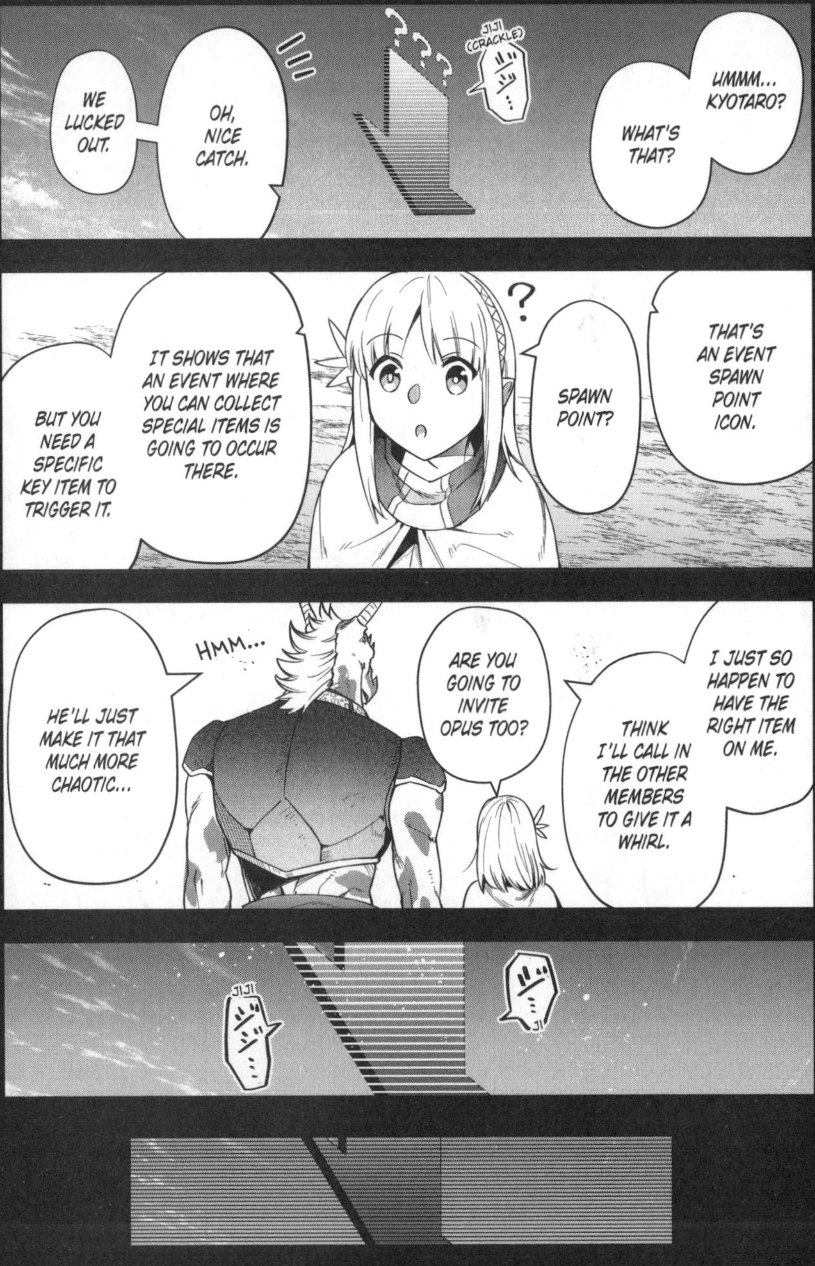
UMMM... KYOTARO?
WHAT'S THAT?
JIJI (CRACKLE)
OH, NICE CATCH.
WE LUCKED OUT.
THAT'S AN EVENT SPAWN POINT ICON.
SPAWN POINT?
IT SHOWS THAT AN EVENT WHERE YOU CAN COLLECT SPECIAL ITEMS IS GOING TO OCCUR THERE.
BUT YOU NEED A SPECIFIC KEY ITEM TO TRIGGER IT.
I JUST SO HAPPEN TO HAVE THE RIGHT ITEM ON ME.
THINK I'LL CALL IN THE OTHER MEMBERS TO GIVE IT A WHIRL.
ARE YOU GOING TO INVITE OPUS TOO?
HMM...
HE'LL JUST MAKE IT THAT MUCH MORE CHAOTIC...
JI
JIJI

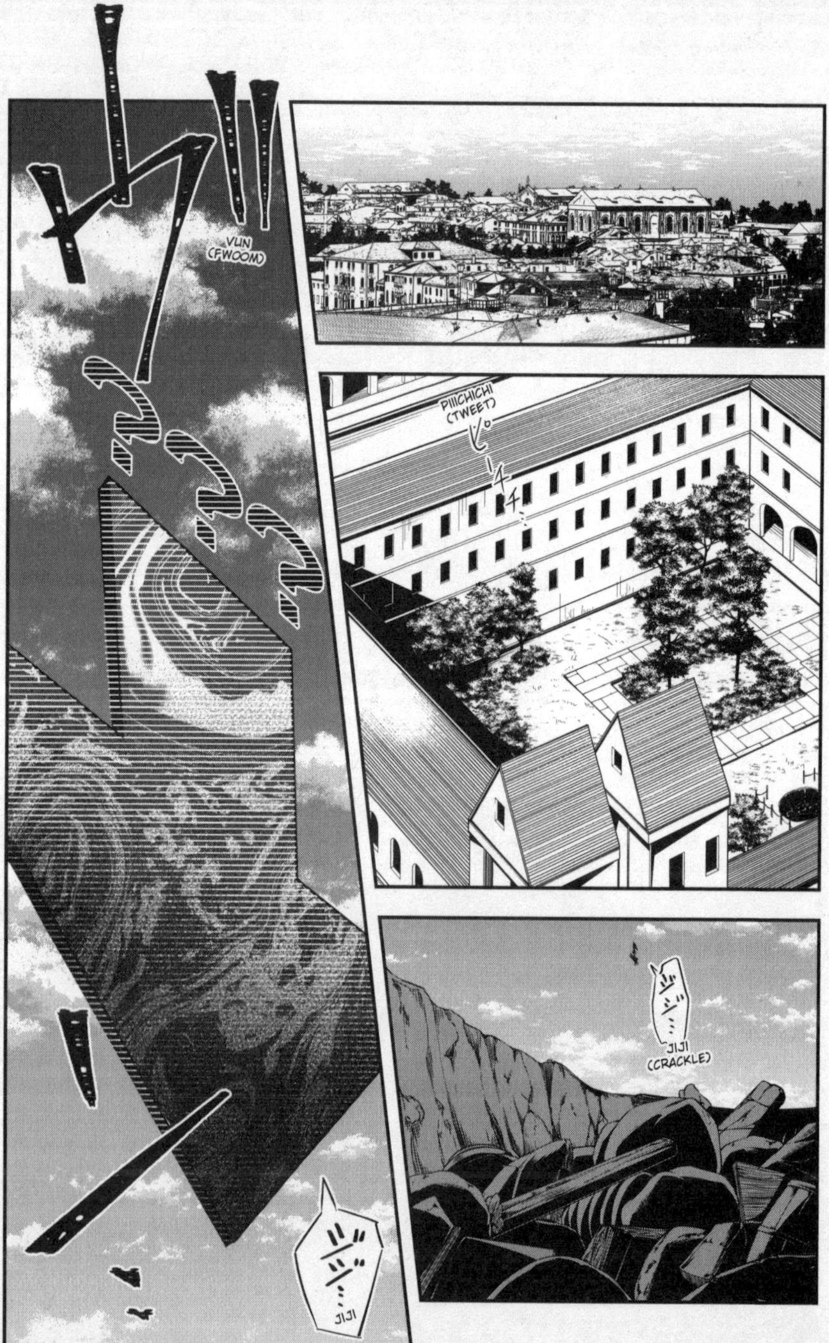
PIIICHICHI
(TWEET)
JIJI
(CRACKLE)
VUN
(FWOOM)
JIJI

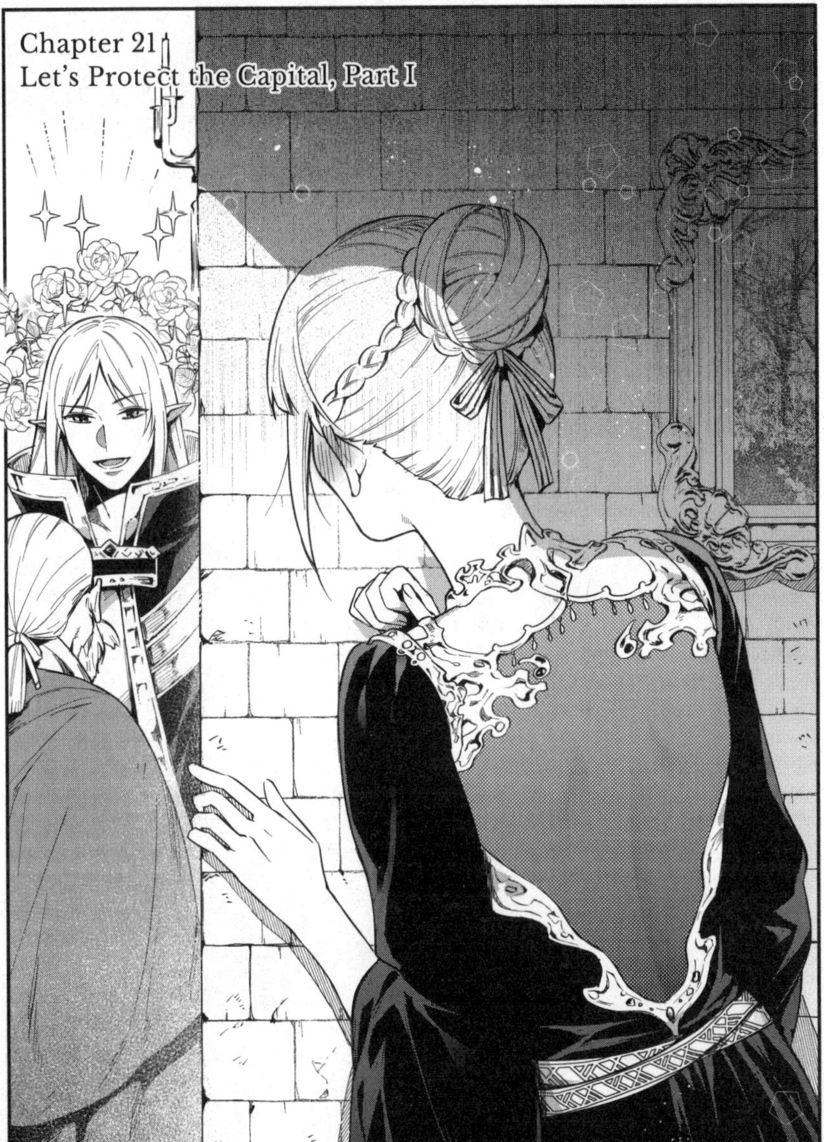
Chapter 21
Let's Protect the Capital, Part I

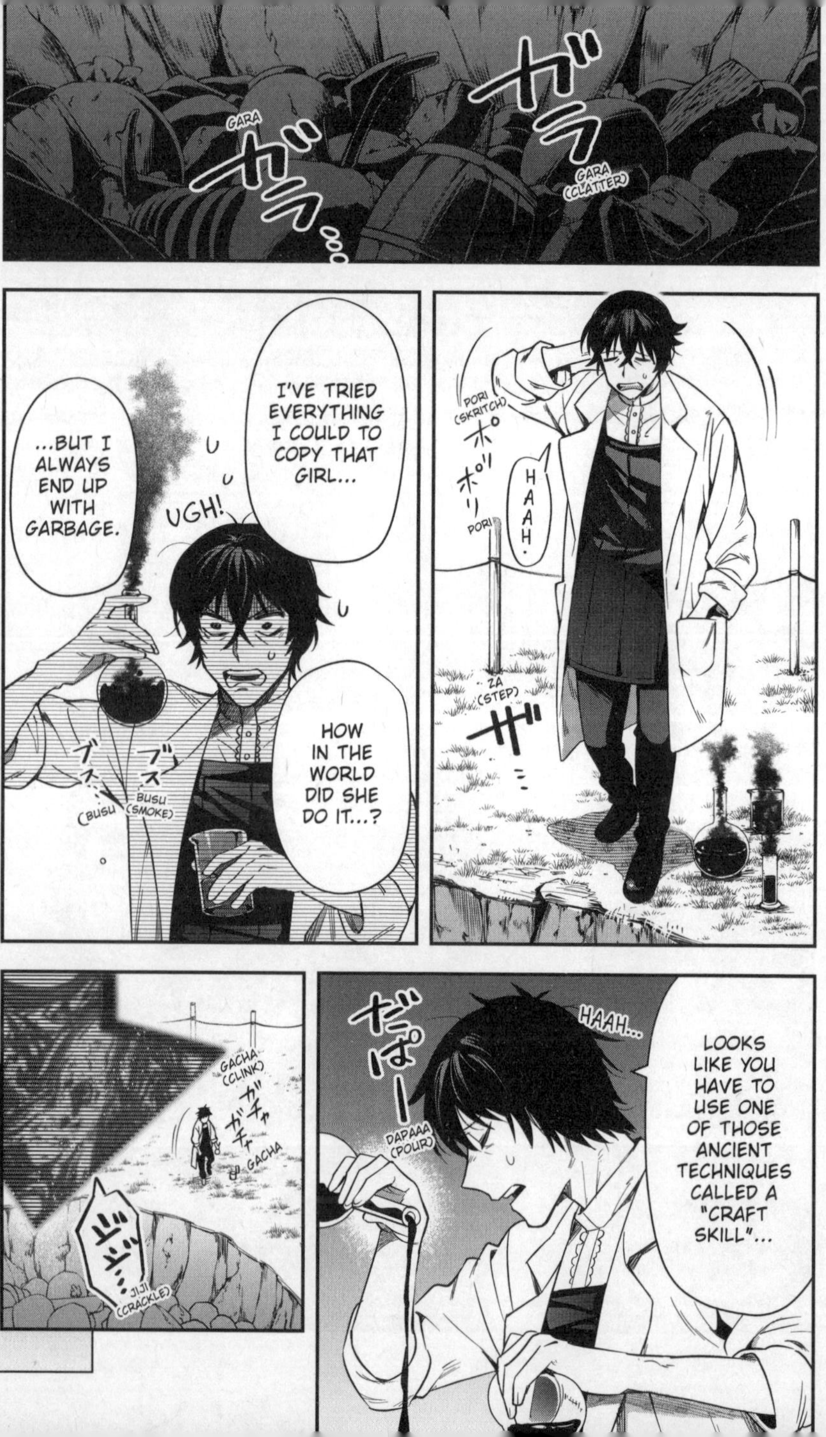
ガラ
GARA (CLATTER)
GARA
ガラ…
PORI (SKRITCH)
ポリ
ポリ
PORI
HAAAH.
ZA (STEP)
ザ
I'VE TRIED EVERYTHING I COULD TO COPY THAT GIRL...
UGH!
...BUT I ALWAYS END UP WITH GARBAGE.
HOW IN THE WORLD DID SHE DO IT...?
ブス
BUSU (SMOKE)
ブス…
(BUSU
LOOKS LIKE YOU HAVE TO USE ONE OF THOSE ANCIENT TECHNIQUES CALLED A "CRAFT SKILL"...
HAAH...
だぱー
DAPAAA (POUR)
GACHA (CLINK)
ガチャ
ガチャ
GACHA
ジジ…
JIJI (CRACKLE)

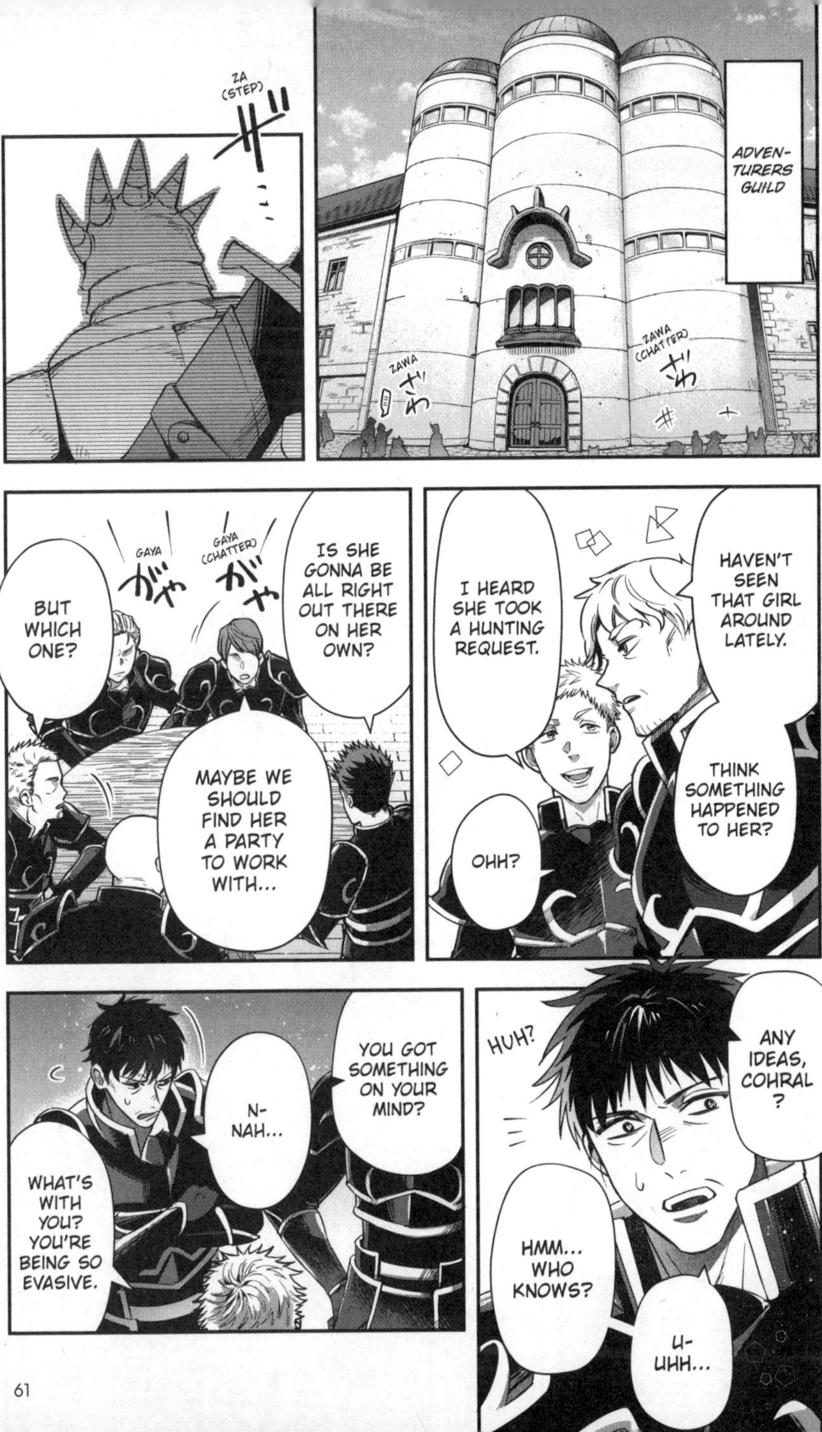
ADVENTURERS GUILD
ZAWA (CHATTER)
ZAWA
ZA (STEP)
HAVEN'T SEEN THAT GIRL AROUND LATELY.
I HEARD SHE TOOK A HUNTING REQUEST.
THINK SOMETHING HAPPENED TO HER?
OHH?
IS SHE GONNA BE ALL RIGHT OUT THERE ON HER OWN?
GAYA (CHATTER)
GAYA
BUT WHICH ONE?
MAYBE WE SHOULD FIND HER A PARTY TO WORK WITH...
ANY IDEAS, COHRAL?
HUH?
HMM... WHO KNOWS?
U-UHH...
YOU GOT SOMETHING ON YOUR MIND?
N-NAH...
WHAT'S WITH YOU? YOU'RE BEING SO EVASIVE.

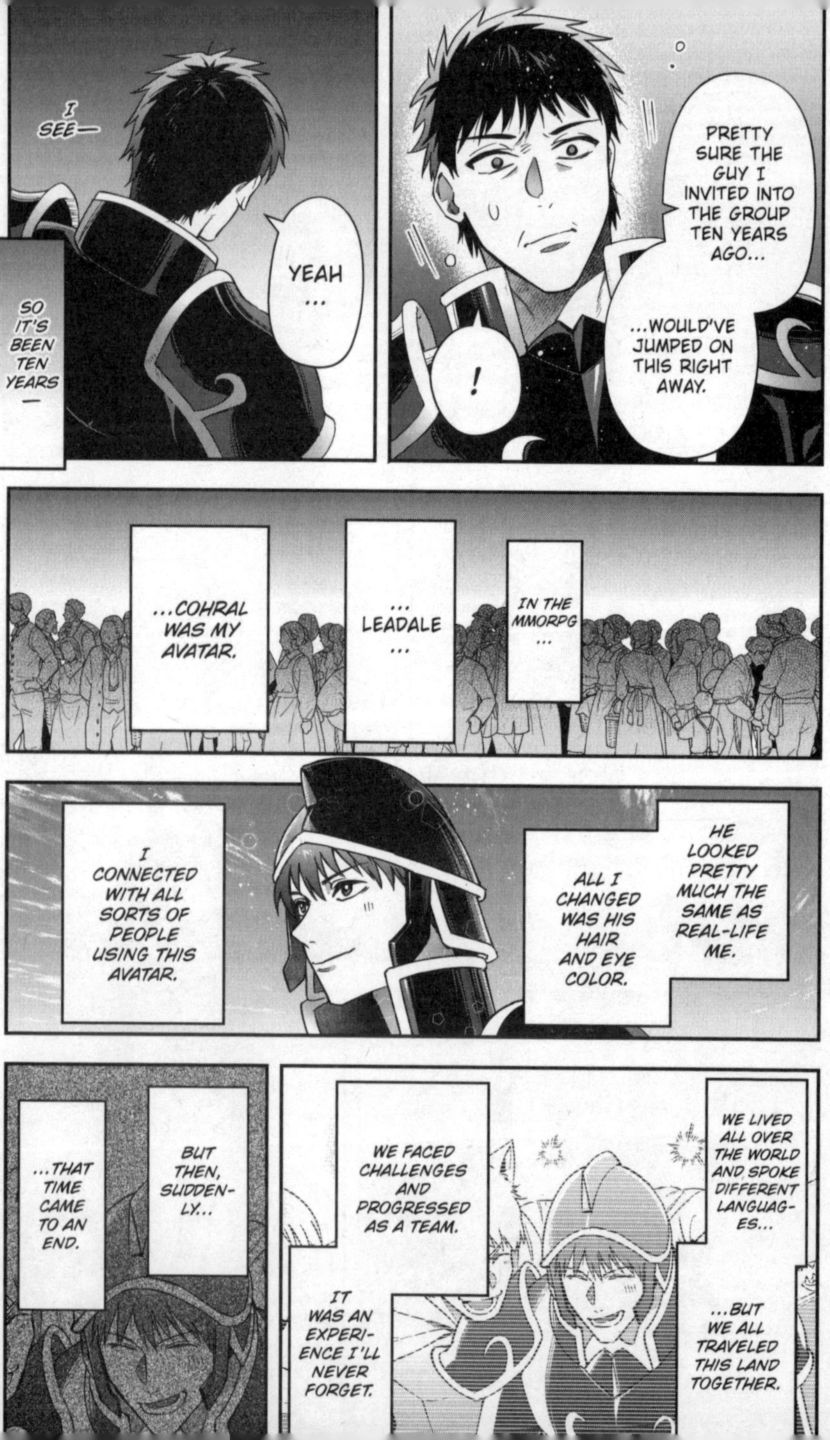
PRETTY SURE THE GUY I INVITED INTO THE GROUP TEN YEARS AGO...
...WOULD'VE JUMPED ON THIS RIGHT AWAY.
!
YEAH...
I SEE—
SO IT'S BEEN TEN YEARS—
IN THE MMORPG...
...LEADALE...
...COHRAL WAS MY AVATAR.
HE LOOKED PRETTY MUCH THE SAME AS REAL-LIFE ME.
ALL I CHANGED WAS HIS HAIR AND EYE COLOR.
I CONNECTED WITH ALL SORTS OF PEOPLE USING THIS AVATAR.
WE LIVED ALL OVER THE WORLD AND SPOKE DIFFERENT LANGUAG-ES...
...BUT WE ALL TRAVELED THIS LAND TOGETHER.
WE FACED CHALLENGES AND PROGRESSED AS A TEAM.
IT WAS AN EXPERI-ENCE I'LL NEVER FORGET.
BUT THEN, SUDDEN-LY...
...THAT TIME CAME TO AN END.

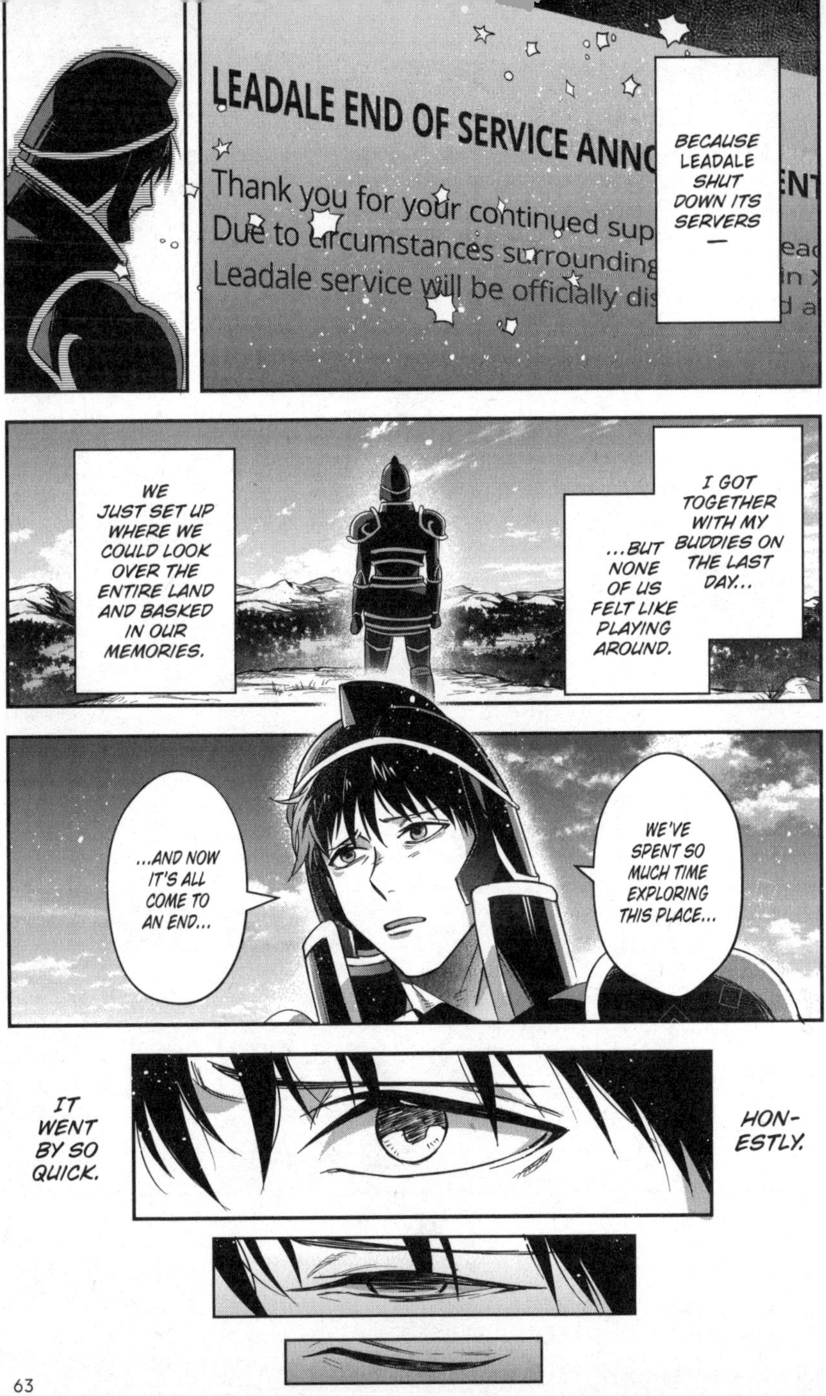
BECAUSE LEADALE SHUT DOWN ITS SERVERS —
LEADALE END OF SERVICE ANNO
Thank you for your continued sup
Due to circumstances surrounding
Leadale service will be officially dis
I GOT TOGETHER WITH MY BUDDIES ON THE LAST DAY...
...BUT NONE OF US FELT LIKE PLAYING AROUND.
WE JUST SET UP WHERE WE COULD LOOK OVER THE ENTIRE LAND AND BASKED IN OUR MEMORIES.
WE'VE SPENT SO MUCH TIME EXPLORING THIS PLACE...
...AND NOW IT'S ALL COME TO AN END...
HON-ESTLY.
IT WENT BY SO QUICK.

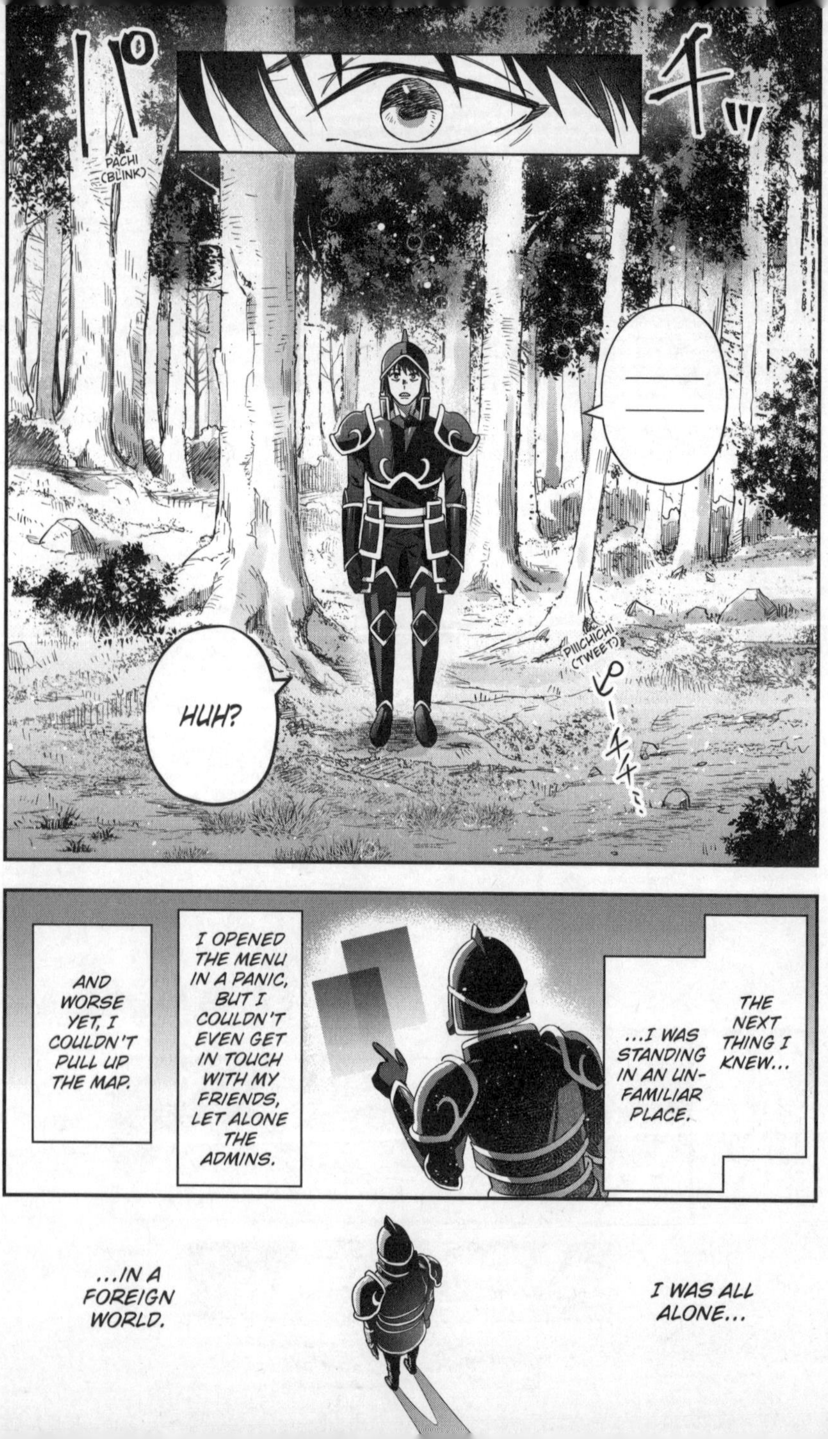
PACHI (BLINK)
——
——
PIIICHICHI (TWEET)
HUH?
THE NEXT THING I KNEW...
...I WAS STANDING IN AN UN-FAMILIAR PLACE.
I OPENED THE MENU IN A PANIC, BUT I COULDN'T EVEN GET IN TOUCH WITH MY FRIENDS, LET ALONE THE ADMINS.
AND WORSE YET, I COULDN'T PULL UP THE MAP.
I WAS ALL ALONE...
...IN A FOREIGN WORLD.

AFTER THAT—
I LUCKED OUT WHEN A HUNTER FROM A NEARBY VILLAGE FOUND ME...
...AND HE TOLD ME A BUNCH OF STORIES THAT SOUNDED LIKE FAIRY TALES.
THE SEVEN KINGDOMS WERE THREE NOW...
...AND NOTHING WAS THE SAME...
...AS IT HAD BEEN TWO HUNDRED YEARS AGO—
I PANICKED FOR A WHOLE WEEK...
...BUT AFTER I ACCEPTED MY NEW REALITY...
...I DECIDED TO LIVE ON AS COHRAL.
I SPENT A BIT OF TIME IN THAT VILLAGE...
...BEFORE SETTING OUT FOR THE CAPITAL...
...WHERE THEY WERE RECRUITING NEW ADVENTURERS.
BUT—EVEN AFTER MAKING UP MY MIND TO LIVE HERE...
...I NEVER STOPPED LOOKING FOR OTHER PLAYERS IN THE SAME SITUATION.

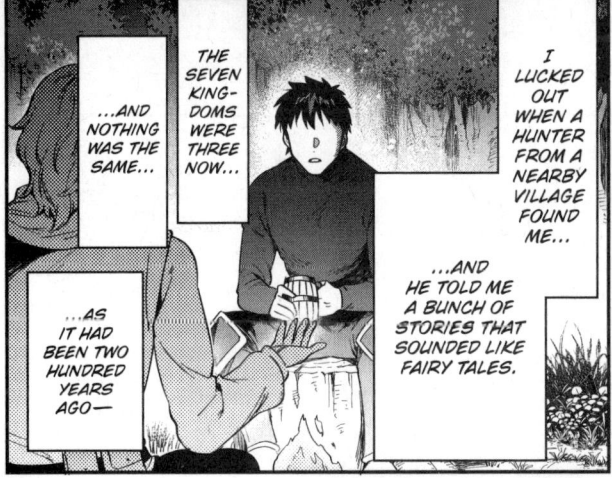

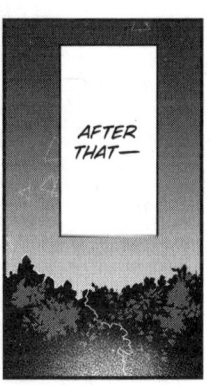

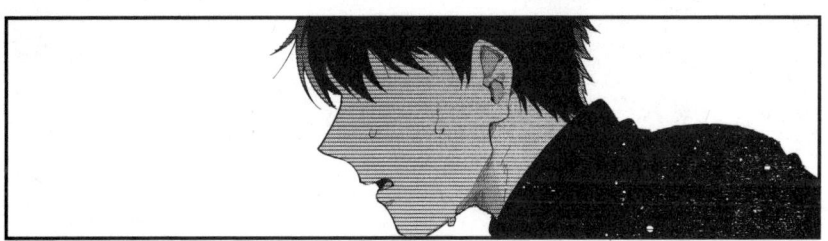

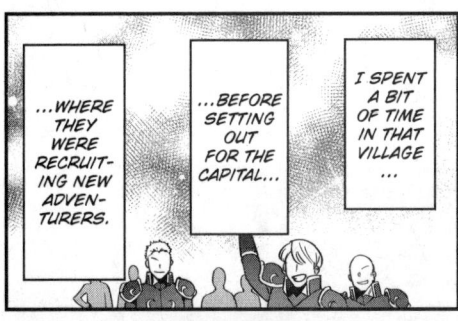

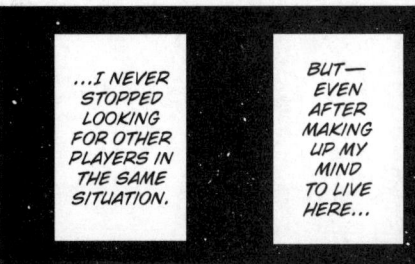

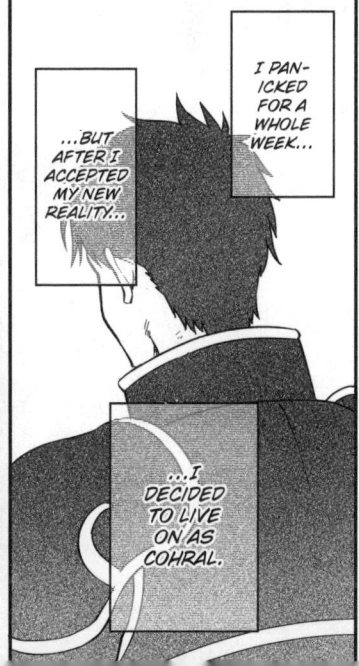

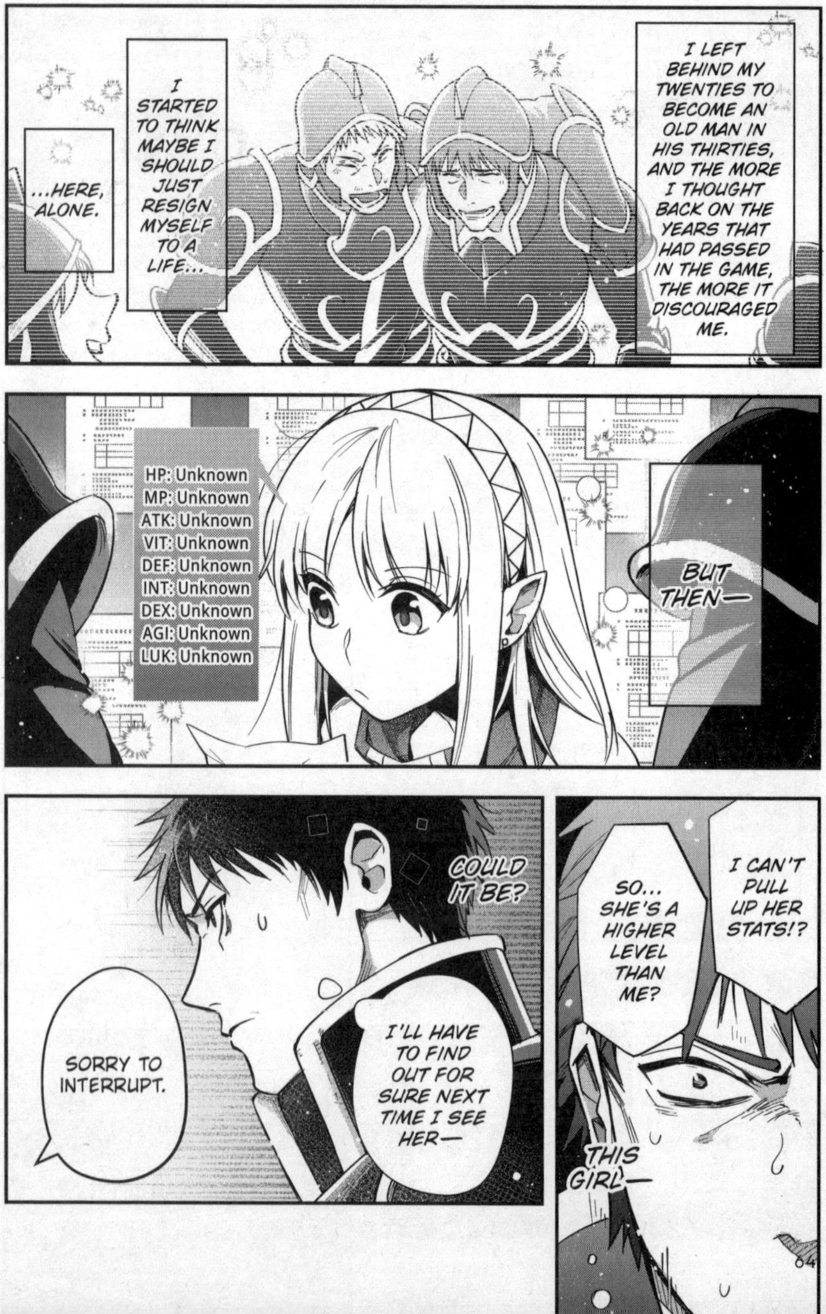
I LEFT BEHIND MY TWENTIES TO BECOME AN OLD MAN IN HIS THIRTIES, AND THE MORE I THOUGHT BACK ON THE YEARS THAT HAD PASSED IN THE GAME, THE MORE IT DISCOURAGED ME.
I STARTED TO THINK MAYBE I SHOULD JUST RESIGN MYSELF TO A LIFE...
...HERE, ALONE.
BUT THEN—
HP: Unknown
MP: Unknown
ATK: Unknown
VIT: Unknown
DEF: Unknown
INT: Unknown
DEX: Unknown
AGI: Unknown
LUK: Unknown
I CAN'T PULL UP HER STATS!?
SO... SHE'S A HIGHER LEVEL THAN ME?
THIS GIRL—
COULD IT BE?
I'LL HAVE TO FIND OUT FOR SURE NEXT TIME I SEE HER—
SORRY TO INTERRUPT.

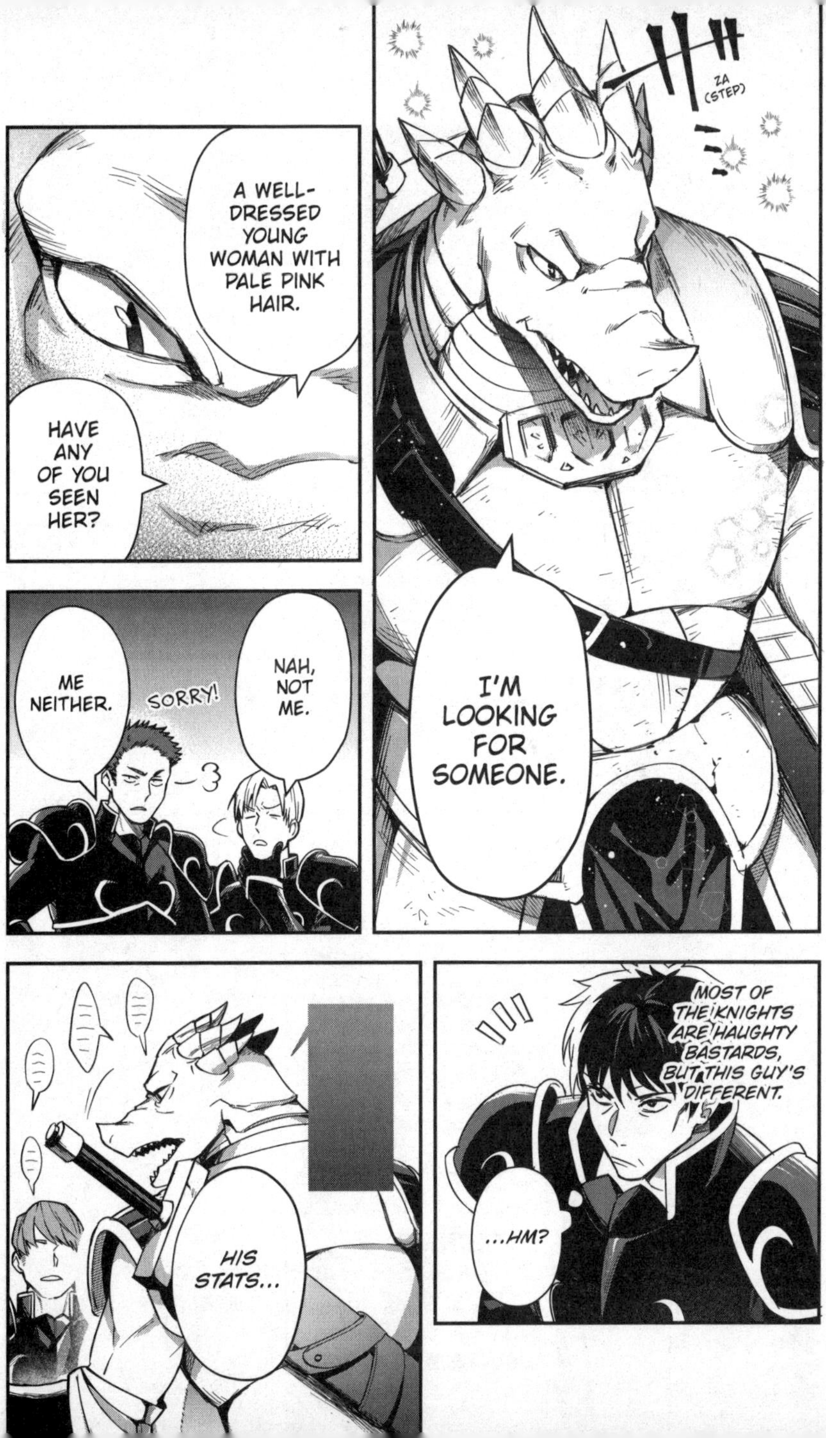
ZA (STEP)
I'M LOOKING FOR SOMEONE.
A WELL-DRESSED YOUNG WOMAN WITH PALE PINK HAIR.
HAVE ANY OF YOU SEEN HER?
NAH, NOT ME.
SORRY!
ME NEITHER.
MOST OF THE KNIGHTS ARE HAUGHTY BASTARDS, BUT THIS GUY'S DIFFERENT.
...HM?
HIS STATS...

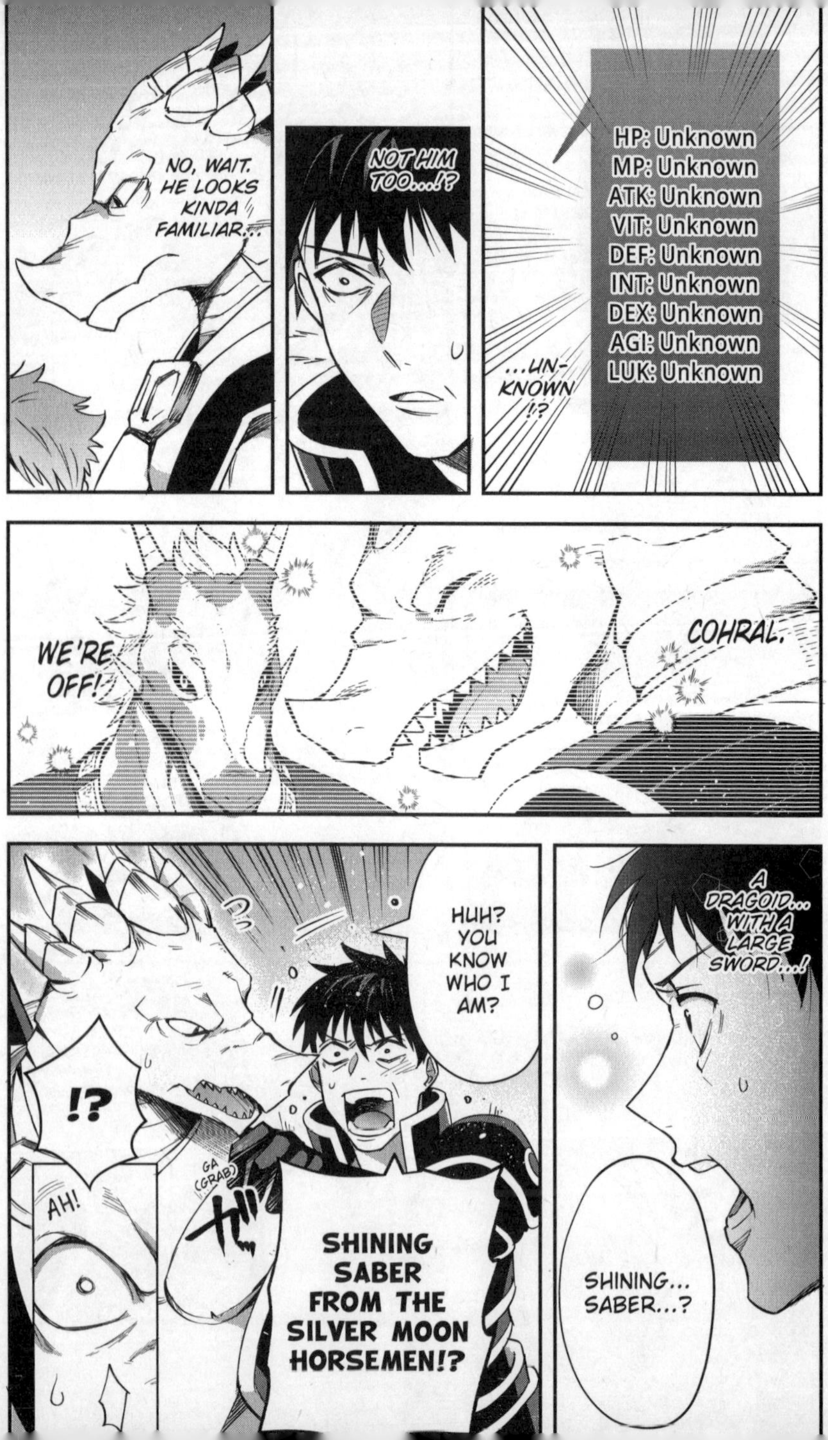
HP: Unknown
MP: Unknown
ATK: Unknown
VIT: Unknown
DEF: Unknown
INT: Unknown
DEX: Unknown
AGI: Unknown
LUK: Unknown
...UN-KNOWN !?
NOT HIM TOO...!?
NO, WAIT. HE LOOKS KINDA FAMILIAR...
COHRAL.
WE'RE OFF!
A DRAGOID... WITH A LARGE SWORD...!
SHINING... SABER...?
HUH? YOU KNOW WHO I AM?
!?
GA (GRAB)
AH!
SHINING SABER FROM THE SILVER MOON HORSEMEN!?

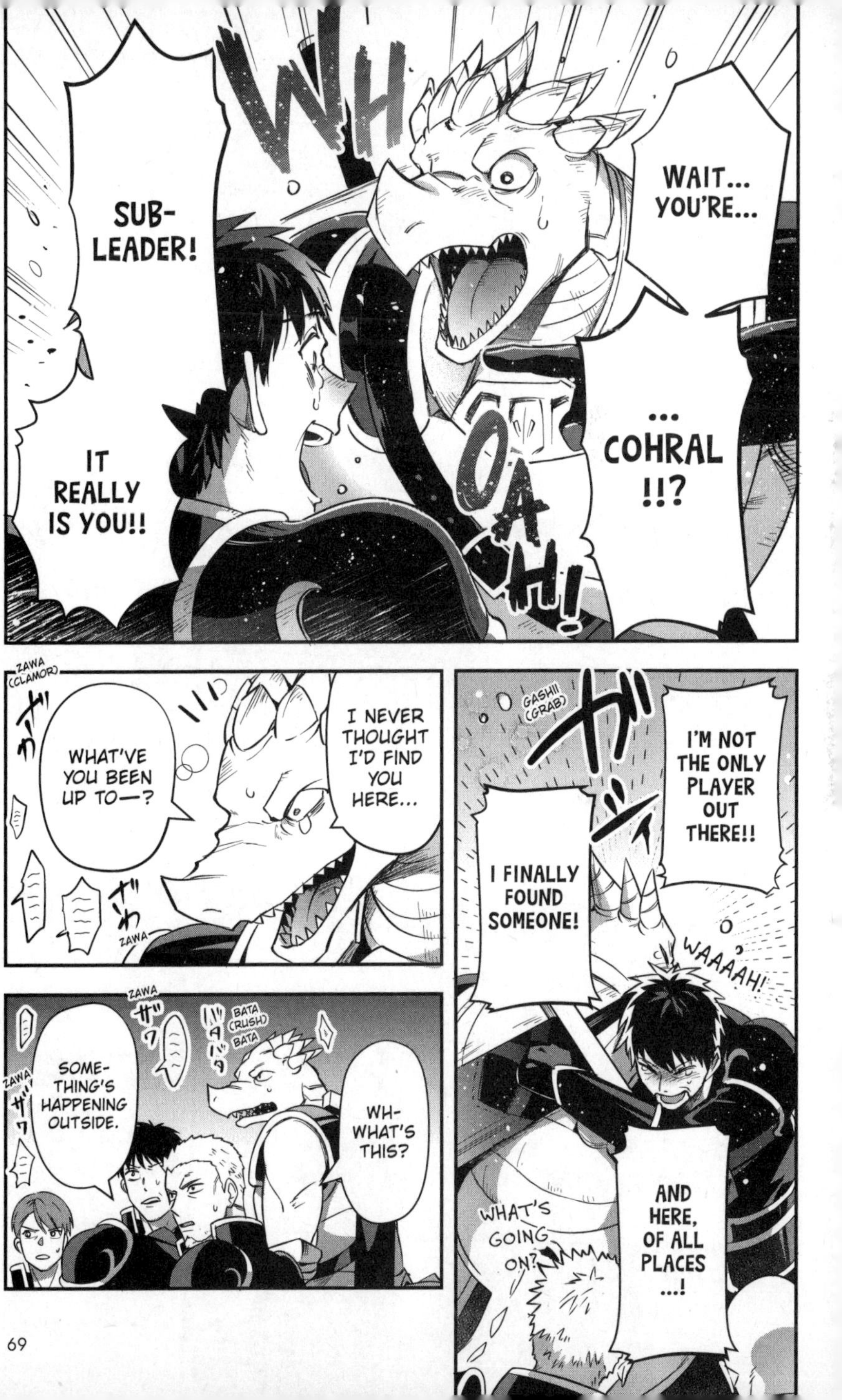
WAIT... YOU'RE...
... COHRAL !!?
WHOAH!
SUB-LEADER!
IT REALLY IS YOU!!
GASHII (GRAB)
I'M NOT THE ONLY PLAYER OUT THERE!!
I FINALLY FOUND SOMEONE!
WAAAAH!
AND HERE, OF ALL PLACES ...!
WHAT'S GOING ON?
ZAWA (CLAMOR)
I NEVER THOUGHT I'D FIND YOU HERE...
WHAT'VE YOU BEEN UP TO—?
ZAWA
BATA (RUSH) BATA
ZAWA
WH-WHAT'S THIS?
SOME-THING'S HAPPENING OUTSIDE.
ZAWA

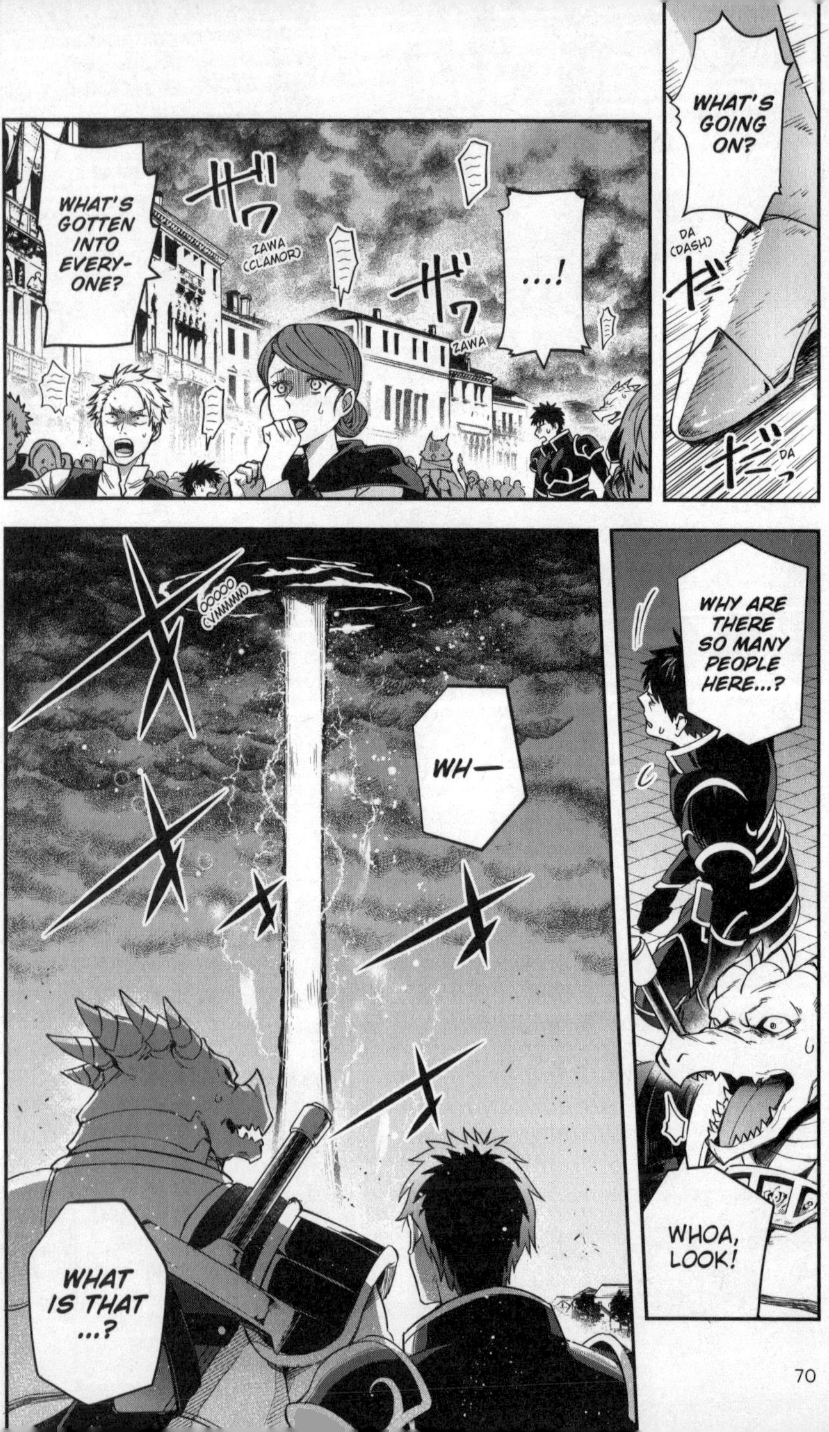
WHAT'S GOING ON?
DA (DASH)
DA
...!
ZAWA
WHAT'S GOTTEN INTO EVERY-ONE?
ZAWA (CLAMOR)
WHY ARE THERE SO MANY PEOPLE HERE...?
WHOA, LOOK!
(VMMMMM)
WH—
WHAT IS THAT ...?

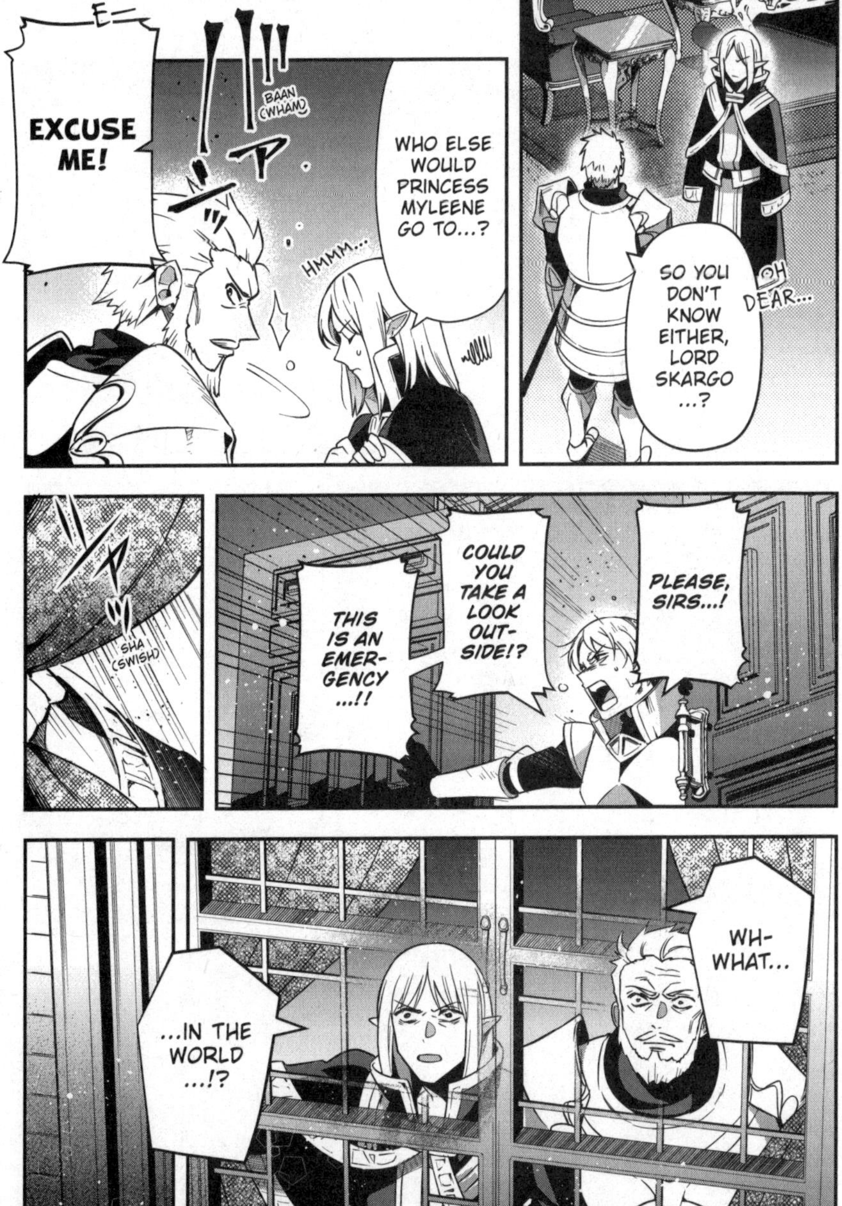
OH DEAR...
SO YOU DON'T KNOW EITHER, LORD SKARGO...?
WHO ELSE WOULD PRINCESS MYLEENE GO TO...?
HMMM...
BAAN (WHAM)
EXCUSE ME!
PLEASE, SIRS...!
COULD YOU TAKE A LOOK OUTSIDE!?
THIS IS AN EMERGENCY...!!
SHA (SWISH)
WH- WHAT...
...IN THE WORLD...!?

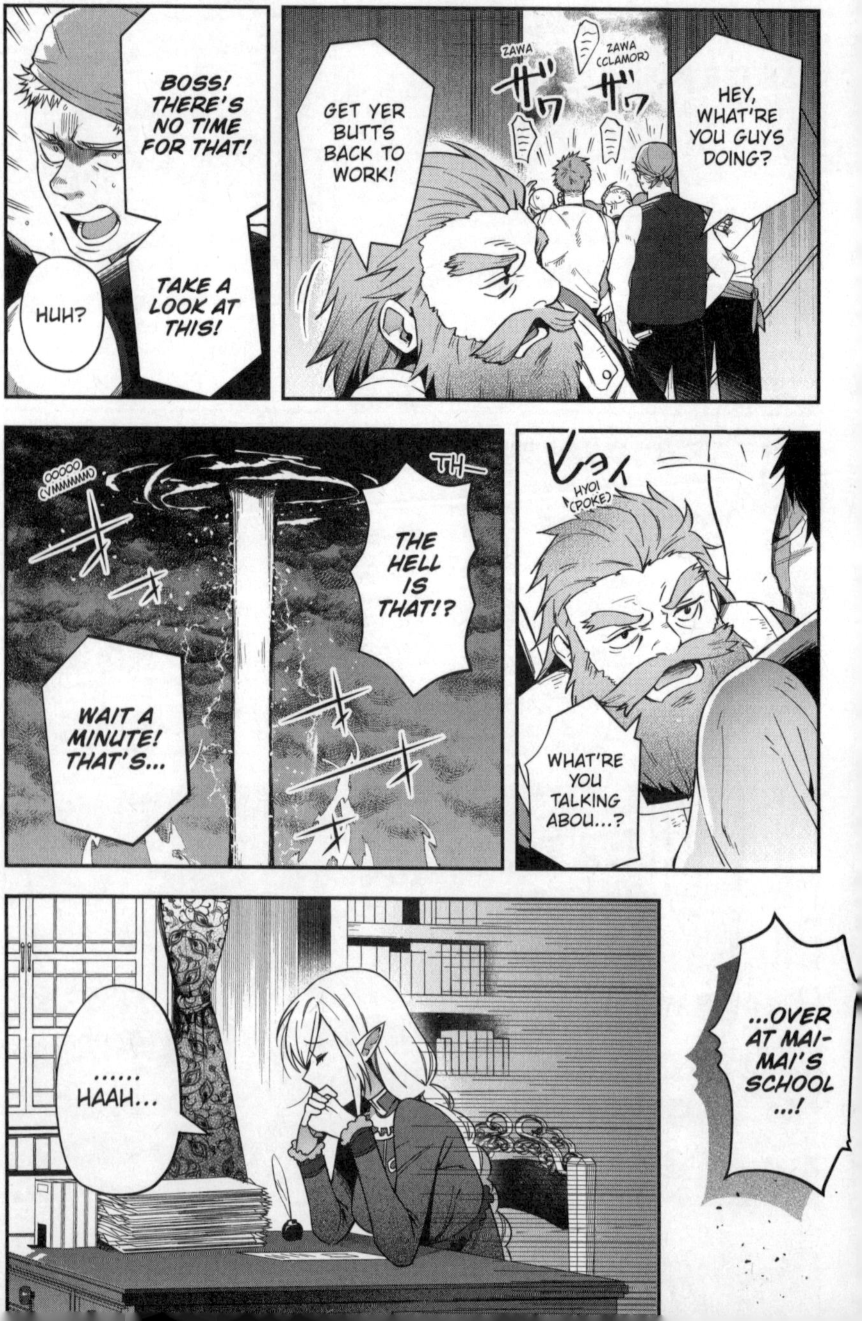

HEY, WHAT'RE YOU GUYS DOING?
ZAWA (CLAMOR)
ZAWA
GET YER BUTTS BACK TO WORK!
BOSS! THERE'S NO TIME FOR THAT!
TAKE A LOOK AT THIS!
HUH?
HYOI (POKE)
WHAT'RE YOU TALKING ABOU...?
TH—
THE HELL IS THAT!?
WAIT A MINUTE! THAT'S...
...OVER AT MAI-MAI'S SCHOOL ...!
...... HAAH...

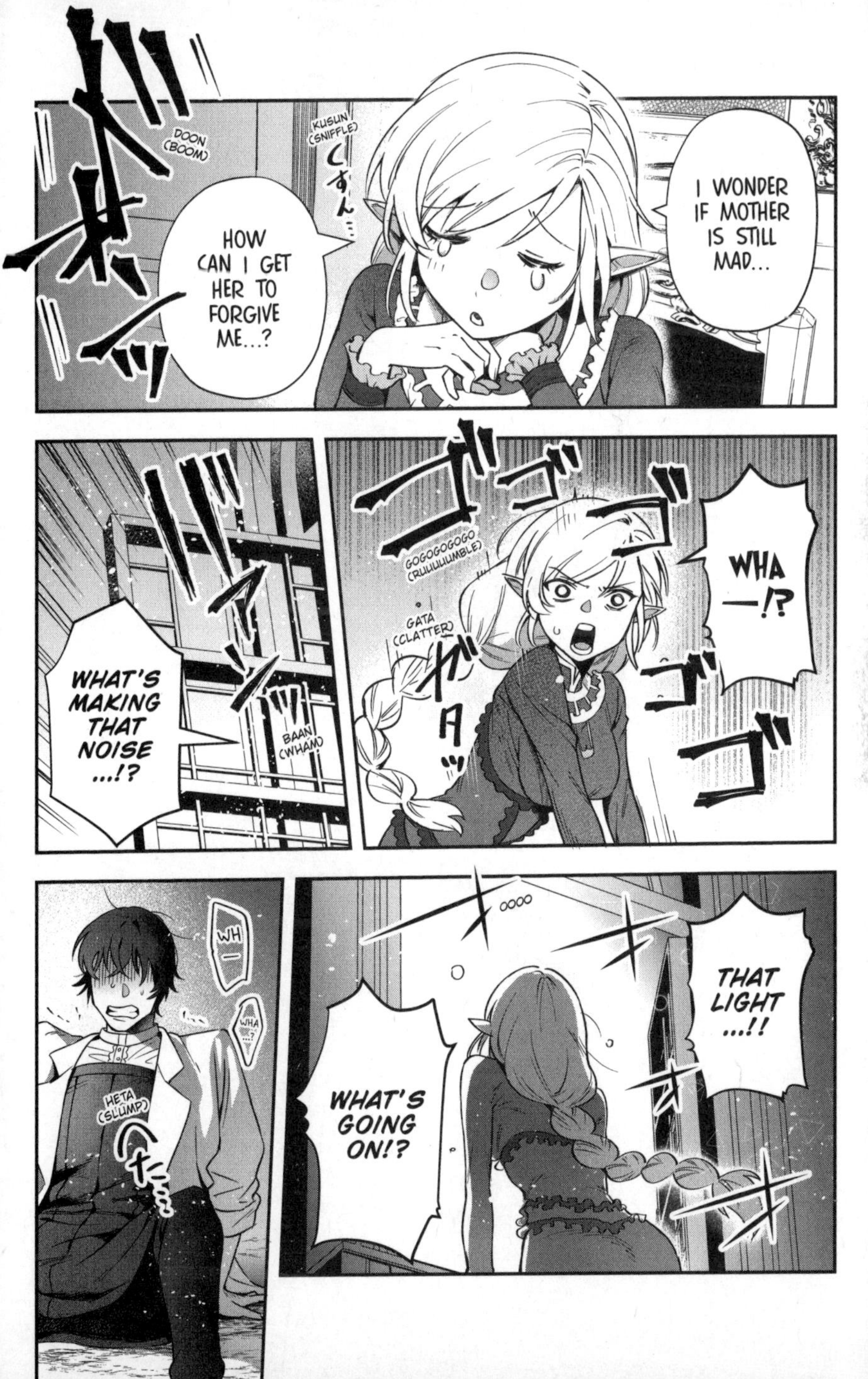
I WONDER IF MOTHER IS STILL MAD...
KUSUN (SNIFFLE)
くすん…
HOW CAN I GET HER TO FORGIVE ME...?
DOON (BOOM)
GOGOGOGOGO (RUUUUUMBLE)
WHA—!?
GATA (CLATTER)
BAAN (WHAM)
WHAT'S MAKING THAT NOISE...!?
THAT LIGHT...!!
WHAT'S GOING ON!?
WH—
WHA—?
HETA (SLUMP)

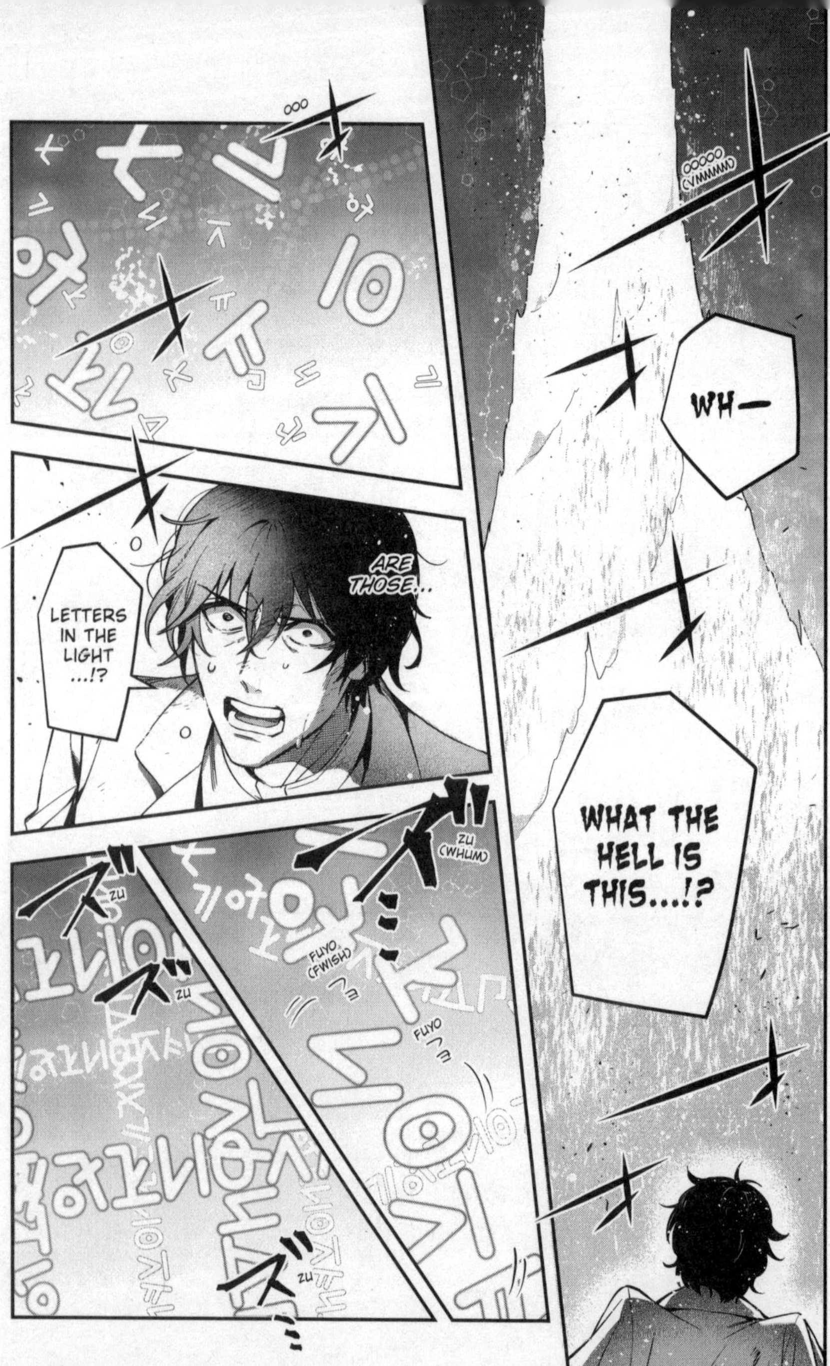
OOOOO (VWWWWW)
WH—
WHAT THE HELL IS THIS...!?
OOO
ARE THOSE...
LETTERS IN THE LIGHT...!?
ZU (WHUM)
FUYO (FWISH)
FUYO
ZU
ZU
ZU

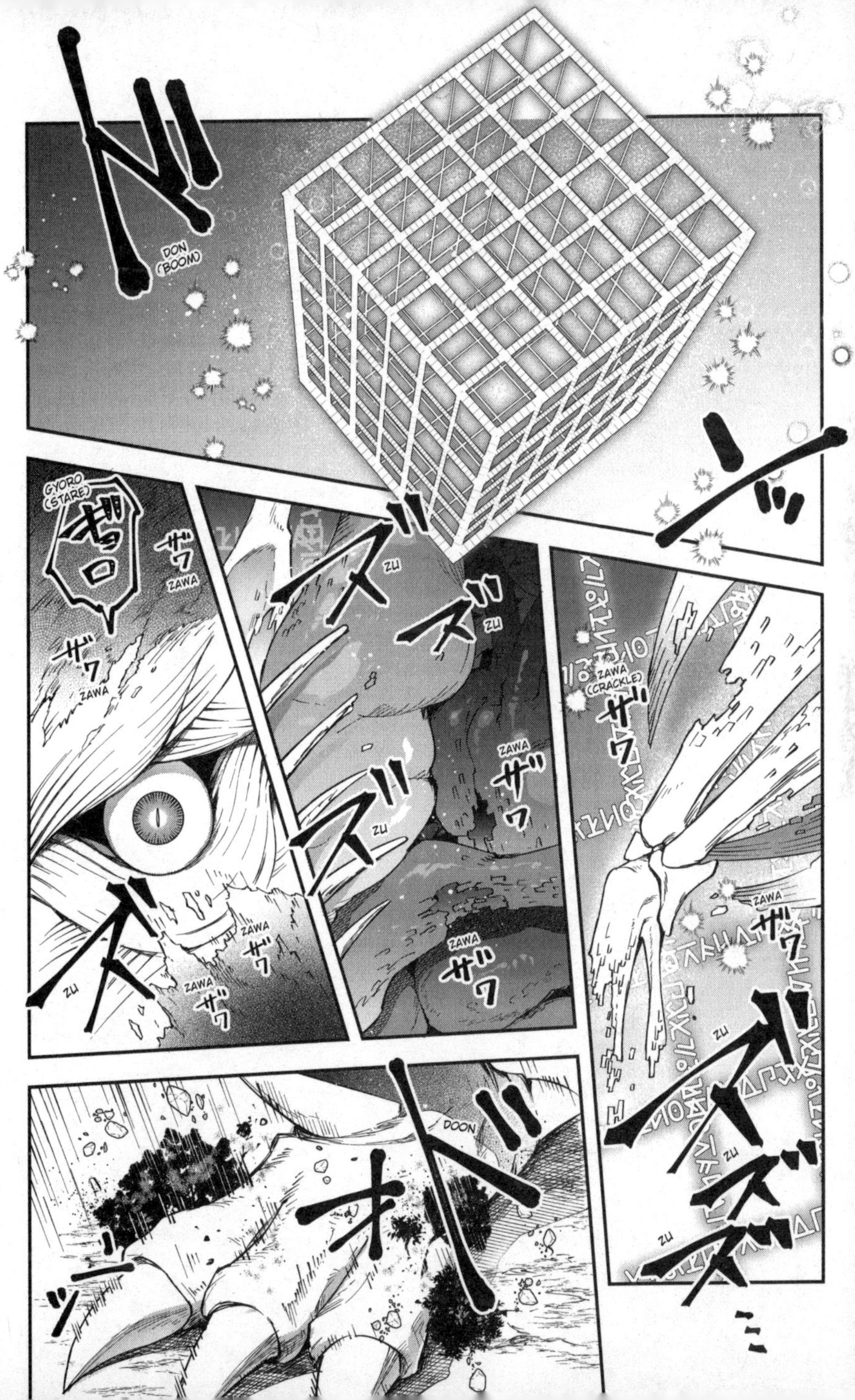

DON (BOOM)
ZAWA (CRACKLE)
ZAWA
ZU
ZU
ZU
ZU
ZU
ZAWA
ZAWA
GYORO (STARE)
ZAWA
ZAWA
ZAWA
ZAWA
ZU
DOON

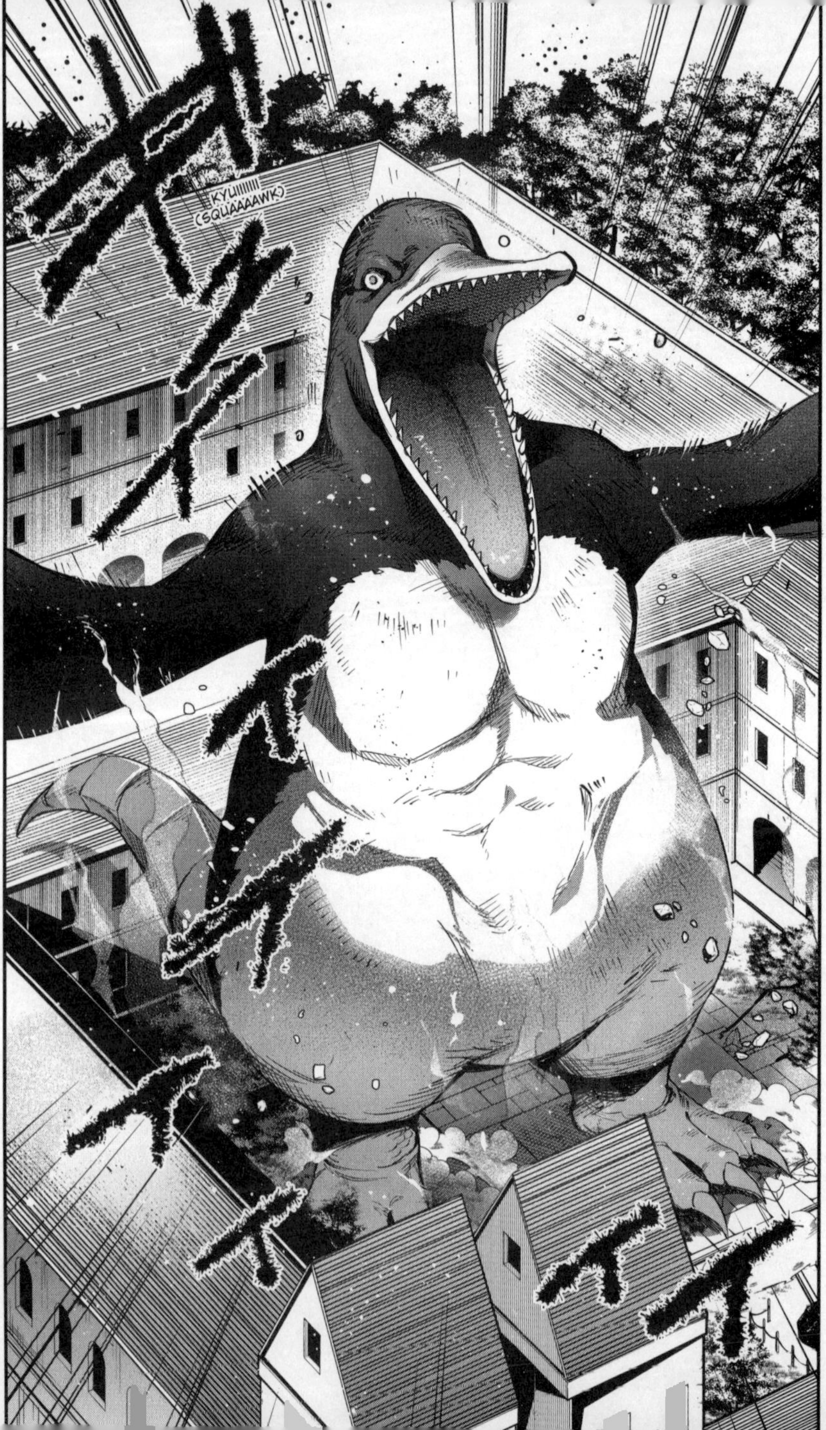
KYUIIIIIIIIII
(SQUAAAAAWK)

In the Land of Leadale

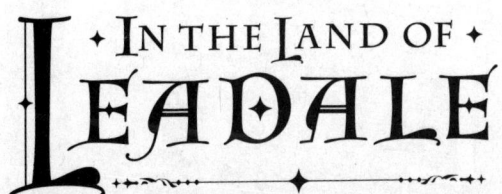

· IN THE LAND OF ·
LEADALE

Chapter 22
Let's Protect the Capital, Part II

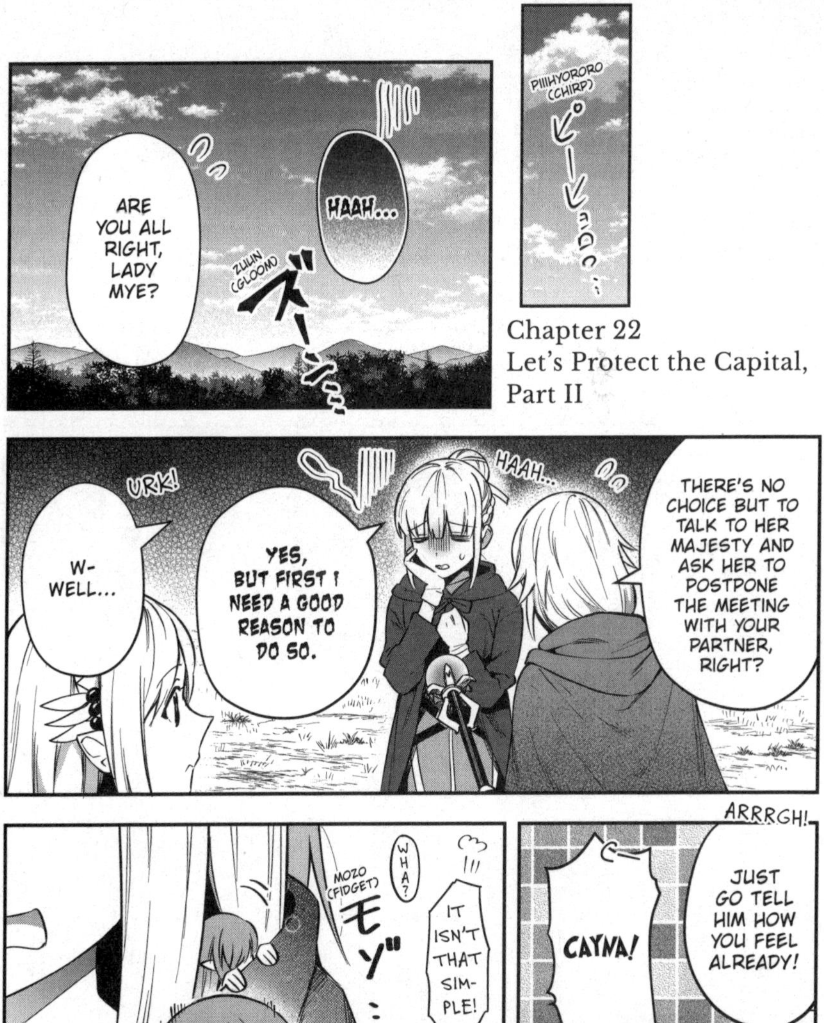
PIIIHYORORO (CHIRP)
ピーヒョロロ…
HAAH...
ZUUN (GLOOM)
ズーン…
ARE YOU ALL RIGHT, LADY MYE?
THERE'S NO CHOICE BUT TO TALK TO HER MAJESTY AND ASK HER TO POSTPONE THE MEETING WITH YOUR PARTNER, RIGHT?
HAAH...
YES, BUT FIRST I NEED A GOOD REASON TO DO SO.
URK!
W-WELL...
ARRRGH!
JUST GO TELL HIM HOW YOU FEEL ALREADY!
CAYNA!
COME ON!
KAAA (BLUSH)
IT ISN'T THAT SIMPLE!
WHA?
MOZO (FIDGET)
モゾ…
BA (SHOCK)

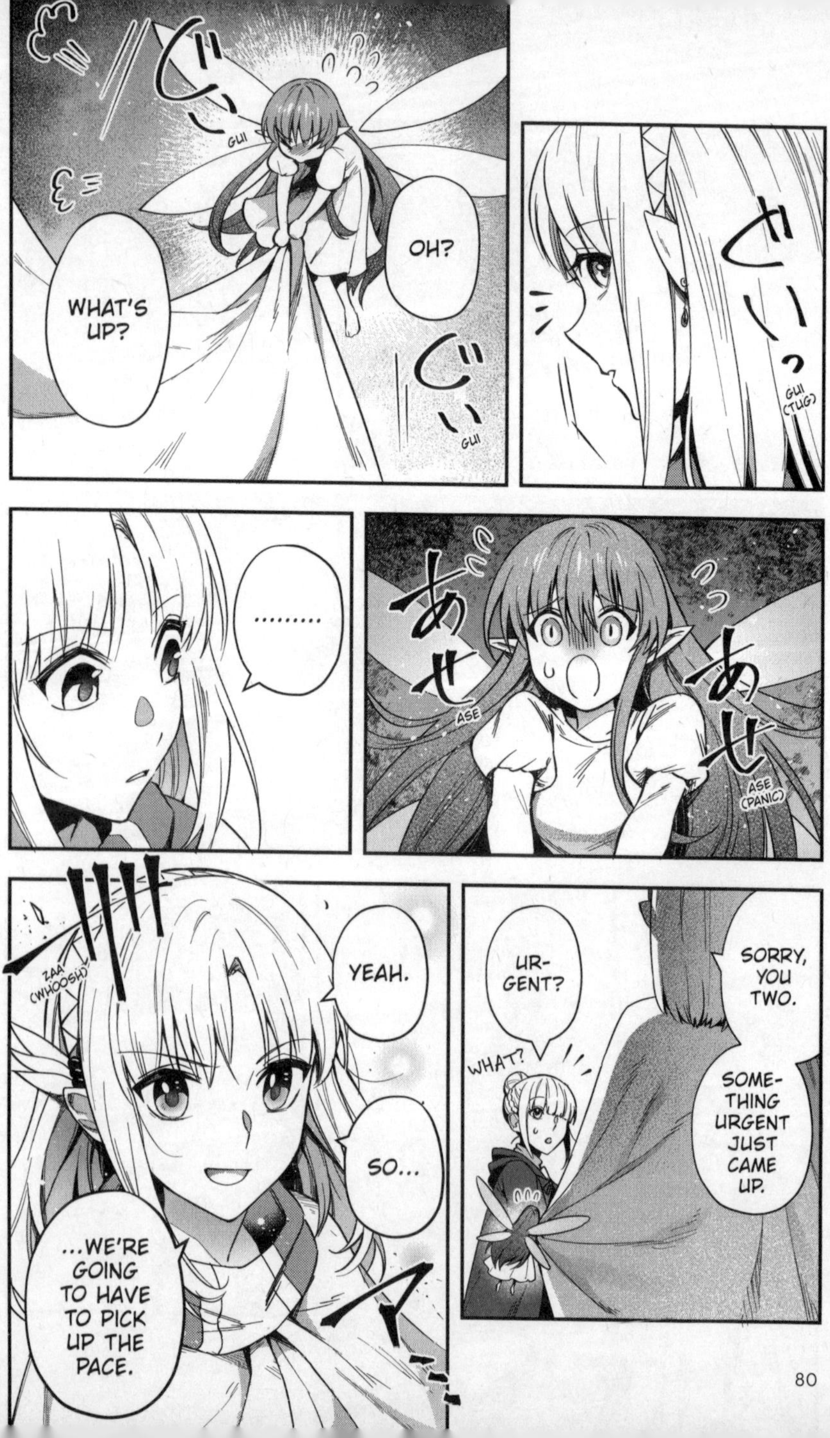
GUI (TUG)
GUI
GUI
OH?
WHAT'S UP?
ASE
ASE (PANIC)
....
SORRY, YOU TWO.
SOMETHING URGENT JUST CAME UP.
URGENT?
WHAT?
YEAH.
ZAA (WHOOSH)
SO...
...WE'RE GOING TO HAVE TO PICK UP THE PACE.

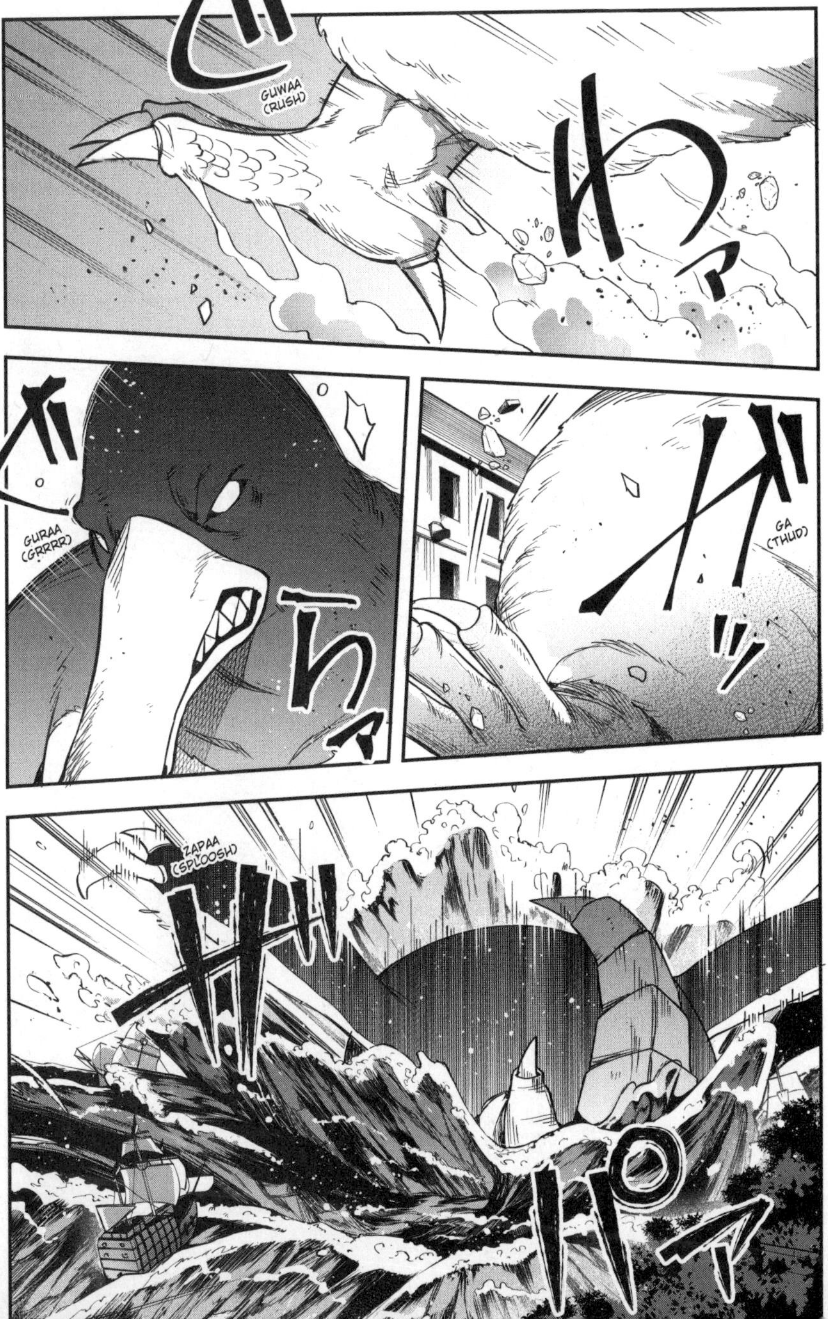
GUWAA (RUSH)
GA (THUD)
GURAA (GRRRR)
ZAPAA (SPLOOSH)

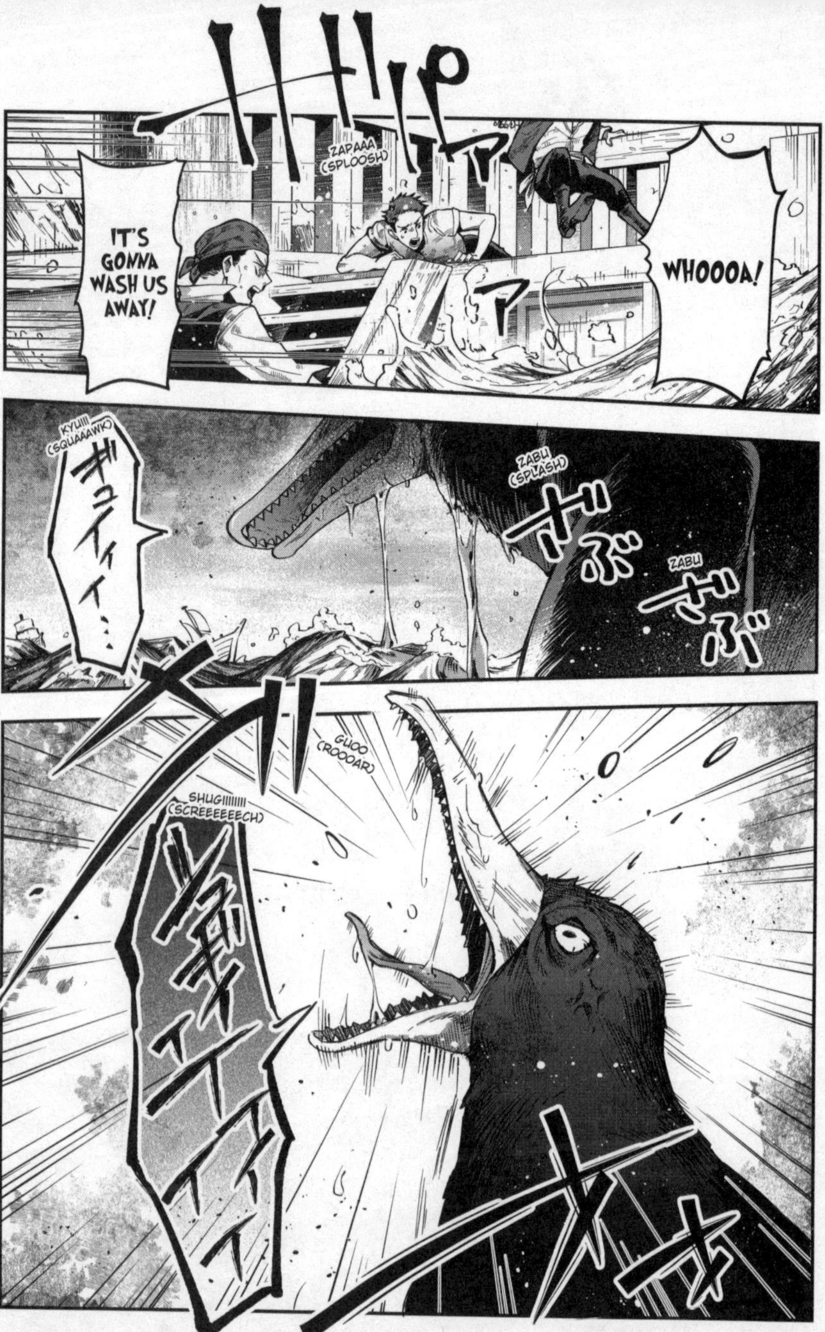
WHOOOA!
ZAPAAA
(SPLOOSH)
IT'S GONNA WASH US AWAY!
ZABU
(SPLASH)
ZABU
KYUIII
(SQUAAAWK)
GUOO
(ROOOAR)
SHUGIIIIIIIIII
(SCREEEEEEECH)

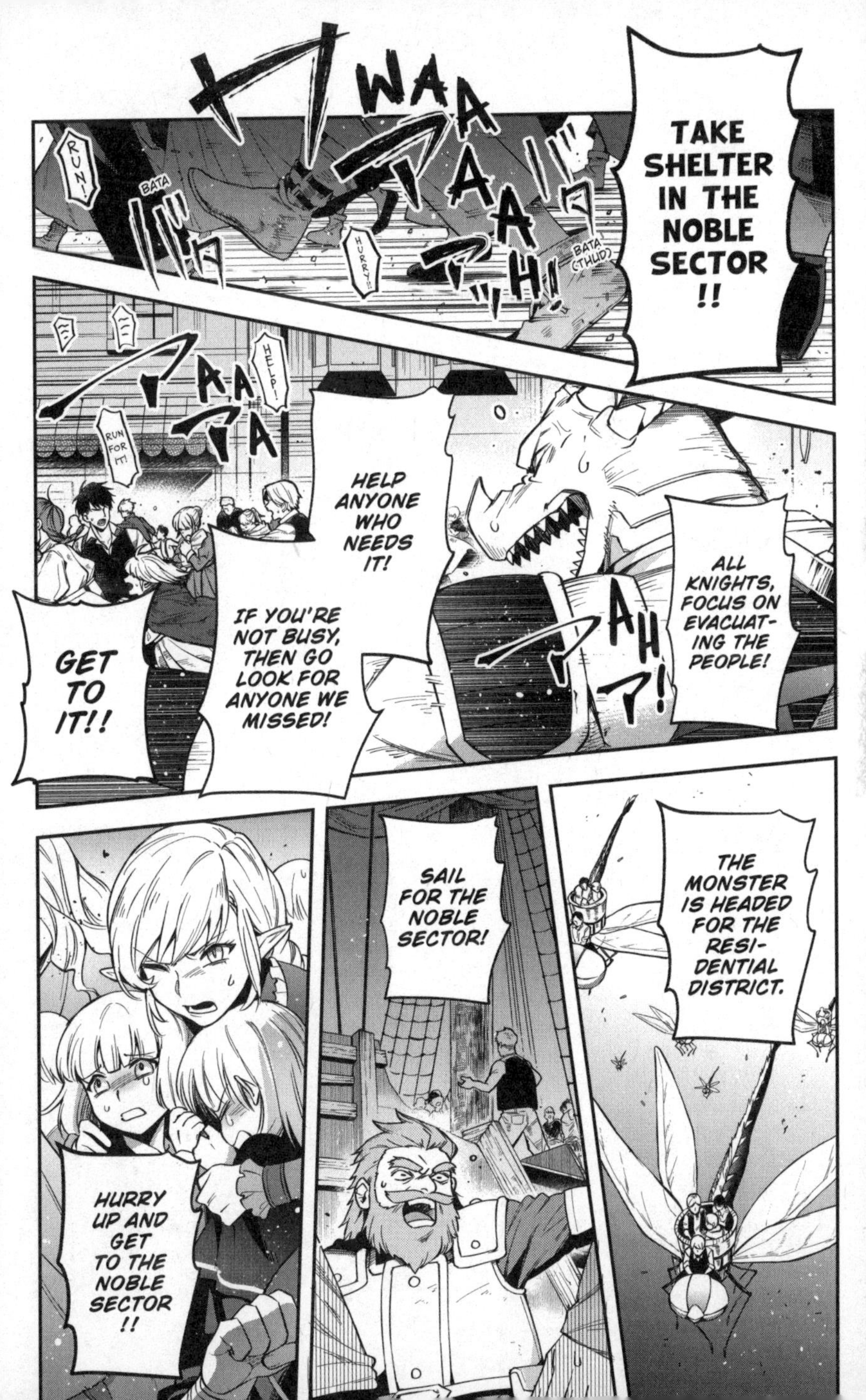
TAKE SHELTER IN THE NOBLE SECTOR!!
WAAAAAH!!
BATA (THUD)
HURRY!!
BATA
RUN!
ALL KNIGHTS, FOCUS ON EVACUATING THE PEOPLE!
AHH!
HELP ANYONE WHO NEEDS IT!
IF YOU'RE NOT BUSY, THEN GO LOOK FOR ANYONE WE MISSED!
GET TO IT!!
AAA
HELP!
RUN FOR IT!
THE MONSTER IS HEADED FOR THE RESIDENTIAL DISTRICT.
SAIL FOR THE NOBLE SECTOR!
HURRY UP AND GET TO THE NOBLE SECTOR!!

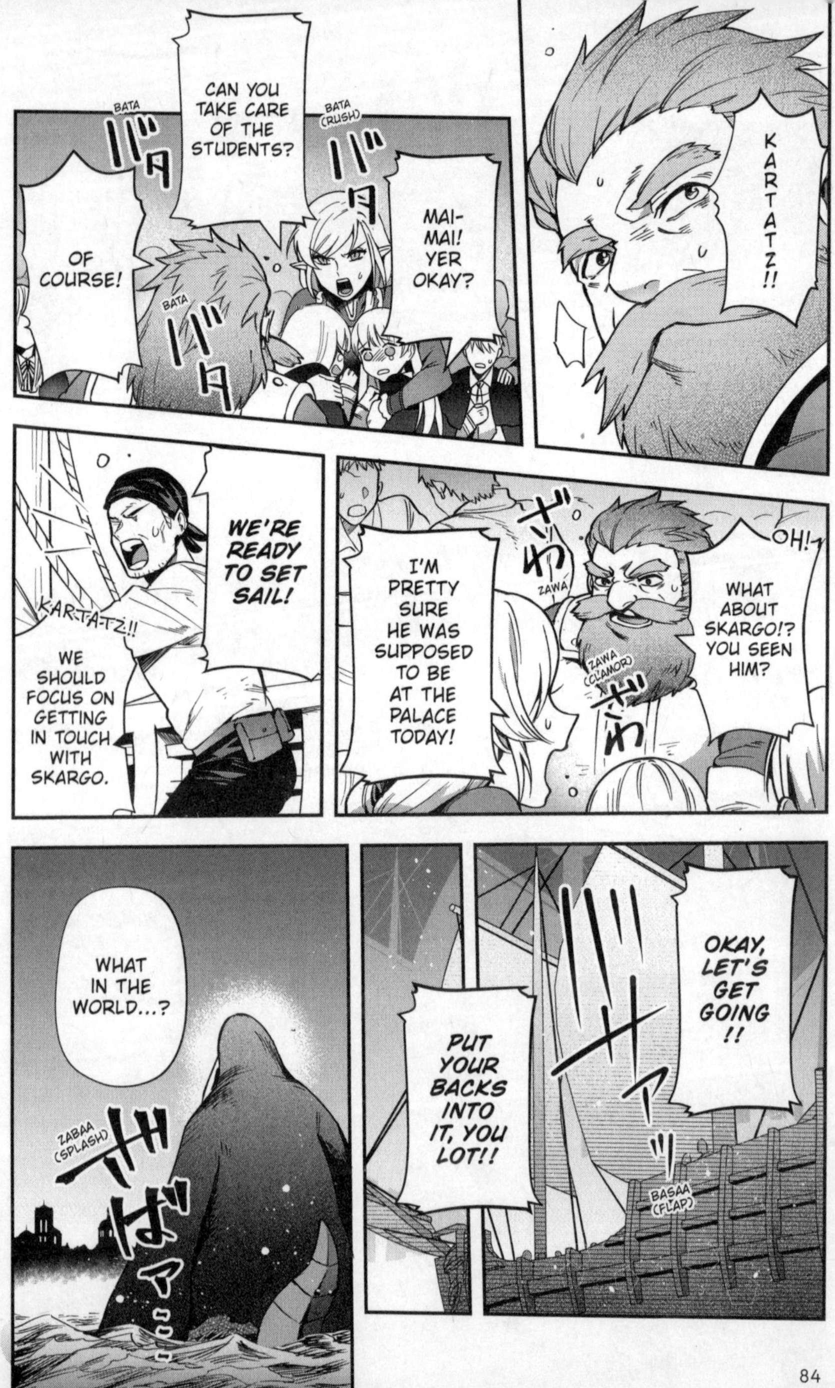
KARTATZ!!
BATA (RUSH)
MAI-MAI! YER OKAY?
CAN YOU TAKE CARE OF THE STUDENTS?
BATA
OF COURSE!
BATA
OH!
WHAT ABOUT SKARGO!? YOU SEEN HIM?
ZAWA
I'M PRETTY SURE HE WAS SUPPOSED TO BE AT THE PALACE TODAY!
ZAWA (CLAMOR)
WE'RE READY TO SET SAIL!
KARTATZ!!
WE SHOULD FOCUS ON GETTING IN TOUCH WITH SKARGO.
OKAY, LET'S GET GOING!!
PUT YOUR BACKS INTO IT, YOU LOT!!
BASAA (FLAP)
WHAT IN THE WORLD...?
ZABAA (SPLASH)

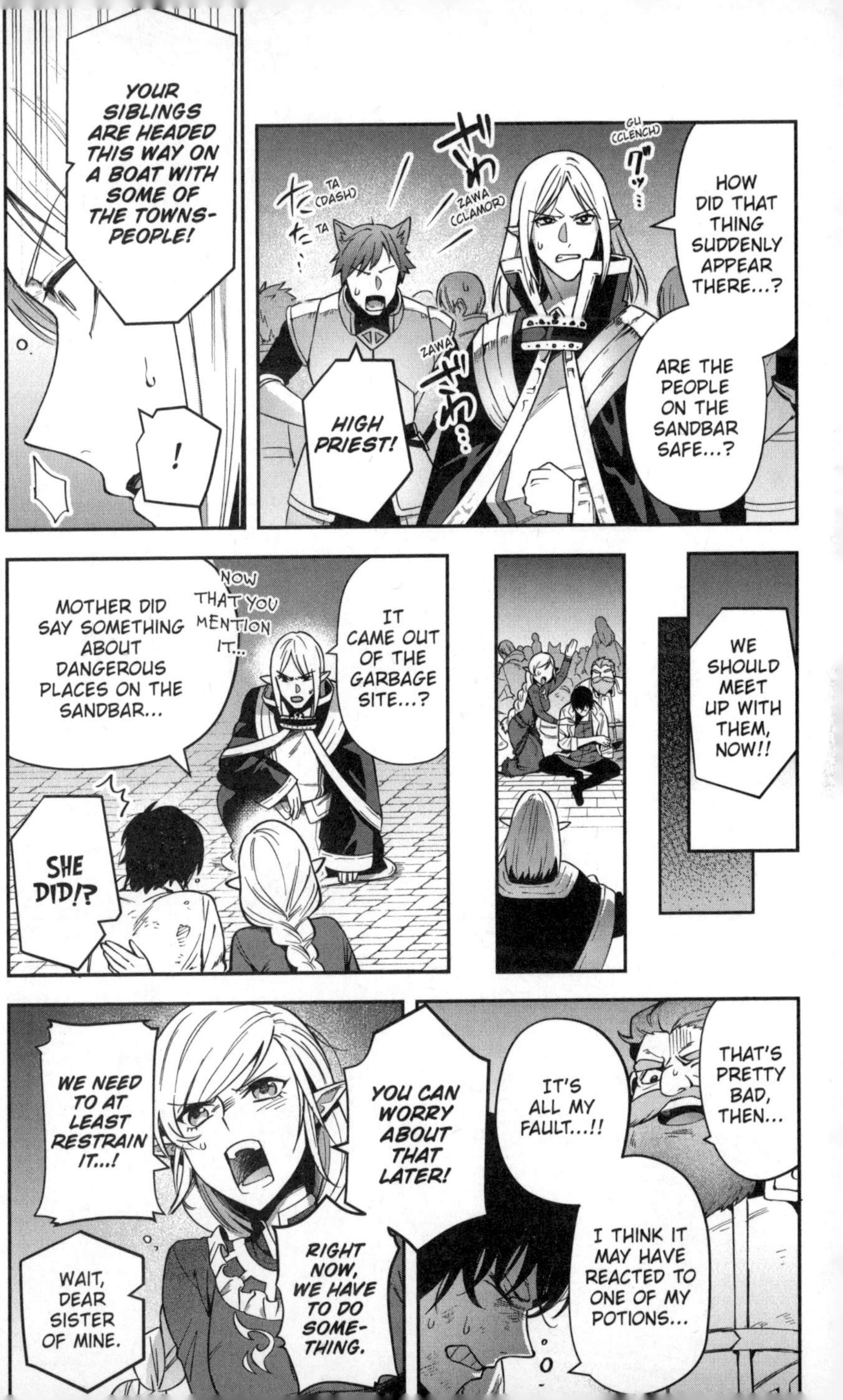
GU (CLENCH)
HOW DID THAT THING SUDDENLY APPEAR THERE...?
ZAWA (CLAMOR)
TA (DASH) TA
ARE THE PEOPLE ON THE SANDBAR SAFE...?
ZAWA
HIGH PRIEST!
YOUR SIBLINGS ARE HEADED THIS WAY ON A BOAT WITH SOME OF THE TOWNS-PEOPLE!
!
WE SHOULD MEET UP WITH THEM, NOW!!
IT CAME OUT OF THE GARBAGE SITE...?
NOW THAT YOU MENTION IT...
MOTHER DID SAY SOMETHING ABOUT DANGEROUS PLACES ON THE SANDBAR...
SHE DID!?
THAT'S PRETTY BAD, THEN...
IT'S ALL MY FAULT...!!
I THINK IT MAY HAVE REACTED TO ONE OF MY POTIONS...
YOU CAN WORRY ABOUT THAT LATER!
WE NEED TO AT LEAST RESTRAIN IT...!
RIGHT NOW, WE HAVE TO DO SOME-THING.
WAIT, DEAR SISTER OF MINE.

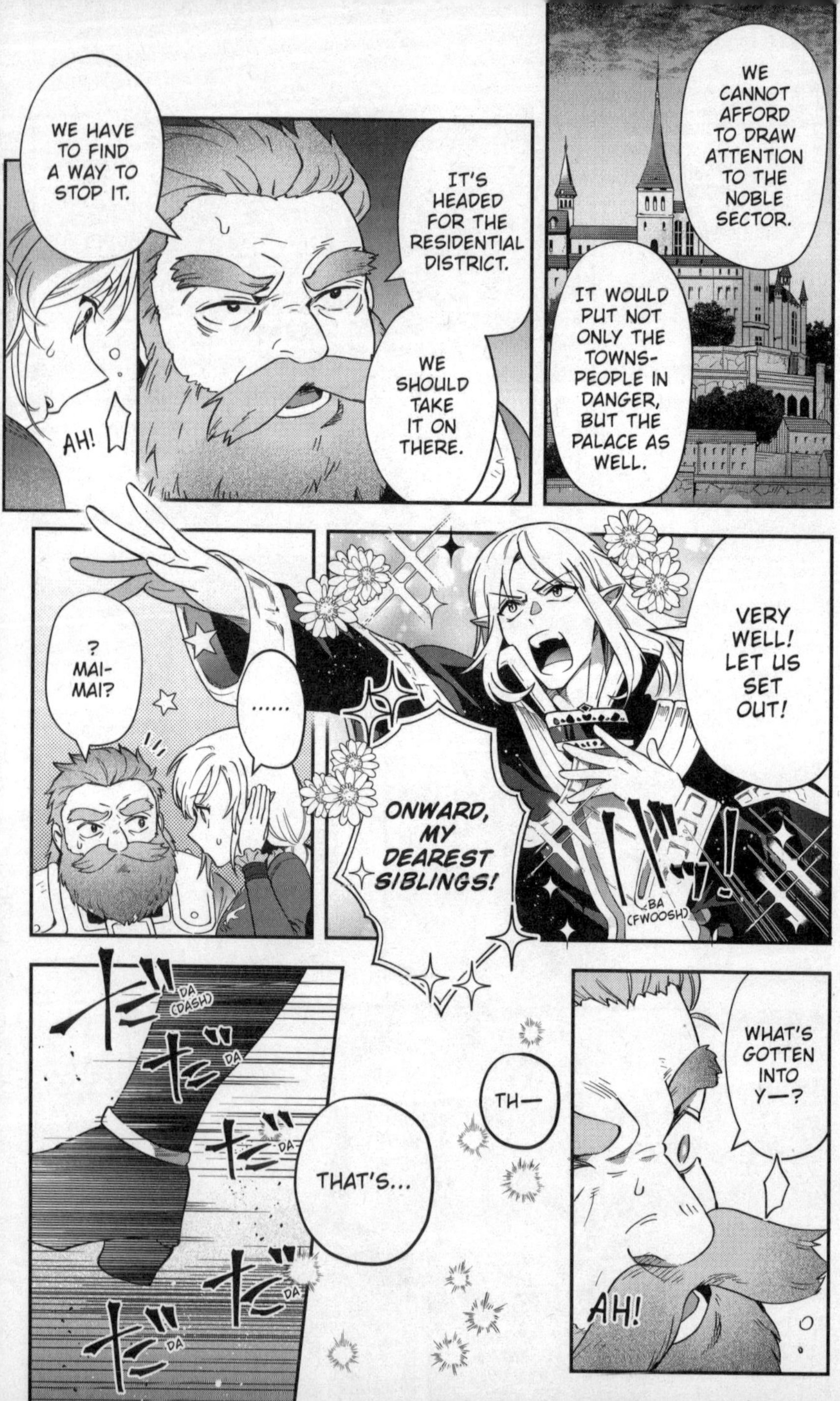
WE CANNOT AFFORD TO DRAW ATTENTION TO THE NOBLE SECTOR.
IT WOULD PUT NOT ONLY THE TOWNS-PEOPLE IN DANGER, BUT THE PALACE AS WELL.
IT'S HEADED FOR THE RESIDENTIAL DISTRICT.
WE SHOULD TAKE IT ON THERE.
WE HAVE TO FIND A WAY TO STOP IT.
AH!
VERY WELL! LET US SET OUT!
ONWARD, MY DEAREST SIBLINGS!
BA (FWOOSH)
......
? MAI-MAI?
WHAT'S GOTTEN INTO Y—?
AH!
TH—
THAT'S...
DA (DASH)
DA
DA
DA
DA

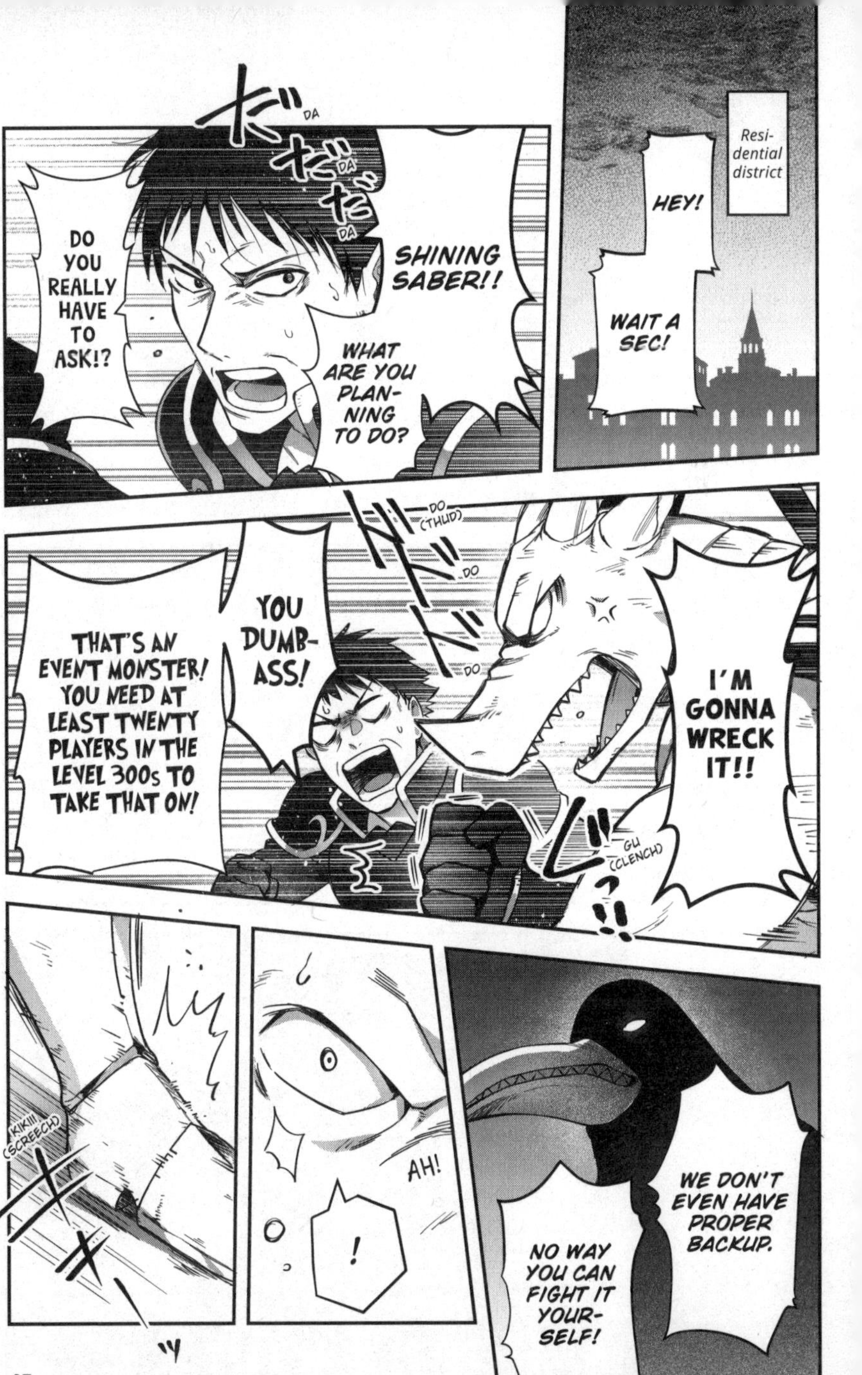
Residential district
HEY!
WAIT A SEC!
DA DA DA
SHINING SABER!!
WHAT ARE YOU PLANNING TO DO?
DO YOU REALLY HAVE TO ASK!?
I'M GONNA WRECK IT!!
DO (THUD) DO DO
GU (CLENCH)
YOU DUMBASS!
THAT'S AN EVENT MONSTER! YOU NEED AT LEAST TWENTY PLAYERS IN THE LEVEL 300s TO TAKE THAT ON!
WE DON'T EVEN HAVE PROPER BACKUP.
NO WAY YOU CAN FIGHT IT YOURSELF!
AH!
!
KIKIII (SCREECH)

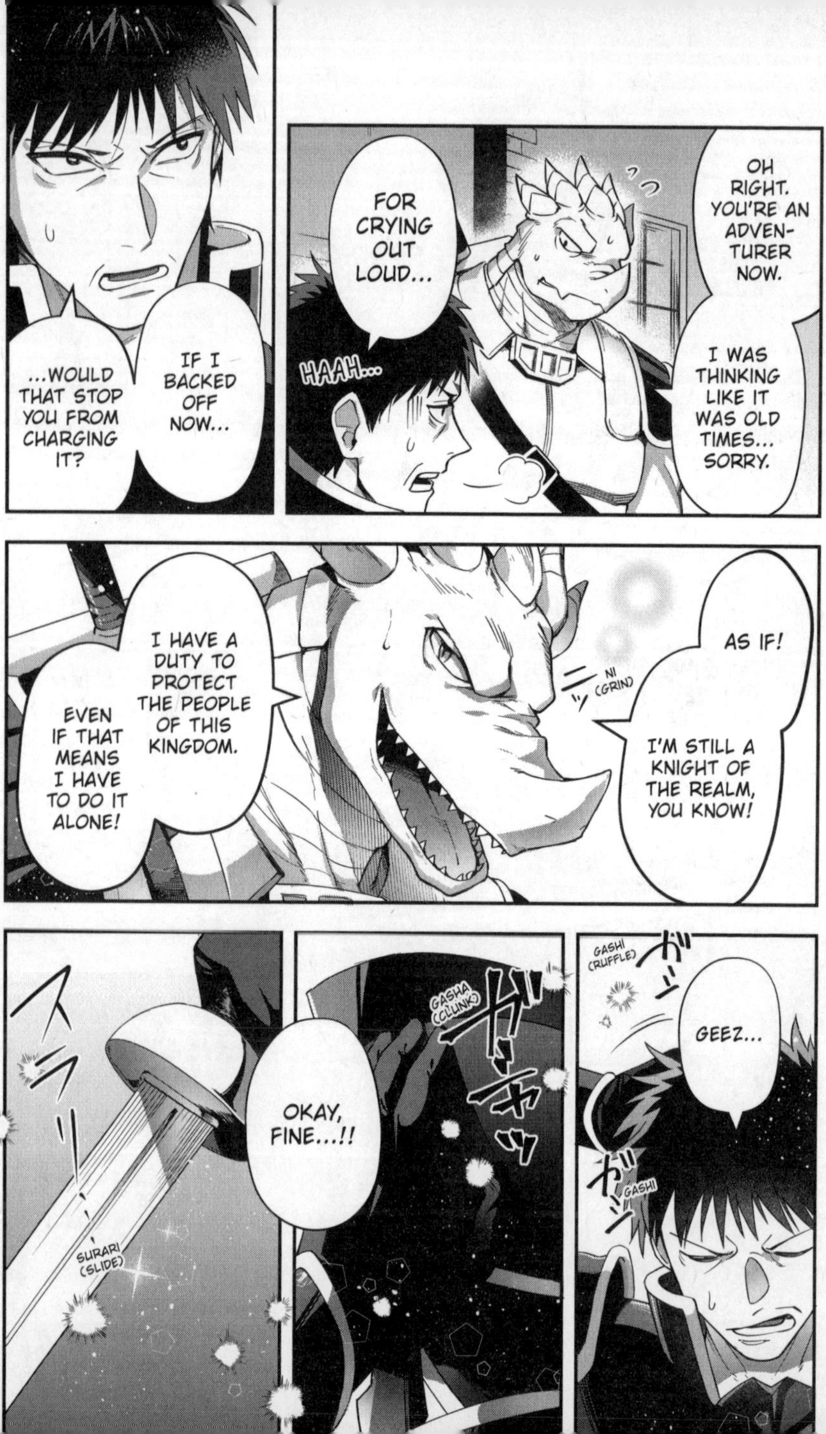
OH RIGHT. YOU'RE AN ADVEN-TURER NOW.
FOR CRYING OUT LOUD...
I WAS THINKING LIKE IT WAS OLD TIMES... SORRY.
HAAH...
IF I BACKED OFF NOW...
...WOULD THAT STOP YOU FROM CHARGING IT?
AS IF!
NI (GRIN)
I'M STILL A KNIGHT OF THE REALM, YOU KNOW!
I HAVE A DUTY TO PROTECT THE PEOPLE OF THIS KINGDOM.
EVEN IF THAT MEANS I HAVE TO DO IT ALONE!
GASHI (RUFFLE)
GEEZ...
GASHI
GASHA (CLUNK)
OKAY, FINE...!!
SURARI (SLIDE)

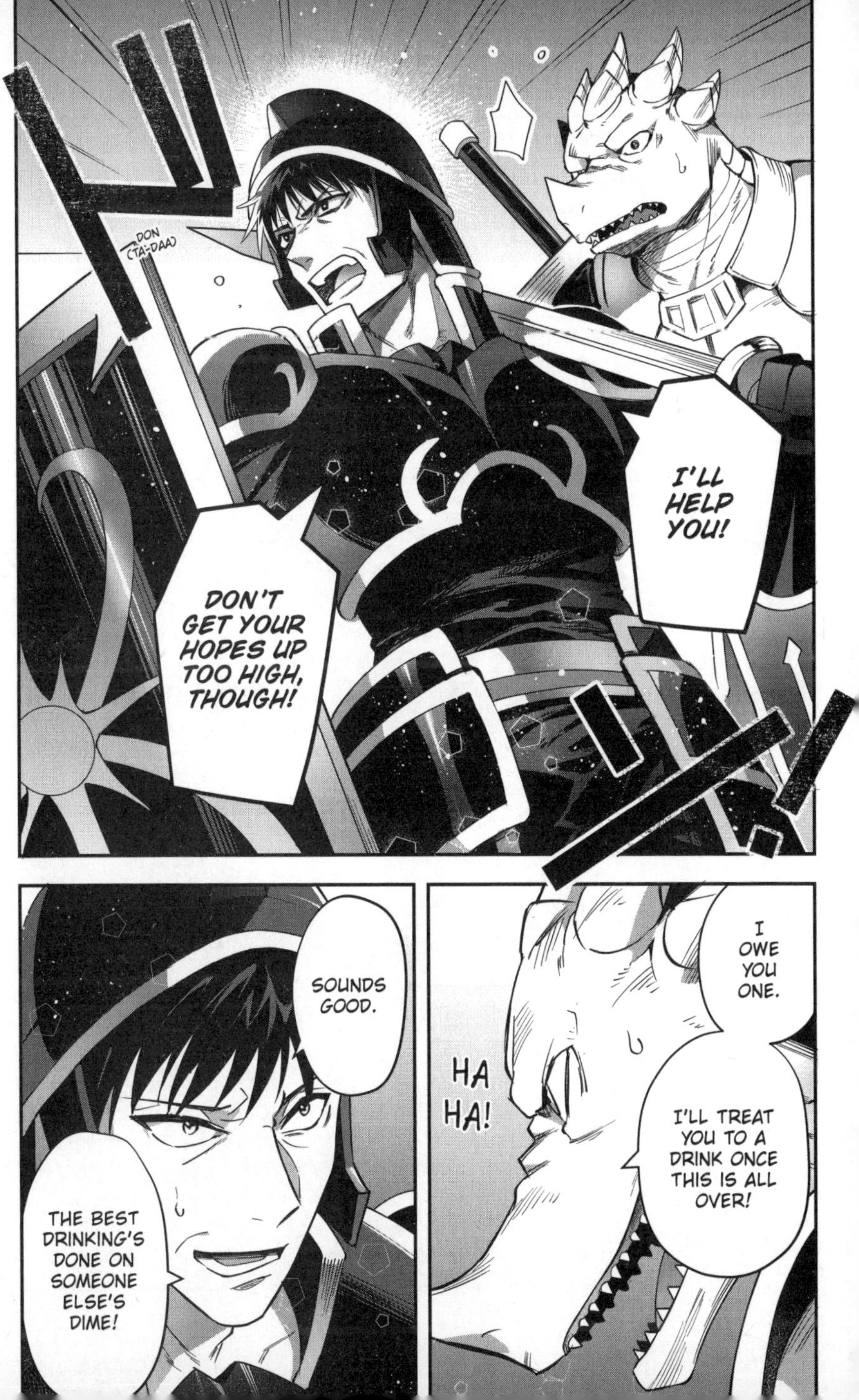
DON (TA-DAA)
I'LL HELP YOU!
DON'T GET YOUR HOPES UP TOO HIGH, THOUGH!
I OWE YOU ONE.
I'LL TREAT YOU TO A DRINK ONCE THIS IS ALL OVER!
HA HA!
SOUNDS GOOD.
THE BEST DRINKING'S DONE ON SOMEONE ELSE'S DIME!

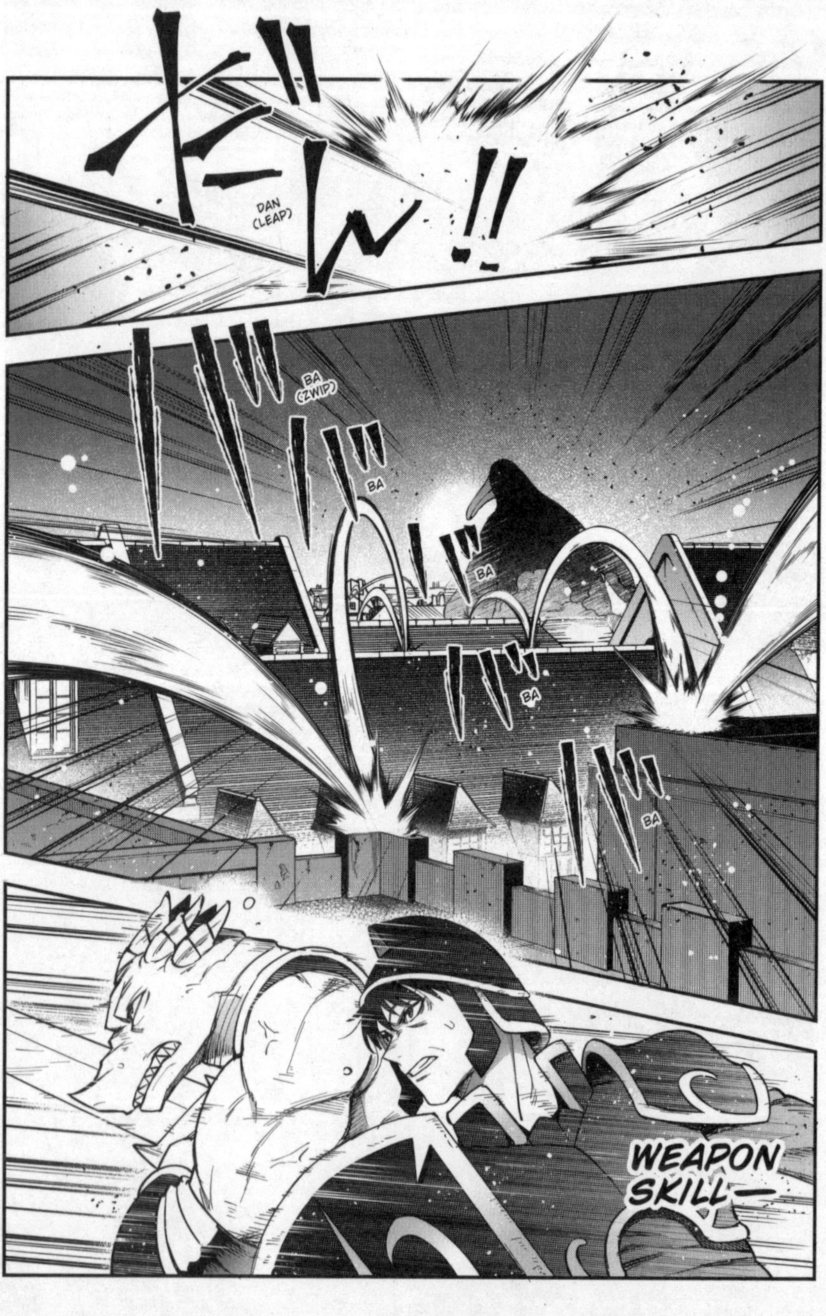
ドーん!!
DAN (LEAP)
BA (ZWIP)
BA
BA
BA
BA
WEAPON SKILL—

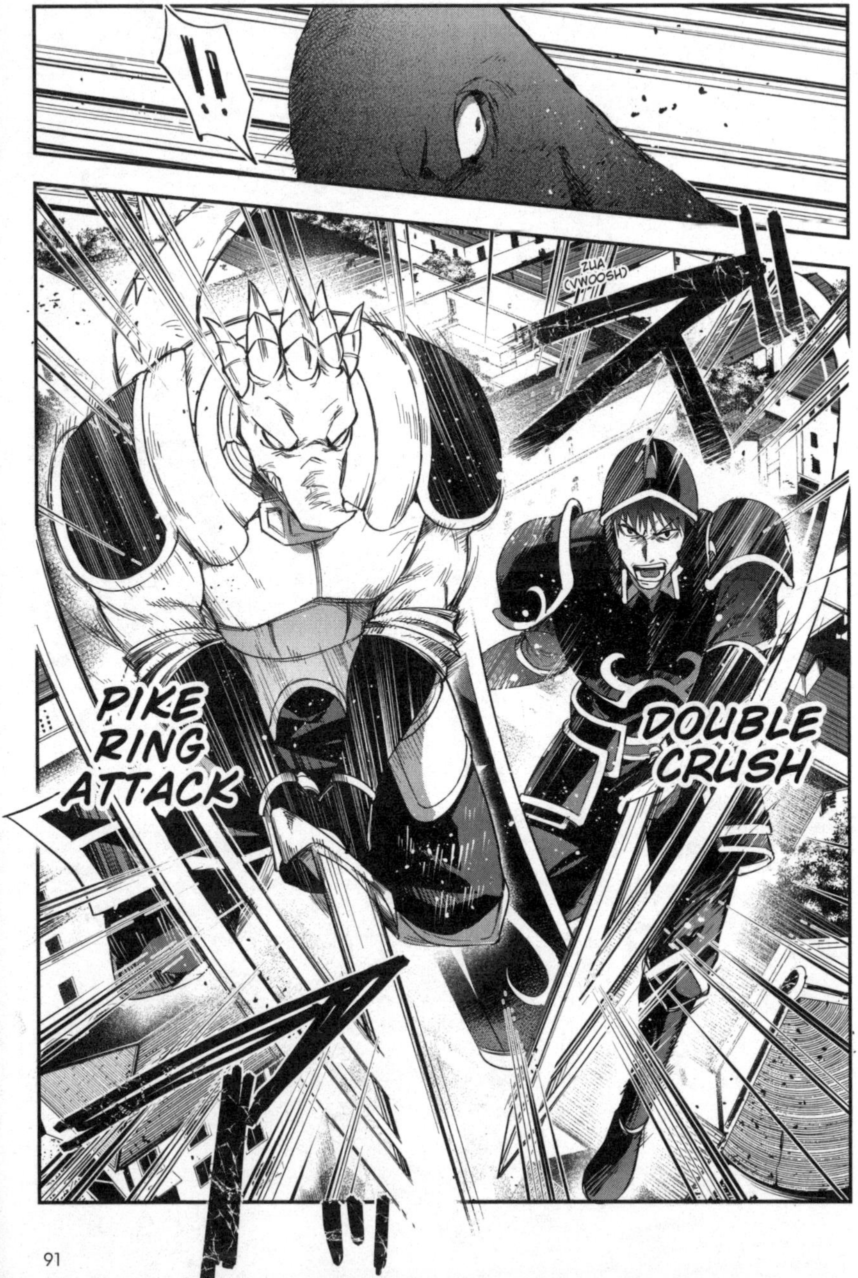
!!
ZUA
(VWOOSH)
DOUBLE
CRUSH
PIKE
RING
ATTACK

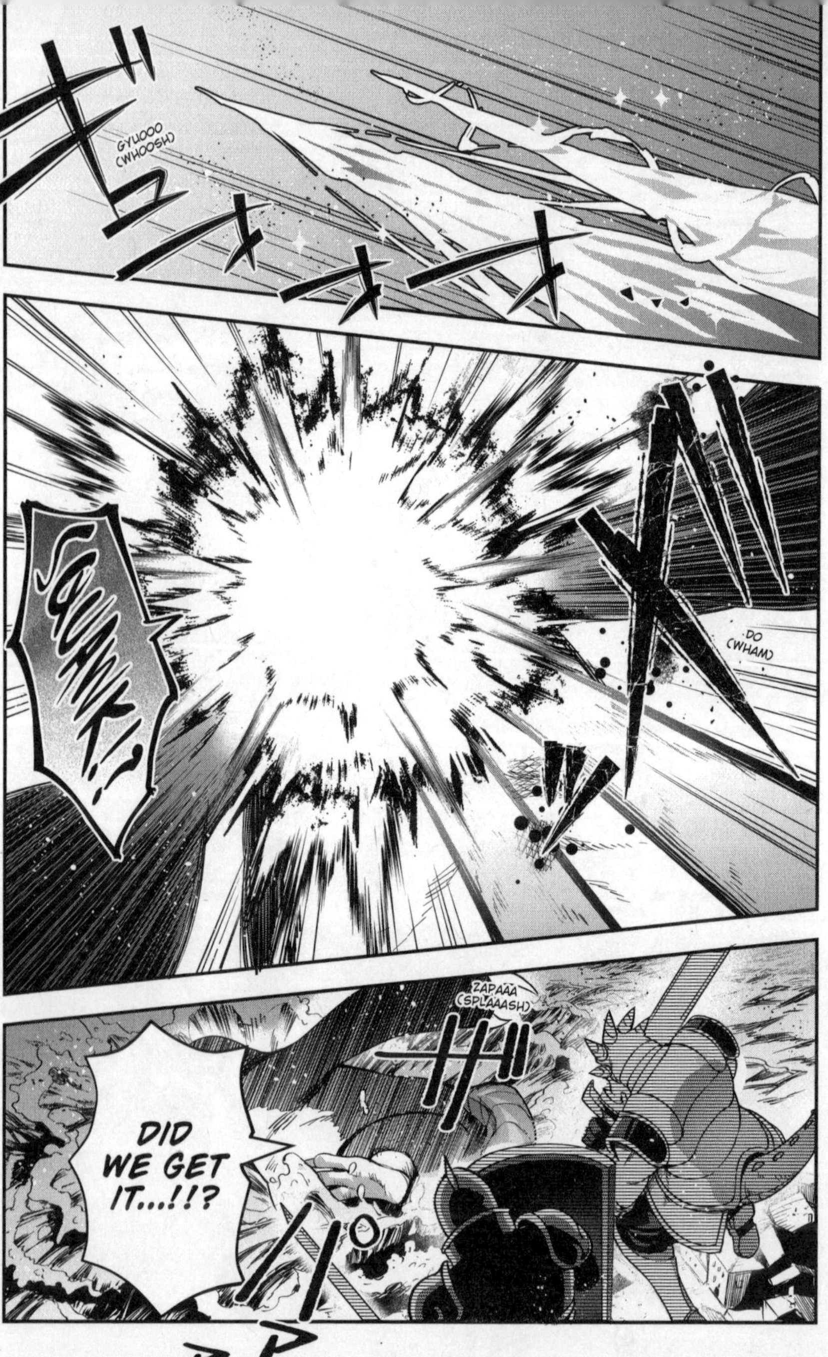
GYUOOO (WHOOSH)
DO (WHAM)
SQUAWK!!?
ZAPAAA (SPLAAASH)
DID WE GET IT...!!?

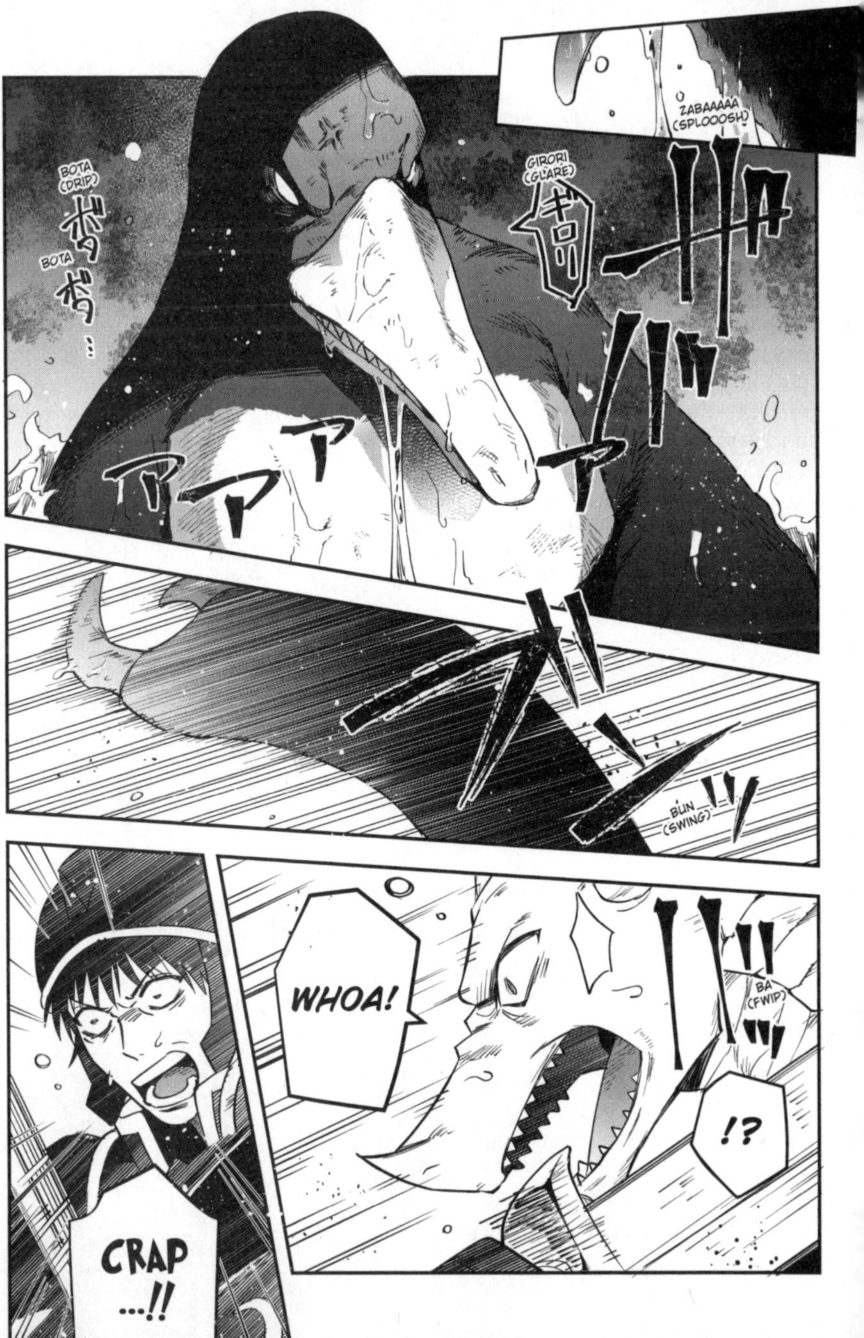

ZABAAAAA (SPLOOOSH)
GIRORI (GLARE)
BOTA (DRIP) BOTA
BUN (SWING)
BA (FWIP)
WHOA!
!?
CRAP ...!!

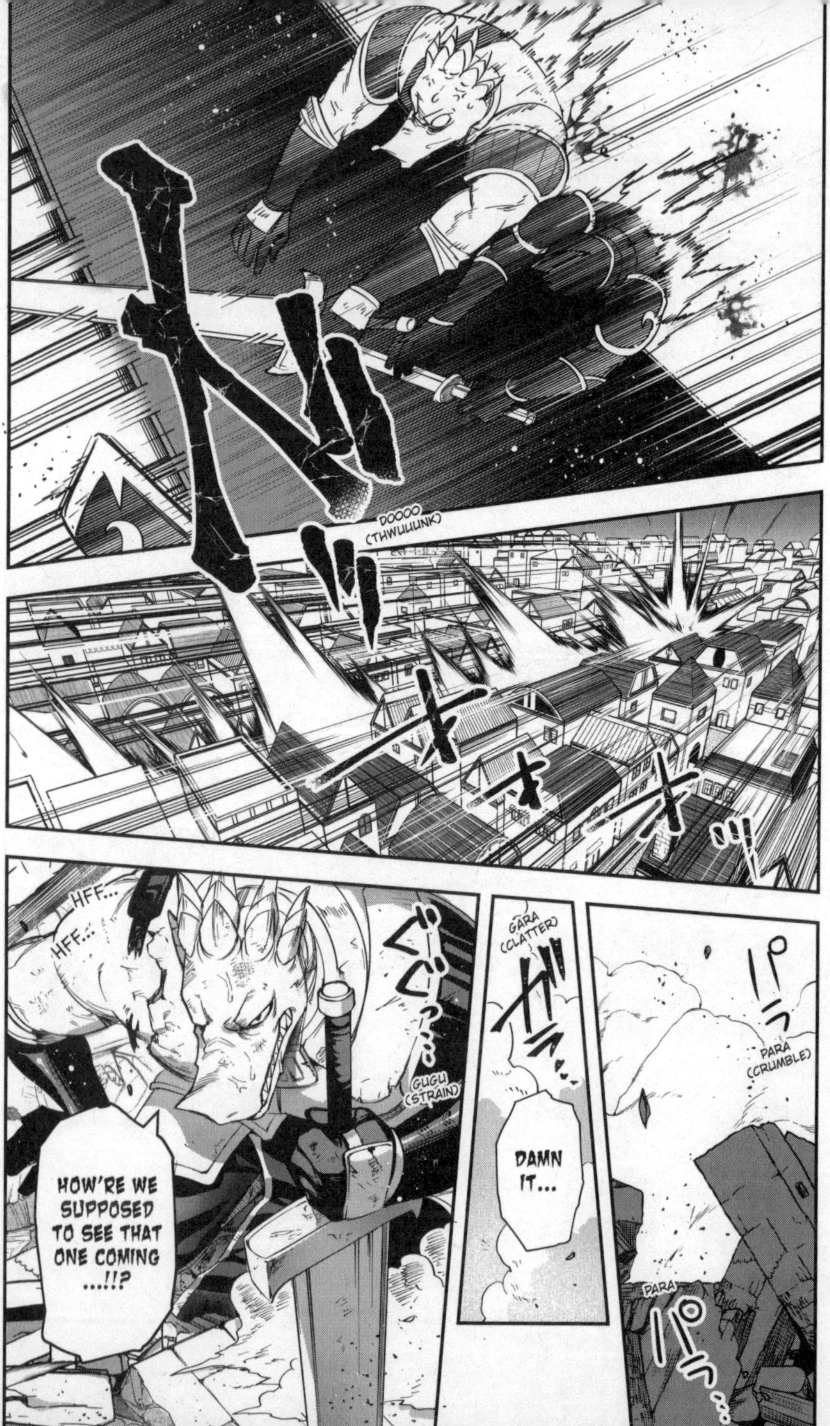
DOOOO
(THWUUUNK)
PARA
(CRUMBLE)
PARA
GARA
(CLATTER)
DAMN IT...
HFF...
HFF...
GUGU
(STRAIN)
HOW'RE WE SUPPOSED TO SEE THAT ONE COMING ...!!?

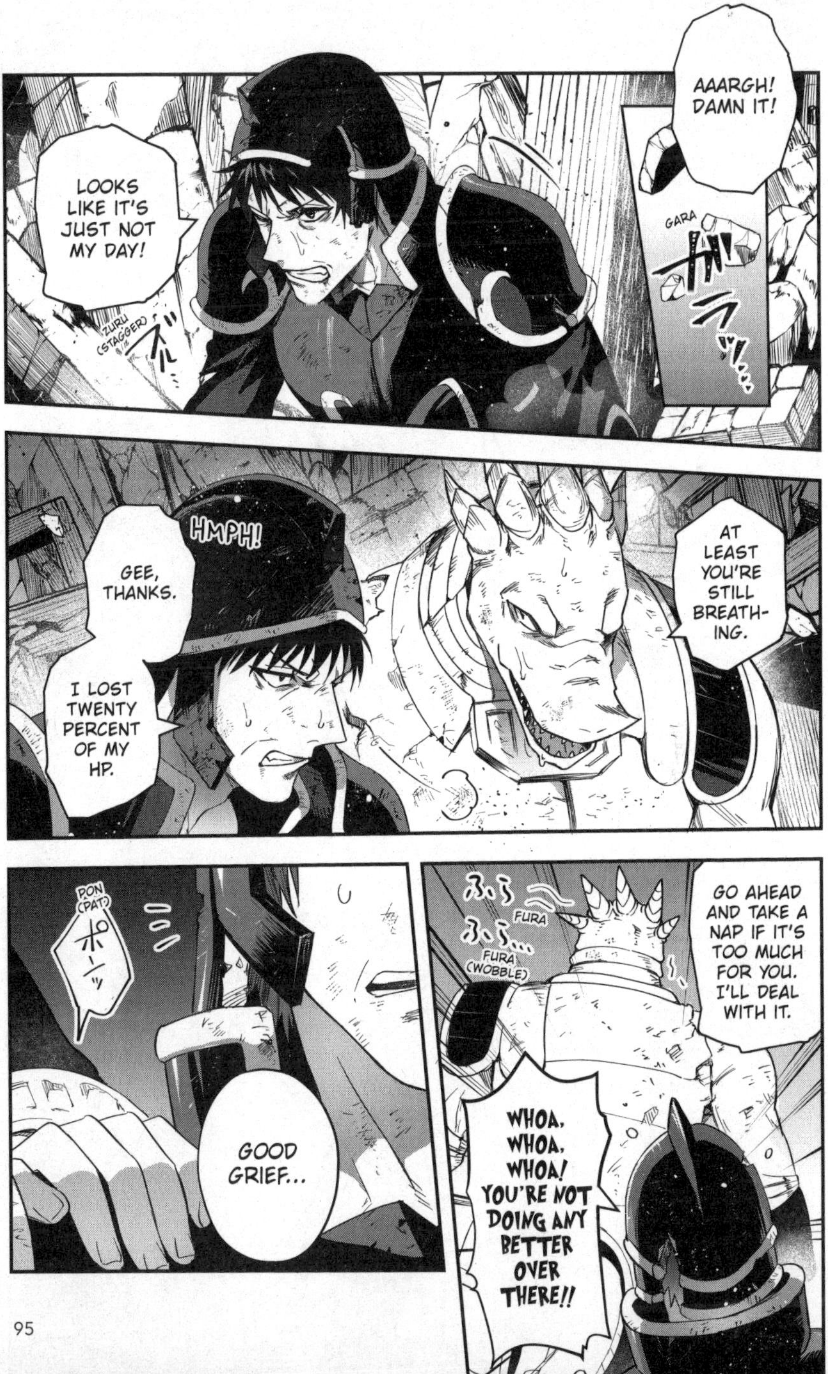
AAARGH! DAMN IT!
GARA
LOOKS LIKE IT'S JUST NOT MY DAY!
ZURU (STAGGER)
AT LEAST YOU'RE STILL BREATH-ING.
HMPH!
GEE, THANKS.
I LOST TWENTY PERCENT OF MY HP.
GO AHEAD AND TAKE A NAP IF IT'S TOO MUCH FOR YOU. I'LL DEAL WITH IT.
FURA
FURA (WOBBLE)
WHOA, WHOA, WHOA! YOU'RE NOT DOING ANY BETTER OVER THERE!!
PON (PAT)
GOOD GRIEF...

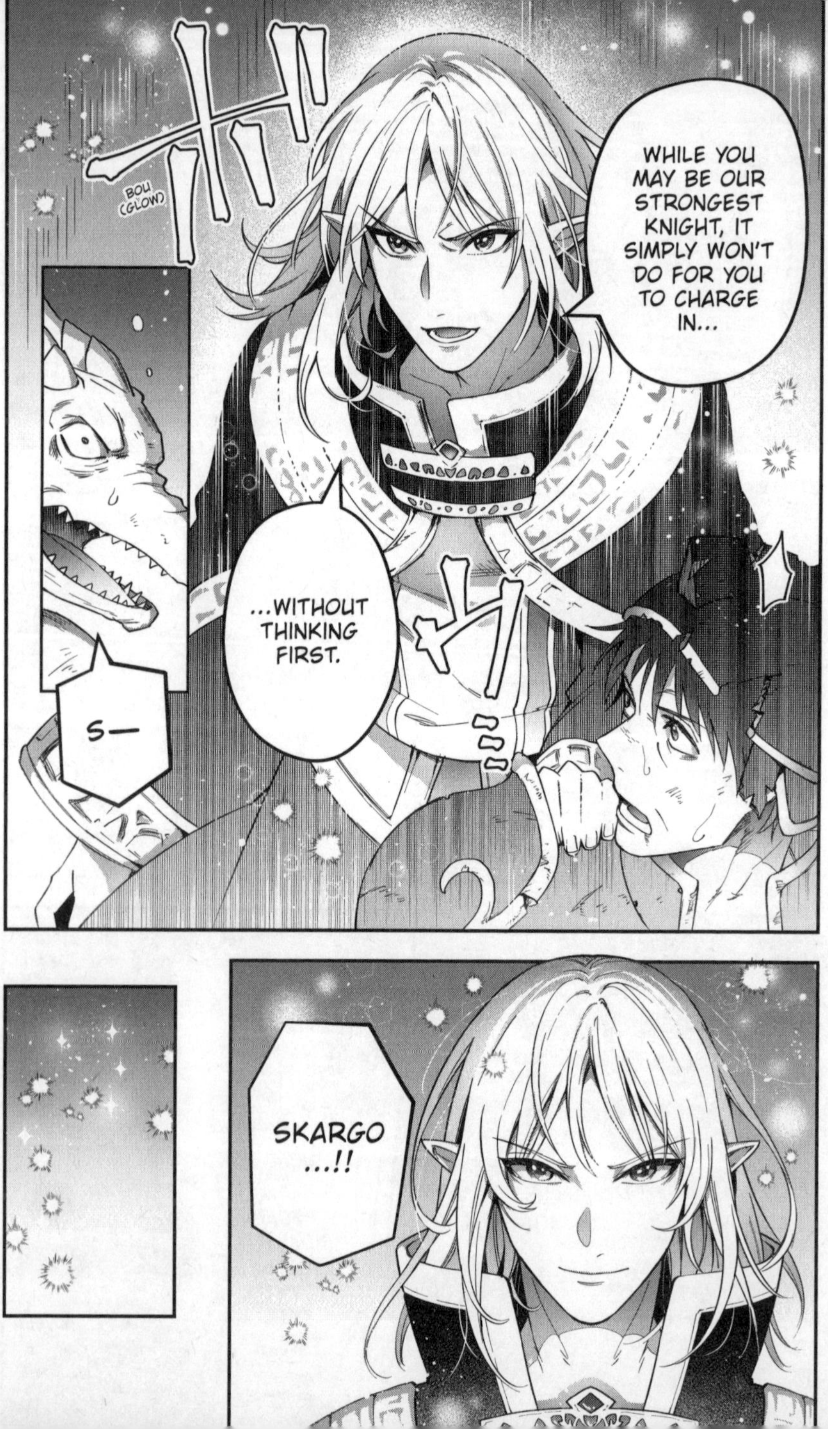
WHILE YOU MAY BE OUR STRONGEST KNIGHT, IT SIMPLY WON'T DO FOR YOU TO CHARGE IN...
BOU (GLOW)
...WITHOUT THINKING FIRST.
S—
SKARGO ...!!

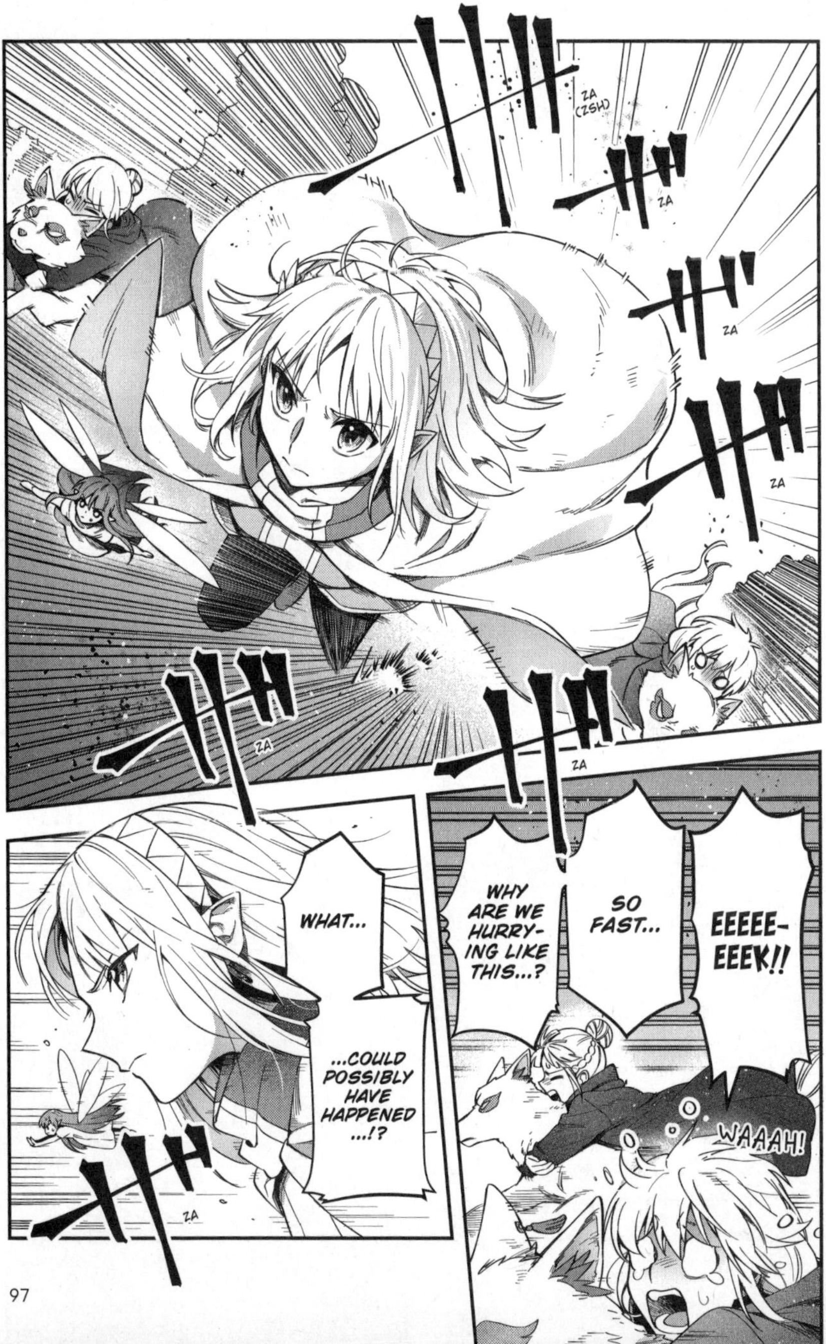
ZA (ZSH)
ZA
ZA
ZA
ZA
ZA
EEEEE-EEEK!!
SO FAST...
WHY ARE WE HURRYING LIKE THIS...?
WAAAH!
WHAT...
...COULD POSSIBLY HAVE HAPPENED ...!?
ZA

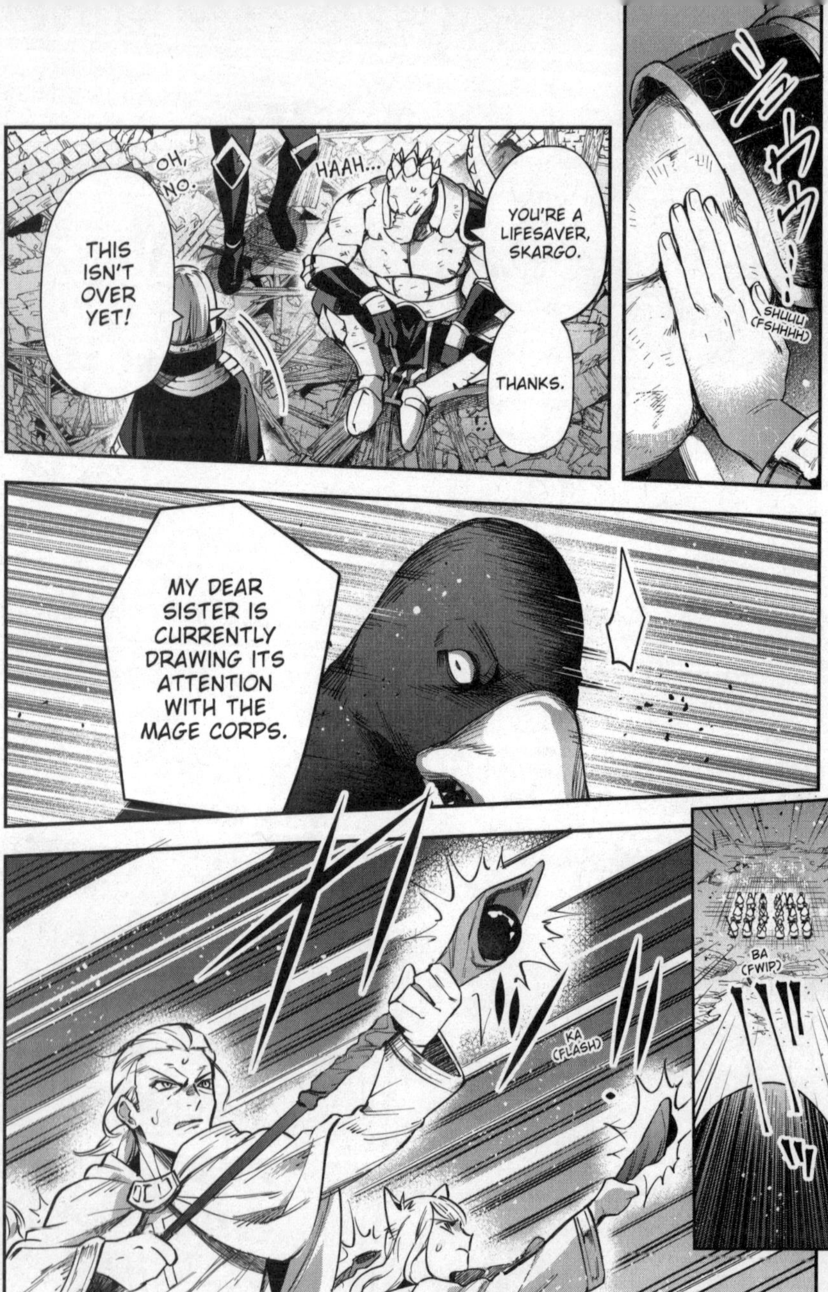
SHUUU
(FSHHHH)
HAAH...
YOU'RE A LIFESAVER, SKARGO.
THANKS.
OH, NO.
THIS ISN'T OVER YET!
MY DEAR SISTER IS CURRENTLY DRAWING ITS ATTENTION WITH THE MAGE CORPS.
BA
(FWIP)
KA
(FLASH)

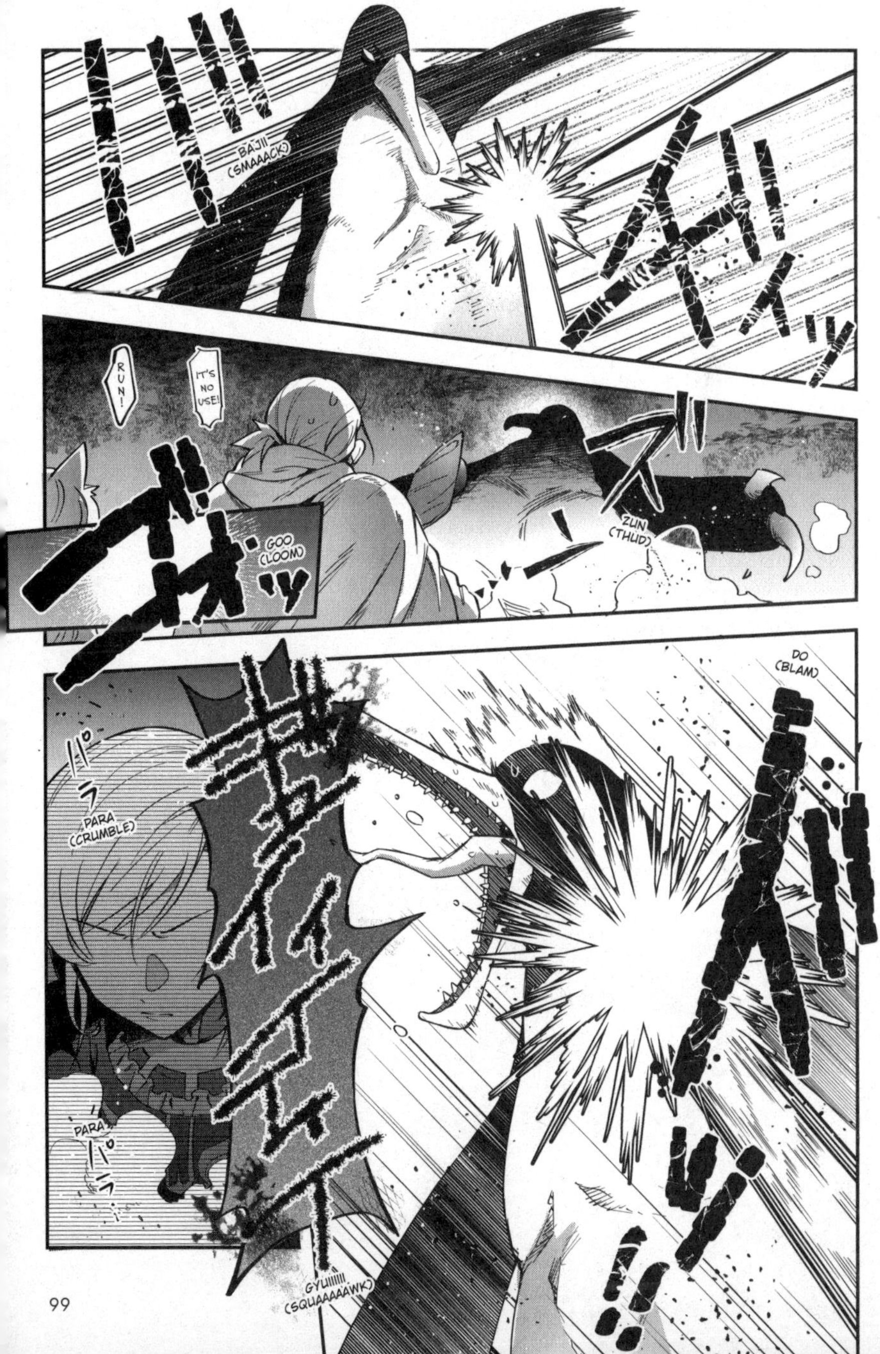
BAJII
(SMAAACK)
IT'S NO USE!
RUN!
ZUN
(THUD)
GOO
(LOOM)
DO
(BLAM)
PARA
(CRUMBLE)
PARA
GYUIIIIII
(SQUAAAAAWK)

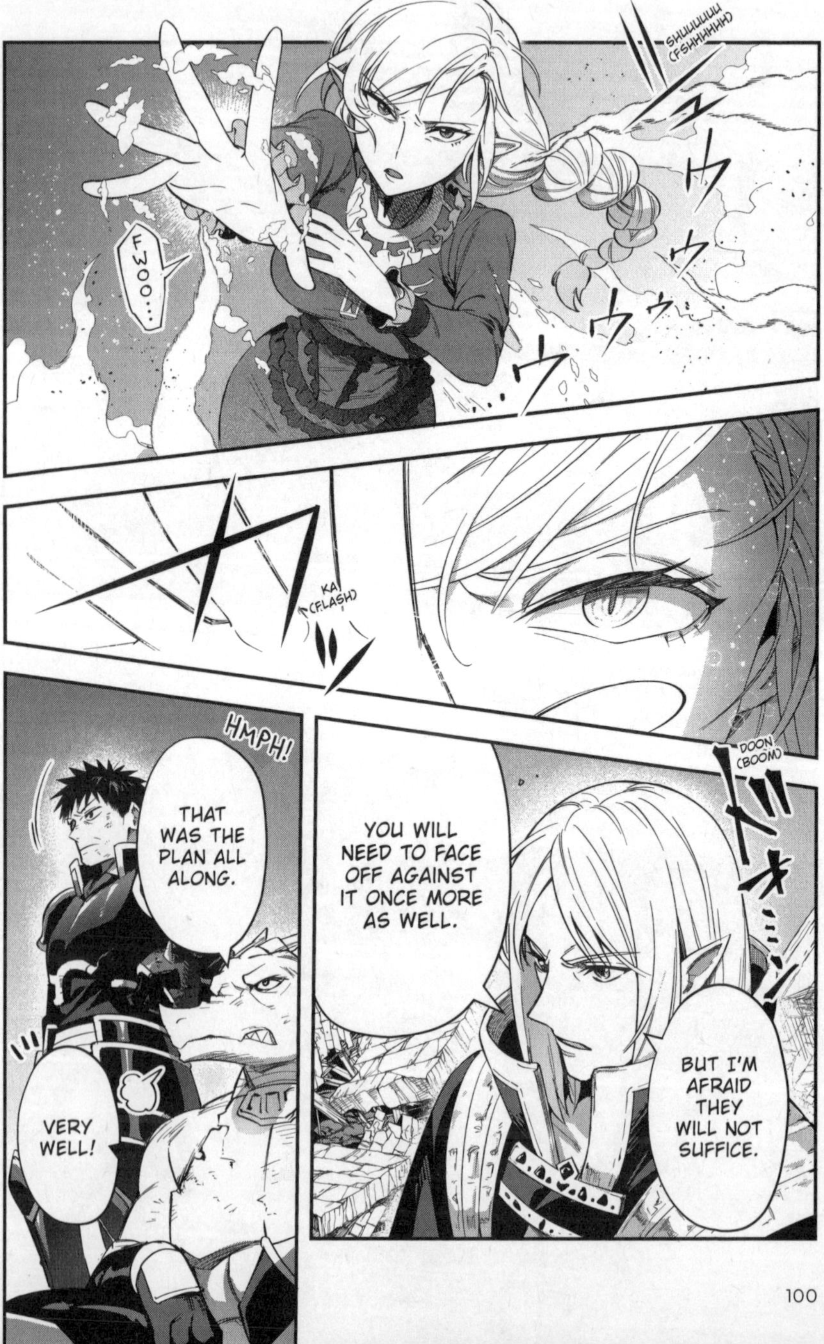
SHUUUUUU (FSHHHHHH)
FWOO...
KA (FLASH)
DOON (BOOM)
BUT I'M AFRAID THEY WILL NOT SUFFICE.
YOU WILL NEED TO FACE OFF AGAINST IT ONCE MORE AS WELL.
HMPH!
THAT WAS THE PLAN ALL ALONG.
VERY WELL!

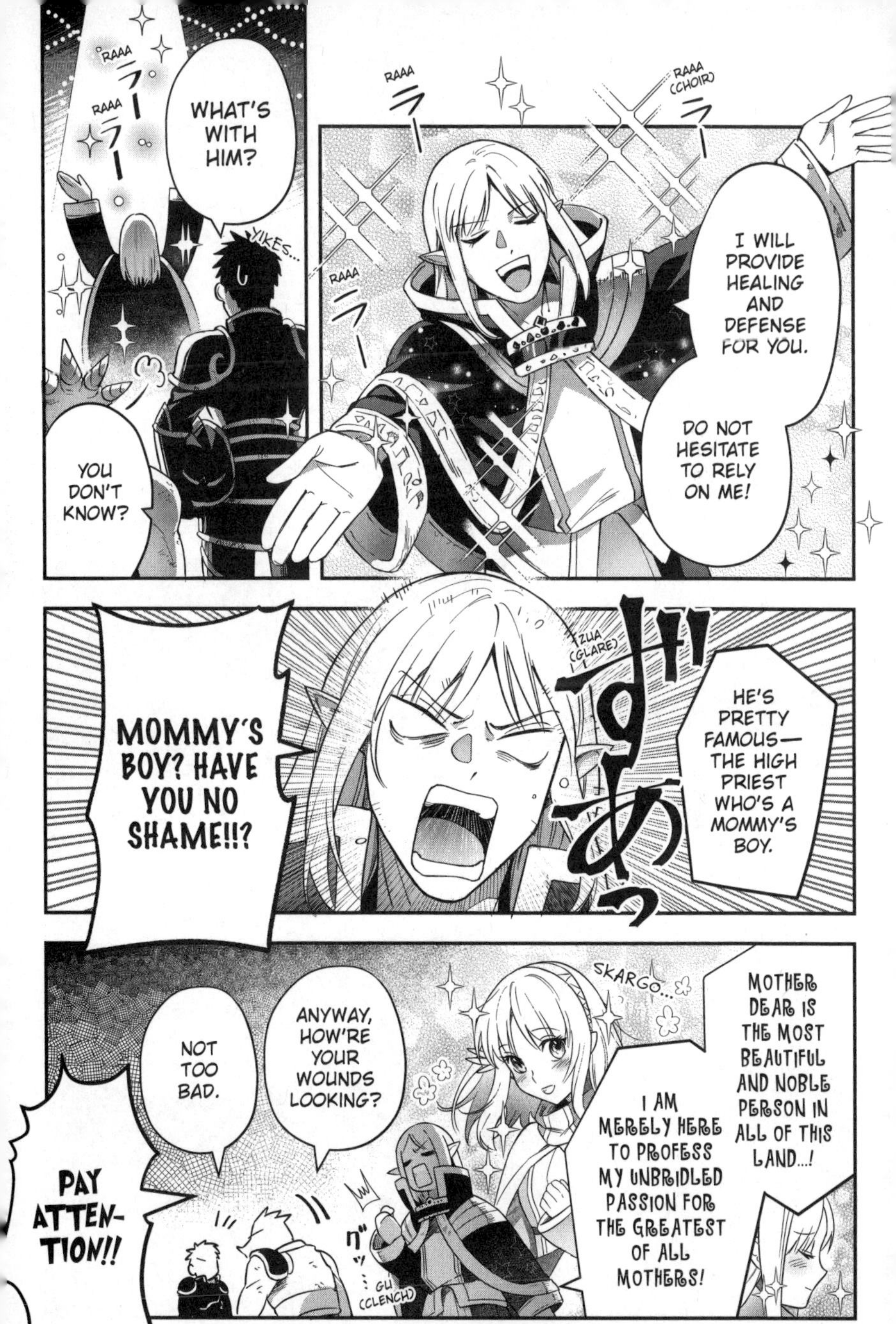
RAAA (CHOIR)
RAAA
RAAA
I WILL PROVIDE HEALING AND DEFENSE FOR YOU.
DO NOT HESITATE TO RELY ON ME!
RAAA
RAAA
WHAT'S WITH HIM?
YIKES...
YOU DON'T KNOW?
HE'S PRETTY FAMOUS—THE HIGH PRIEST WHO'S A MOMMY'S BOY.
ZUA (GLARE)
MOMMY'S BOY? HAVE YOU NO SHAME!!?
MOTHER DEAR IS THE MOST BEAUTIFUL AND NOBLE PERSON IN ALL OF THIS LAND...!
SKARGO...
I AM MERELY HERE TO PROFESS MY UNBRIDLED PASSION FOR THE GREATEST OF ALL MOTHERS!
GU (CLENCH)
ANYWAY, HOW'RE YOUR WOUNDS LOOKING?
NOT TOO BAD.
PAY ATTEN-TION!!
*HIS IMAGINATION

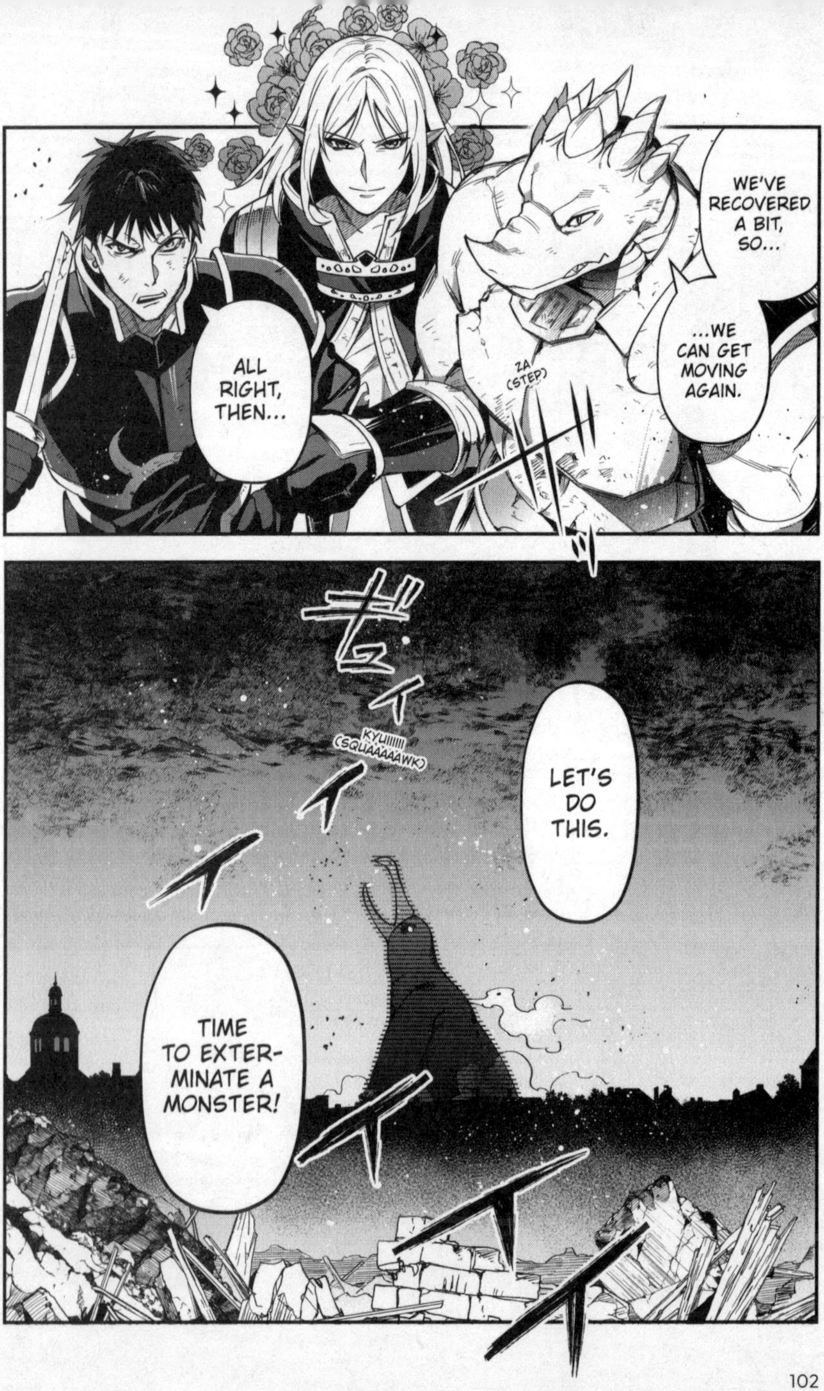
WE'VE RECOVERED A BIT, SO...
...WE CAN GET MOVING AGAIN.
ZA (STEP)
ALL RIGHT, THEN...
KYUIIIIII (SQUAAAAAWK)
LET'S DO THIS.
TIME TO EXTER-MINATE A MONSTER!

In the Land of Leadale

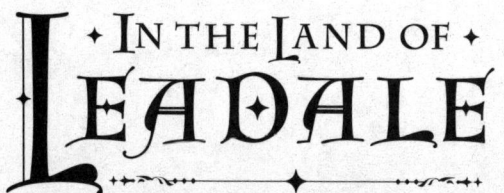

IN THE LAND OF
LEADALE

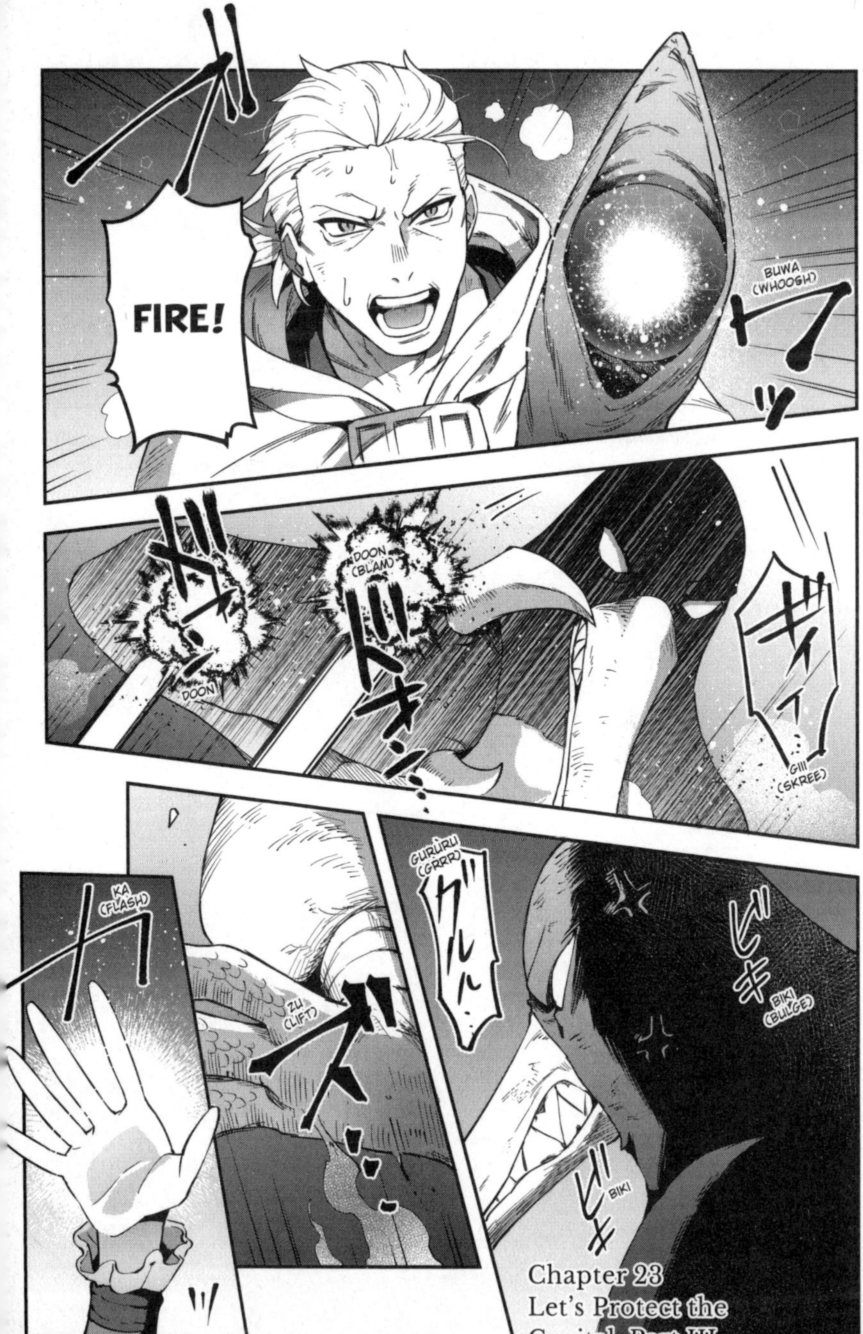
FIRE!
BUWA (WHOOGH)
GIII (SKREE)
DOON (BLAM)
DOON
GURURU (GRRR)
BIKI (BULGE)
BIKI
Chapter 23
Let's Protect the Capital, Part III
ZU (LIFT)
KA (FLASH)

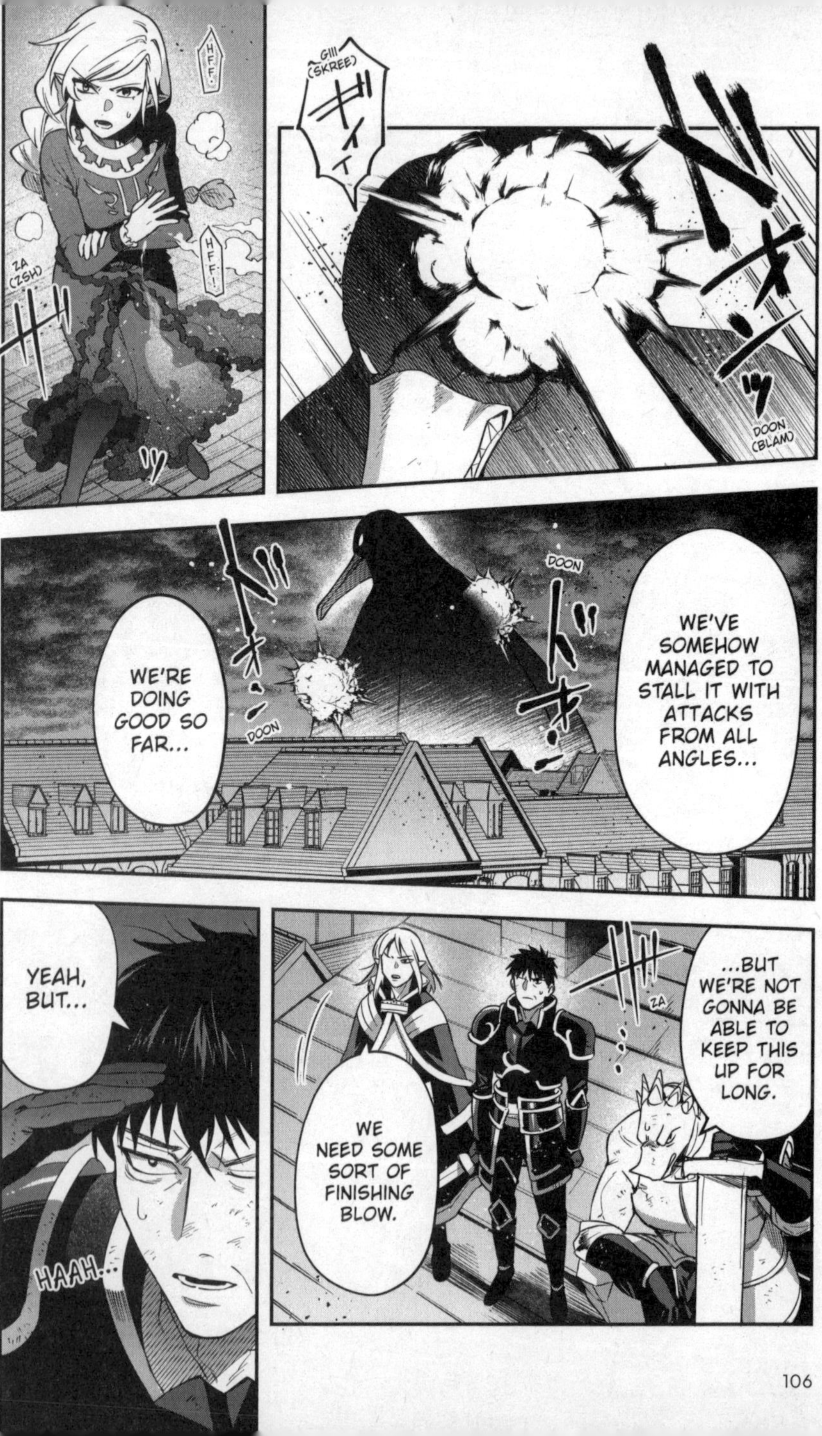
GIII (SKREE)
DOON (BLAM)
HFF.
HFF!
ZA (ZSH)
DOON
WE'VE SOMEHOW MANAGED TO STALL IT WITH ATTACKS FROM ALL ANGLES...
WE'RE DOING GOOD SO FAR...
DOON
...BUT WE'RE NOT GONNA BE ABLE TO KEEP THIS UP FOR LONG.
ZA
WE NEED SOME SORT OF FINISHING BLOW.
YEAH, BUT...
HAAH...

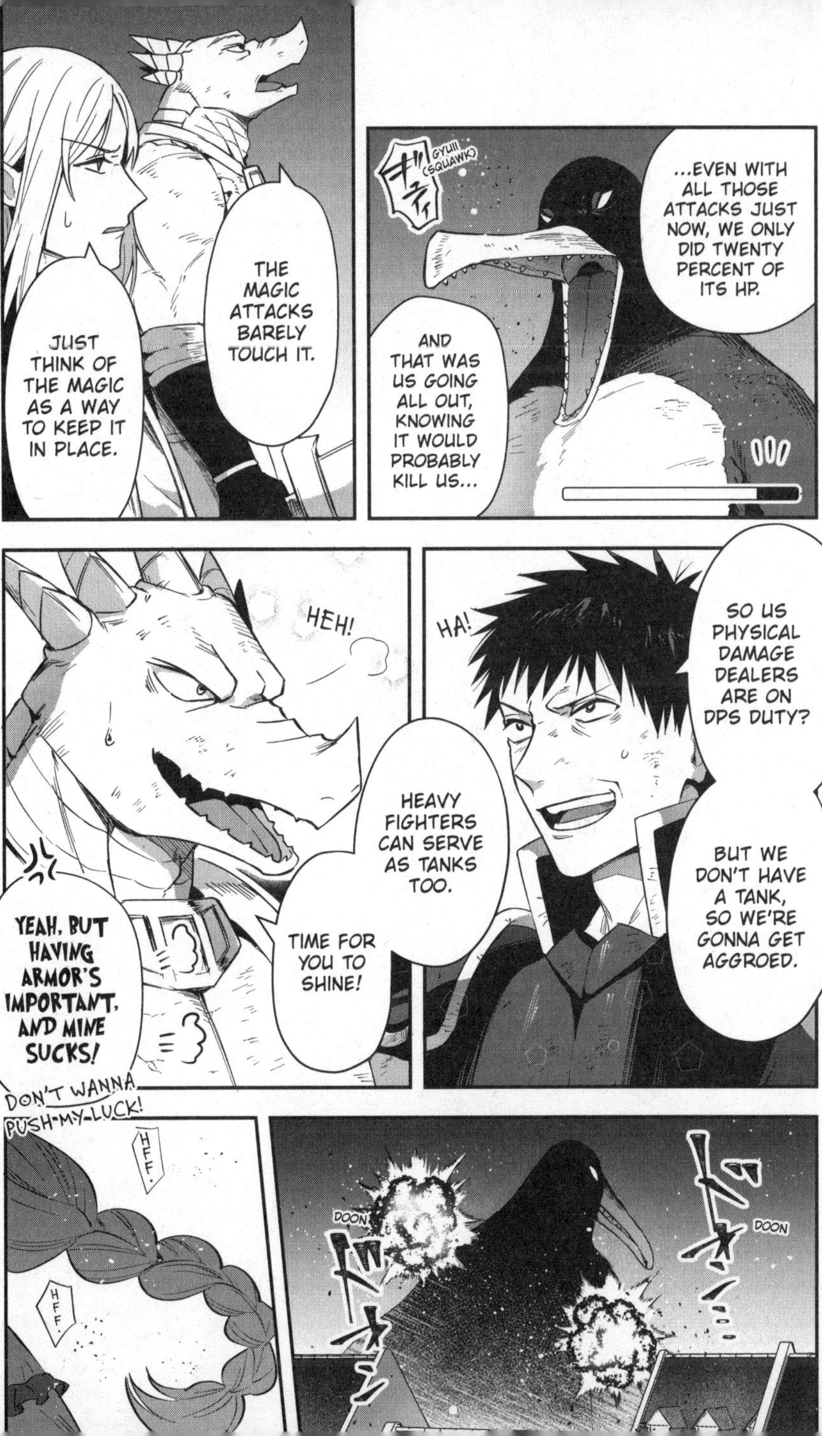
GYUII (SQUAWK)
...EVEN WITH ALL THOSE ATTACKS JUST NOW, WE ONLY DID TWENTY PERCENT OF ITS HP.
AND THAT WAS US GOING ALL OUT, KNOWING IT WOULD PROBABLY KILL US...
THE MAGIC ATTACKS BARELY TOUCH IT.
JUST THINK OF THE MAGIC AS A WAY TO KEEP IT IN PLACE.
SO US PHYSICAL DAMAGE DEALERS ARE ON DPS DUTY?
HA!
BUT WE DON'T HAVE A TANK, SO WE'RE GONNA GET AGGROED.
HEAVY FIGHTERS CAN SERVE AS TANKS TOO.
TIME FOR YOU TO SHINE!
HEH!
YEAH, BUT HAVING ARMOR'S IMPORTANT, AND MINE SUCKS!
DON'T WANNA PUSH MY LUCK!
DOON
DOON
HFF.
HFF.

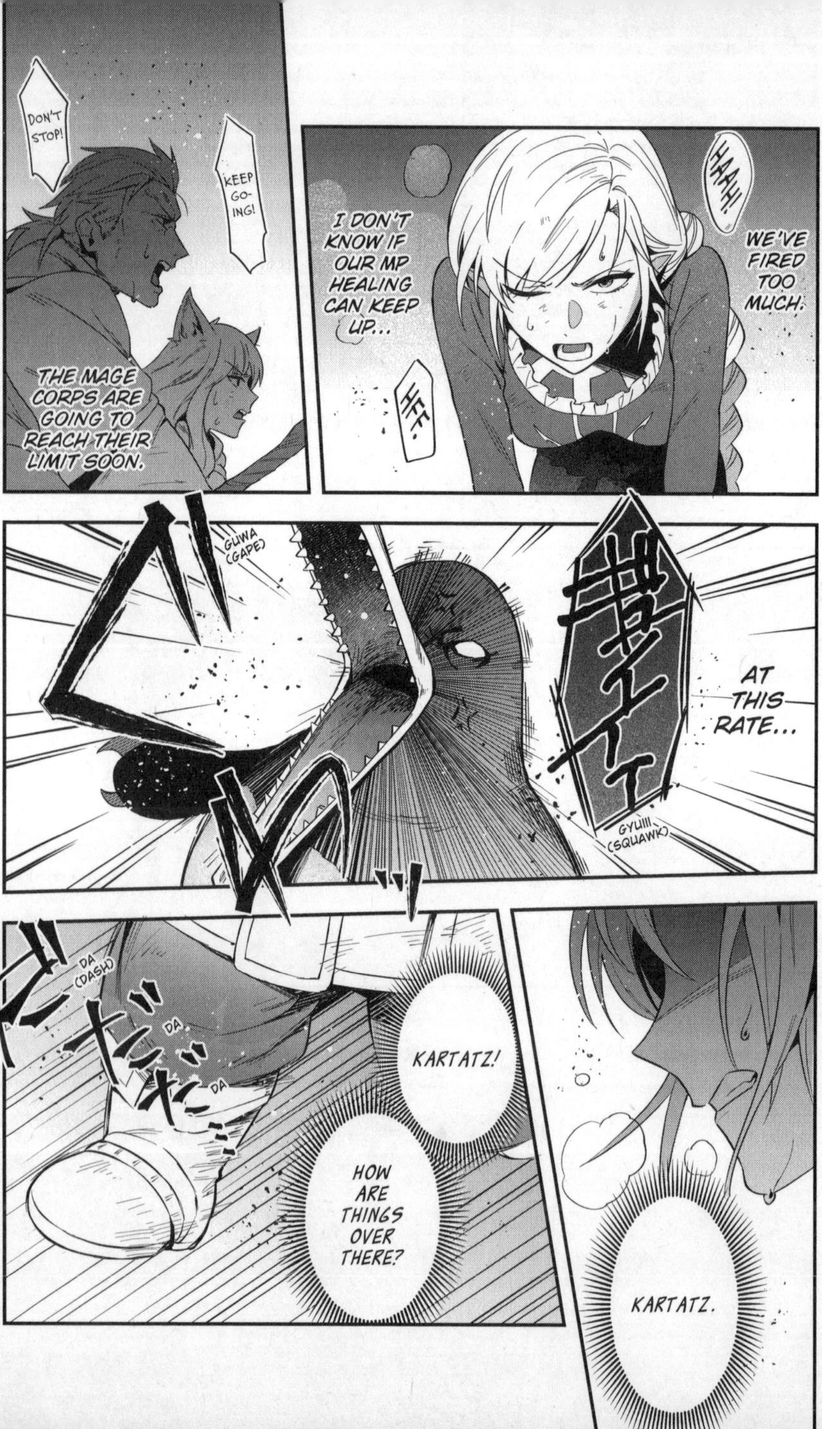
HAAH!
WE'VE FIRED TOO MUCH.
I DON'T KNOW IF OUR MP HEALING CAN KEEP UP...
HFF.
DON'T STOP!
KEEP GO-ING!
THE MAGE CORPS ARE GOING TO REACH THEIR LIMIT SOON.
AT THIS RATE...
GYUIII (SQUAWK)
GUWA (GAPE)
KARTATZ.
KARTATZ!
HOW ARE THINGS OVER THERE?
DA (DASH)
DA
DA

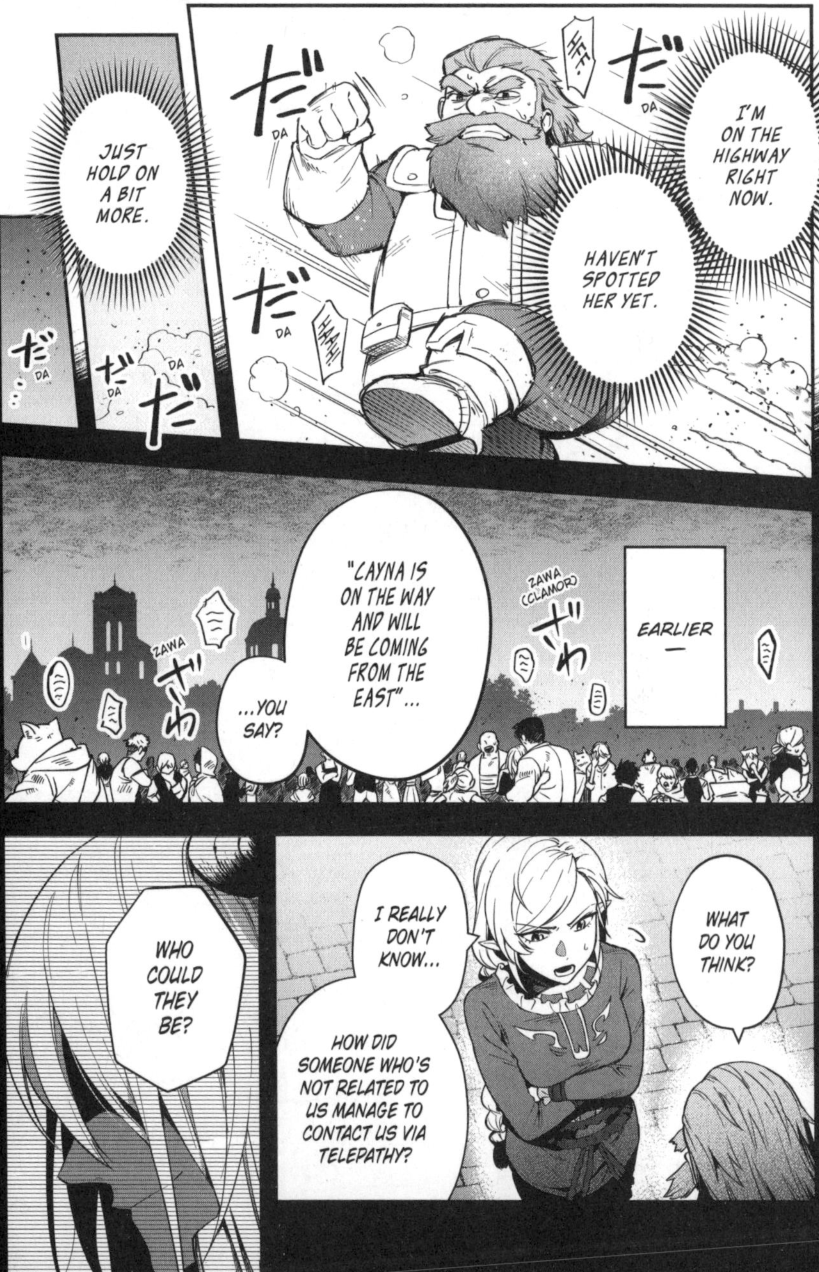

HFF.
だ
DA
I'M ON THE HIGHWAY RIGHT NOW.
HAVEN'T SPOTTED HER YET.
だ
DA
だ
DA
HAAH!
JUST HOLD ON A BIT MORE.
だ
DA
だ
DA
だ
DA
EARLIER—
ざわ
ZAWA (CLAMOR)
"CAYNA IS ON THE WAY AND WILL BE COMING FROM THE EAST"...
...YOU SAY?
ざわ
ZAWA
WHAT DO YOU THINK?
I REALLY DON'T KNOW...
HOW DID SOMEONE WHO'S NOT RELATED TO US MANAGE TO CONTACT US VIA TELEPATHY?
WHO COULD THEY BE?

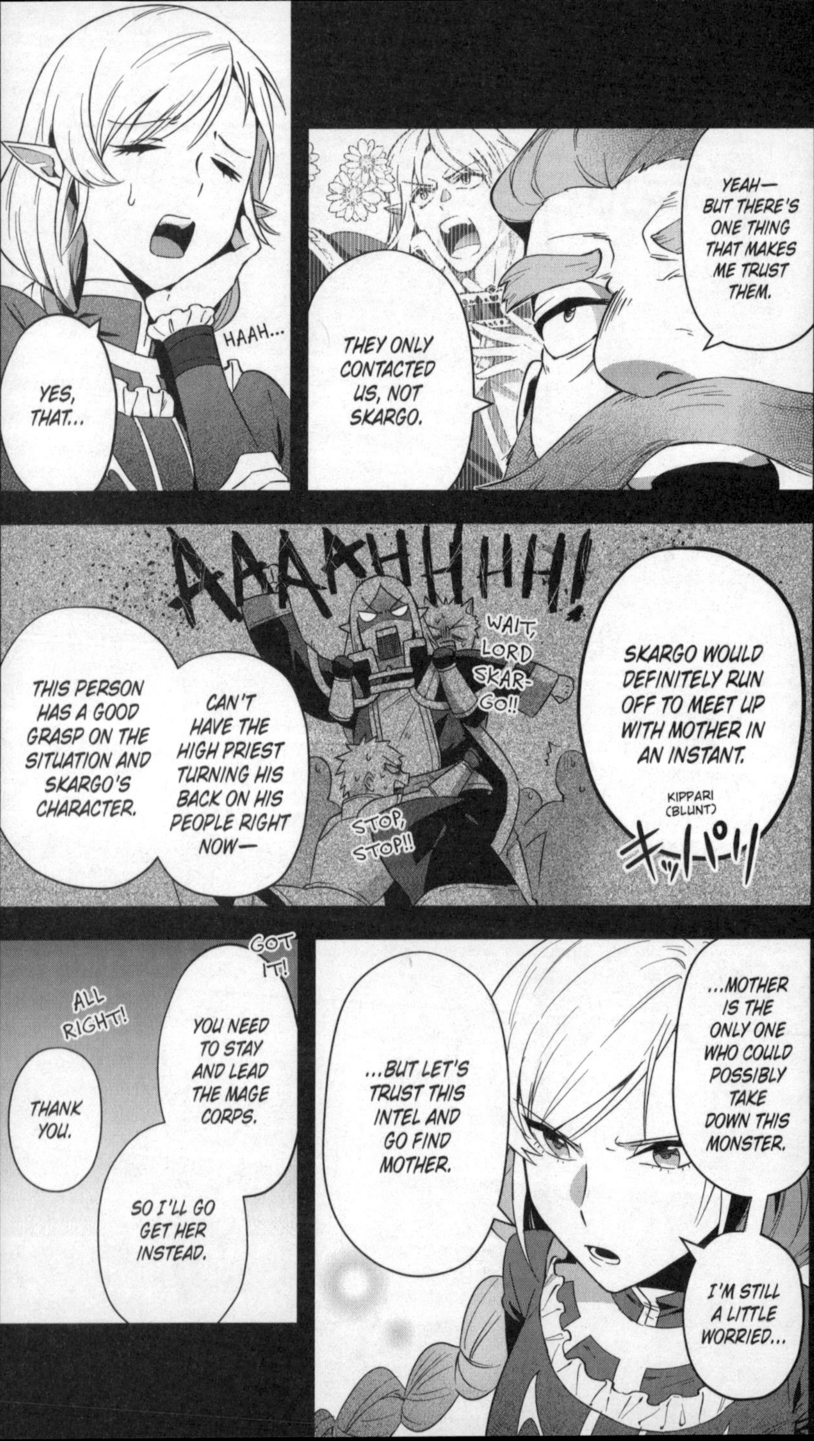
YEAH— BUT THERE'S ONE THING THAT MAKES ME TRUST THEM.
THEY ONLY CONTACTED US, NOT SKARGO.
HAAH...
YES, THAT...
SKARGO WOULD DEFINITELY RUN OFF TO MEET UP WITH MOTHER IN AN INSTANT.
KIPPARI (BLUNT)
キッパリ
AAAHHHHH!
WAIT, LORD SKAR-GO!!
STOP, STOP!!
CAN'T HAVE THE HIGH PRIEST TURNING HIS BACK ON HIS PEOPLE RIGHT NOW—
THIS PERSON HAS A GOOD GRASP ON THE SITUATION AND SKARGO'S CHARACTER.
...MOTHER IS THE ONLY ONE WHO COULD POSSIBLY TAKE DOWN THIS MONSTER.
I'M STILL A LITTLE WORRIED...
...BUT LET'S TRUST THIS INTEL AND GO FIND MOTHER.
GOT IT!
YOU NEED TO STAY AND LEAD THE MAGE CORPS.
SO I'LL GO GET HER INSTEAD.
ALL RIGHT!
THANK YOU.

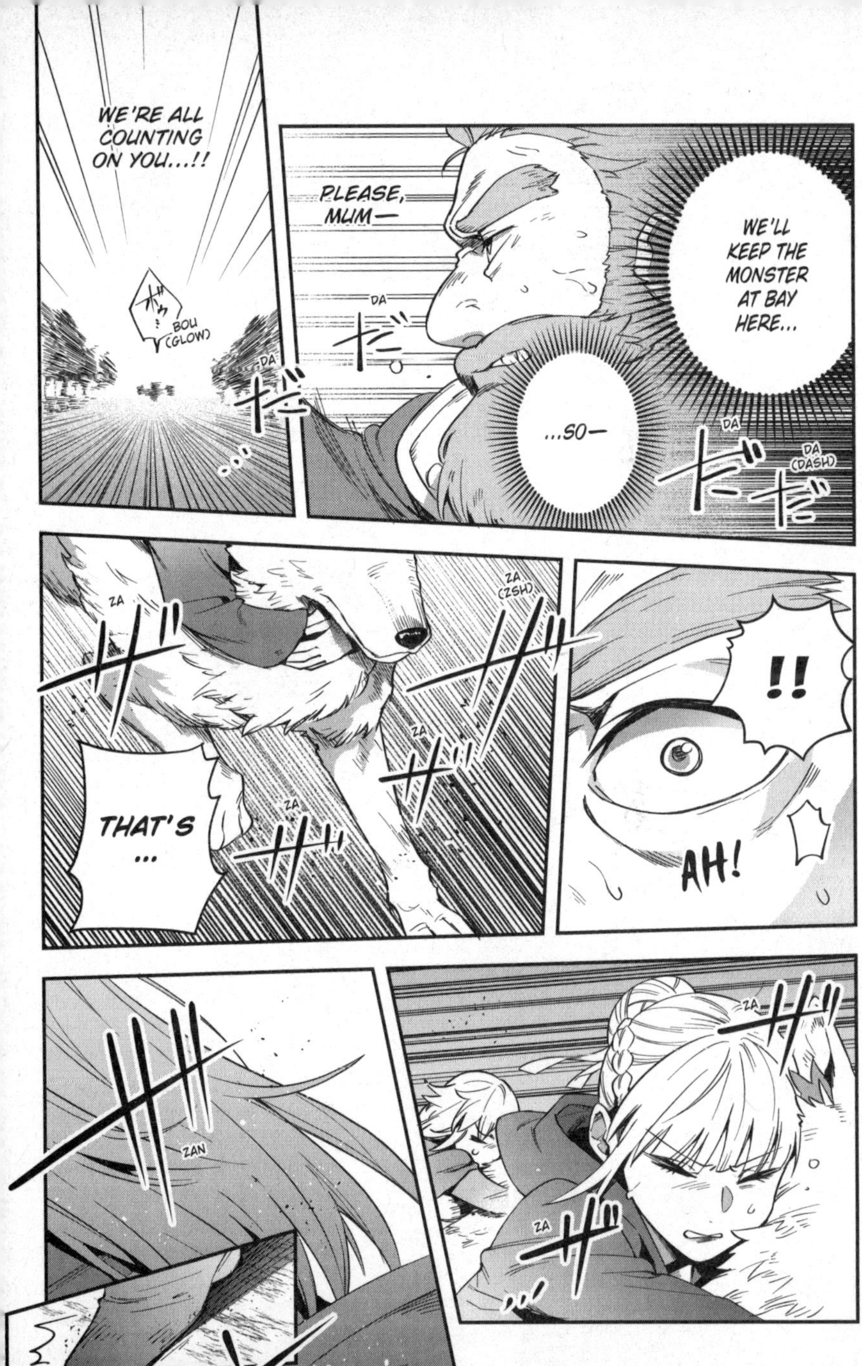
PLEASE, MUM—
WE'LL KEEP THE MONSTER AT BAY HERE...
DA
...SO—
DA
DA (DASH)
WE'RE ALL COUNTING ON YOU...!!
BOU (GLOW)
DA
!!
AH!
ZA (ZSH)
ZA
ZA
ZA
THAT'S ...
ZA
ZA
ZAN

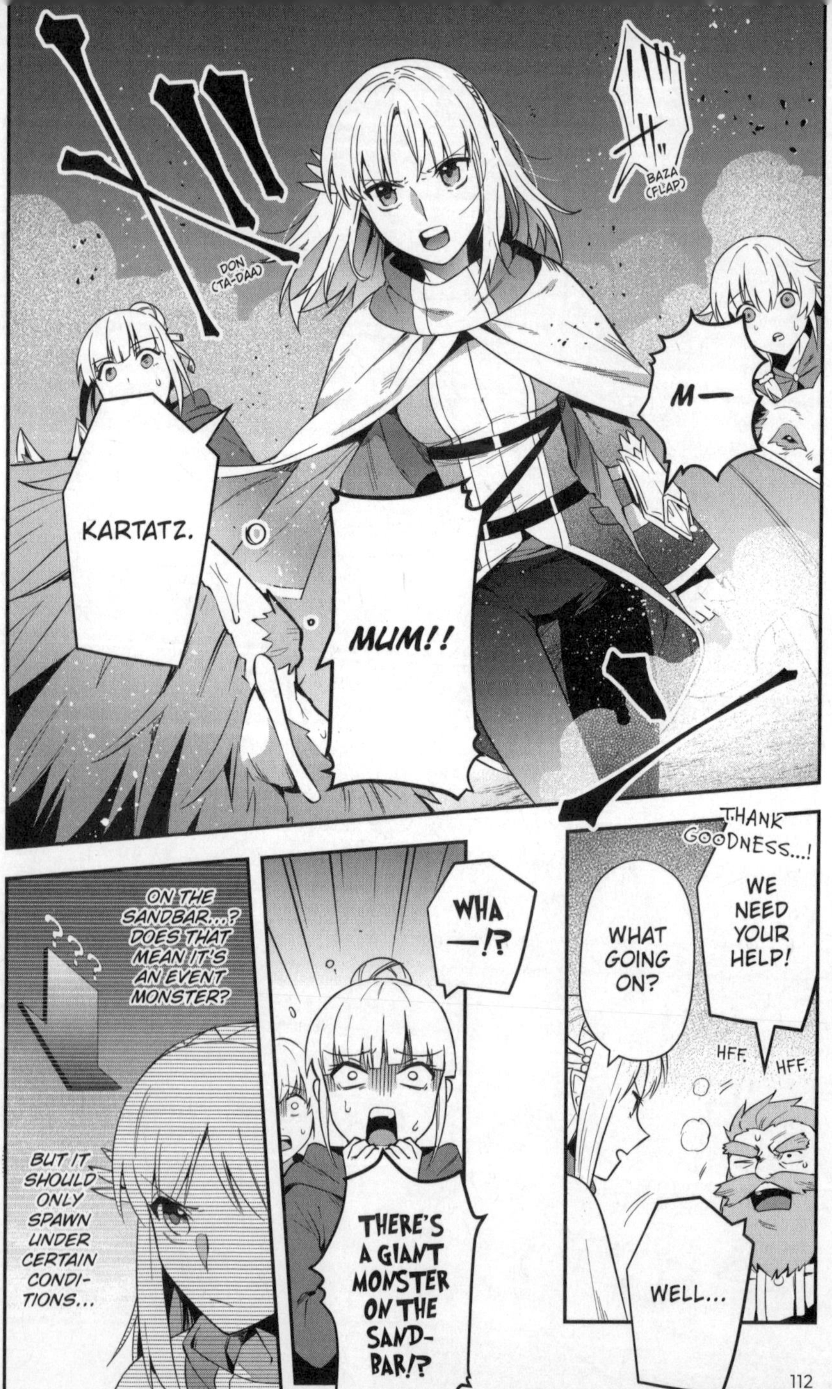
BAZA (FLAP)
DON (TA-DAA)
M—
MUM!!
KARTATZ.
THANK GOODNESS...!
WE NEED YOUR HELP!
WHAT GOING ON?
HFF. HFF.
WELL...
WHA—!?
THERE'S A GIANT MONSTER ON THE SANDBAR!?
ON THE SANDBAR...? DOES THAT MEAN IT'S AN EVENT MONSTER?
BUT IT SHOULD ONLY SPAWN UNDER CERTAIN CONDITIONS...

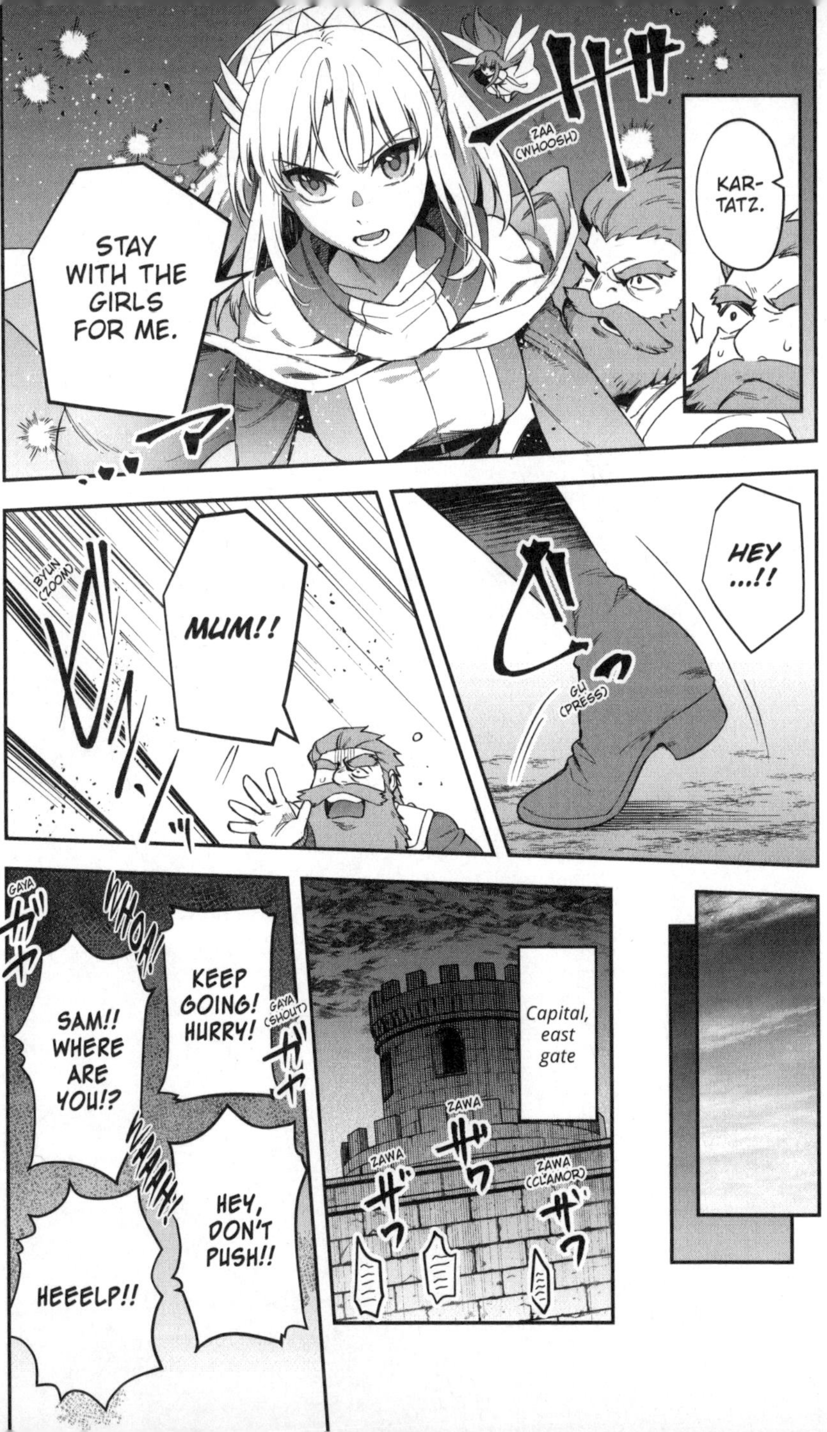
KAR-TATZ.
ZAA (WHOOSH)
STAY WITH THE GIRLS FOR ME.
HEY ...!!
GU (PRESS)
MUM!!
BYUN (ZOOM)
Capital, east gate
ZAWA (CLAMOR)
ZAWA
ZAWA
GAYA (SHOUT)
KEEP GOING! HURRY!
WHOA!
GAYA
SAM!! WHERE ARE YOU!?
WAAAH!
HEY, DON'T PUSH!!
HEEELP!!

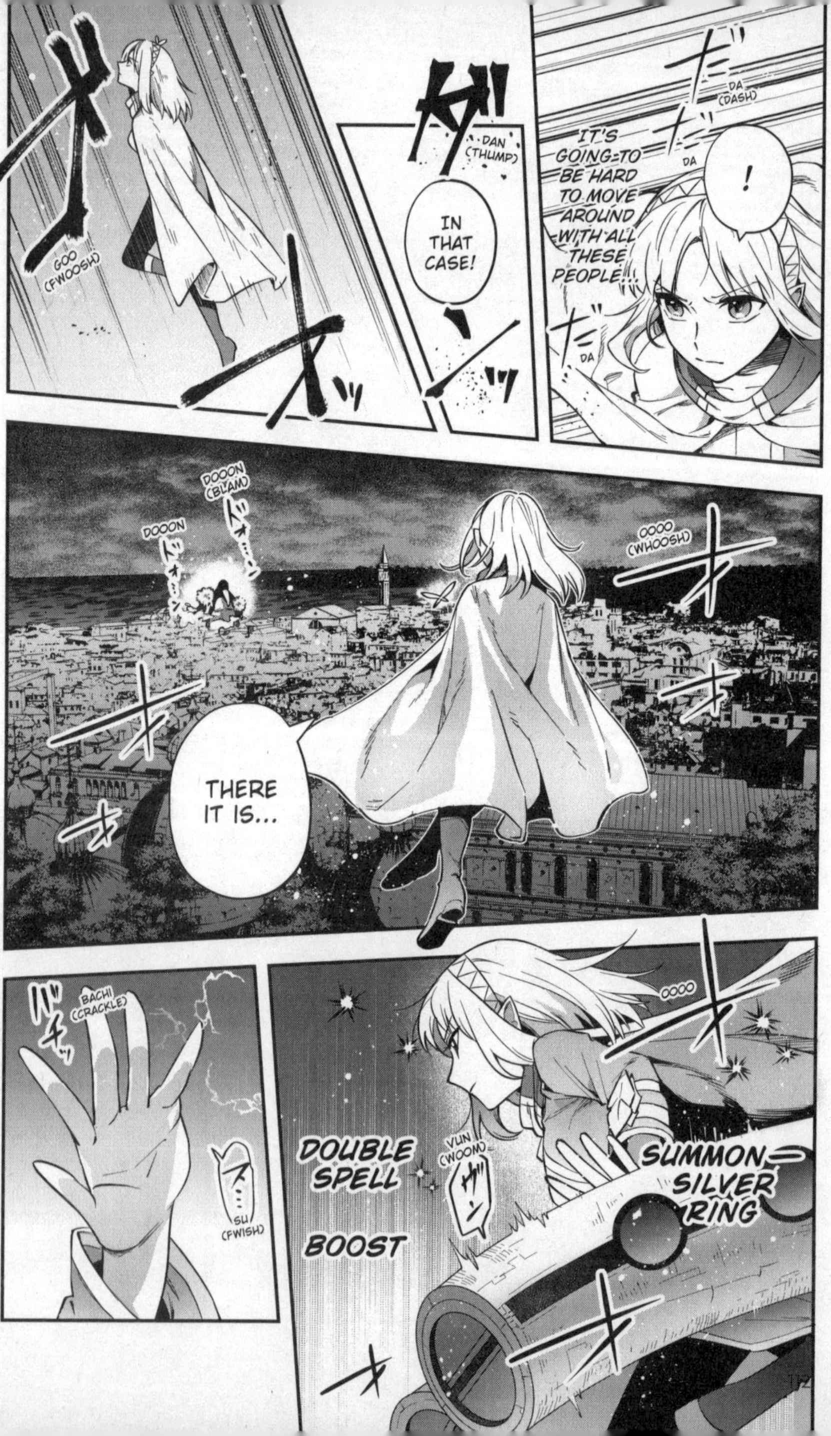
DA (DASH)
!
IT'S GOING TO BE HARD TO MOVE AROUND WITH ALL THESE PEOPLE...
DA
DA
DAN (THUMP)
IN THAT CASE!
GOO (FWOOSH)
OOOO (WHOOSH)
DOOON (BLAM)
DOOON
THERE IT IS...
OOOO
SUMMON SILVER RING
DOUBLE SPELL
VUN (WOOM)
BOOST
BACHI (CRACKLE)
SU (FWISH)

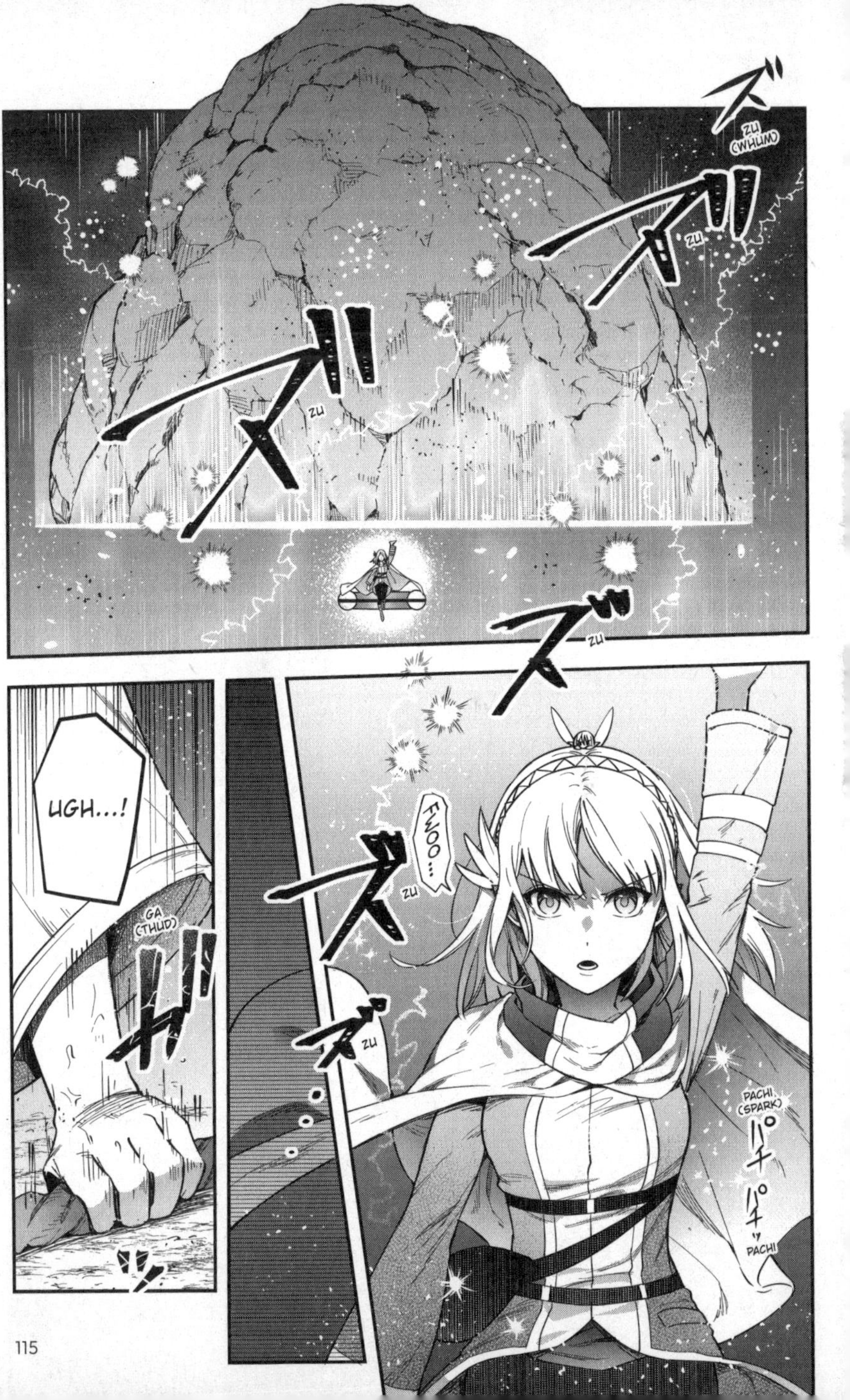
ZU
(WHUM)
ZU
ZU
ZU
FWOO...
ZU
ZU
PACHI
(SPARK)
PACHI
UGH...!
GA
(THUD)

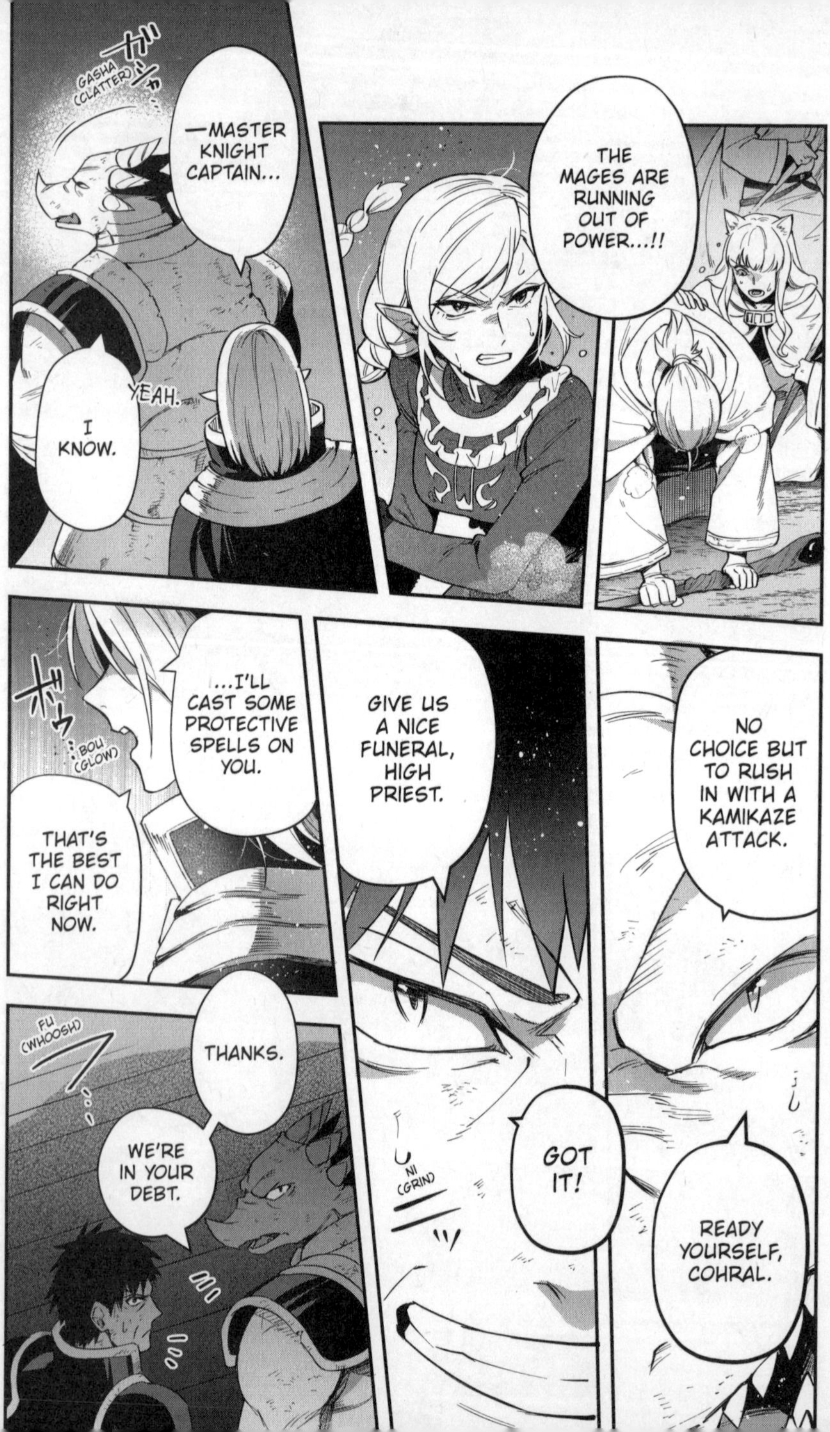
THE MAGES ARE RUNNING OUT OF POWER...!!
—MASTER KNIGHT CAPTAIN...
GASHA (CLATTER)
YEAH.
I KNOW.
NO CHOICE BUT TO RUSH IN WITH A KAMIKAZE ATTACK.
GIVE US A NICE FUNERAL, HIGH PRIEST.
...I'LL CAST SOME PROTECTIVE SPELLS ON YOU.
BOU (GLOW)
THAT'S THE BEST I CAN DO RIGHT NOW.
READY YOURSELF, COHRAL.
GOT IT!
NI (GRIN)
THANKS.
FU (WHOOSH)
WE'RE IN YOUR DEBT.

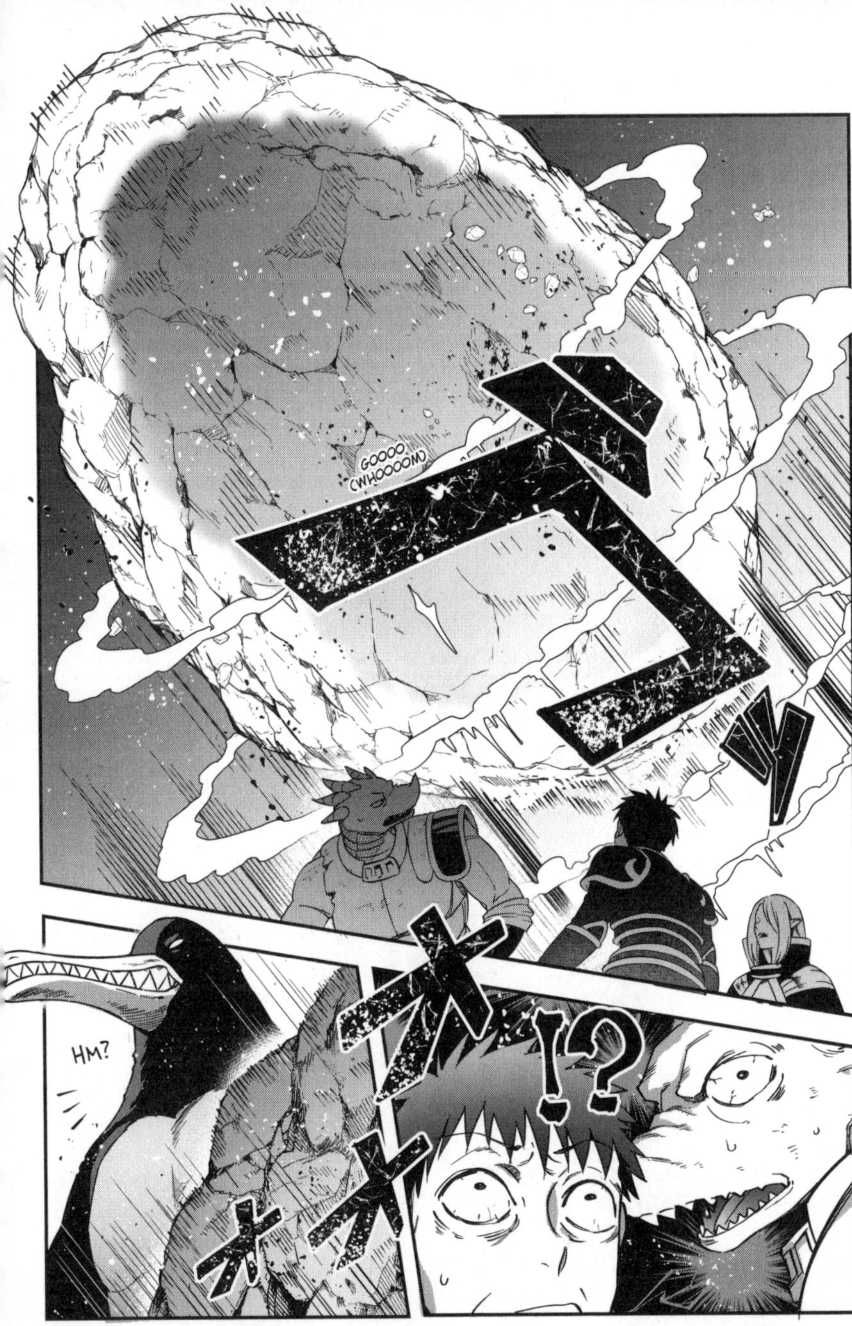

ゴッ
GOOOO
(WHOOOOM)
オオ!?
HM?

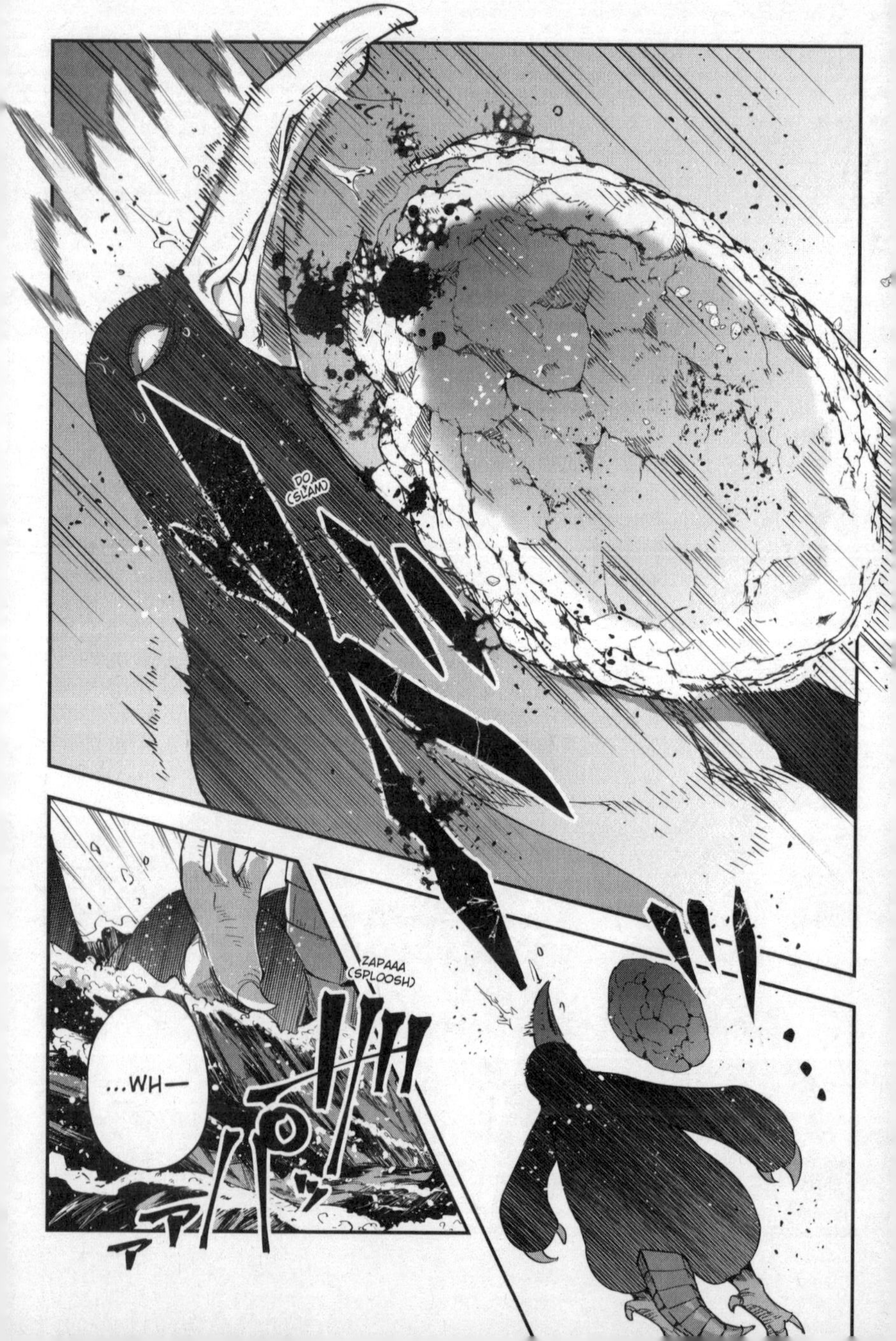
DO (SLAM)
ZAPAAA (SPLOOSH)
...WH—

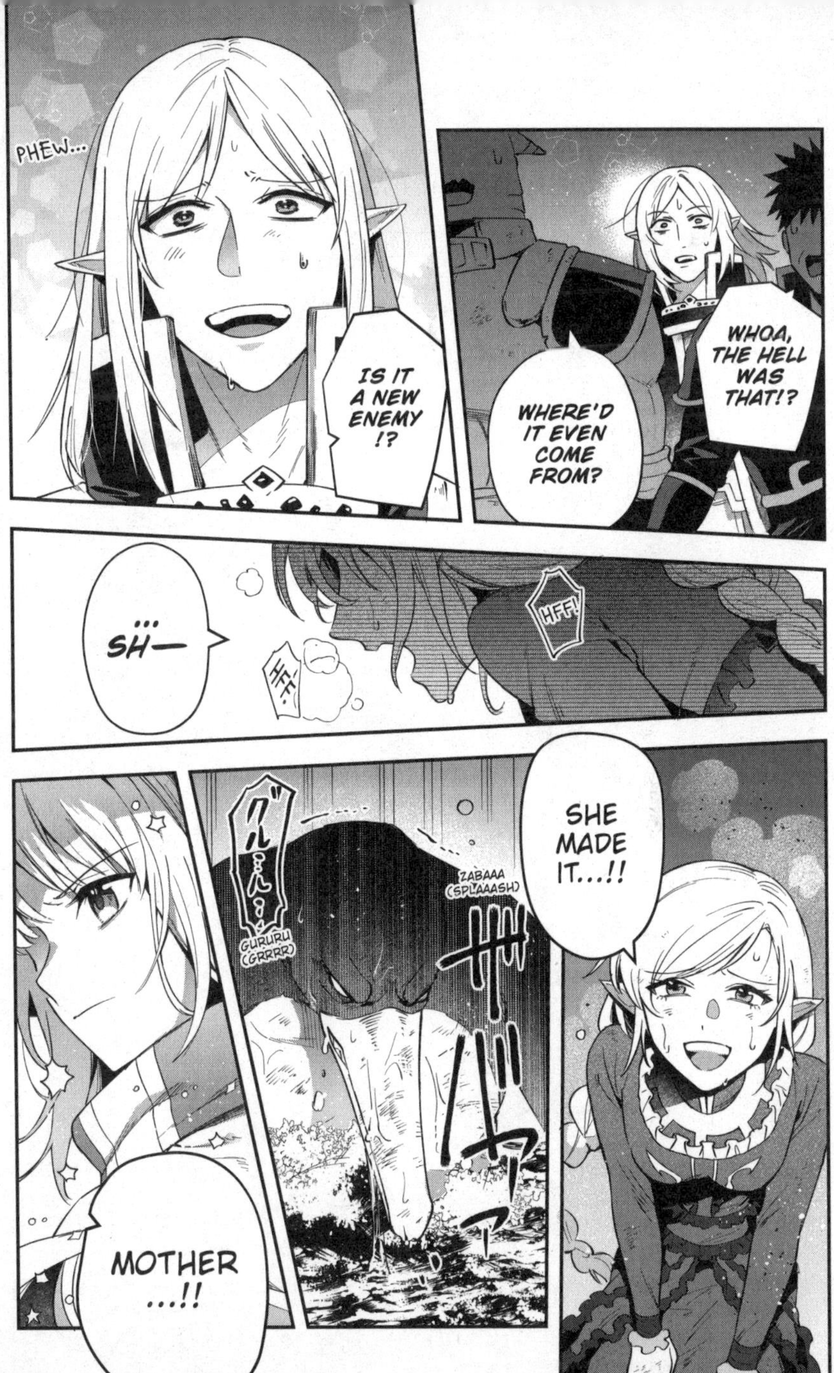
WHOA, THE HELL WAS THAT!?
WHERE'D IT EVEN COME FROM?
PHEW...
IS IT A NEW ENEMY !?
HFF!
HFF!
... SH—
SHE MADE IT...!!
ZABAAA (SPLAAASH)
GURURU (GRRRR)
MOTHER ...!!

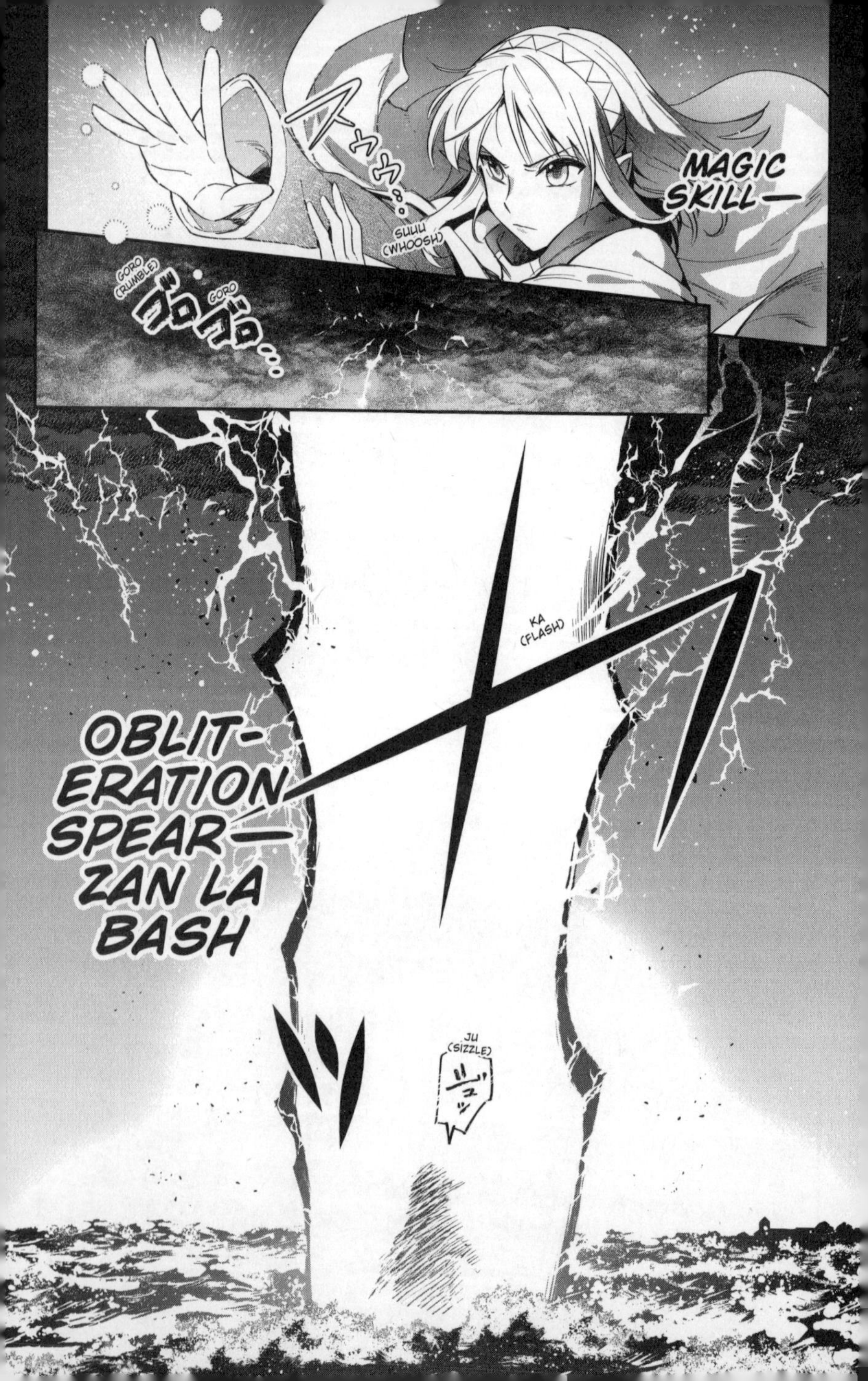
MAGIC SKILL—
SUUU (WHOOSH)
GORO (RUMBLE) GORO
KA (FLASH)
OBLIT-ERATION SPEAR—ZAN LA BASH
JU (SIZZLE)

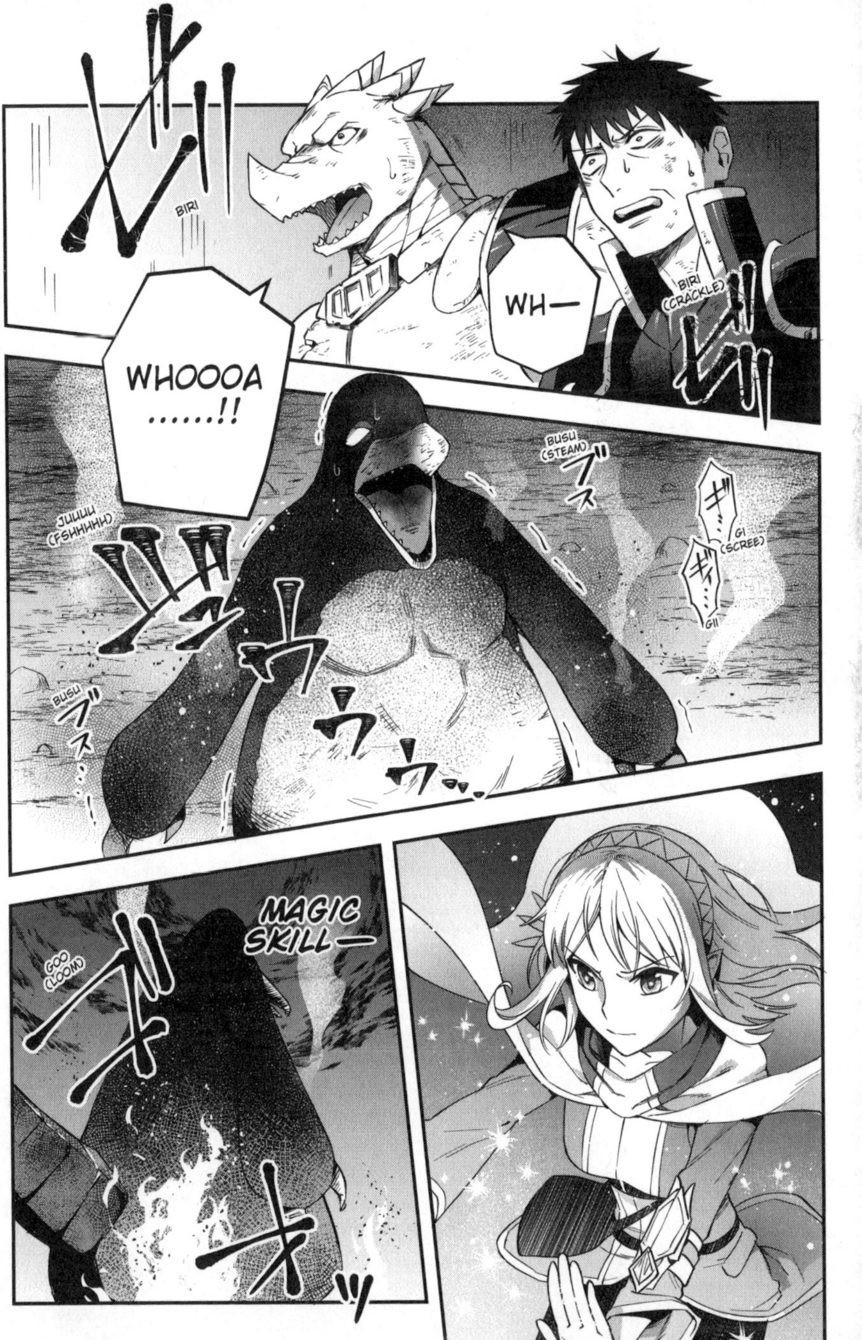
BIRI (CRACKLE)
WH—
BIRI
WHOOOA ......!!
BUSU (STEAM)
ブス
GI (SCREE)
ギ…
ギィ…
GII
JUUUU (FSHHHHH)
BUSU
ブス…
MAGIC SKILL—
GOO (LOOM)

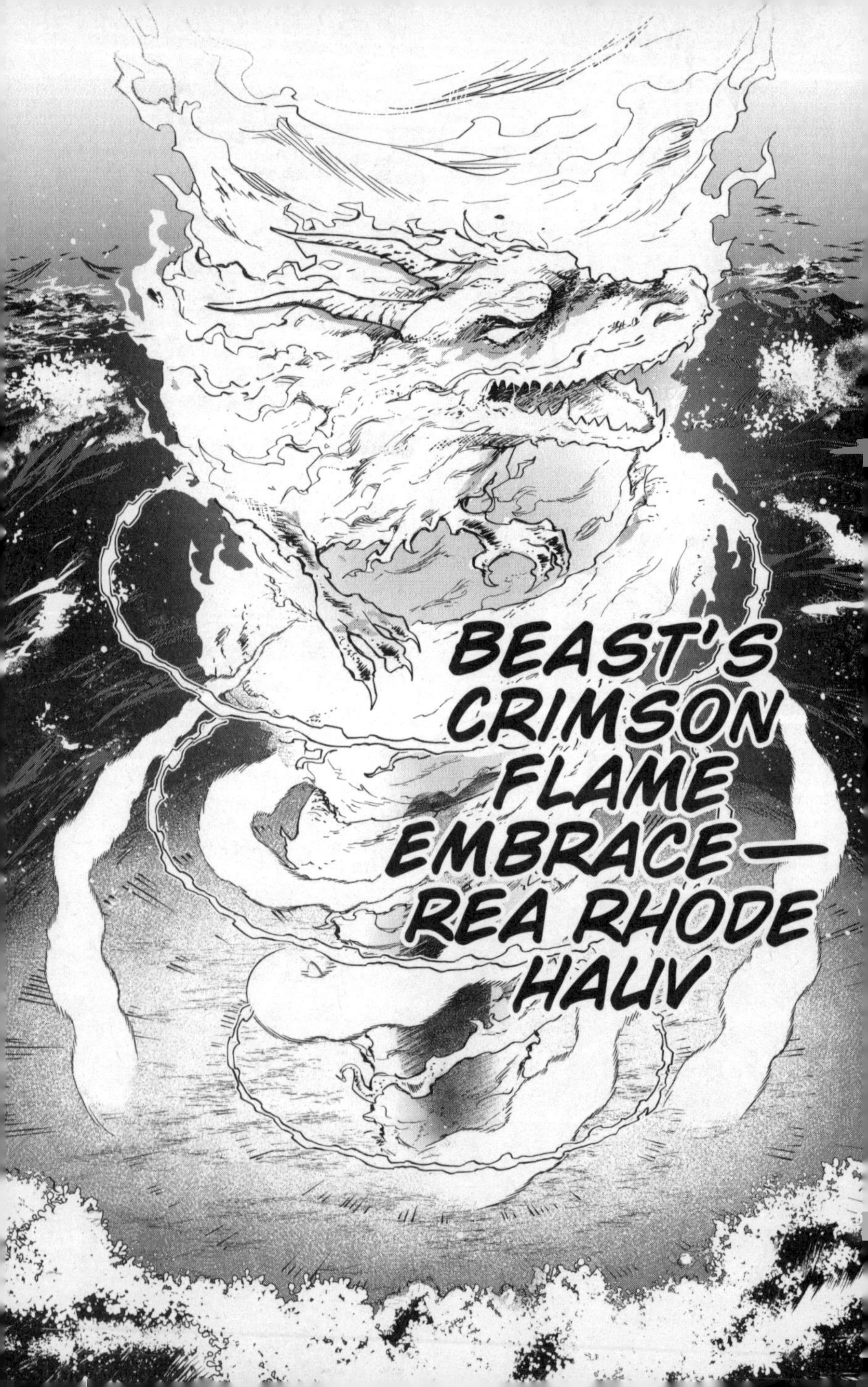
BEAST'S CRIMSON FLAME EMBRACE—REA RHODE HAUV

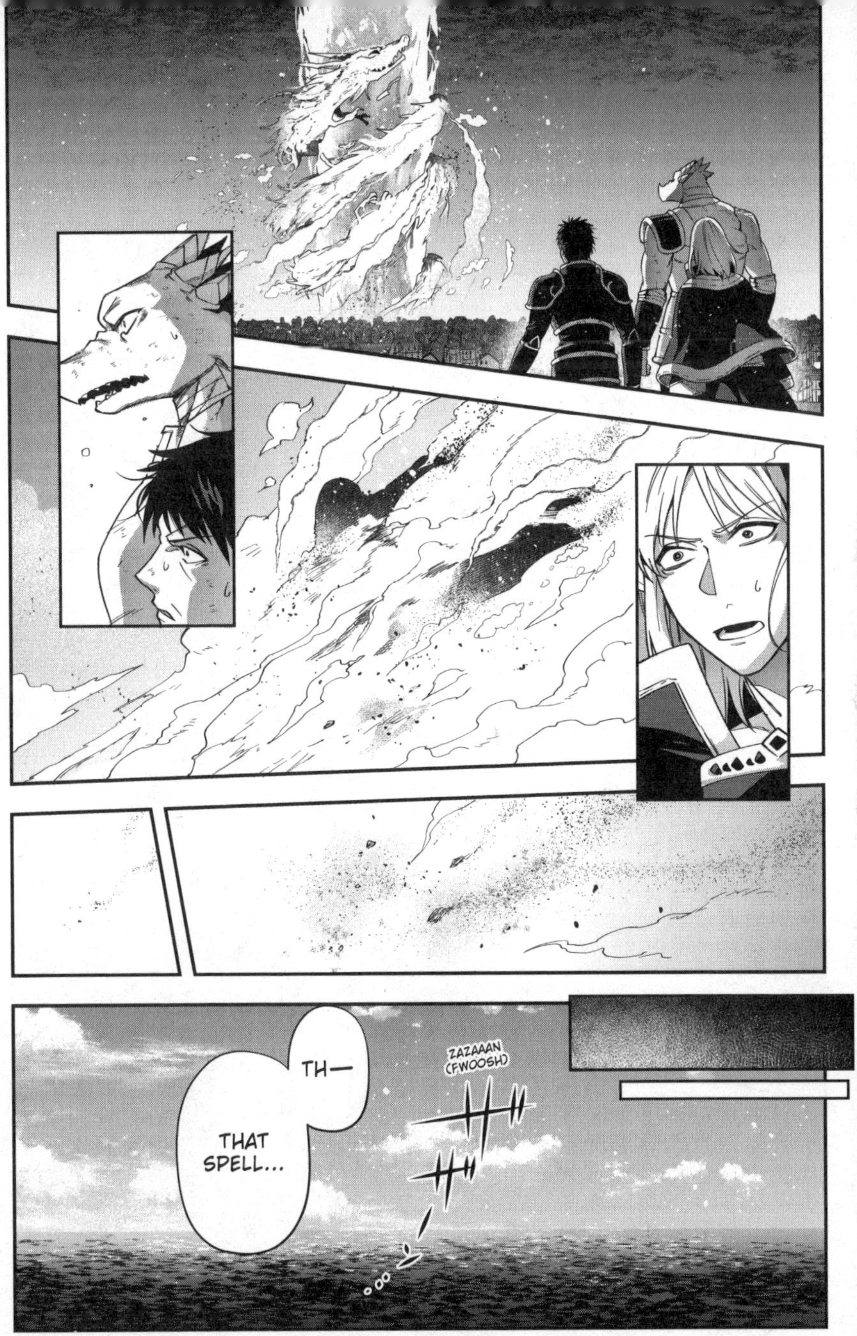
ZAZAAAN
(FWOOSH)
TH—
THAT SPELL...

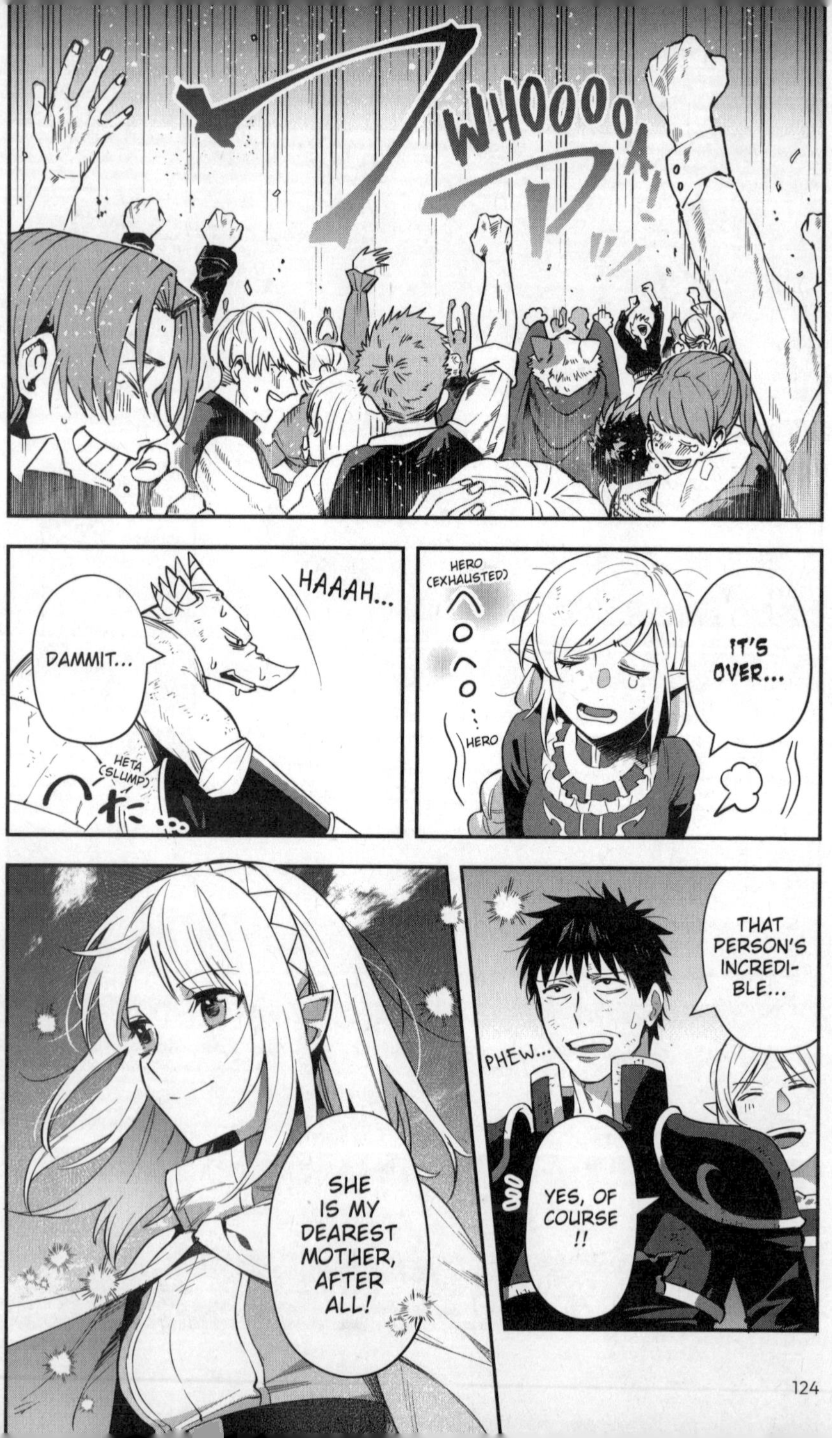
WHOOOOA!!
HERO (EXHAUSTED)
HERO
IT'S OVER...
HAAAH...
DAMMIT...
HETA (SLUMP)
THAT PERSON'S INCREDIBLE...
PHEW...
YES, OF COURSE !!
SHE IS MY DEAREST MOTHER, AFTER ALL!

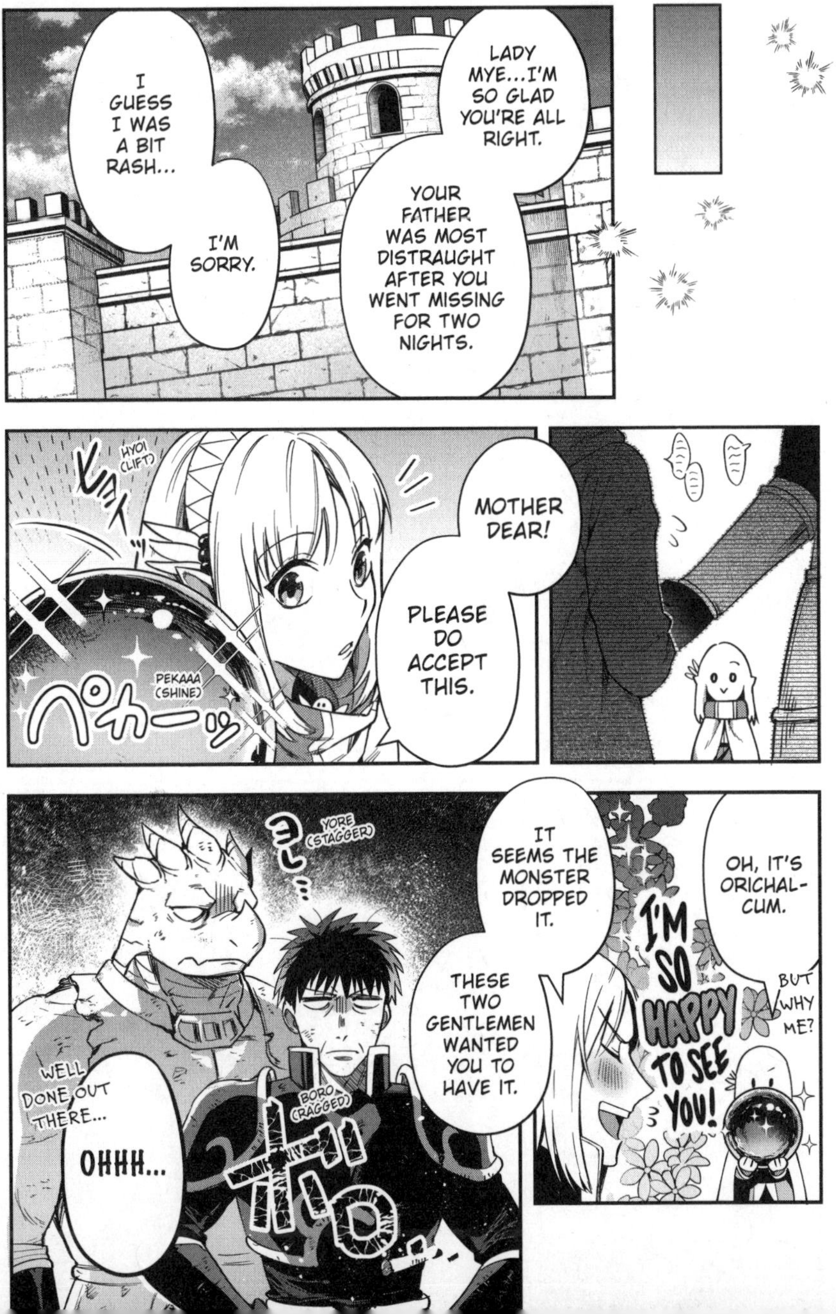
LADY MYE...I'M SO GLAD YOU'RE ALL RIGHT.
YOUR FATHER WAS MOST DISTRAUGHT AFTER YOU WENT MISSING FOR TWO NIGHTS.
I GUESS I WAS A BIT RASH...
I'M SORRY.
MOTHER DEAR!
PLEASE DO ACCEPT THIS.
HYOI (LIFT)
PEKAAA (SHINE)
OH, IT'S ORICHALCUM.
BUT WHY ME?
I'M SO HAPPY TO SEE YOU!
IT SEEMS THE MONSTER DROPPED IT.
THESE TWO GENTLEMEN WANTED YOU TO HAVE IT.
YORE (STAGGER)
BORO (RAGGED)
WELL DONE OUT THERE...
OHHH...

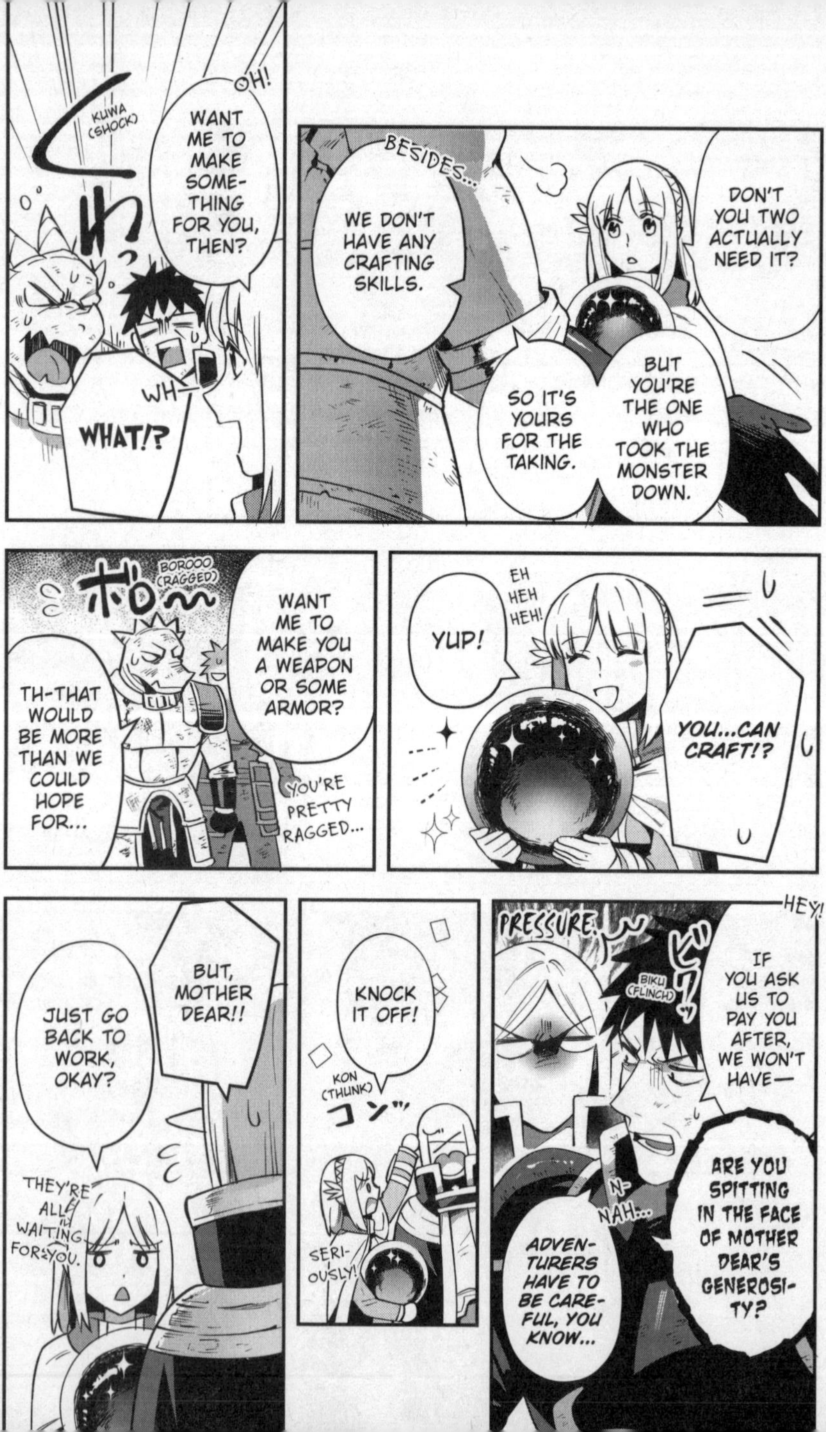
DON'T YOU TWO ACTUALLY NEED IT?
BESIDES...
WE DON'T HAVE ANY CRAFTING SKILLS.
BUT YOU'RE THE ONE WHO TOOK THE MONSTER DOWN.
SO IT'S YOURS FOR THE TAKING.
OH!
WANT ME TO MAKE SOMETHING FOR YOU, THEN?
KUWA (SHOCK)
WH-
WHAT!?
YOU...CAN CRAFT!?
EH HEH HEH!
YUP!
WANT ME TO MAKE YOU A WEAPON OR SOME ARMOR?
BOROOO (RAGGED)
TH-THAT WOULD BE MORE THAN WE COULD HOPE FOR...
YOU'RE PRETTY RAGGED...
HEY!
IF YOU ASK US TO PAY YOU AFTER, WE WON'T HAVE—
PRESSURE
BIKU (FLINCH)
ARE YOU SPITTING IN THE FACE OF MOTHER DEAR'S GENEROSITY?
N-NAH...
ADVENTURERS HAVE TO BE CAREFUL, YOU KNOW...
KNOCK IT OFF!
KON (THUNK)
SERIOUSLY!
BUT, MOTHER DEAR!!
JUST GO BACK TO WORK, OKAY?
THEY'RE ALL WAITING FOR YOU.

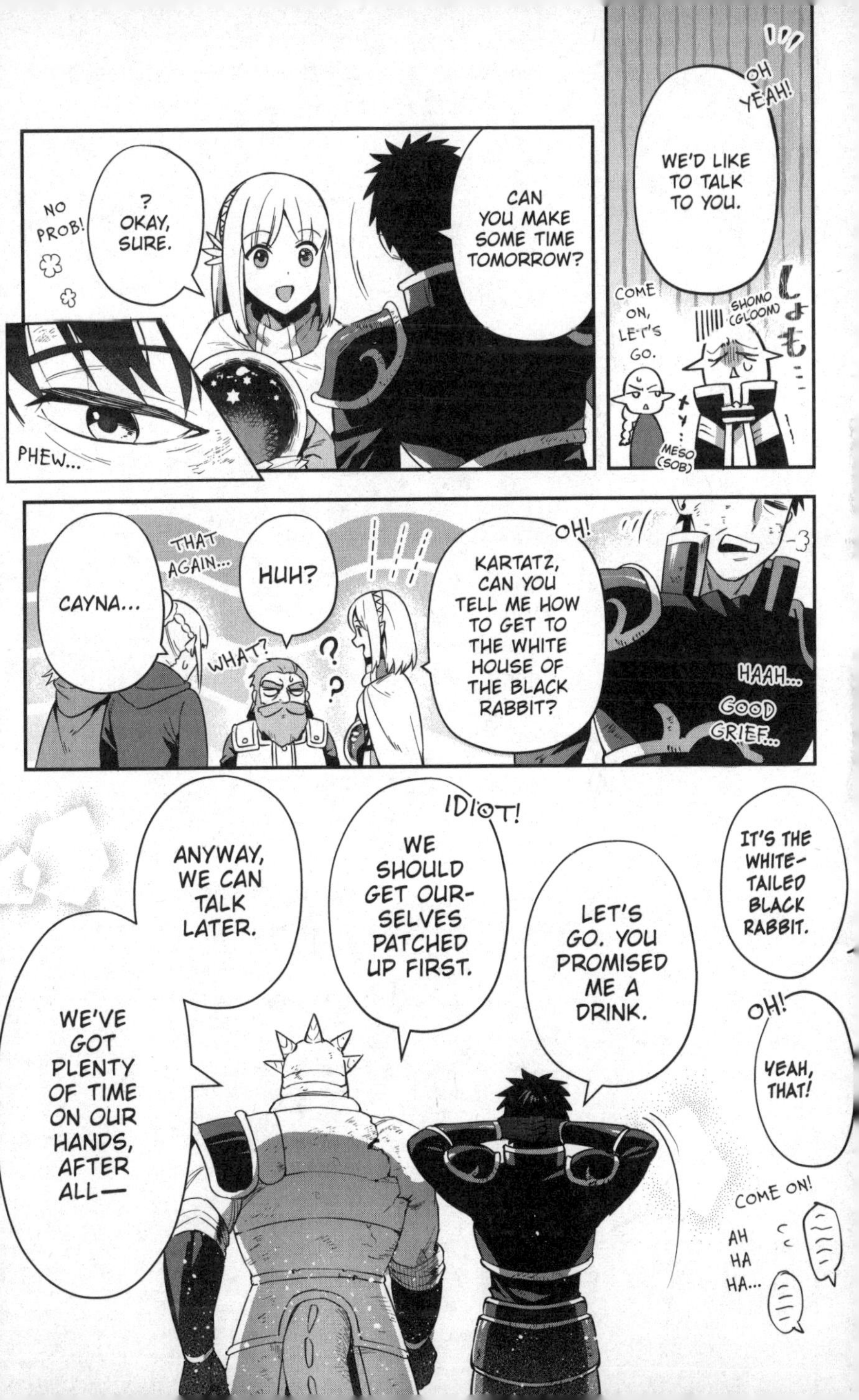
OH YEAH!
WE'D LIKE TO TALK TO YOU.
COME ON, LET'S GO.
しょも
SHOMO (GLOOM)
メソ
MESO (SOB)
CAN YOU MAKE SOME TIME TOMORROW?
? OKAY, SURE.
NO PROB!
PHEW...
OH!
KARTATZ, CAN YOU TELL ME HOW TO GET TO THE WHITE HOUSE OF THE BLACK RABBIT?
HAAH... GOOD GRIEF...
HUH?
WHAT?
THAT AGAIN...
CAYNA...
IT'S THE WHITE-TAILED BLACK RABBIT.
OH!
YEAH, THAT!
LET'S GO. YOU PROMISED ME A DRINK.
IDIOT!
WE SHOULD GET OURSELVES PATCHED UP FIRST.
ANYWAY, WE CAN TALK LATER.
WE'VE GOT PLENTY OF TIME ON OUR HANDS, AFTER ALL—
COME ON!
AH HA HA...

IN THE LAND OF LEADALE

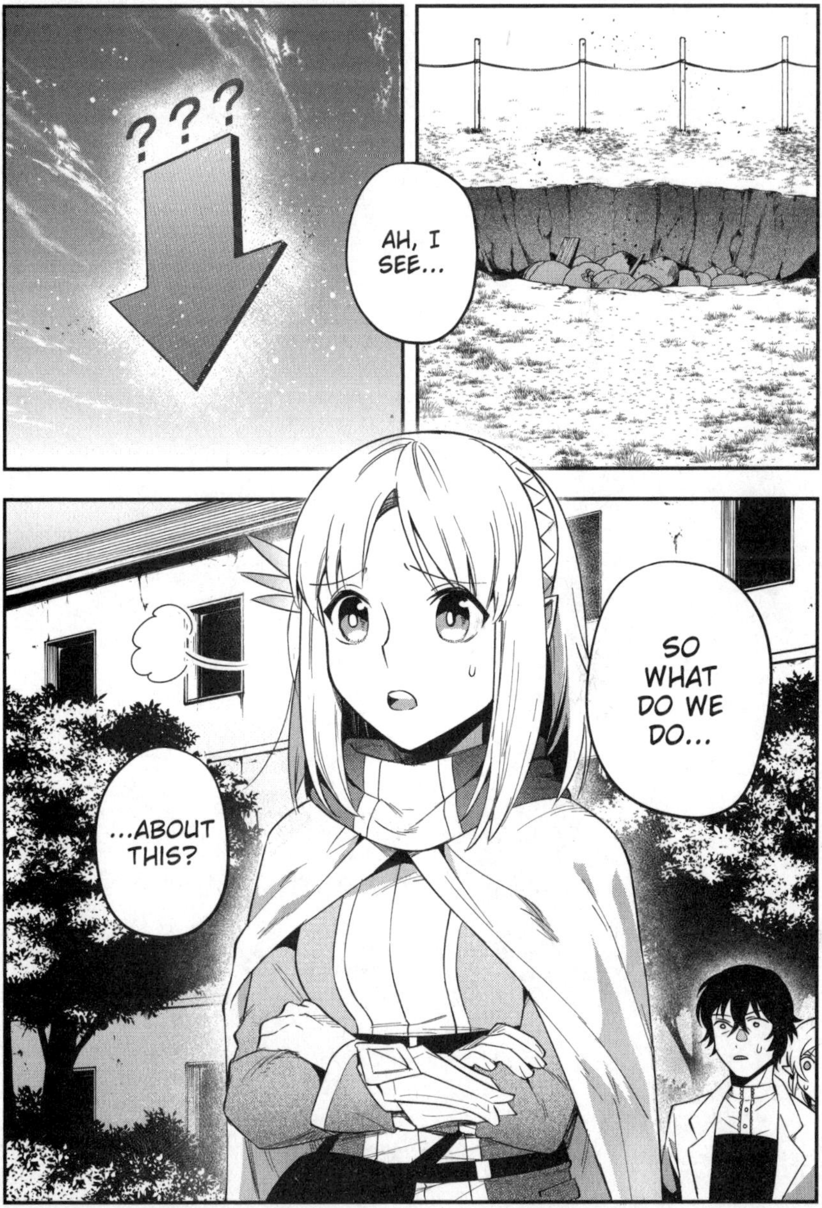
AH, I SEE...
???
SO WHAT DO WE DO...
...ABOUT THIS?

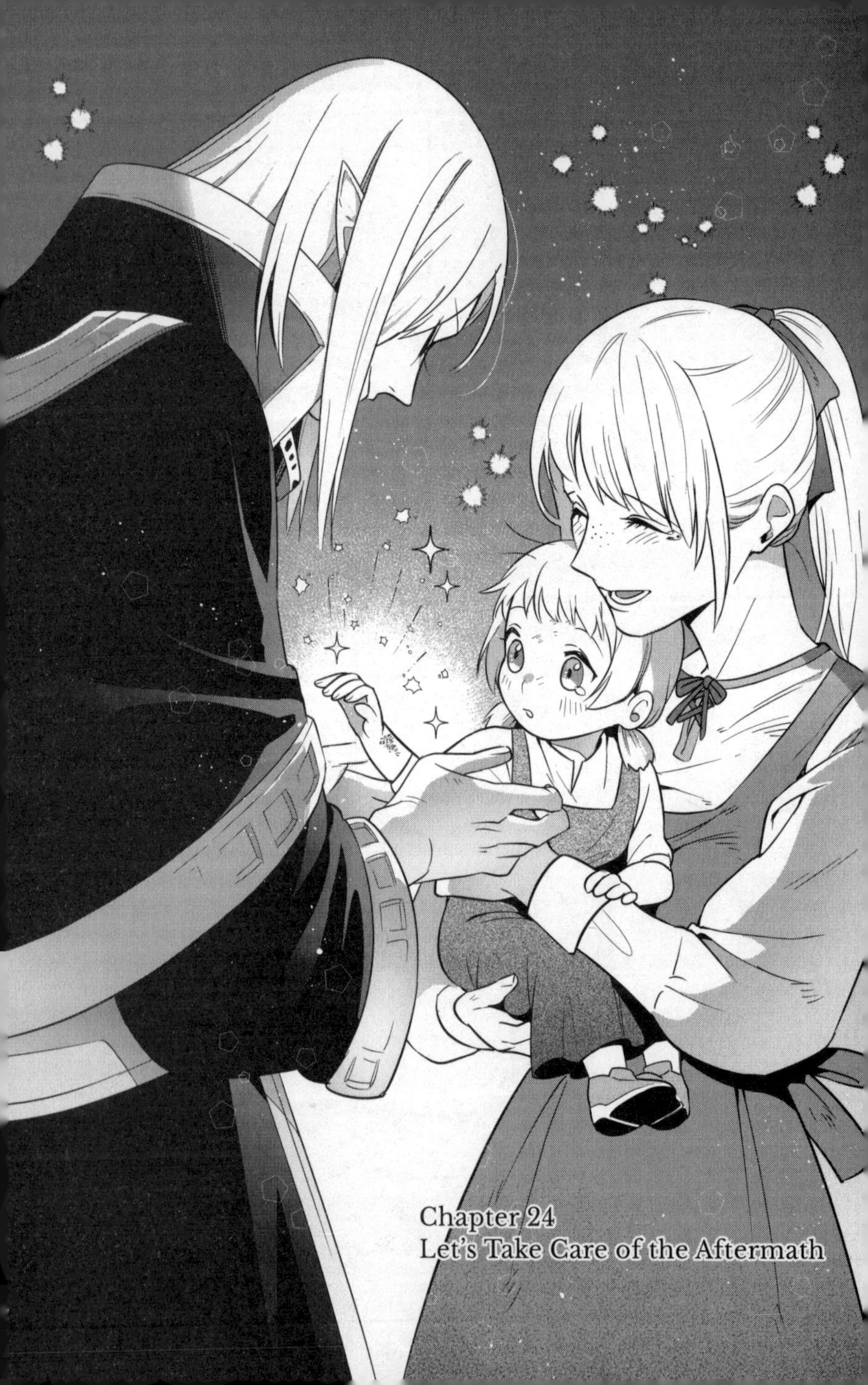
Chapter 24
Let's Take Care of the Aftermath

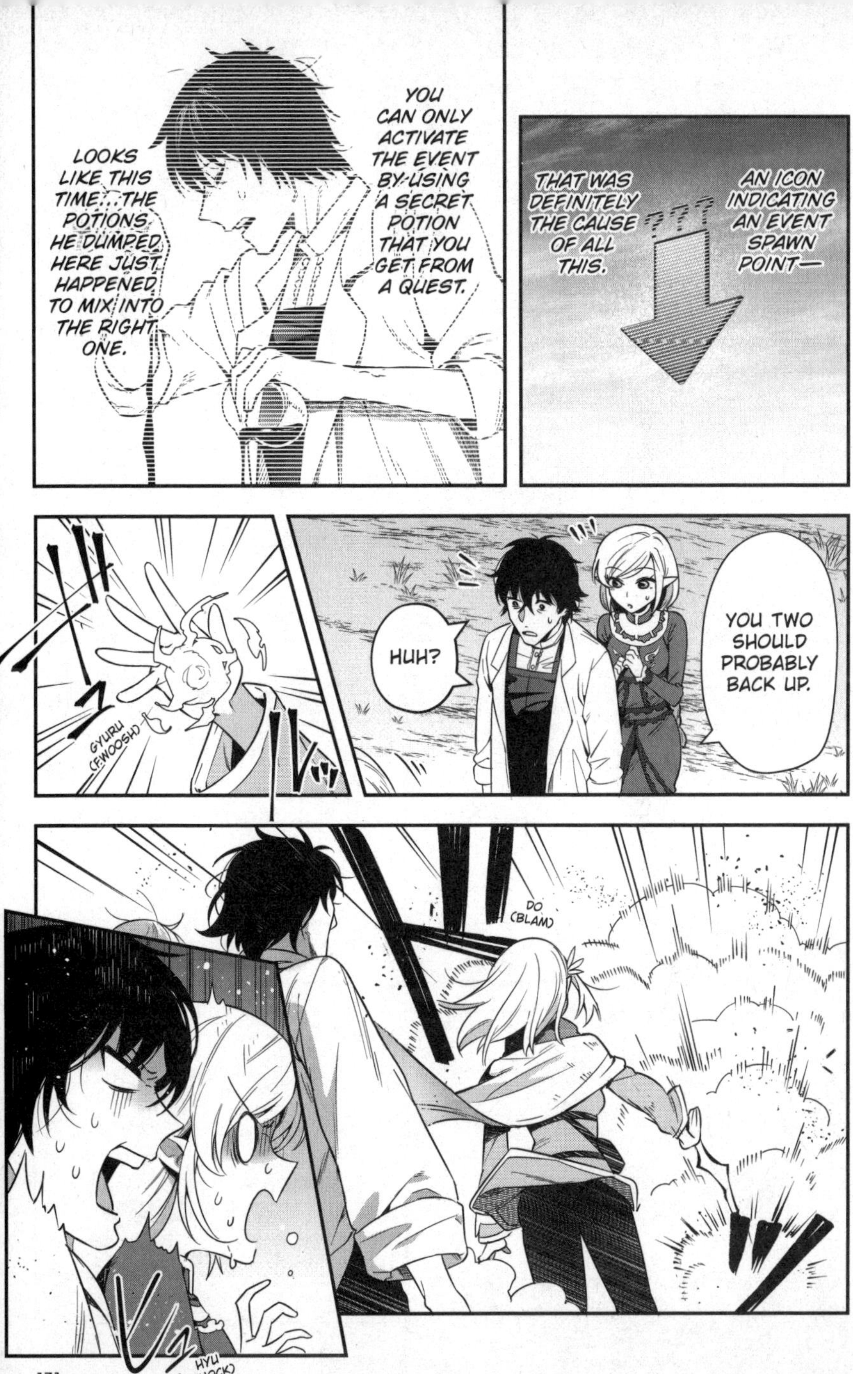
AN ICON INDICATING AN EVENT SPAWN POINT—
???
THAT WAS DEFINITELY THE CAUSE OF ALL THIS.
YOU CAN ONLY ACTIVATE THE EVENT BY USING A SECRET POTION THAT YOU GET FROM A QUEST.
LOOKS LIKE THIS TIME...THE POTIONS HE DUMPED HERE JUST HAPPENED TO MIX INTO THE RIGHT ONE.
YOU TWO SHOULD PROBABLY BACK UP.
HUH?
GYURU (F'WOOSH)
DO (BLAM)
HYU (SHOCK)

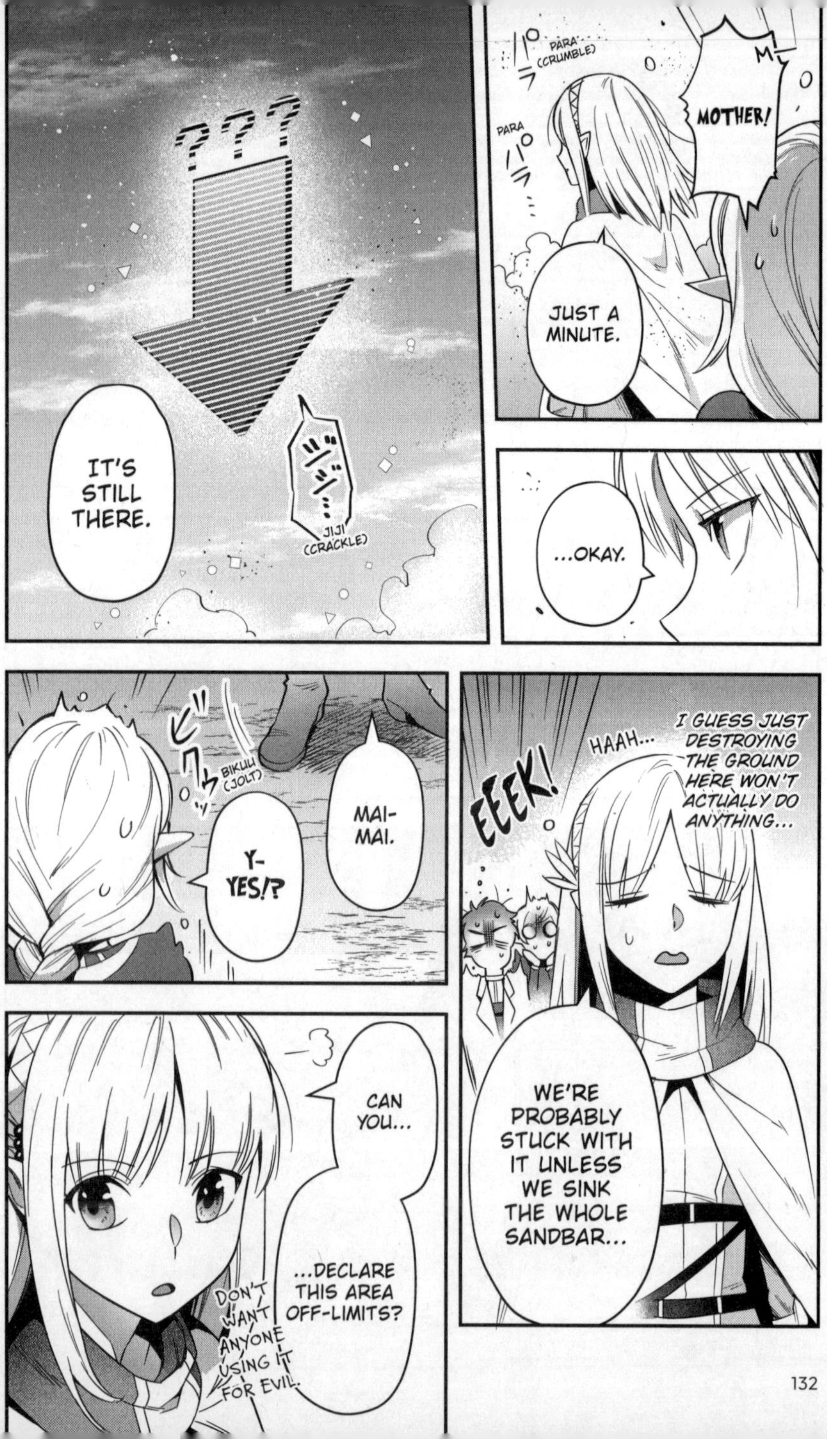
M—
MOTHER!
PARA (CRUMBLE)
PARA
JUST A MINUTE.
...OKAY.
???
JIJI (CRACKLE)
IT'S STILL THERE.
HAAH...
I GUESS JUST DESTROYING THE GROUND HERE WON'T ACTUALLY DO ANYTHING...
EEEK!
WE'RE PROBABLY STUCK WITH IT UNLESS WE SINK THE WHOLE SANDBAR...
MAI-MAI.
BIKUU (JOLT)
Y-YES!?
CAN YOU...
...DECLARE THIS AREA OFF-LIMITS?
DON'T WANT ANYONE USING IT FOR EVIL.

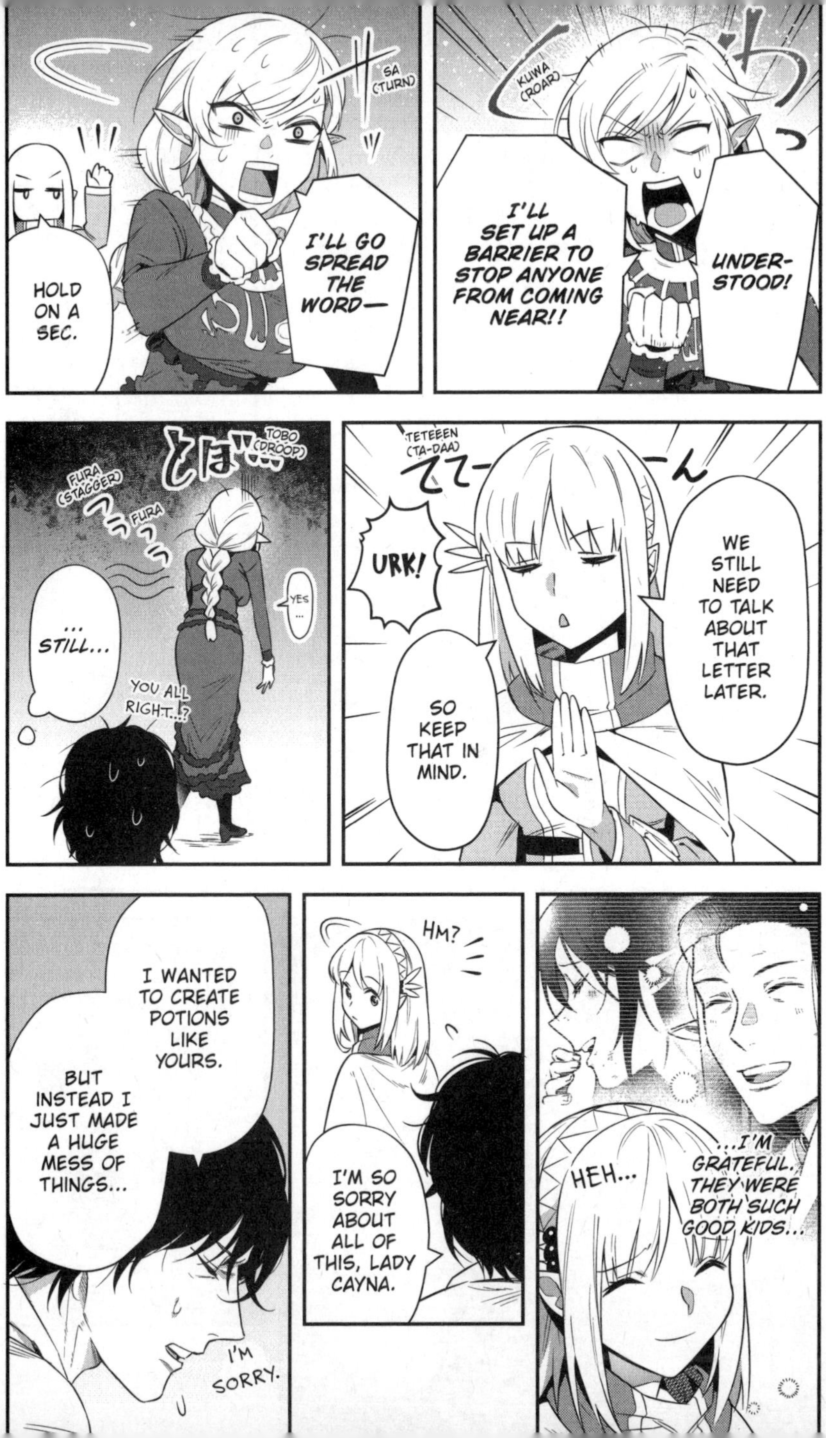
KUWA (ROAR)
UNDER-STOOD!
I'LL SET UP A BARRIER TO STOP ANYONE FROM COMING NEAR!!
SA (TURN)
I'LL GO SPREAD THE WORD—
HOLD ON A SEC.
TETEEEN (TA-DAA)
WE STILL NEED TO TALK ABOUT THAT LETTER LATER.
URK!
SO KEEP THAT IN MIND.
TOBO (DROOP)
FURA (STAGGER)
FURA
YES...
...STILL...
YOU ALL RIGHT...?
...I'M GRATEFUL. THEY WERE BOTH SUCH GOOD KIDS...
HEH...
HM?
I'M SO SORRY ABOUT ALL OF THIS, LADY CAYNA.
I WANTED TO CREATE POTIONS LIKE YOURS.
BUT INSTEAD I JUST MADE A HUGE MESS OF THINGS...
I'M SORRY.

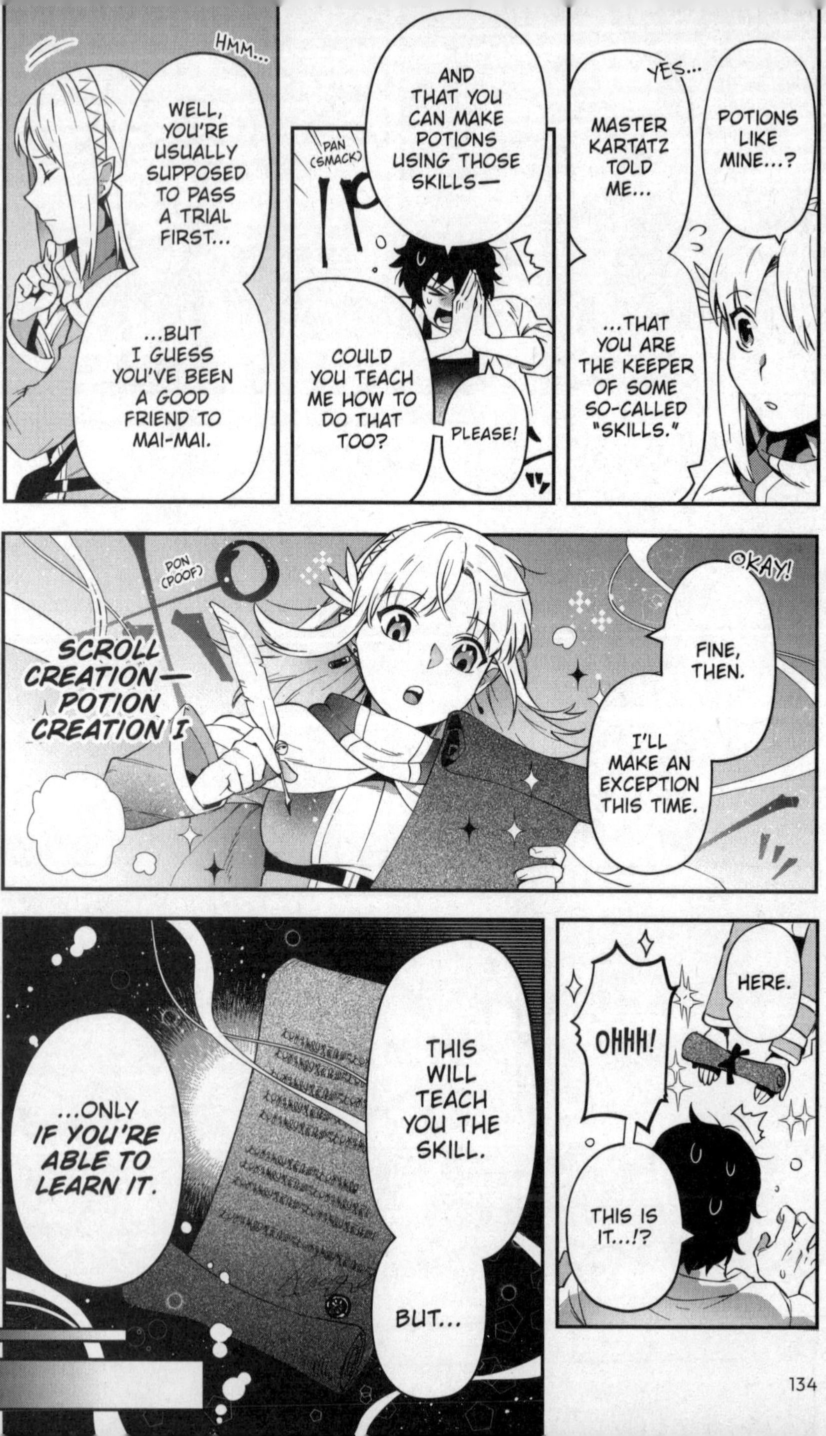
POTIONS LIKE MINE...?
YES...
MASTER KARTATZ TOLD ME...
...THAT YOU ARE THE KEEPER OF SOME SO-CALLED "SKILLS."
AND THAT YOU CAN MAKE POTIONS USING THOSE SKILLS—
PAN (SMACK)
COULD YOU TEACH ME HOW TO DO THAT TOO?
PLEASE!
HMM...
WELL, YOU'RE USUALLY SUPPOSED TO PASS A TRIAL FIRST...
...BUT I GUESS YOU'VE BEEN A GOOD FRIEND TO MAI-MAI.
OKAY!
FINE, THEN.
I'LL MAKE AN EXCEPTION THIS TIME.
PON (POOF)
SCROLL CREATION—POTION CREATION I
HERE.
OHHH!
THIS IS IT...!?
THIS WILL TEACH YOU THE SKILL.
BUT...
...ONLY IF YOU'RE ABLE TO LEARN IT.

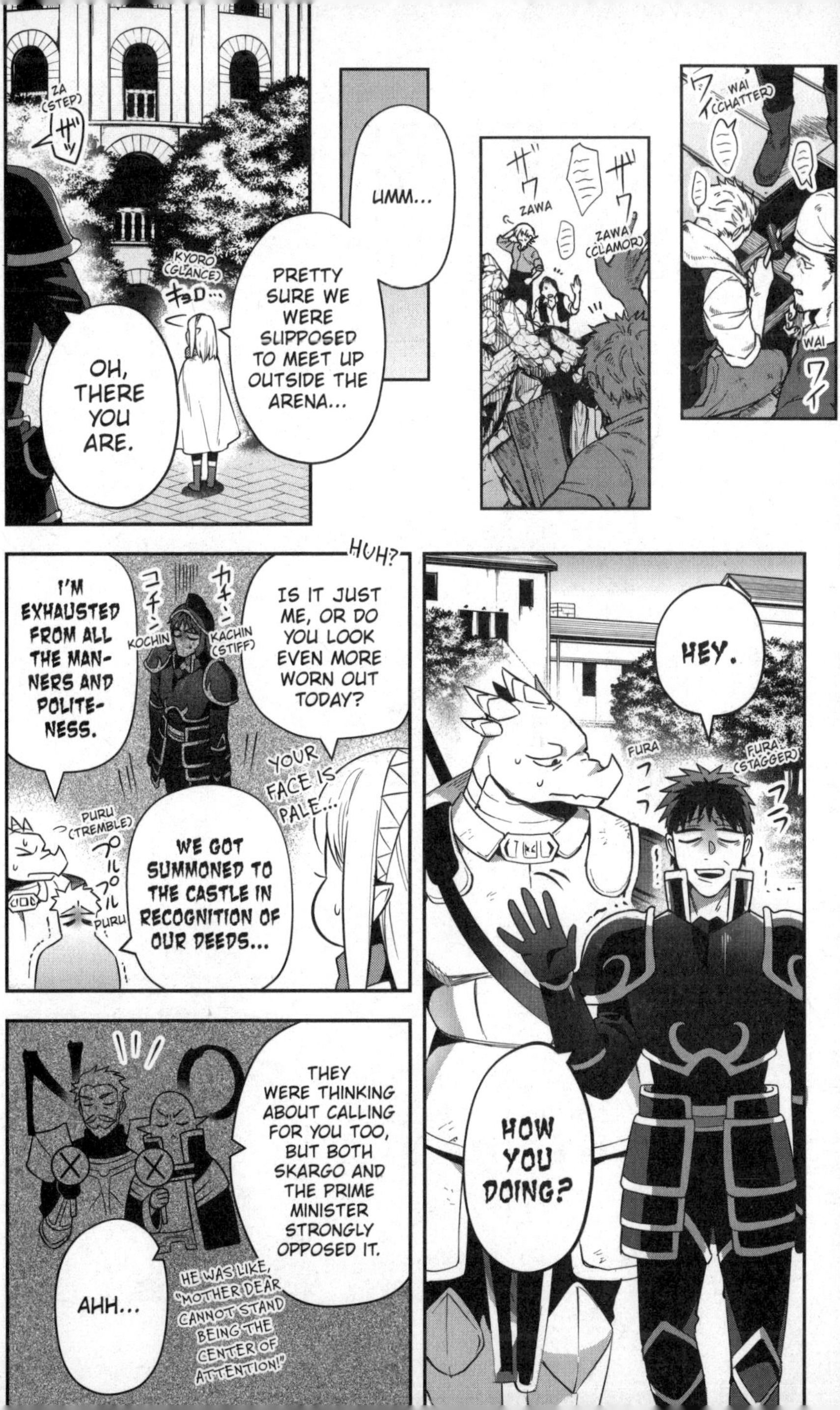

WAI (CHATTER)
WAI
ZAWA
ZAWA (CLAMOR)
UMM...
ZA (STEP)
PRETTY SURE WE WERE SUPPOSED TO MEET UP OUTSIDE THE ARENA...
KYORO (GLANCE)
OH, THERE YOU ARE.
HEY.
FURA
FURA (STAGGER)
HOW YOU DOING?
HUH?
IS IT JUST ME, OR DO YOU LOOK EVEN MORE WORN OUT TODAY?
KACHIN (STIFF)
KOCHIN
I'M EXHAUSTED FROM ALL THE MANNERS AND POLITENESS.
YOUR FACE IS PALE...
WE GOT SUMMONED TO THE CASTLE IN RECOGNITION OF OUR DEEDS...
PURU (TREMBLE)
PURU
THEY WERE THINKING ABOUT CALLING FOR YOU TOO, BUT BOTH SKARGO AND THE PRIME MINISTER STRONGLY OPPOSED IT.
HE WAS LIKE, "MOTHER DEAR CANNOT STAND BEING THE CENTER OF ATTENTION!"
AHH...

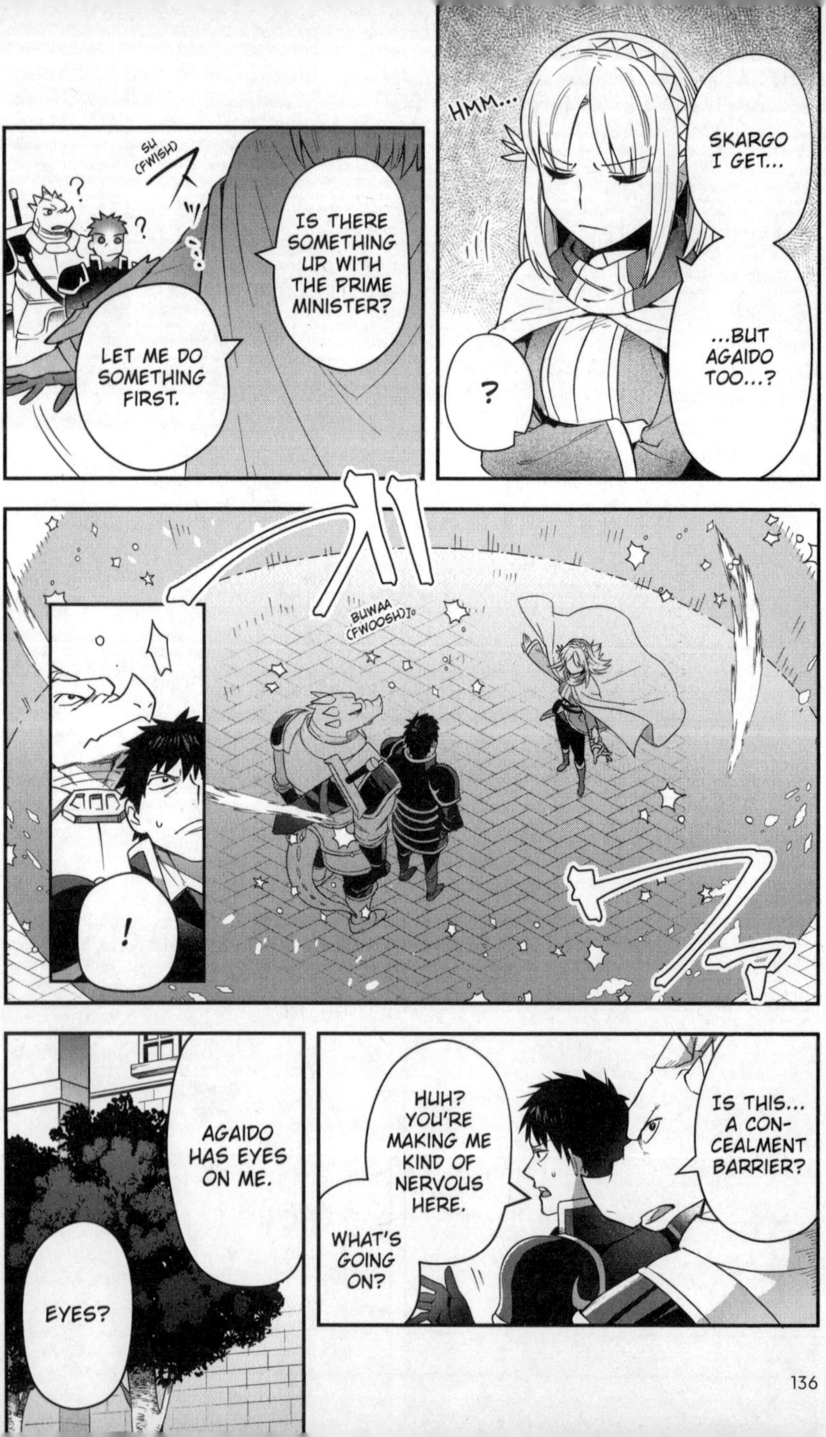
HMM...
SKARGO I GET...
...BUT AGAIDO TOO...?
?
SU (FWISH)
IS THERE SOMETHING UP WITH THE PRIME MINISTER?
LET ME DO SOMETHING FIRST.
BUWAA (FWOOSH)
!
IS THIS... A CON-CEALMENT BARRIER?
HUH? YOU'RE MAKING ME KIND OF NERVOUS HERE.
WHAT'S GOING ON?
AGAIDO HAS EYES ON ME.
EYES?

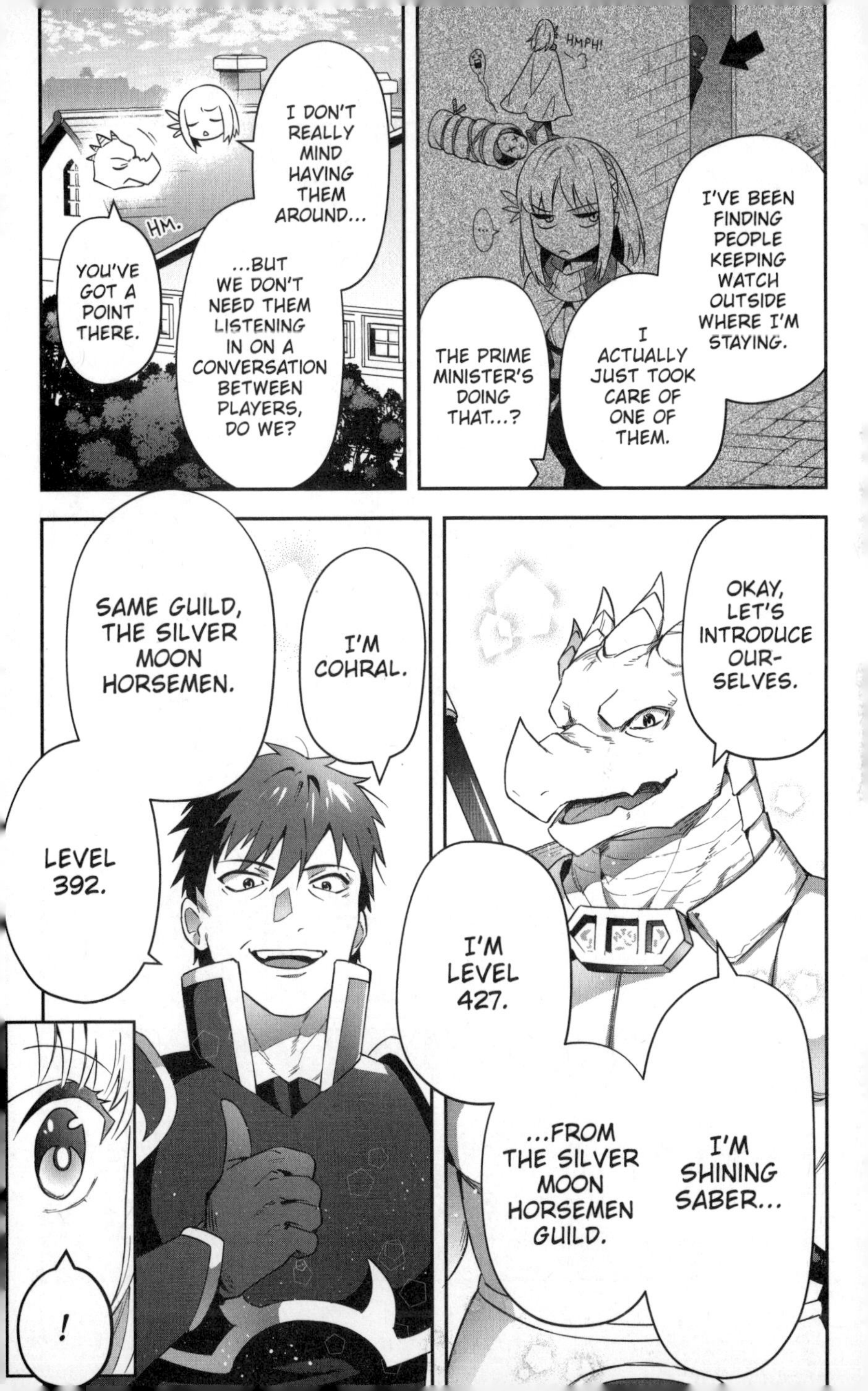
HMPH!
I'VE BEEN FINDING PEOPLE KEEPING WATCH OUTSIDE WHERE I'M STAYING.
I ACTUALLY JUST TOOK CARE OF ONE OF THEM.
THE PRIME MINISTER'S DOING THAT...?
I DON'T REALLY MIND HAVING THEM AROUND...
...BUT WE DON'T NEED THEM LISTENING IN ON A CONVERSATION BETWEEN PLAYERS, DO WE?
HM.
YOU'VE GOT A POINT THERE.
OKAY, LET'S INTRODUCE OUR-SELVES.
I'M SHINING SABER...
...FROM THE SILVER MOON HORSEMEN GUILD.
I'M LEVEL 427.
I'M COHRAL.
SAME GUILD, THE SILVER MOON HORSEMEN.
LEVEL 392.
!

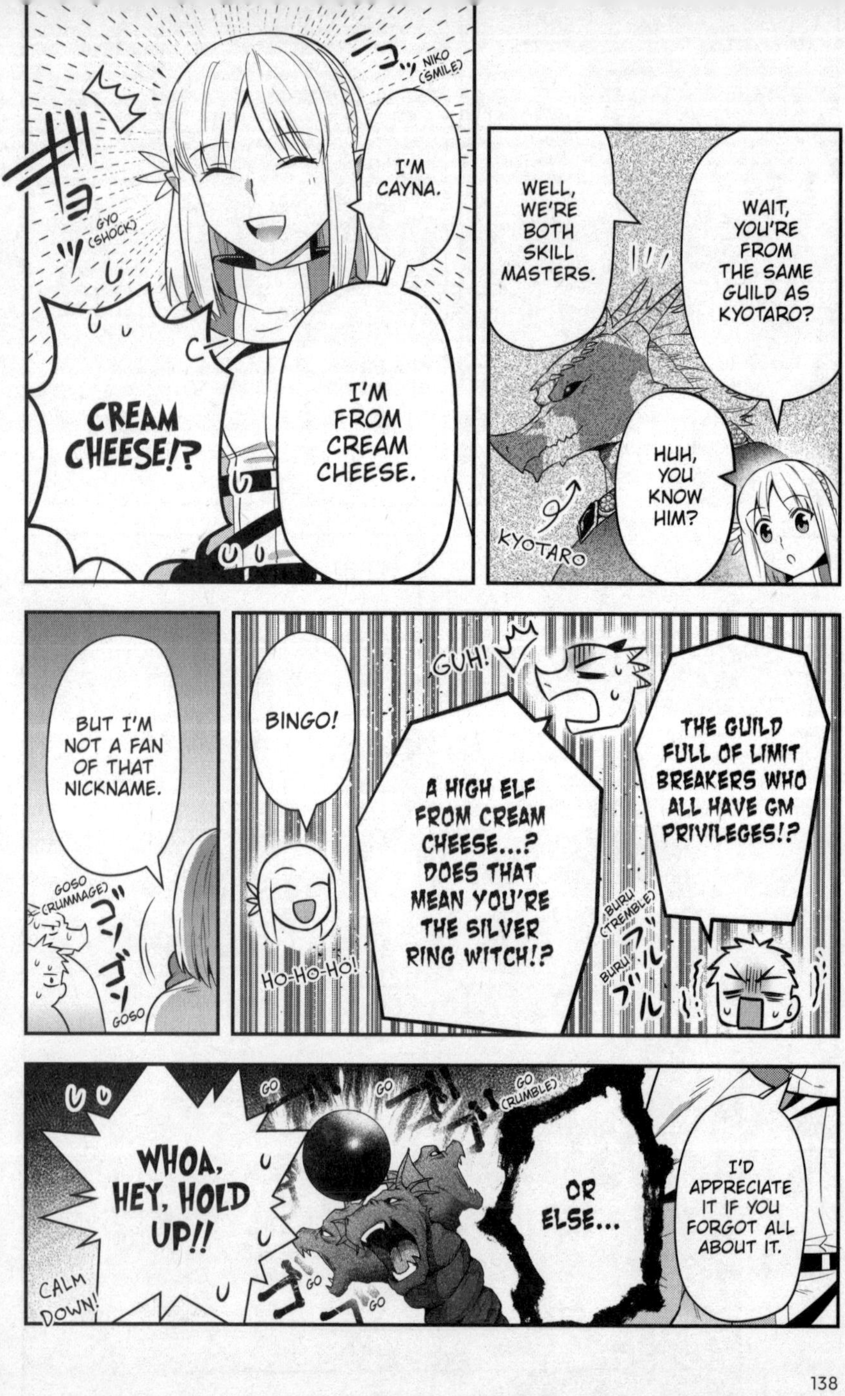
WAIT, YOU'RE FROM THE SAME GUILD AS KYOTARO?
WELL, WE'RE BOTH SKILL MASTERS.
HUH, YOU KNOW HIM?
KYOTARO
NIKO (SMILE)
I'M CAYNA.
I'M FROM CREAM CHEESE.
GYO (SHOCK)
CREAM CHEESE!?
THE GUILD FULL OF LIMIT BREAKERS WHO ALL HAVE GM PRIVILEGES!?
GUH!
A HIGH ELF FROM CREAM CHEESE...? DOES THAT MEAN YOU'RE THE SILVER RING WITCH!?
BINGO!
BURU (TREMBLE)
BURU
HO-HO-HO!
BUT I'M NOT A FAN OF THAT NICKNAME.
GOSO (RUMMAGE)
GOSO
I'D APPRECIATE IT IF YOU FORGOT ALL ABOUT IT.
OR ELSE...
GO (CRUMBLE)
GO
GO
WHOA, HEY, HOLD UP!!
CALM DOWN!
GO
GO

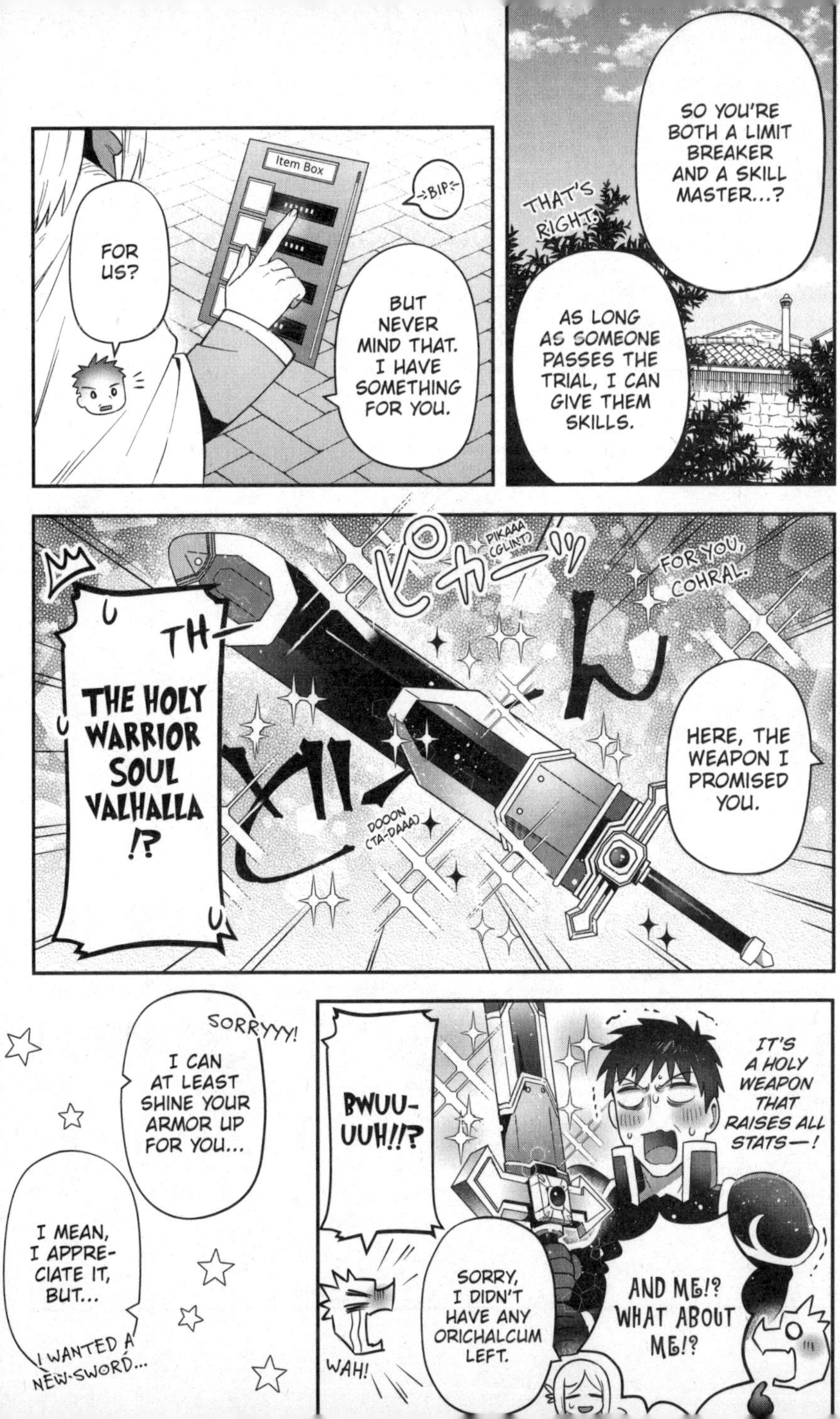
SO YOU'RE BOTH A LIMIT BREAKER AND A SKILL MASTER...?
THAT'S RIGHT.
AS LONG AS SOMEONE PASSES THE TRIAL, I CAN GIVE THEM SKILLS.
BIP
Item Box
FOR US?
BUT NEVER MIND THAT. I HAVE SOMETHING FOR YOU.
FOR YOU, COHRAL.
PIKAAA (GLINT)
HERE, THE WEAPON I PROMISED YOU.
DOOON (TA-DAAA)
TH—
THE HOLY WARRIOR SOUL VALHALLA!?
IT'S A HOLY WEAPON THAT RAISES ALL STATS—!
BWUU-UUH!!?
AND ME!? WHAT ABOUT ME!?
SORRY, I DIDN'T HAVE ANY ORICHALCUM LEFT.
WAH!
SORRYYY!
I CAN AT LEAST SHINE YOUR ARMOR UP FOR YOU...
I MEAN, I APPRECIATE IT, BUT...
I WANTED A NEW SWORD...

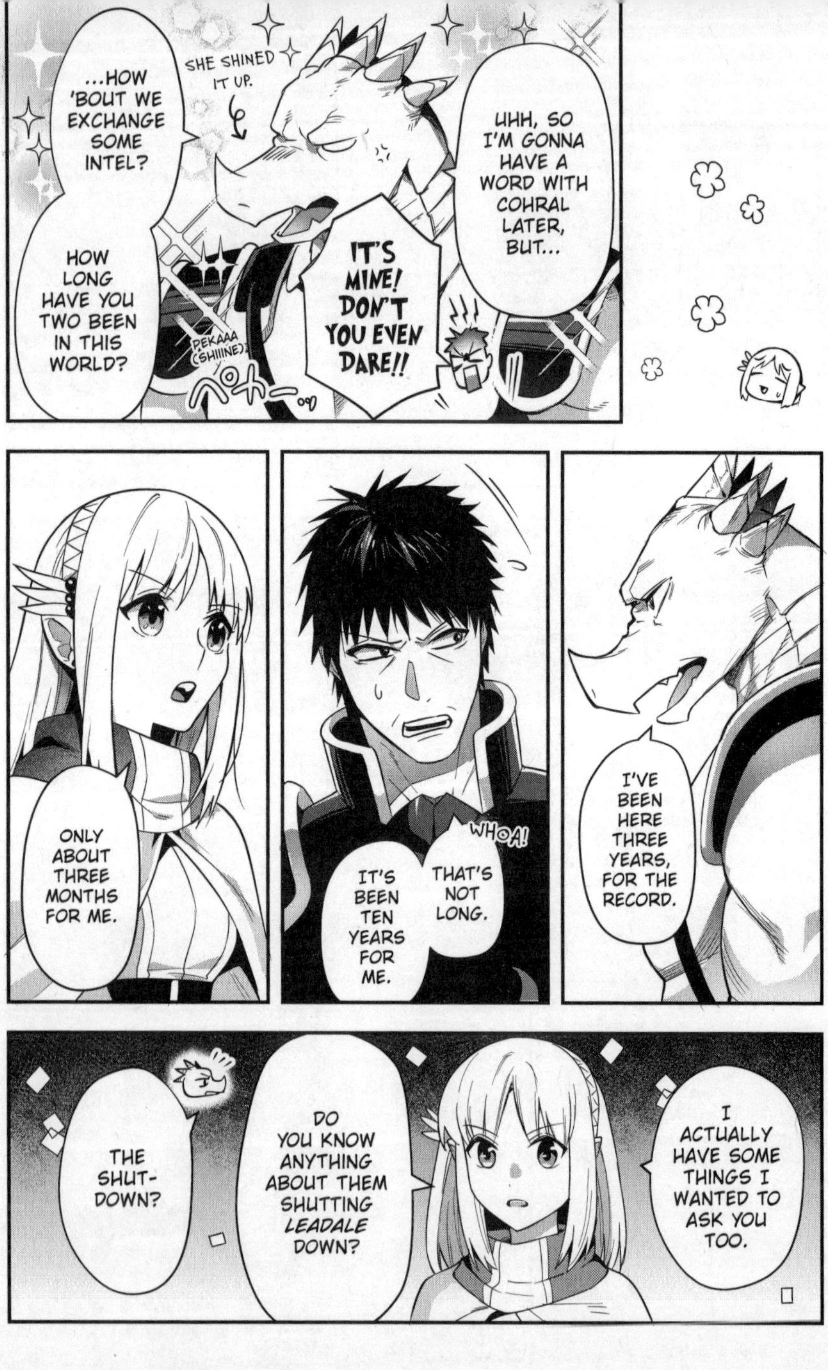
UHH, SO I'M GONNA HAVE A WORD WITH COHRAL LATER, BUT...
IT'S MINE! DON'T YOU EVEN DARE!!
SHE SHINED IT UP.
...HOW 'BOUT WE EXCHANGE SOME INTEL?
PEKAAA (SHIIINE)
HOW LONG HAVE YOU TWO BEEN IN THIS WORLD?
I'VE BEEN HERE THREE YEARS, FOR THE RECORD.
WHOA!
THAT'S NOT LONG.
IT'S BEEN TEN YEARS FOR ME.
ONLY ABOUT THREE MONTHS FOR ME.
I ACTUALLY HAVE SOME THINGS I WANTED TO ASK YOU TOO.
DO YOU KNOW ANYTHING ABOUT THEM SHUTTING *LEADALE* DOWN?
THE SHUT-DOWN?

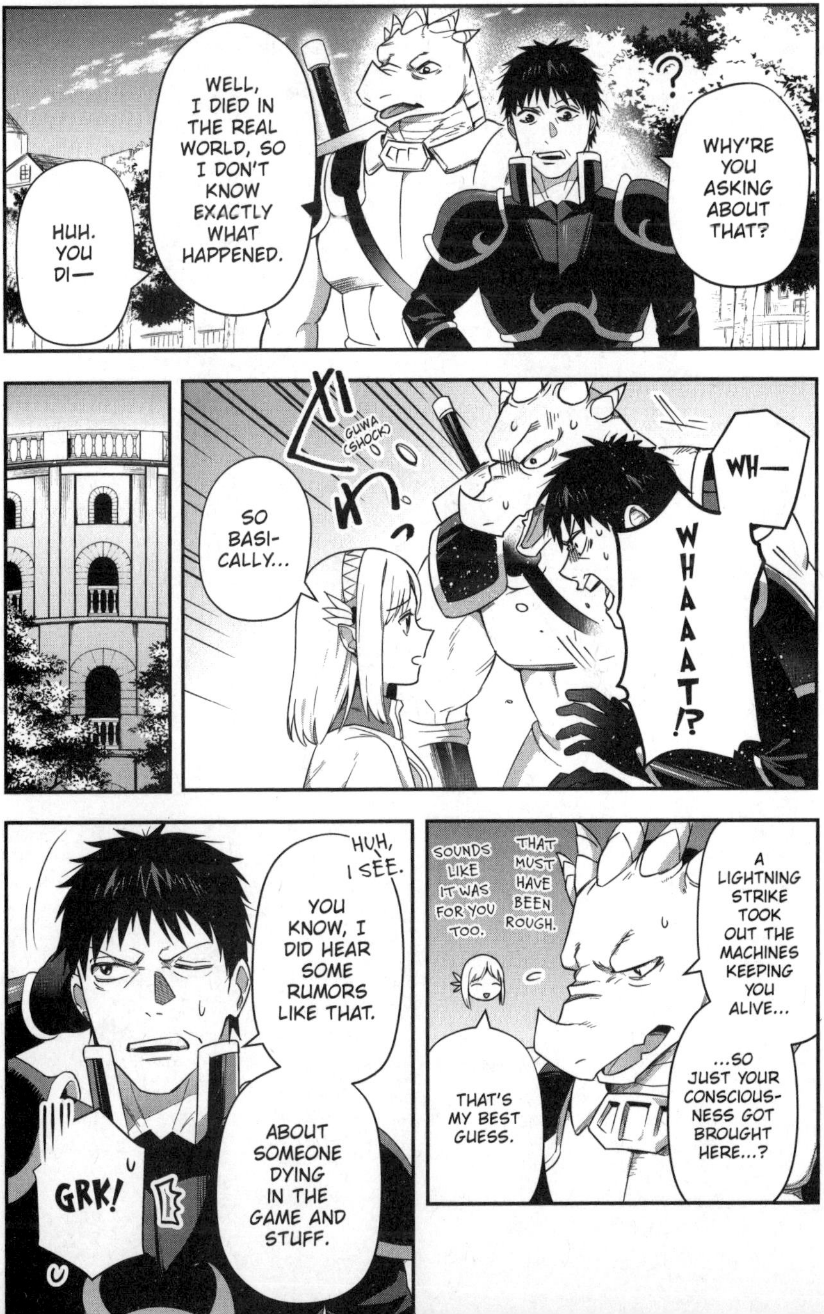
WHY'RE YOU ASKING ABOUT THAT?
WELL, I DIED IN THE REAL WORLD, SO I DON'T KNOW EXACTLY WHAT HAPPENED.
HUH. YOU DI—
WH—
WHAAAT!?
GUWA (SHOCK)
SO BASI-CALLY...
A LIGHTNING STRIKE TOOK OUT THE MACHINES KEEPING YOU ALIVE...
...SO JUST YOUR CONSCIOUS-NESS GOT BROUGHT HERE...?
THAT'S MY BEST GUESS.
THAT MUST HAVE BEEN ROUGH.
SOUNDS LIKE IT WAS FOR YOU TOO.
HUH, I SEE.
YOU KNOW, I DID HEAR SOME RUMORS LIKE THAT.
ABOUT SOMEONE DYING IN THE GAME AND STUFF.
GRK!

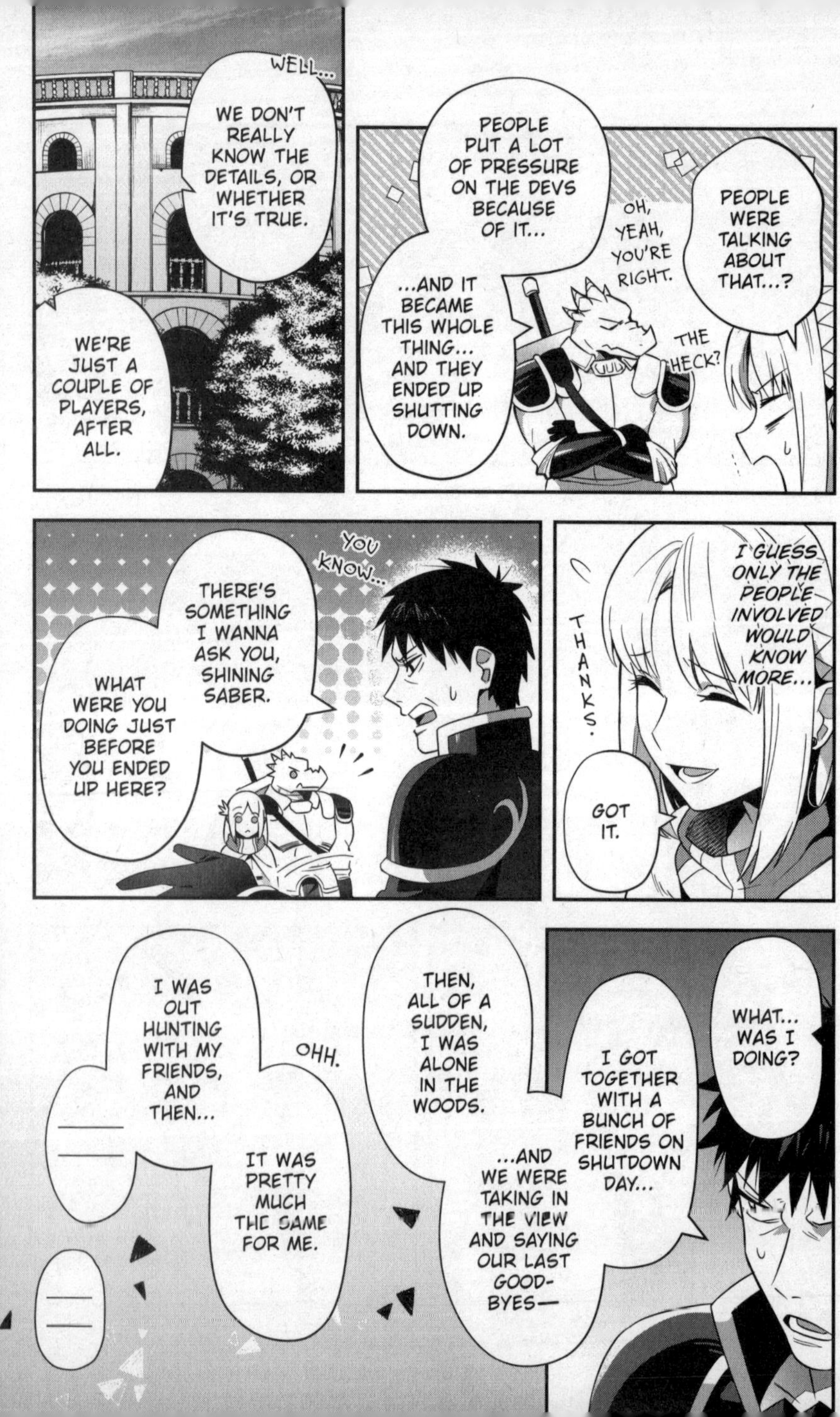
PEOPLE WERE TALKING ABOUT THAT...?
THE HECK?
OH, YEAH, YOU'RE RIGHT.
PEOPLE PUT A LOT OF PRESSURE ON THE DEVS BECAUSE OF IT...
...AND IT BECAME THIS WHOLE THING... AND THEY ENDED UP SHUTTING DOWN.
WELL...
WE DON'T REALLY KNOW THE DETAILS, OR WHETHER IT'S TRUE.
WE'RE JUST A COUPLE OF PLAYERS, AFTER ALL.
I GUESS ONLY THE PEOPLE INVOLVED WOULD KNOW MORE...
THANKS.
GOT IT.
YOU KNOW...
THERE'S SOMETHING I WANNA ASK YOU, SHINING SABER.
WHAT WERE YOU DOING JUST BEFORE YOU ENDED UP HERE?
WHAT... WAS I DOING?
I GOT TOGETHER WITH A BUNCH OF FRIENDS ON SHUTDOWN DAY...
...AND WE WERE TAKING IN THE VIEW AND SAYING OUR LAST GOOD-BYES—
THEN, ALL OF A SUDDEN, I WAS ALONE IN THE WOODS.
OHH.
IT WAS PRETTY MUCH THE SAME FOR ME.
I WAS OUT HUNTING WITH MY FRIENDS, AND THEN...
——
——

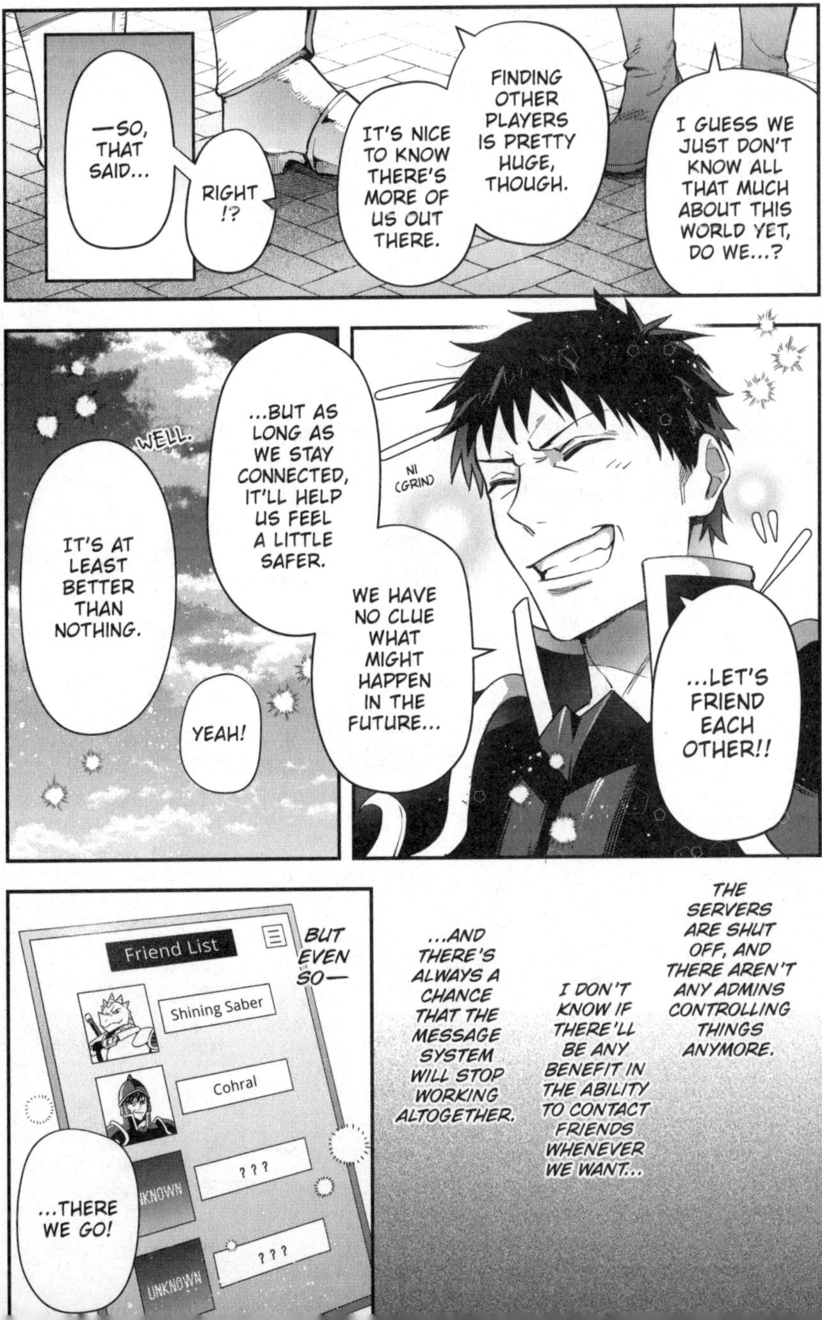
I GUESS WE JUST DON'T KNOW ALL THAT MUCH ABOUT THIS WORLD YET, DO WE...?
FINDING OTHER PLAYERS IS PRETTY HUGE, THOUGH.
IT'S NICE TO KNOW THERE'S MORE OF US OUT THERE.
RIGHT!?
—SO, THAT SAID...
...LET'S FRIEND EACH OTHER!!
NI (GRIN)
WE HAVE NO CLUE WHAT MIGHT HAPPEN IN THE FUTURE...
...BUT AS LONG AS WE STAY CONNECTED, IT'LL HELP US FEEL A LITTLE SAFER.
WELL.
IT'S AT LEAST BETTER THAN NOTHING.
YEAH!
THE SERVERS ARE SHUT OFF, AND THERE AREN'T ANY ADMINS CONTROLLING THINGS ANYMORE.
I DON'T KNOW IF THERE'LL BE ANY BENEFIT IN THE ABILITY TO CONTACT FRIENDS WHENEVER WE WANT...
...AND THERE'S ALWAYS A CHANCE THAT THE MESSAGE SYSTEM WILL STOP WORKING ALTOGETHER.
BUT EVEN SO—
Friend List
Shining Saber
Cohral
???
UNKNOWN
???
UNKNOWN
...THERE WE GO!

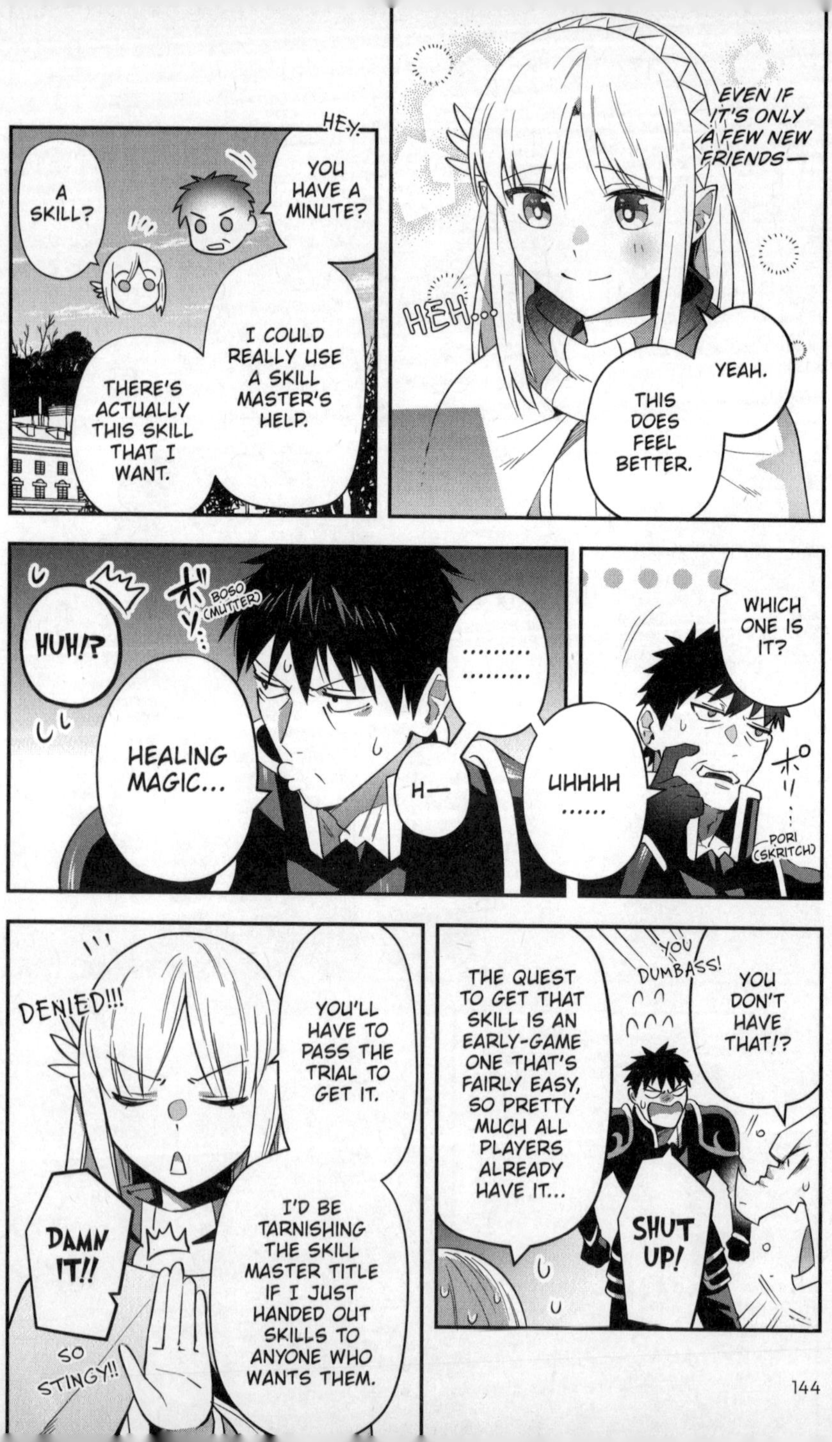
EVEN IF IT'S ONLY A FEW NEW FRIENDS—
HEH...
YEAH.
THIS DOES FEEL BETTER.
HEY.
YOU HAVE A MINUTE?
A SKILL?
I COULD REALLY USE A SKILL MASTER'S HELP.
THERE'S ACTUALLY THIS SKILL THAT I WANT.
WHICH ONE IS IT?
UHHHH ......
PORI (SKRITCH)
....
H—
HEALING MAGIC...
BOSO (MUTTER)
HUH!?
YOU DON'T HAVE THAT!?
YOU DUMBASS!
THE QUEST TO GET THAT SKILL IS AN EARLY-GAME ONE THAT'S FAIRLY EASY, SO PRETTY MUCH ALL PLAYERS ALREADY HAVE IT...
SHUT UP!
YOU'LL HAVE TO PASS THE TRIAL TO GET IT.
DENIED!!!
I'D BE TARNISHING THE SKILL MASTER TITLE IF I JUST HANDED OUT SKILLS TO ANYONE WHO WANTS THEM.
DAMN IT!!
SO STINGY!!

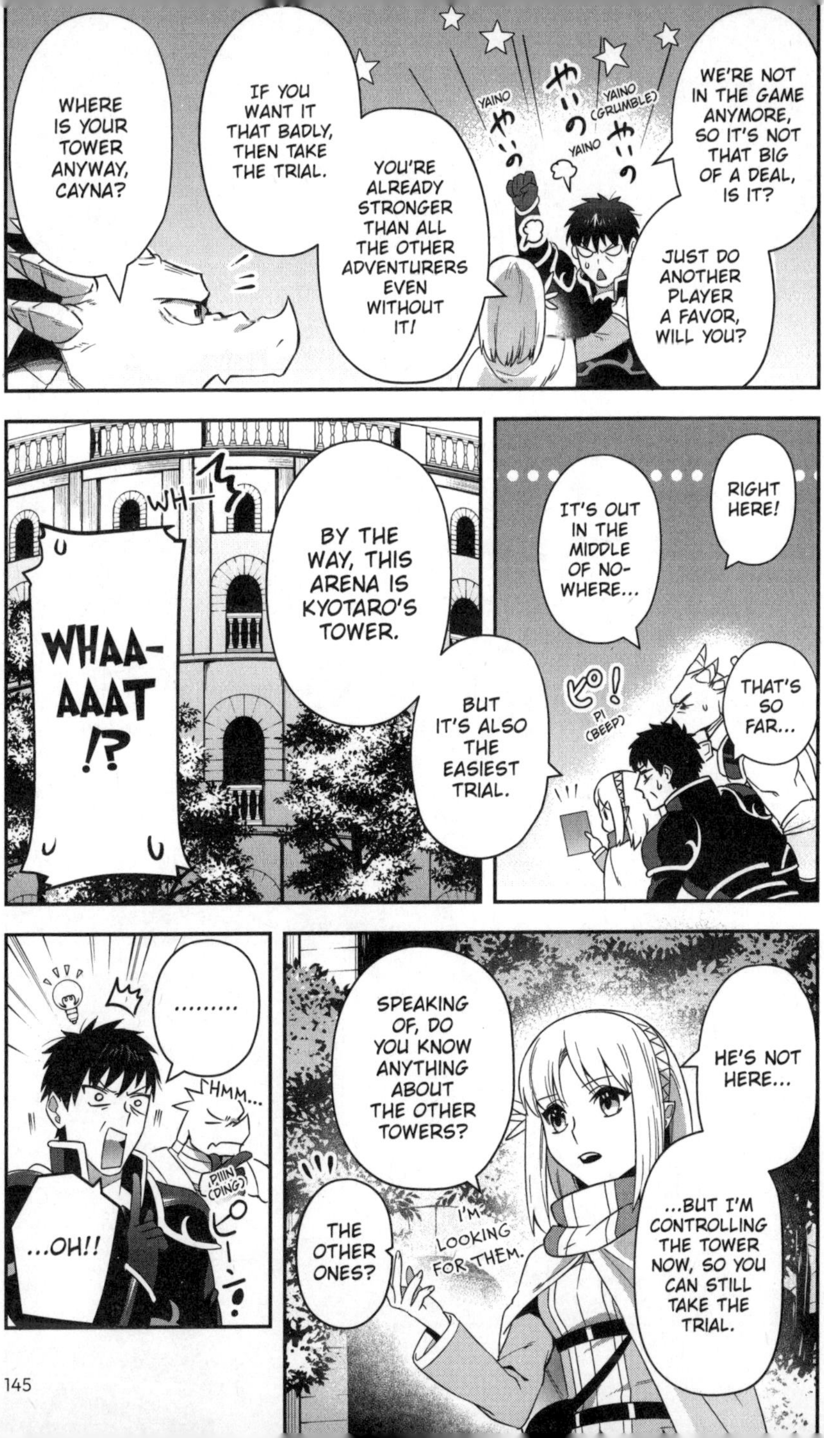
WE'RE NOT IN THE GAME ANYMORE, SO IT'S NOT THAT BIG OF A DEAL, IS IT?
JUST DO ANOTHER PLAYER A FAVOR, WILL YOU?
YAINO YAINO (GRUMBLE) YAINO
IF YOU WANT IT THAT BADLY, THEN TAKE THE TRIAL.
YOU'RE ALREADY STRONGER THAN ALL THE OTHER ADVENTURERS EVEN WITHOUT IT!
WHERE IS YOUR TOWER ANYWAY, CAYNA?
RIGHT HERE!
IT'S OUT IN THE MIDDLE OF NOWHERE...
THAT'S SO FAR...
PI (BEEP)
BY THE WAY, THIS ARENA IS KYOTARO'S TOWER.
BUT IT'S ALSO THE EASIEST TRIAL.
WH—
WHAA-AAAT!?
HE'S NOT HERE...
...BUT I'M CONTROLLING THE TOWER NOW, SO YOU CAN STILL TAKE THE TRIAL.
SPEAKING OF, DO YOU KNOW ANYTHING ABOUT THE OTHER TOWERS?
I'M LOOKING FOR THEM.
THE OTHER ONES?
....
HMM...
PIIIN (DING)
...OH!!

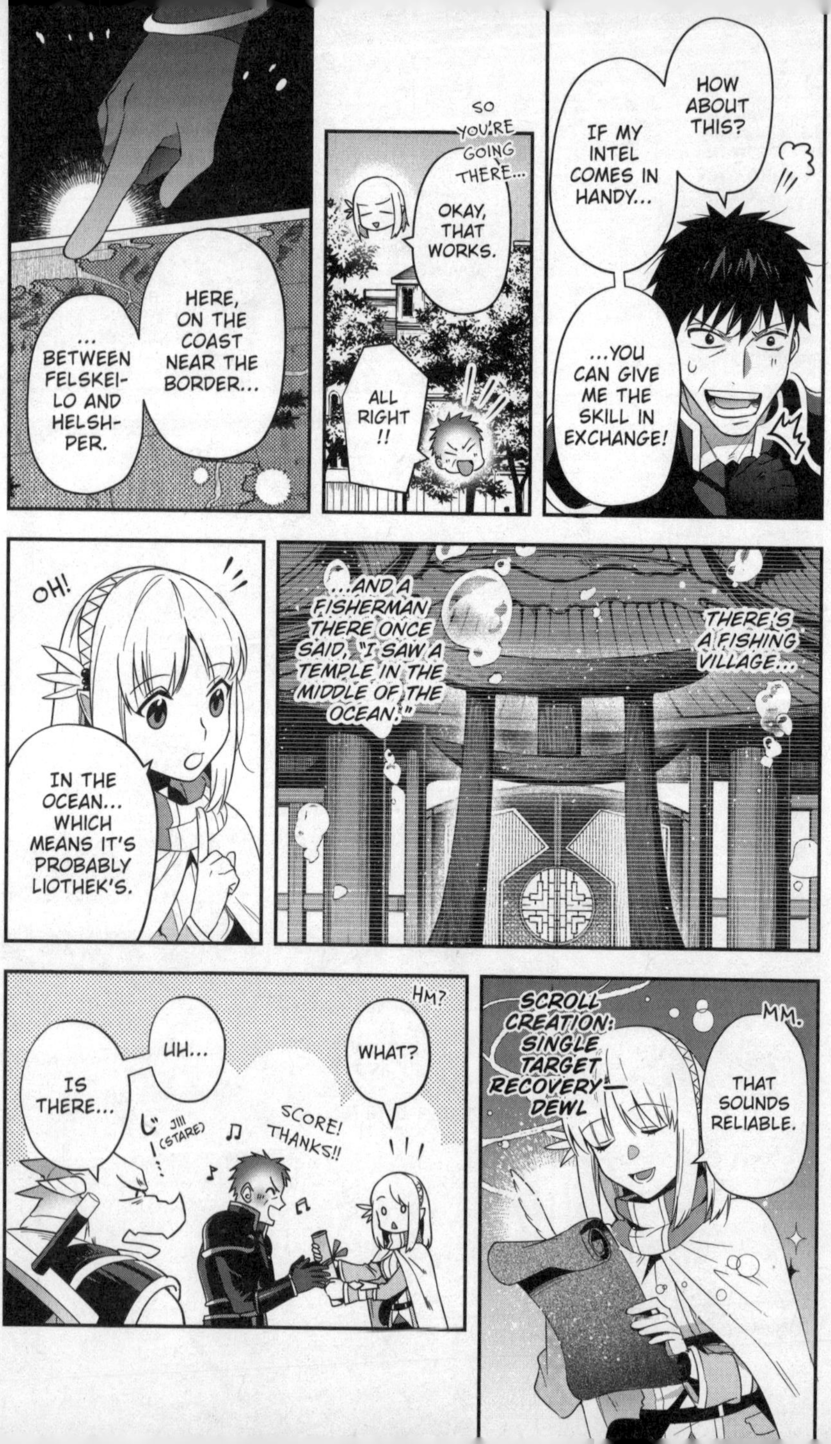
HOW ABOUT THIS?
IF MY INTEL COMES IN HANDY...
...YOU CAN GIVE ME THE SKILL IN EXCHANGE!
SO YOU'RE GOING THERE...
OKAY, THAT WORKS.
ALL RIGHT!!
HERE, ON THE COAST NEAR THE BORDER...
...BETWEEN FELSKEILO AND HELSHPER.
THERE'S A FISHING VILLAGE...
...AND A FISHERMAN THERE ONCE SAID, "I SAW A TEMPLE IN THE MIDDLE OF THE OCEAN."
OH!
IN THE OCEAN... WHICH MEANS IT'S PROBABLY LIOTHEK'S.
MM.
THAT SOUNDS RELIABLE.
SCROLL CREATION: SINGLE TARGET RECOVERY—DEWL
HM?
WHAT?
SCORE! THANKS!!
じ!
JIII (STARE)
UH...
IS THERE...

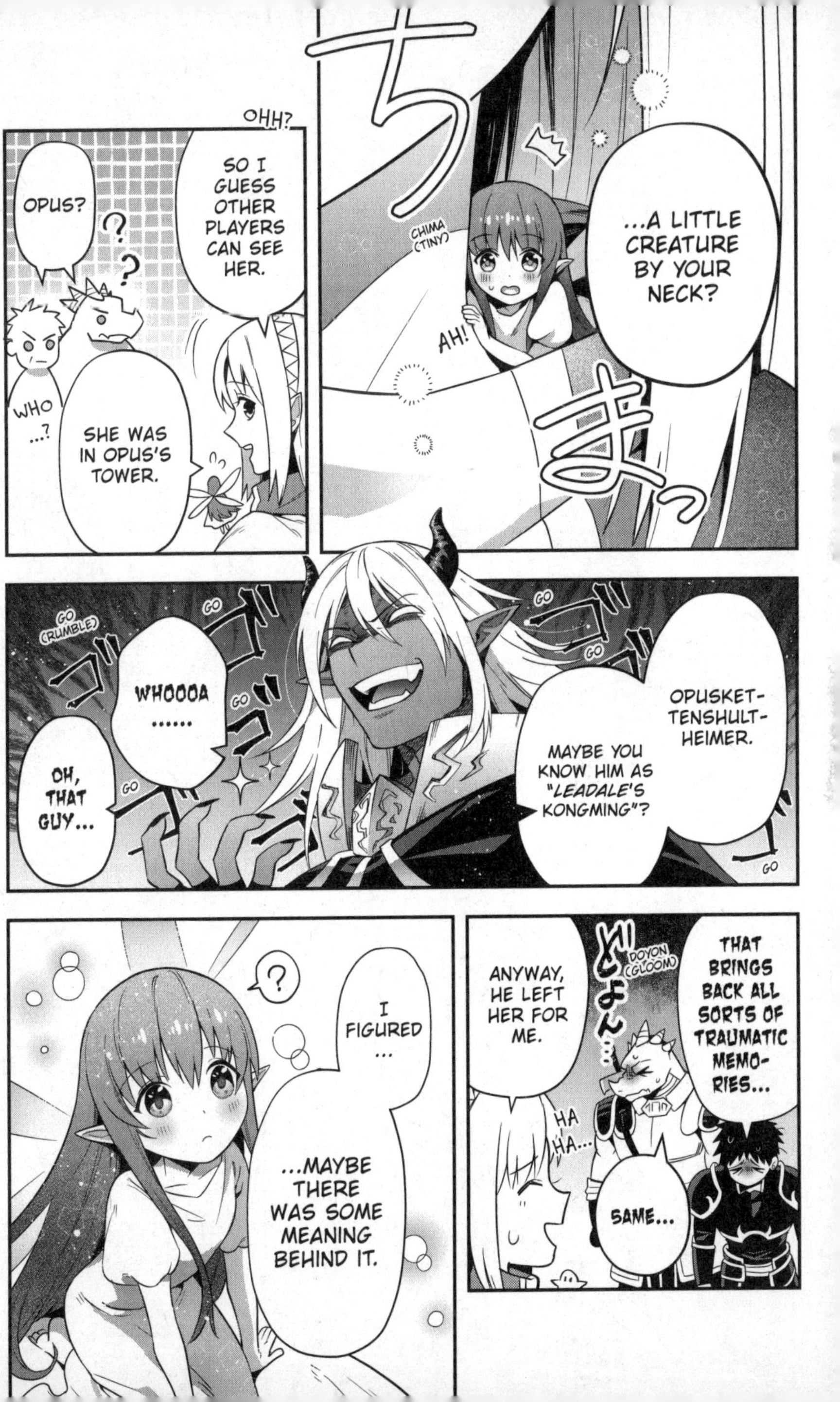
ち
...A LITTLE CREATURE BY YOUR NECK?
CHIMA (TINY)
AH!
まっ
OHH?
SO I GUESS OTHER PLAYERS CAN SEE HER.
OPUS?
??
SHE WAS IN OPUS'S TOWER.
WHO ...?
GO
OPUSKET-TENSHULT-HEIMER.
MAYBE YOU KNOW HIM AS "LEADALE'S KONGMING"?
GO
GO
GO
WHOOOA ......
GO
GO (RUMBLE)
OH, THAT GUY...
GO
THAT BRINGS BACK ALL SORTS OF TRAUMATIC MEMORIES...
DOYON (GLOOM)
どよん...
ANYWAY, HE LEFT HER FOR ME.
HA HA...
SAME...
I FIGURED ...
?
...MAYBE THERE WAS SOME MEANING BEHIND IT.

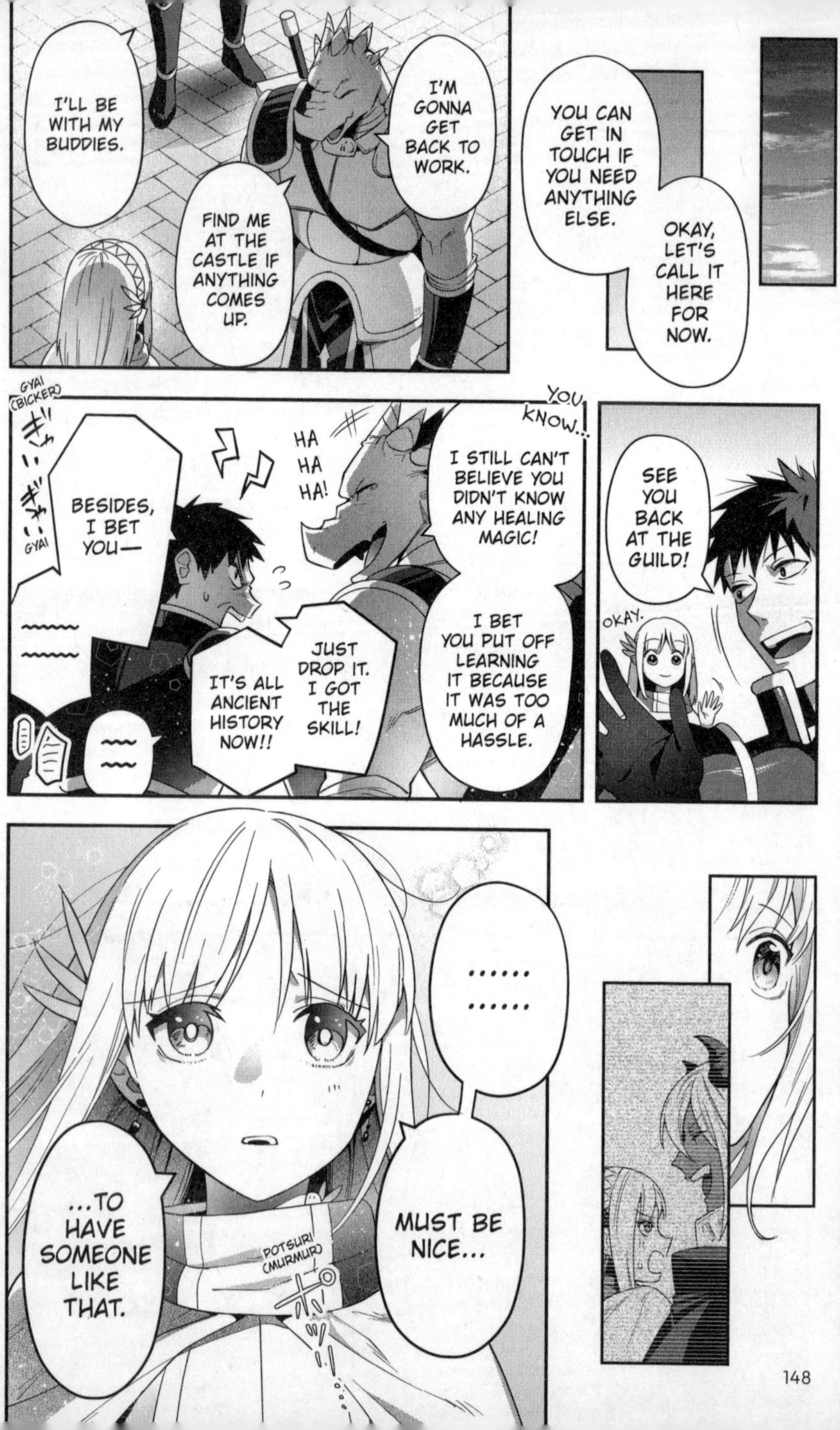
OKAY, LET'S CALL IT HERE FOR NOW.
YOU CAN GET IN TOUCH IF YOU NEED ANYTHING ELSE.
I'M GONNA GET BACK TO WORK.
FIND ME AT THE CASTLE IF ANYTHING COMES UP.
I'LL BE WITH MY BUDDIES.
SEE YOU BACK AT THE GUILD!
OKAY.
YOU KNOW...
I STILL CAN'T BELIEVE YOU DIDN'T KNOW ANY HEALING MAGIC!
HA HA HA!
I BET YOU PUT OFF LEARNING IT BECAUSE IT WAS TOO MUCH OF A HASSLE.
JUST DROP IT. I GOT THE SKILL!
IT'S ALL ANCIENT HISTORY NOW!!
BESIDES, I BET YOU—
GYAI (BICKER)
GYAI
......
......
MUST BE NICE...
...TO HAVE SOMEONE LIKE THAT.
POTSURI (MURMUR)

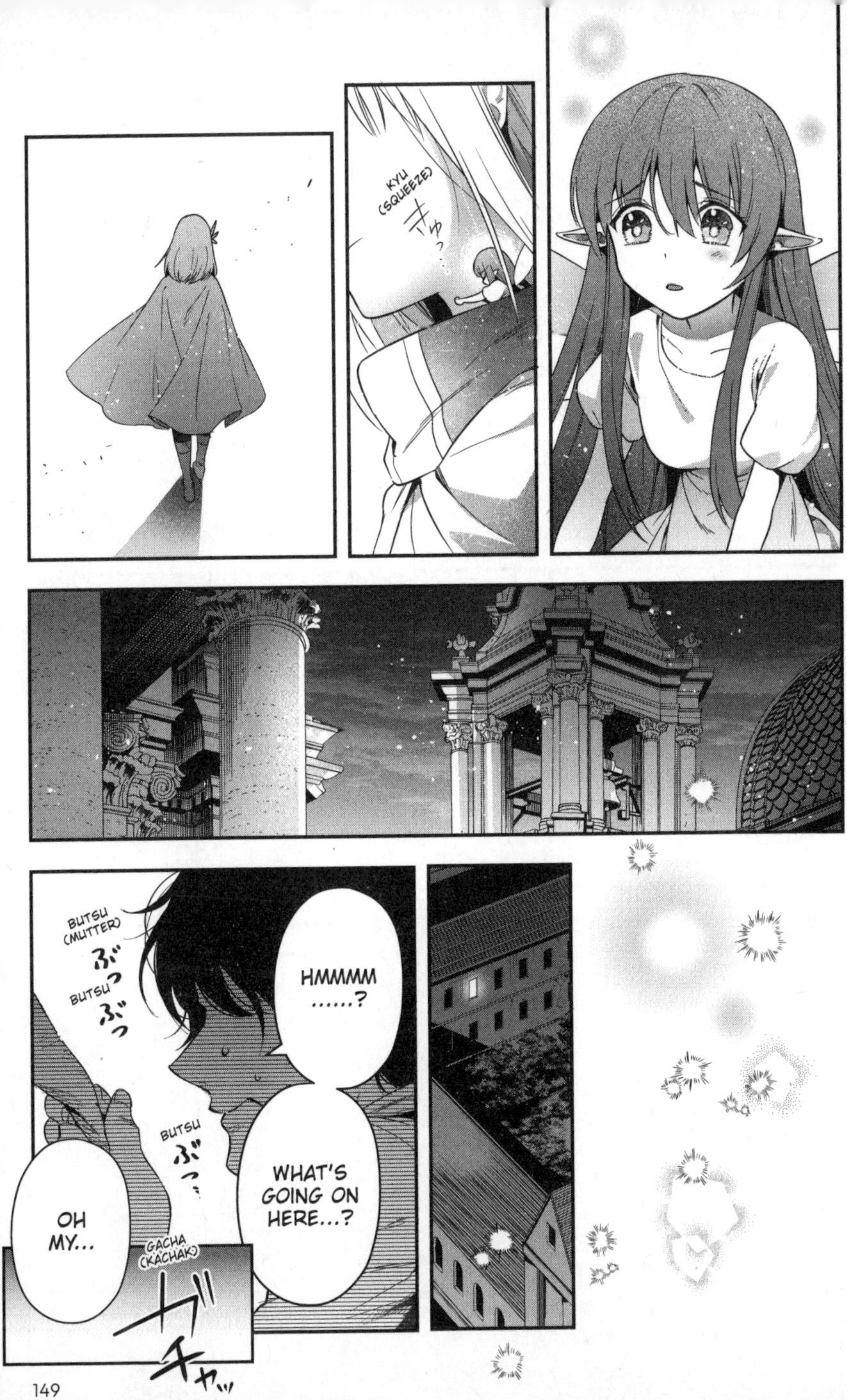
KYU (SQUEEZE)
きゅっ…
HMMMM ......?
WHAT'S GOING ON HERE...?
BUTSU (MUTTER)
ぶっ
BUTSU
ぶっ
BUTSU
ぶっ
OH MY...
GACHA (KACHAK)
ガチャッ

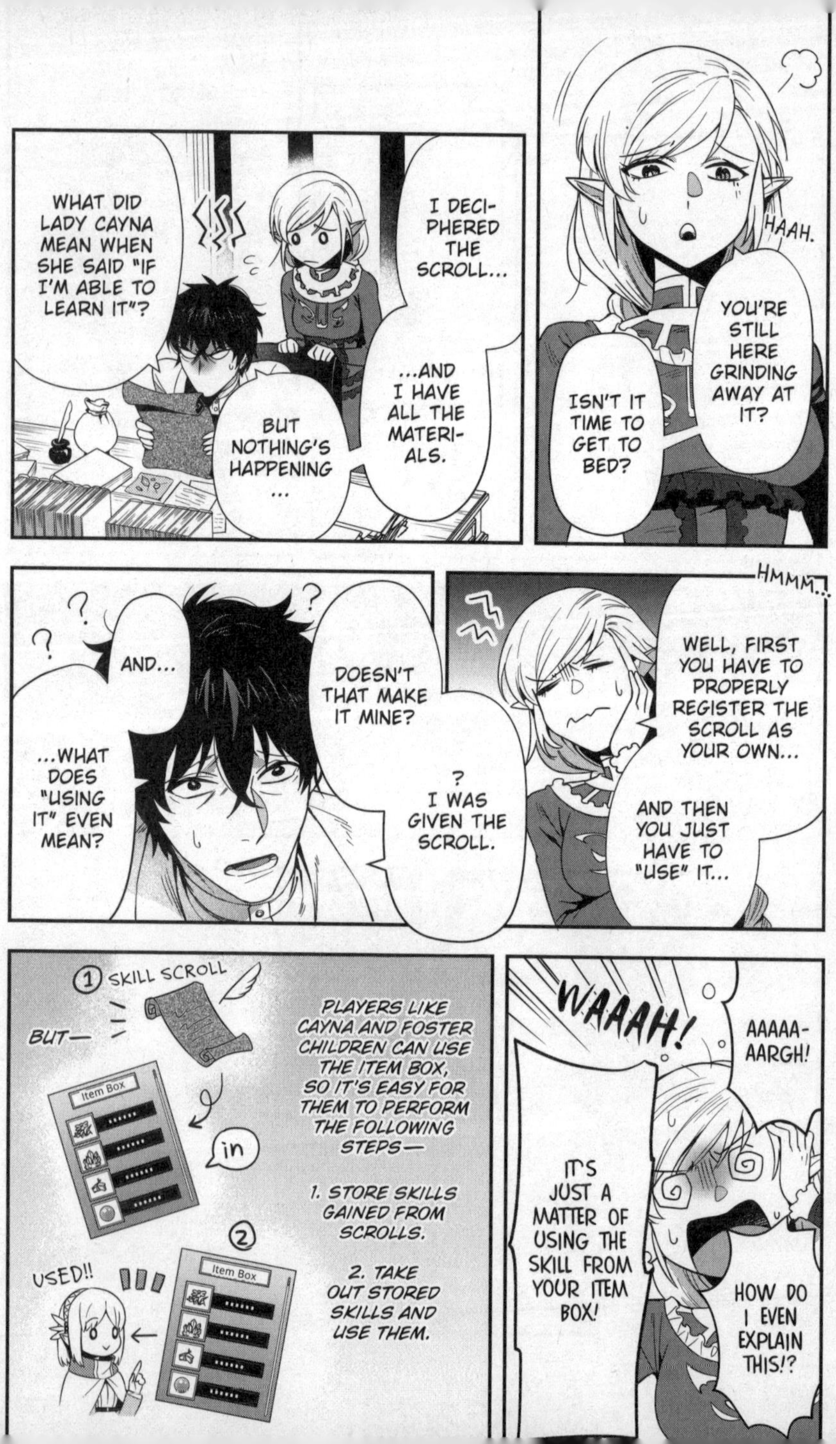
HAAH.
YOU'RE STILL HERE GRINDING AWAY AT IT?
ISN'T IT TIME TO GET TO BED?
I DECI-PHERED THE SCROLL...
...AND I HAVE ALL THE MATERI-ALS.
BUT NOTHING'S HAPPENING...
WHAT DID LADY CAYNA MEAN WHEN SHE SAID "IF I'M ABLE TO LEARN IT"?
HMMM...
WELL, FIRST YOU HAVE TO PROPERLY REGISTER THE SCROLL AS YOUR OWN...
AND THEN YOU JUST HAVE TO "USE" IT...
? I WAS GIVEN THE SCROLL.
DOESN'T THAT MAKE IT MINE?
AND...
...WHAT DOES "USING IT" EVEN MEAN?
WAAAH!
AAAAA-AARGH!
IT'S JUST A MATTER OF USING THE SKILL FROM YOUR ITEM BOX!
HOW DO I EVEN EXPLAIN THIS!?
PLAYERS LIKE CAYNA AND FOSTER CHILDREN CAN USE THE ITEM BOX, SO IT'S EASY FOR THEM TO PERFORM THE FOLLOWING STEPS—
1. STORE SKILLS GAINED FROM SCROLLS.
2. TAKE OUT STORED SKILLS AND USE THEM.
1 SKILL SCROLL
BUT—
Item Box
in
2
Item Box
USED!!

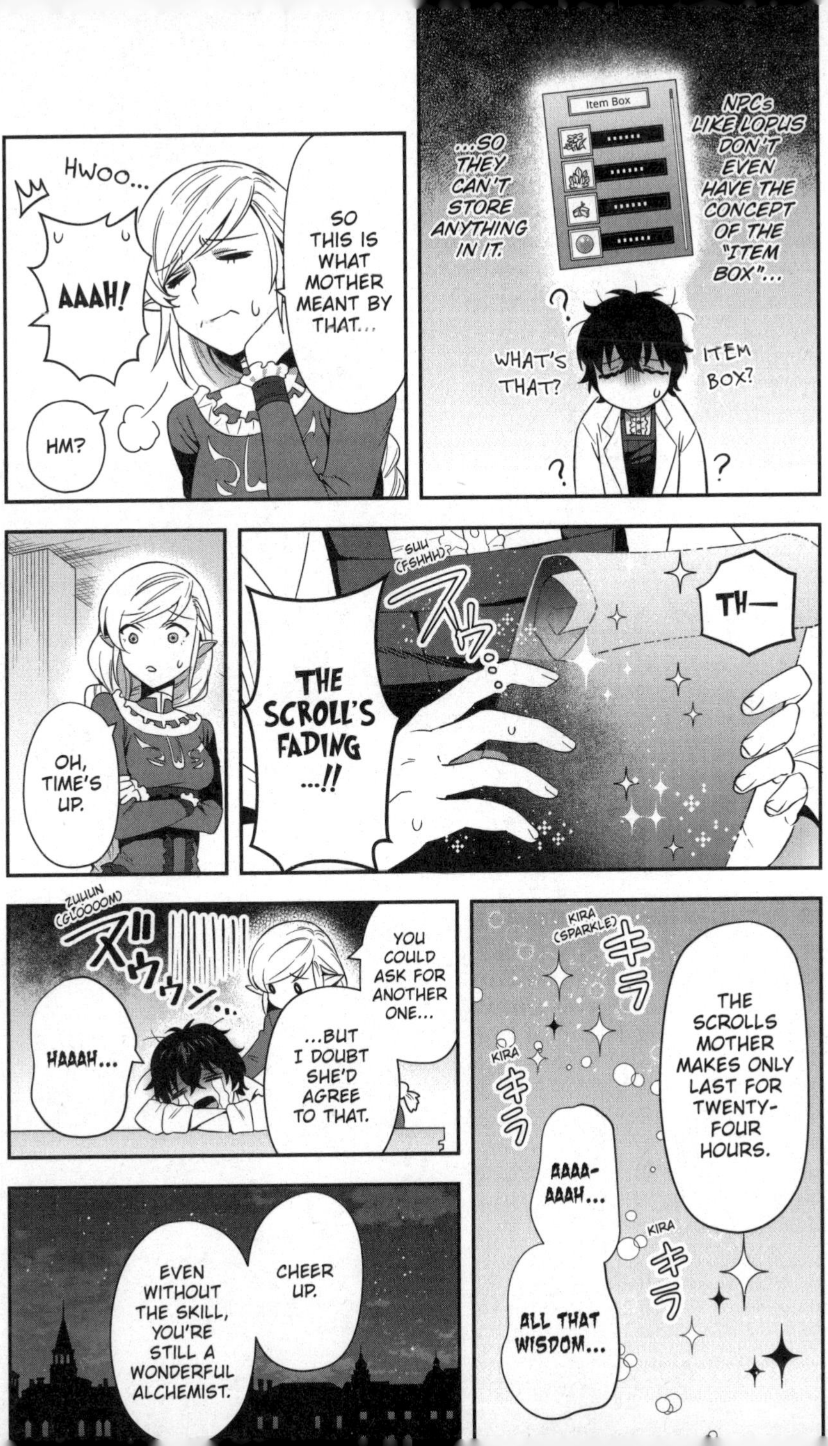
Item Box
NPCs LIKE LOPUS DON'T EVEN HAVE THE CONCEPT OF THE "ITEM BOX"...
...SO THEY CAN'T STORE ANYTHING IN IT.
ITEM BOX?
WHAT'S THAT?
SO THIS IS WHAT MOTHER MEANT BY THAT...
HWOO...
AAAH!
HM?
TH—
SUU (FSHHH)
THE SCROLL'S FADING ...!!
OH, TIME'S UP.
KIRA (SPARKLE)
THE SCROLLS MOTHER MAKES ONLY LAST FOR TWENTY-FOUR HOURS.
KIRA
AAAA-AAAH...
KIRA
ALL THAT WISDOM...
ZUUUN (GLOOOOM)
YOU COULD ASK FOR ANOTHER ONE...
...BUT I DOUBT SHE'D AGREE TO THAT.
HAAAH...
CHEER UP.
EVEN WITHOUT THE SKILL, YOU'RE STILL A WONDERFUL ALCHEMIST.

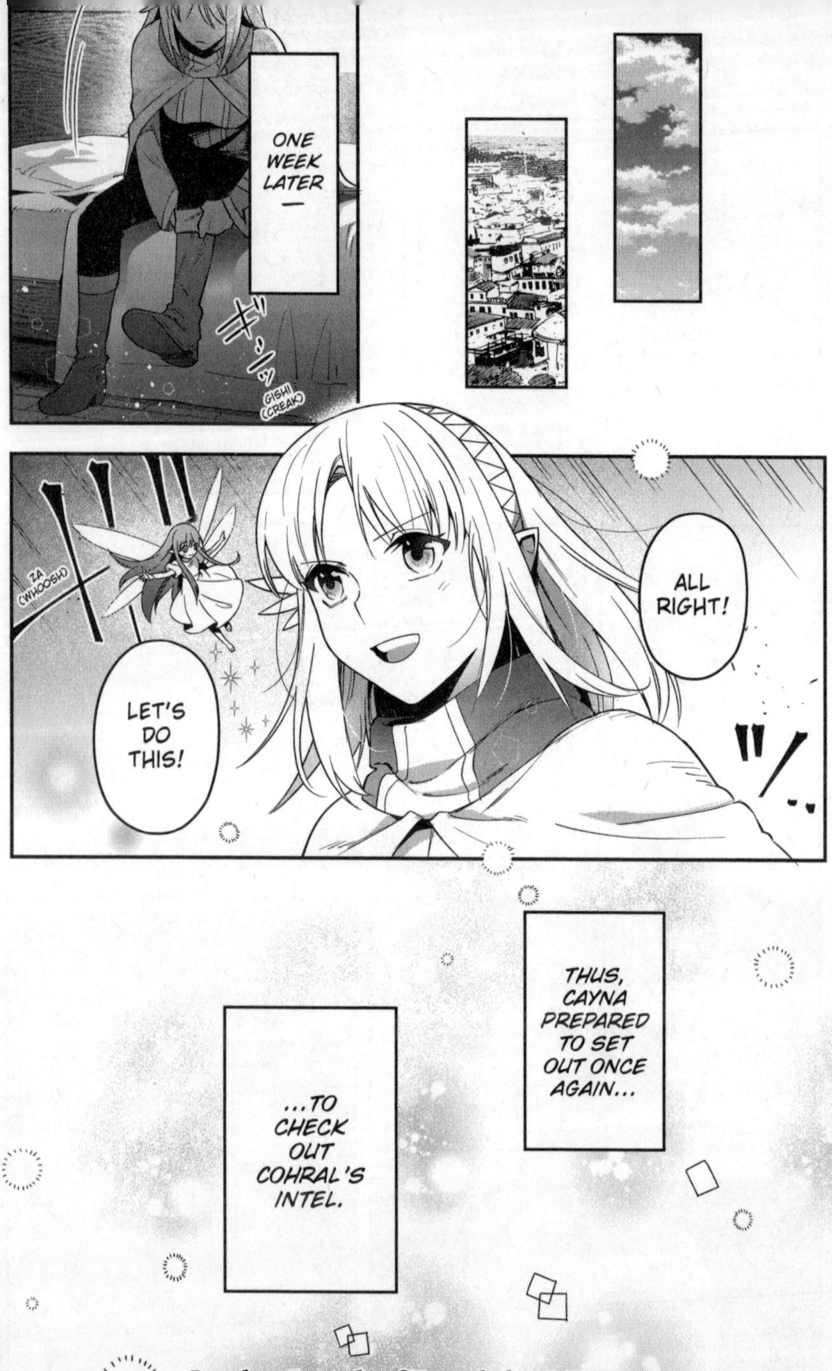
ONE WEEK LATER —
GISHI (CREAK)
ALL RIGHT!
LET'S DO THIS!
ZA (WHOOSH)
THUS, CAYNA PREPARED TO SET OUT ONCE AGAIN...
...TO CHECK OUT COHRAL'S INTEL.

In the Land of Leadale 5 END

IN THE LAND OF
LEADALE

· IN THE LAND OF ·
LEADALE

Bonus Story
Time Waits for No One

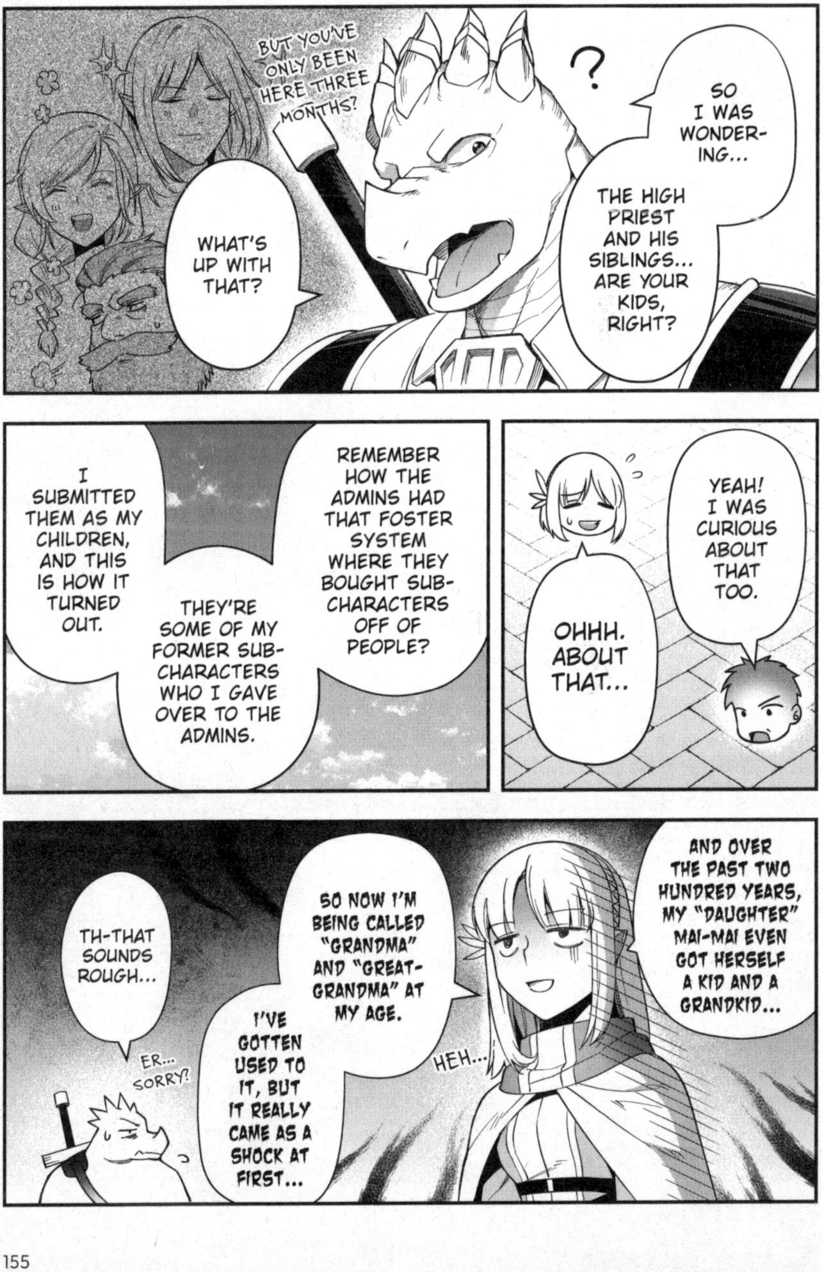
SO I WAS WONDERING...
THE HIGH PRIEST AND HIS SIBLINGS... ARE YOUR KIDS, RIGHT?
BUT YOU'VE ONLY BEEN HERE THREE MONTHS?
WHAT'S UP WITH THAT?
YEAH! I WAS CURIOUS ABOUT THAT TOO.
OHHH. ABOUT THAT...
REMEMBER HOW THE ADMINS HAD THAT FOSTER SYSTEM WHERE THEY BOUGHT SUB-CHARACTERS OFF OF PEOPLE?
THEY'RE SOME OF MY FORMER SUB-CHARACTERS WHO I GAVE OVER TO THE ADMINS.
I SUBMITTED THEM AS MY CHILDREN, AND THIS IS HOW IT TURNED OUT.
AND OVER THE PAST TWO HUNDRED YEARS, MY "DAUGHTER" MAI-MAI EVEN GOT HERSELF A KID AND A GRANDKID...
SO NOW I'M BEING CALLED "GRANDMA" AND "GREAT-GRANDMA" AT MY AGE.
HEH...
I'VE GOTTEN USED TO IT, BUT IT REALLY CAME AS A SHOCK AT FIRST...
TH-THAT SOUNDS ROUGH...
ER... SORRY?

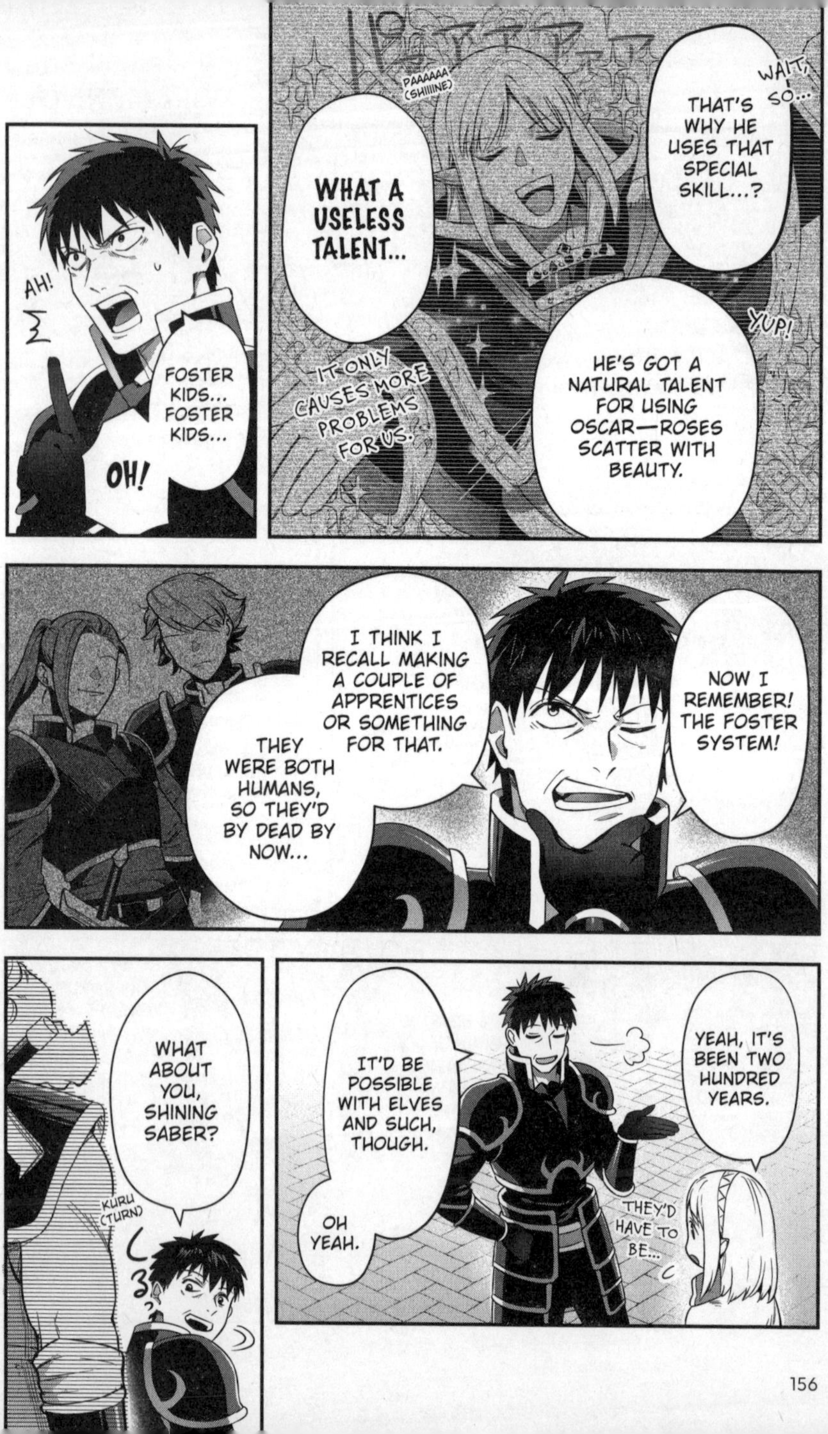
WAIT, SO...
THAT'S WHY HE USES THAT SPECIAL SKILL...?
PAAAAAA (SHIIIINE)
WHAT A USELESS TALENT...
YUP!
HE'S GOT A NATURAL TALENT FOR USING OSCAR—ROSES SCATTER WITH BEAUTY.
IT ONLY CAUSES MORE PROBLEMS FOR US.
AH!
FOSTER KIDS... FOSTER KIDS...
OH!
NOW I REMEMBER! THE FOSTER SYSTEM!
I THINK I RECALL MAKING A COUPLE OF APPRENTICES OR SOMETHING FOR THAT.
THEY WERE BOTH HUMANS, SO THEY'D BY DEAD BY NOW...
YEAH, IT'S BEEN TWO HUNDRED YEARS.
THEY'D HAVE TO BE...
IT'D BE POSSIBLE WITH ELVES AND SUCH, THOUGH.
OH YEAH.
WHAT ABOUT YOU, SHINING SABER?
KURU (TURN)

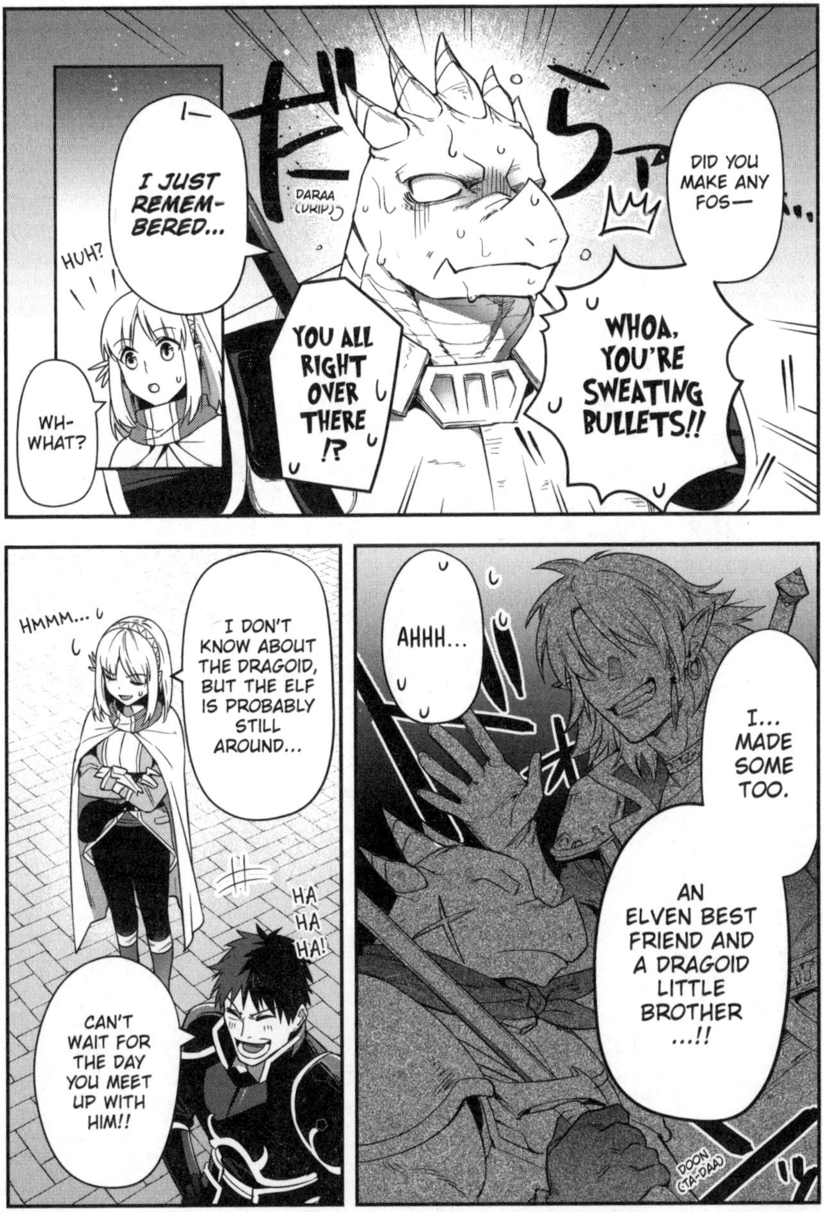
DID YOU MAKE ANY FOS—
WHOA, YOU'RE SWEATING BULLETS!!
YOU ALL RIGHT OVER THERE!?
DARAA (DRIP)
I— I JUST REMEMBERED...
HUH?
WH-WHAT?
AHHH...
I... MADE SOME TOO.
AN ELVEN BEST FRIEND AND A DRAGOID LITTLE BROTHER...!!
DOON (TA-DAA)
HMMM...
I DON'T KNOW ABOUT THE DRAGOID, BUT THE ELF IS PROBABLY STILL AROUND...
HA HA HA!
CAN'T WAIT FOR THE DAY YOU MEET UP WITH HIM!!

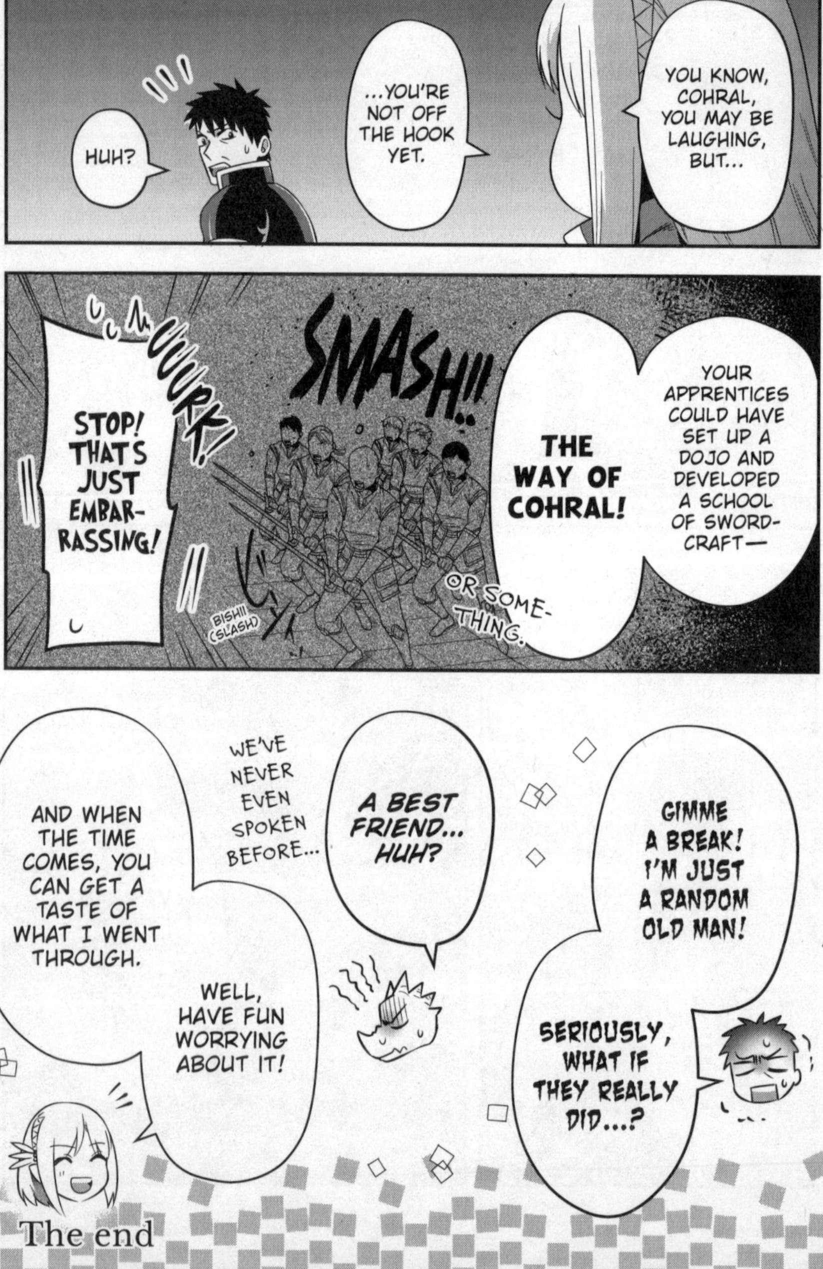
YOU KNOW, COHRAL, YOU MAY BE LAUGHING, BUT...
...YOU'RE NOT OFF THE HOOK YET.
HUH?
YOUR APPRENTICES COULD HAVE SET UP A DOJO AND DEVELOPED A SCHOOL OF SWORD-CRAFT—
THE WAY OF COHRAL!
OR SOME-THING.
SMASH!!
BISHII (SLASH)
UUUURK!
STOP! THAT'S JUST EMBAR-RASSING!
GIMME A BREAK! I'M JUST A RANDOM OLD MAN!
SERIOUSLY, WHAT IF THEY REALLY DID...?
A BEST FRIEND... HUH?
WE'VE NEVER EVEN SPOKEN BEFORE...
AND WHEN THE TIME COMES, YOU CAN GET A TASTE OF WHAT I WENT THROUGH.
WELL, HAVE FUN WORRYING ABOUT IT!
The end

AFTERWORD

*Thank you so much to everyone who picked up this book.
Thanks to all of your warm encouragement and support,
we've made it to Volume 5. The entire time I was drawing,
I struggled through with the hope that I could present things
in a way that's easy for people to understand.
My back's been hurting me lately, but I'll muddle through
and keep working hard. Please, everyone, try to keep an eye
on your health.*

*Ceez, tenmaso—
Thanks to your amazing story and character designs,
we've made it five volumes in. I'm incredibly grateful.*

*Ryo Suzukaze—
I didn't have to worry about getting lost with your detailed
composition. Thank you so much for everything. I look forward to
working with you in the future too.*

*My assistants Negi Asagi, Chiai, and Ito Mitsuba—
If it weren't for you, I wouldn't be able to keep putting out manga.
Thank you so, so much. Here's to a long time working together.*

*The designer, Yokoyama—
Thank you for another beautiful layout. Drawing covers is rough,
but I can put my all into it because I have your designs to look
forward to.*

*My editor, Yamagawa—
I'm soooo sorry for everything, and thank you so much. I would
have quit if it weren't for you. Please stick with me in the future!*

IN THE LAND OF LEADALE

5

ART: Dashio Tsukimi
ORIGINAL STORY: Ceez
CHARACTER DESIGN: Tenmaso
COMPOSITION: Ryo Suzukaze

TRANSLATION: Leighann Harvey
LETTERING: Elena Pizarro

This book is a work of fiction. Names, characters, places, and incidents are the product of the author's imagination or are used fictitiously. Any resemblance to actual events, locales, or persons, living or dead, is coincidental.

RIADEIRU NO DAICHI NITE Vol 5
©Dashio Tsukimi 2022
©Ceez 2022
First published in Japan in 2022 by KADOKAWA CORPORATION, Tokyo
English translation rights arranged with KADOKAWA CORPORATION, Tokyo
through Tuttle-Mori Agency, Inc.

English translation © 2024 by Yen Press, LLC

Yen Press, LLC supports the right to free expression and the value of copyright. The purpose of copyright is to encourage writers and artists to produce the creative works that enrich our culture.

The scanning, uploading, and distribution of this book without permission is a theft of the author's intellectual property. If you would like permission to use material from the book (other than for review purposes), please contact the publisher. Thank you for your support of the author's rights.

Yen Press
150 West 30th Street, 19th Floor
New York, NY 10001

Visit us at yenpress.com
facebook.com/yenpress
twitter.com/yenpress
yenpress.tumblr.com
instagram.com/yenpress

First Yen Press Edition: January 2024
Edited by Yen Press Editorial: Jacquelyn Li
Designed by Yen Press Design: Liz Parlett

Yen Press is an imprint of Yen Press, LLC.
The Yen Press name and logo are trademarks of Yen Press, LLC.

The publisher is not responsible for websites (or their content) that are not owned by the publisher.

Library of Congress Control Number: 2022931495

ISBNs: 978-1-9753-7380-1 (paperback)
978-1-9753-7381-8 (ebook)

10 9 8 7 6 5 4 3 2 1

WOR

Printed in the United States of America